# Medea's Daughter

# Medea's Daughter

## A Novel

## Thomas T. Thomas

MEDEA'S DAUGHTER

Paperback ISBN: 978-0-9861054-6-3
Ebook ISBN: 978-0-9861054-5-6

# Contents

I was angry with my friend;
I told my wrath, my wrath did end.
I was angry with my foe:
I told it not, my wrath did grow.

—*William Blake*

**June 1970**

# 1. Graduation Day

WITH THE SUN beating down on her head and shoulders, Danielle Wheelock wondered why she had bothered to come to her graduation ceremony at all. To distract herself, she tried to analyze the architecture of her surroundings and figure out how the football stadium had become such a furnace.

Because of the prevailing onshore winds, Badger Stadium at the University of Lake Ontario—about sixty miles east along the lakeshore from Rochester, New York—had been constructed so that the open end of the encircling stands, where nothing but the scoreboard stood, faced *away* from the lake. This prevented either team from gaining an advantage in kickoffs, long passes, and kicks for extra points—or so she supposed. Actually, Dani had only gone to one football game in her entire college career, back when she was a freshman. But still, she understood the game's mechanics. And she knew from her courses in structural design that architectural and civil engineers were instructed to take a building's intended function into account as much as its desired form. Too bad they never considered today's function in their design.

That was why she was sitting on a folding chair in the hot June sun, wearing a black robe and a mortarboard hat that collected solar energy better than a photovoltaic panel, with not a bit of breeze off the lake to stir the air inside the stadium. On top of that, she had worn her best outfit for the event, with good shoes that had fashionably narrow toes and the heels tapering down to half a square inch. Those heels had sunk an inch into the turf with every step as she filed in with her graduating class. Now the front edge of the chair's seat was biting into the back of her thighs, because its tube legs were also sinking into the ground at an awkward angle toward the back. And the toes of those stylish shoes were starting to compress the metatarsal bones in the balls of her feet, creating more pain. It was going to be worse when she had to get up and parade in

3

line—hobbling, no doubt—to the improvised stage to receive her diploma. So she quietly slipped her feet out of her shoes and pushed them back under her chair.

Dani hadn't wanted to come to her graduation at all. She had planned to skip the ceremony and let the College of Engineering mail her the sheepskin. She did value her B.S. in Mechanical Engineering, along with her three-point-five grade point average, but only for where they could take her in life. The actual artifact, for all its fancy calligraphy and faux-wax seals, was just a piece of thin leather in a satin binder.

But Dani's mother had insisted. Jane Wheelock seemed to feel personally responsible for her daughter's finishing the last two years of college—even though she had been absent for most of Dani's life.

"It's not every day you get to be the center of attention like this," Jane had told her grimly. "So make the most of it, my dear."

The one person who really belonged up there in the stands was missing. Her father, William Henry, had done the most to care for and raise her. He had once been a full professor at the University of Lake Ontario, although that was in the College of Liberal Arts, where he had taught the classics. Still, he was Dani's inspiration to enroll and had urged her to follow her interests and go into engineering. William Henry was the most important man in her life, and yet he could not get away from his current job—readying a holiday resort for the summer season on Lake Simcoe, up in Canada—to be with his daughter at her graduation. But he did send her a nice watch, a Rolex Orchid on an expansion band decorated with seashells. That was something.

"Your father has chosen that Welsh woman over you," Jane had remarked with characteristic spite, referring to the woman who owned and ran the resort. "That watch is just a sop—and *she* probably paid for it."

After the obligatory speeches by the university's president and the deans of their represented colleges, along with an invocation by the chaplain from the School of Religion, the ceremony settled into the traditional commencement address. This year the speaker was a senior vice president from International Business Machines, a U.L.O. alumnus and the person most responsible for computerizing the campus with an IBM System/360 in the basement of Helmsman Hall. He spoke—for forty-five minutes by Dani's new watch—about the country's great future, about technical advancements in science and computers, and how the graduating class seated before him could contribute to that greatness and its advancements. All the while, Dani's head was getting hotter and the sweat was running through her braided hair, down her neck, under the collar of the black rayon gown, and into the summer-print dress she was wearing underneath it.

Soon, she was not hearing the man's words at all, as they echoed out of the public-address system. Instead she just followed the rhythms and modulations of his voice. Was his oratory descending, as if coming in for a landing? Was he speaking in shorter and shorter sentences, as if his thought train was winding down? Was he using longer and longer pauses, searching the faces before him for eye contact, while imagining the lives he was changing with his prepared speech?

Finally, as her mind faded into a red haze from the direct sunlight and its molten reflection off every bit of metal on the field and in the stands, she heard the man pause for one last time, or pause without starting up again, followed three beats later by applause from the graduates sitting around her and their parents filling the first seven rows of the stadium.

Dani herself started clapping just in time to stop when the university president asked the graduating class of 1970 to come forward to receive their diplomas. The string quartet from the School of Music, amplified and made grainy by the public address system, struck up the traditional march from *Pomp and Circumstance*. People in the rows around her gathered themselves, preparing to file out onto the cinder running track and approach the stage.

When Dani bent to get her shoes, she found that the stiff leather at the back, which normally cupped her heel and helped keep her balance, had become jammed under the chair's front rung. She tried to pull them free, but her expensive Italian pumps were stuck fast. Those narrow heels had been driven deep into the turf. She tried to assume a dignified half-crouch, tilt the chair back with one hand, and work the shoes loose by pulling with her other hand, but without effect. It was already past time for her to stand up and start moving. People were pressing up behind her from farther along in the row.

So it was that Danielle Wheelock collected her sheepskin in her stocking feet with bits of gravel embedded in the soles of her pantyhose.

## 2. Part-Time Job

THE DAY AFTER her daughter's graduation, Jane Wheelock helped Dani clean out her dorm room in Durrell Hall.

She stood outside in the hallway holding a garment bag with Dani's three nice dresses and a couple of long skirts, all of them bought with Jane's money and all neatly arranged on hangers, including the floral print Dani had worn the day before. For the rest of her wardrobe, her daughter was stuffing blue jeans, various shirts and knit tops, and underwear into paper bags. At Jane's feet was a carton containing a pair of engineer boots, a pair of cowboy boots, two pairs of sneakers, three pairs of plain brown loafers, and the Italian high-heeled pumps, again bought by Jane, which she had recovered from the football field after the graduation ceremony. The good shoes were now stained, scuffed, and broken, having been walked on by a couple of dozen people shuffling down the row after Dani had abandoned them.

It was a shame that Dani didn't have more, well, *feminine* clothes—frilly, girlish things that would attract the boys. But then, what could you expect? Her tomboy daughter had been mostly raised by her father, while Jane herself was out on the West Coast and … otherwise engaged.

The rest of Dani's luggage was books, boxes and boxes of technical books, course textbooks in mathematics, physics, and chemistry, books filled with engineering reference tables, and one lone box of popular novels in paperback. Aside from those, there was only Dani's portable record player and a metal case containing her favorite albums.

"Where are we taking all this … stuff?" Jane asked for the third time that day.

"First, we have to drop off my key and the room form at the housing office."

"Yes, but after that? Do you have a hotel? A friend's apartment? Anything?"

"Well ..." Dani paused and straightened up from the bureau drawer she was emptying. She was a head taller than Jane and lanky, taking after her father that way, as in so much else. "To tell you the truth, I thought I would get some response on all those job applications by now. Then I would be on my way to ... wherever."

"So! The answer is no."

"That's right, Mother."

"What will you do for money? You have student loans to pay off, you know."

"Yes, I owe the school twenty-eight hundred dollars that I'll pay off eventually."

"I suppose I could put you on at the Third Base ..." This was the bar in Byzantium, the college town attached to the university, where Jane worked six nights a week from six in the evening till two in the morning. Business was good there, at least until the town cleared out for term break. But things would pick up again once the summer session started, and the lull would give Dani time to learn the job and get her orders straight.

"Schlepping drinks isn't going to pay enough," Dani said.

"It'll do to get you started. The country's in a recession, after all." Jane paused and pointed at the bag of jeans and tee shirts. "Of course, you'll need better clothes than this."

"It's a college crowd, isn't it? They won't mind a waitress—"

"Actually, the word we use is 'hostess,' " Jane corrected her.

"—whatever! I'll be dressed like them. This isn't the fifties."

Jane decided not to argue. "We could store all this at my place, I guess. And put you up on the couch—just while you're finding your feet."

"Just that long," Dani agreed with a massive sigh.

———

As a student, Dani Wheelock had always worked hard. Between attending classes, reading for her coursework and tackling homework problems, and then her evening job tending the reference desk at the Engineering Library in Stones Hall, she usually put in a twelve-hour day. But most of the work was mental, and all of it was done sitting down. "Hostessing" at the Third Base was physically the hardest job she ever had.

For one thing, Dani was on her feet for eight hours straight, aside from two breaks of fifteen minutes each, which were also the only time she was allowed to go to the bathroom. And it wasn't all mindless activity, because she had to learn the customers' faces and match them with their drink orders. Some of those orders, too, could be for obscure liquor brands and strange cocktail mixes that the college kids would think up just to stump the bartender. But her mother Jane, who captained the bar, managed to field every one of them—sometimes to the applause of the table that ordered it.

"How do you remember all that?" Dani asked her one night.

"I've got years in the business. And Tony has good stock."

"But you've got a little black book back there, too? Right?"

"I'll tell you a secret, my child." Jane lowered her voice. "You watch where the orders are coming from. After a table's downed two rounds, these kids don't really know what they're drinking. So you mix whatever's handy and charge for the good stuff."

"But …" Dani was shocked. "Isn't that … *cheating*?"

"No. Just business. Keeping my customers satisfied."

Dani was learning about that, too. For the first few nights, despite her mother's orders, she showed up wearing blue jeans, tennis shoes, and whatever top was clean out of the laundry. And for those days she collected maybe eighty-five cents in tips from her whole shift. But Dani saw the girl who worked the noon-to-six, a single mother named Sally, tuck away four or five dollars each day—and that was from hours when the Third Base was half empty. Dani complained about this to Jane, and her mother had another ready-made answer.

"Look at how she's dressed. Miniskirt, hose, heels, and a scoop-neck shell top. She's twice your age, but she knows what these boys like. And she uses the body she's got to her advantage. The women in the party don't count. It's the men who pay the tab."

So Dani spent her first week's wages to buy similar clothes and wore them—although the shoes burned like hell after she had been on her feet for six hours. She also came to recognize the bar's regular customers, greeted them by name, and remembered what they were drinking. That was good for an extra fifty cents left with the change on her tray.

All in all, working at the Third Base wasn't bad—for her first job in the real world. But Dani knew she didn't want to do this for the rest of her life. Not like her mother. Not even if that was the only work she could get.

As it turned out, she wouldn't have to. When they arrived back at the apartment at two in the morning during her second week on the job, Jane collected the mail from their box. In with her own letters was one for Dani, forwarded from Durrell Hall. The return address was the Personnel Department of Mannheim Construction, Inc., in San Francisco, California. Dani took it without enthusiasm, expecting to find another rejection, like the ones she had already received late in the spring quarter, before her graduation.

"Aren't you going to open it?" Jane asked.

"I know what's in it. It will keep till morning."

Jane snorted. "Now you're clairvoyant, are you?"

"Oh, all *right*," Dani said, tearing the gummed flap and pulling out the single, folded sheet. "Dear Miss Wheelock," she read aloud. "Thank you for your interest in joining our firm, as expressed in your *blah-blah-blah … blah … ooh … *Oh!" Dani stopped reading and absorbed the news.

"What?" Jane asked.

"I've got an interview."

"When is it? And where?"

"Friday—day after tomorrow. In San Francisco." Dani's mind was already working out the timing and connections. "But that's too soon! I'm not ready!"

"Nonsense. We'll get you a plane ticket."

"But ... I don't have anything to wear."

"Get you a business suit. And shoes."

"But I don't have *money* for that."

"How about we give you an advance at the bar?" Jane said.

"I don't know. ... How would I ever pay back that much?"

"We'll dock your salary when you return from the Coast."

"But suppose they take me, and I don't ever come back?"

"Then, my dear, I'll write it off to doing my good deed."

———

Jane Wheelock thought her daughter would be coming back, all right, so she didn't mind splurging to make her ready for the job interview. The first thing they did when they got up the next day was buy a round-trip ticket on United Airlines, leaving Greater Rochester International Airport at midnight, transferring through O'Hare in Chicago in the dark, and arriving at San Francisco—with the layover and change in time zones—at six in the morning. Dani's appointment was for ten with the Mannheim people, so that gave her plenty of leeway to get into town, find the address, and arrive relaxed and smiling.

After buying the ticket, Jane took her daughter shopping. They chose an ensemble suit in black linen with a gorgeous sheen to the material. The suit featured a knee-length pencil skirt and cropped bolero jacket. Dani could mix and match those pieces and go anywhere—even back to work at the bar.

"But, Mother! Do I really need a jacket? I'll be stifling!"

"Trust me, I know summer out there in San Francisco."

They bought a plain white silk blouse, black pumps with heels that did not exaggerate Dani's height, and a handbag that would work with the outfit.

"But I carry my wallet in my hip pocket."

"Not in that skirt, you don't. No pockets."

Although Dani expected to fly back the same day, right after the interview, Jane insisted she take a bag with one of her nice dresses, a change of underwear, and toiletries.

"Plan ahead, darling. You never know what might happen."

"Mother, I'm an engineer. We know how the world works."

Jane chose to ignore that comment. Dani had much to learn.

Because they were splurging, and the girl's future pay-checks—come what may—would be good for it, Jane cashed a personal check for thirty dollars in walking-around money. After all, her daughter might never get to see San Francisco again.

# 3. Interview in San Francisco

TWO YEARS EARLIER, Dani had been beaten by a Hell's Angel–type biker, Eric Bell, who had followed her mother back to Upstate New York from the West Coast after Jane stole a kilogram of heroin from him. Or that was the story Jane told the family. Bell had found Dani while looking for Jane and conducted a savage interrogation to find out where her mother had gone. Anyway, Bell was now safely dead.

Dani's injuries from the beating included—among other things she didn't like to think about—a broken cheekbone that, despite surgery to repair, created an asymmetry on the left side of her face, about which Dani was self-conscious whenever she looked in the mirror. The damaged sinuses also gave her an excellent barometer that ached whenever a low-pressure front swept in from Lake Ontario, which happened about every third day in the summertime.

Now she found that her face pained her on airplane rides, too. It was something to do with reduced cabin pressure—she had read that, on a plane at about 30,000 feet, the pressure dropped to between eleven and twelve pounds per square inch, equivalent to about 10,000 feet of elevation and measurably reduced from the fourteen-point-seven pounds at sea level. By the time she had landed and taken off at O'Hare, then landed again in San Francisco, Dani's face felt swollen and her head was pounding. The two aspirins she got from the stewardess somewhere over Nevada didn't touch the ache.

She also felt sweaty and tired. Because she didn't have a place to change, she had worn her new linen suit to the airport. With the jacket, it was too heavy for crossing part of Upstate New York in June in a car without air conditioning. The material was just right for the cool air on the plane and in Chicago's air-conditioned terminal. And when she landed in California and stepped out onto the ramp, Dani found that the jacket was a blessing in the cold, damp air coming off San Francisco Bay.

But otherwise, she was a mess. She had slept in the suit on the plane, and the skirt was now wrinkled across her hips like an accordion and creased down the back like a set of vertical pleats. No amount of sponging—or steaming, even if she had the time—would take out those creases. Also, the armpits of her new blouse had creeping yellow stains. And she had snagged her nylons on a rough edge somewhere under the seat in front of her.

On the cab ride into the city, Dani at first gave the driver the address of Mannheim Construction, Inc., at someplace called Centennial Plaza. Then she realized no one would be in the office at six o'clock. And next she realized she was famished. So instead she asked for the address of "a nice place to get breakfast."

From the airport, the cab at first drove on a long, straight causeway that edged the Bay, then climbed over a steep hill that separated Visitacion Valley on the left from the start of Third Street on the right—which, the driver said, wound its way past Bay View and the Navy yard at Hunters Point and up into the downtown area. But he was taking her the way that was longer but faster, he said: on Highway 101, cutting over to the stub end of Interstate 280, past Army Street, and around the east side of Potrero Hill. From that elevation, the driver pointed out the view across the flatlands of Dogpatch, Mission Bay, and South of Market to the city skyline, rising out of the mist into the sunshine. For a girl raised in a small college town on the Great Lakes, the City by the Bay looked amazing.

She clearly made out the seven hills on which it perched— like Rome on its own seven, as her father, the classics professor, would have noted. The hill slopes were outlined with row upon row of three- and four-story buildings, punctuated here and there by skyscrapers like the Bank of America, the Transamerica Pyramid, the Fairmont Tower, and the Mark Hopkins Hotel. The driver named these landmarks in turn as they approached downtown. He also pointed out the four towers of the suspension bridge that went east across the Bay, through Yerba Buena

Island, and on toward Oakland, which she glimpsed just off to the right in the morning haze.

The office tower of Centennial Plaza and the Mannheim Construction headquarters were just beyond Rincon Hill, the driver said, which was the "jumping off place" for the San Francisco end of the bridge. Then he apologized for the city's rapidly rising skyline—"ice trays in the sky," he called them—because they hid the famous Coit Tower on Telegraph Hill, on the far north side of the city. That place offered "the best views in town," he said. "Or used to."

When they got into the area around Union Square, the driver dropped her on Powell Street at a diner with the name "Sears Fine Foods." The fare for the ride from the airport was four dollars and twenty cents. Dani didn't feel right giving the man less than a fifty-cent tip, because he had been such an excellent tour guide. Then she felt sheepish about asking for her thirty cents in change from five dollars—but she asked for it anyway. At this rate, plus whatever breakfast was going to cost, that thirty dollars from her mother wouldn't last long.

After eating the diner's "world famous" Swedish pancakes—another two dollars and fifty cents gone—it was closer to eight o'clock and time for Dani to think about getting to her appointment. But first, she had to repair her appearance. She took her small suitcase into the ladies' room, shut herself in a stall with a couple of wet paper towels, and stripped out of her wrinkled suit. She wiped her neck, armpits, and other parts of her body with the towels, then put on the same summer dress she had worn to graduation. At least it was clean and fresh. And with the black jacket over it, her appearance was *kind of* businesslike.

Finally ready to meet the day, she packed up her bag and went out onto Powell Street, looking for another cab that could take her down to Centennial Plaza. One of the city's open-air cable cars went by with its bell clanging, and Dani was tempted to hop on. The twenty-five-cent fare was surely going to be less than a second cab ride, no matter how instructive.

But, for all the cable car's charm, she didn't know where it was going.

Although, truth to tell, she didn't know where *she* was going, either.

————

Cynthia Hammond, a recruiter in the Personnel Department of Mannheim Construction, Inc., studied her ten o'clock appointment as the receptionist showed the tall young woman into her office. She checked the paperwork in front of her: Wheelock, Danielle Ann, June graduate of University of Lake Ontario, 3.5 GPA, and a bachelor of science in mechanical engineering. On paper, she looked perfect. But in person was another matter.

The girl was pretty enough, with auburn hair done up in a French braid and hazel eyes. A bunch of recessive genes there, Hammond guessed. She had a long, straight nose turned up at the end over a wide mouth with full lips in an otherwise unremarkable face. Unfortunately, she wore too much lipstick, and it was a deep shade of red that was meant to go with darker colors and did not complement her yellow cotton dress with its enormous orange flowers—the kind of pattern one saw on the untucked shirts of tourists returning from Hawaii. The dress was tight in the bodice with a flared skirt that ended above the knee. And Cynthia would guess that, under that stiff little black jacket, the dress was sleeveless. All the outfit needed was a pair of cowboy boots to make it truly absurd, but at least Miss Wheelock had chosen black pumps with a low heel. So this was not a completely incompetent woman. One could at least hope she was a competent engineer.

As the girl sat down, Hammond fixed her with a steely eye. "Why do you want to come to work for Mannheim?" she asked by way of greeting.

"I heard you were the best at what you do."

"We are. And did you apply anywhere else?"

"Well, um, yes. ... I wanted to hedge my bets."

"That was sensible. Our hiring is very selective."

Under normal circumstances, that would be true. But Personnel was also under pressure from on-high to increase the presence of women engineers in the company. It was a public-relations move, to boost Mannheim's chances at federal contracts under the new affirmative action guidelines—but theirs not to reason why. Unfortunately, the female engineers from better schools like MIT and Caltech had already been scooped up. Which left this lone young woman from a second-rate college in Upstate New York that wasn't even in Rensselaer's league. But still, Hammond refused to be hurried about these things. The company had a reputation to maintain.

She studied the girl's application, which was typed with two spelling errors. Minus points there. "I see you made the dean's list in your last two years."

"I worked hard for that."

"No one thinks you didn't."

In the résumé section under "Special Achievements" Wheelock had included an interesting fact. "And you wrote a paper on Joseph Strauss and the Golden Gate Bridge. Was that for one of your mechanical engineering courses?"

"It was a class on structural engineering."

"You know we do mostly civil work here, don't you? Buildings and infrastructure, rather than mechanical projects."

"That's why I mentioned the paper. And I do understand that Mannheim's area of expertise is not exactly my specialty. But I figure most of your industrial projects also have mechanical systems, things with motors and pumps, like elevators, water supplies, heating and ventilating. So you must have some mechanicals on your staff."

"As a matter of fact," Hammond said, "we do have an opening for an engineering analyst in our Power Division. They assure me that, aside from the foundations and the administrative offices, those things are *all* mechanical." She watched the girl's face to see how she reacted to the lowly position of "analyst."

"That sounds *very* interesting," Wheelock said with a smile.

"Then I will arrange an interview with the project engineer."

"I'm looking forward to working here," the girl added.

"I am sure you are." Hammond smiled in return.

———

The Hammond woman in Personnel had told Dani to report to another building some distance away at two o'clock that afternoon, which left her four hours for lunch. She ate at a small Italian café on Steuart Street—another three dollars gone!—and spent the rest of the time walking on the Embarcadero, which was a Spanish word for the city's waterfront.

It was an industrial landscape made up of the landward façades of the numbered piers, with glimpses of open water and pilings in between. The piers were more like big, noisy warehouses than docks, and when Dani stuck her head into the open door of one, she was quickly chased out by a man driving a forklift. The street running along the waterfront was overshadowed by the pillars of an elevated, double-decked freeway that seemed to ring the city and obstruct the views of all but the tallest downtown office buildings. A city guidebook she had picked up at the restaurant—another twenty-five cents—said the famous Fisherman's Wharf, a place of fine seafood restaurants, crab shacks, a waxworks, and a penny arcade, was located at the upper end of the Embarcadero, about two miles to the north, but that was too far for her to walk both ways, and she didn't want to pay for the cab ride back.

Dani got back to her appointment at two o'clock and signed in with the guard at the security desk. The Power Division—or at least the part she was visiting—was on the third floor of an older building in the South of Market area that had probably been converted from a factory. The interior was open space filled with drafting tables and desks inside a maze of waist-high partitions. By asking three people in succession, Dani found her way to the cubicle of Michael Manuglian, the man she was going to see. From the expressions on the faces of the people directing her, she guessed he was not popular with the staff.

At the indicated desk, she stood before a burly young man with dark hair and hard eyes. He was in his shirtsleeves with his tie pulled down and his shirt collar unbuttoned.

"Yes?" he said, glaring up at her.

"I'm Danielle Wheelock. Miss Hammond sent me?"

Manuglian shook his head and looked around the room, as if expecting Miss Hammond to suddenly appear and explain everything. "All right," he said when he didn't find her. "So?"

"I'm supposed to interview for the engineering job?"

"Tell them we don't need a secretary," he replied.

"I'm not a secretary. I'm a mechanical engineer."

"Huh!" He blew out his cheeks. "But you're a woman."

Dani decided there was no nice way to treat this man. If she was going to lose this job opportunity—her only job opportunity at this point—and go back to the Third Base and serve drinks, then she would lose it standing on her own two feet and fighting.

"That does not automatically make me a moron... sir. I graduated in the top ten percent of my class. I have a degree in mechanical engineering—which is the position you've got to fill."

He shrugged at that. "Where'd you go to school?"

"At the University of Lake Ontario," she replied.

"Never heard of it. So ... is that place any good?"

"Two from my class went straight to NASA this spring. A third enrolled in the graduate engineering program at Berkeley. I decided to come to Mannheim because I want to build power plants."

"You know we do a lot of nuclear work," he said with a hard look, as if he was trying to discourage her.

"So?" Dani replied in turn. She really had no opinion about the politics of energy supply. "Steam is steam, isn't it?" she said. "Do you want me to sit down and calculate a heat transfer to prove it?"

He sighed and waved her into the chair opposite him across the desk. Then he took up a folder from a pile at his left hand. Inside was her application and hand-typed résumé.

"You're a tough kid, aren't you?" Manuglian said.

"When I have to be." She was still in full fight mode.

"You'll need it to survive around here. Especially from me."

Dani looked him straight in the eye. "Well, I do like a challenge."

From that point on, the man seemed to relax, and he conducted a relatively normal job interview. He asked about her coursework and her professors. He talked about the projects Mannheim had in hand and the jobs they were bidding. The one thing he didn't discuss was the duties of the position on offer.

"What do you expect from me?" Dani finally asked.

"You do what you're told. You work the hours we need. You come up with the right numbers, and you check your math. You ... cope."

"That's the analyst's job?"

"No, that's engineering work."

"You know I won't make coffee ..."

"Everybody here pours his—or her—own."

But still, Manuglian appeared to be undecided. He said he would need time to think about the position and get back to her. She was in town for the weekend, right? So, he said, she should leave a local number with the Personnel office. And with that Dani was out on the street again.

She hailed a cab and asked the driver to take her to a "nice enough" hotel. He drove her up Market Street, turned off on Geary, and then left on Mason Street, dropping her and her suitcase in front of the King George Hotel, a narrow building in red- and green-painted stonework with a high, ornate cornice at the roof line. The awning that extended from the front door to the curb showed the silhouette of a bearded man. The taxi ride with tip cost her another three dollars.

Inside, at the registration desk, she found that a room would cost her twenty dollars a night. That was going to exhaust her "walking around money" two days before she ever got to Monday morning. But Dani was too tired to go look someplace else and afraid of what she would find closer to the financial district or in the dark places along the waterfront.

Before she went up to her room, she called United Airlines to change her return flight. The reservation clerk wanted an extra thirty dollars on top of her hundred and fifty dollar round-trip fare because, he said, she was extending her stay over a weekend, and that was the holiday rate. He gave her the address of a downtown office where she could pay the extra amount and exchange her ticket.

She then asked the hotel concierge where the nearest Western Union office was, and he gave an address around the corner on Powell Street. The next morning she would have to contact Jane and ask her to wire more money. Dani realized she was getting in over her head, incurring a debt that would take her months to pay off.

That night, she went to bed without dinner in a seventh-floor room with a charming bow window that overlooked Mason Street. She listened to the hum of traffic in the city and the distant rattle and clang of the cable cars along Powell Street until she fell asleep.

Dani spent Saturday arranging the wire order, changing her ticket, and then riding the cable cars and visiting Coit Tower, with its 1930s-era Work Projects Administration murals, because the admission ticket was just a dollar. The views of the city itself weren't as interesting as the panorama of the Golden Gate Bridge, the Marin Headlands, Alcatraz, and a hundred little sailboats beating back and forth between them. She ate a hotdog from the stand in tiny Pioneer Park, at the base of the tower, as her only meal that day. She spent Sunday in her hotel room reading a book she had brought along, because she was effectively broke and was saving for cab fare on the trip back to the airport.

At eleven o'clock on Monday, three hours before her flight to the East Coast, Dani got a call from Miss Hammond. They were offering her a starting salary of $12,500 a year to work as an engineering analyst—which was more than her father had made in any one year as a full professor. They wanted her to begin work in a week. Dani asked if she should come into the office and sign anything, but Hammond said, "No, we'll mail you the paperwork." So she need not have stayed the weekend after all. "Have a nice flight home," Hammond told her.

As she was being driven out to the airport, Dani collected her impressions of the place where she was going to live and work for at least the next several years. It was colder than she had ever experienced in June. It was also not the fabled city of "sex, drugs, and rock'n'roll" that she had expected. Instead, San Francisco seemed stiff, hard, and buttoned down. Like a miniature New York City, but with a bit more charm.

# 4. Continuing Education

IT HAPPENED EVERY year. *Sensei* John Schumacher would see his Wednesday and Sunday night karate classes evaporate, from thirty-odd students down to about ten, as most of them went home for the summer term and did not return until the fall. And then there was the percentage who graduated from the University of Lake Ontario and went away forever. One stalwart, however, was Dani Wheelock. She had been a regular, year-round student and, even after graduation, had kept on attending his classes. Although she had an evening job at one of the downtown bars the other five nights of the week, she took time off, sacrificing pay and tips, to make it to class.

Schumacher remembered how she had come to him two years ago, and that had been during the summer, too, between her sophomore and junior years. Her face had been bashed in by a crazy drug dealer named Eric Bell—although not that Dani was involved with drugs in any way—and she was still healing from the surgery. She said she wanted to learn to fight back.

"You know karate isn't necessarily going to do that for you," he had told the tall, lanky young woman. "It takes years of training for the average student to become a match for even the most casual street fighter." He paused. "Longer for a woman, because of differences in size and strength."

"I don't want to be a victim," she had insisted. "Not ever again."

"You can learn mental discipline, perhaps. You'll just go down fighting."

"But, then too, I *might* win," she said, jutting out her chin. *Tough girl.*

"You would also get hurt. Maybe even worse, because you resisted."

"Yeah, but I would be getting hurt on *my* terms."

23

So Schumacher had accepted Wheelock's class fees, put her in the back row, and forgot about her. Most students dropped out in the first six weeks, when they discovered how much boring repetition karate training required. And how minutely technical it was, to the point of distraction.

The beginning student had to learn how to place and hold his feet, balance his weight between them, and regulate his breathing in order to relax his muscles—and do all of this at the same time. Performing the simplest of side blocks entailed dozens of small movements, controlling the positions of shoulder, elbow, fist, and knuckles, in order to create an exact, mechanical, sweeping arc every time. Performing strikes and kicks required perfect alignment of the striking surface with wrist and elbow, or ankle and knee, shifting balance without committing it to forward motion, keeping the joints from locking bone-on-bone, and tightening the muscles of the body core and the striking arm or leg, in sequence with the breath, while keeping the rest of the limbs in a state of relaxed readiness. Even the toughest, most aggressive, most eager male students found the training too tedious. But Dani Wheelock had stayed with it. She took to all this like a ballerina doing pliés at the barre.

*Sensei* Schumacher had personally trained her on the first of the forms, called *kata*s, that simulated a mock battle with a set of invisible opponents: a precise choreography of blocks, punches, and kicks. She moved with the grace of a cat, gliding across the floor on her bare feet. And so he began to take notice of her, sparred with her occasionally to check her range and timing, and gave her moments of special attention as she advanced through the ranks, denoted by the stitched-cotton belts worn with the pajama-like uniform called a *gi,* progressing from white to green belt. After two years, Wheelock had completed the eight hand-and-foot *kata*s in the Isshinryu style and was ready to test for brown belt. After that, she would train with the style's weapons, the short swords called *sai* and the long staff called *bo.* And eventually, in another year or so, she might pass for black belt. It was a shame she had begun training so late in her academic career, because Schumacher wanted to take this young woman to that level, which most students thought of as an end point, but for the adept was really the starting point.

When she missed her first Sunday night class in two years, he thought Dani might have moved on, like all the other graduates. But there she was again on Wednesday. After the class period finished, he thought to ask her about that. Instead, she approached him.

"*Sensei* ..."

"Yes, Dani?"

"I'm going to be leaving town now," she said.

"Oh? I hope you're going to someplace good."

"I have an engineering job in San Francisco."

"That is ... a long way away. I wish you luck."

"I was hoping, before I go ..." She twisted one toe against the wooden floor of the workout area. "If you would test me for brown belt? I know it's presumptuous of me to ask. But it would help if I wanted to join a *dojo* out there."

"You know the belt rank doesn't mean anything," he said.

"I know. It's just a personal marker. But it might help me get accepted."

"I don't have to test you. I've watched you for months now. You pass. Go buy yourself the belt."

Her face brightened at that, and she started to thank him.

"But," he said quickly. "Even if you can find another Isshinryu school on the West Coast—and I haven't heard of any—they won't recognize your belt. They may advance you faster, based on what you've learned here, but they will have their own belt classifications. And their own standards of training."

"Then could you help me find a *dojo* with a good teacher?"

"Sure. It's the least I can do. When are you leaving?"

"Tomorrow. I have to be at work on Monday."

And then *Sensei* Schumacher did something he had never done with any student. He placed his hands on the young woman's shoulders, leaned in, and gave her a light kiss on the forehead. "Be well, Dani. Take care of yourself."

# 5. Interview on Haight Street

WITH ANOTHER LOAN from her mother—one she now knew she could pay back, and get started on her student loans—Dani bought a one-way ticket to San Francisco for the following Saturday. She also had enough extra to keep herself until the first paycheck came in, which wouldn't be for at least two weeks.

This time she would be traveling in daylight. She had booked a window seat on the right side of the aircraft fuselage, out of the direct sunlight as the plane headed west. She spent the flight gazing down, from a height of seven miles in the air, as the countryside unrolled beneath her.

Dani found that, for all she had read, and everything other people said, about how vast the continent was, she had never understood how empty it also was. Once they were out of Chicago and had passed the farmlands and small towns of Iowa and Nebraska, the land seemed to be swept clean. She followed the thin, beige lines of isolated roads as they crossed dark-brown scrub and low hills, stretching for miles without a crossroads or a farmhouse in sight. Wyoming, Utah, and Nevada—when she could guess that her plane had crossed a state line—were the emptiest: just wrinkled black mountains and flat gray-brown desert. It was a relief to arrive in California with more green forests, fields, and orchards. But perhaps the change was due to the jetliner descending slowly and bringing the ground more into focus.

From the airport, Dani again took a taxi. Rather than going into the downtown area, this time she headed toward the center of the peninsula, a hollow lying between the city's prominent hills and the long slope down to the ocean. Her mother had given her an address on Haight Street where she said Dani might find a room.

The cab dropped her and her suitcases in front of a narrow old Victorian-style house, one in a row of such houses along that side of the street. It was three stories tall and no wider than the doorway itself and the big bay window beside it; so Dani hoped it went a ways back into the block, with an air shaft or something to let in light along the sides against the neighboring buildings. The first floor was above street level, up a flight of cracked, terrazzo steps, and she humped her bags up to the arched and colonnaded doorway.

On closer inspection, the place was less encouraging. The exterior clapboards were dented and chipped, with dark streaks where nails had been driven to hold them together. The white paint curled away from the ornate dentils and scrolled woodwork around the door and window frames. The windows themselves were uncurtained and deep in dust. Dani wondered if anyone still lived there.

She pressed the painted-over button that should have rung a bell somewhere inside, but nothing happened for a long time. As this was the weekend, she thought the residents—if there were any—might all have gone to the beach, or something. But finally the door moved, bumped against some obstruction inside, and opened a crack.

"Yes?" said half of a young woman's face, with a blue eye and frizzy yellow hair.

"I'm inquiring about a room," Dani said politely.

"A room?" the woman said. "Do we have a room?"

"I'm told you do," Dani replied. But she was becoming uncertain. She suspected her mother's information was by now some years out of date. After all, there was no sign outside saying anything about rooms to rent. The house might have changed hands.

"You'll have to speak to the Chairman of the Housing Committee," the woman said.

"I see. And is he available?" Dani asked reasonably.

"Yeah, I guess so." She turned away from the door and bellowed. "Adrian! You have a visitor." Then she turned back to Dani. "Takes him a minute to put his pants on when he's stoned."

With that, the young woman disappeared down the dark interior hallway, leaving Dani standing on the steps and the door swinging slowly open under its own weight. After that minute, she heard footsteps drumming on inside stairs, and a middle-aged man in jeans and a tie-dyed tee shirt, barefoot, and with a gray ponytail pulling back on his scalp, stepped into the open space.

"Yeah?" He studied her through bleary eyes. "Do I know you?"

"Are you the housing chairman? I'm looking for a room to rent."

"Room … yeah." He straightened. "Six is available. I think. Or will be, when Darryl decides to get his shit together."

"And when do you think that will be?" she asked.

"Five o'clock. Maybe four, if we push him. He's moving down to Carmel."

"Oh. All right." She had thought it might be a week, with notice. "May I come in?"

"Sure thing." Adrian backed out of the doorway, let her enter the hallway, and pointed to the first door on the right, which was more of an open archway. "This is the common room, where you can hang if you want."

Dani set her suitcases by the wall and squatted on a bean-bag chair. The thing was completely sacked out and quickly rearranged itself to deposit her rump on the hardwood floor. She was glad she had decided to travel informally, just jeans and a top, rather than in her suit or a dress. "What's Number Six like?" she asked.

"Second floor in the back," Adrian said, dropping into lotus position on a stretch of thin carpet next to her chair. "You over-look the community garden and rabbit hutches. It's got a bed and a dresser. Mattress not too bad. You bring your own sheets and towels, of course."

"Of course," she said. "Does it have a bathroom?"

He gave her a funny look. "You share with the back half of the house. Work out morning schedules among yourselves. Or take it up with the Grievance Committee."

Dani wasn't sure she liked the sound of that. "Are the people here ... nice?"

"Agh ... s'not a bad group. Most of them have good dope, and they're willing to share. But, really, you're like, three years too late to the party."

"What party was that?" she asked.

"Sixty-seven? Summer of Love?"

"Oh, yes. I have heard about that."

"Beautiful time, man! Reality sucks."

"What is the rent on that room?" she asked.

"Yeah, right. All business. Sure. House dues are thirty bucks a week. Fifty, if you expect to eat here, and then you help with cooking and washing up. That's a hundred and twenty a month, without the food. Two hundred, with."

"That's a nice break."

"How so?" he asked.

"Well, there are four and a third weeks, average, in any month. So basic dues should be a hundred and *thirty*, on average. And with board, more like two hundred sixteen and ... sixty-five cents." Four years of engineering courses had made Dani quick with numbers in her head.

"No kidding? Four and a half weeks?"

"A third—well, you're close enough."

"I never knew that," he said. "Maybe we should put you in charge of house finances."

"It's just simple arithmetic, really."

"Turns out, we've been shortchanging ourselves for years," he said with a frown. "What's your name anyway?"

"Dani—short for Danielle—Wheelock."

"Wheelock? Where've I heard that name before?"

Her mother, of course. But best not to mention it.

"Have you?" she said. "I don't know. I'm from back East."

"Shoot!" He shook his head. "It'll come to me eventually."

# Summer 1970

# 1. The Farragut Steel Report

ON HER FIRST day of work, Dani Wheelock rode the No. 7 Muni bus from her new neighborhood in the Haight District into the downtown Financial District, where Mannheim Construction, Inc., had its various office buildings. To make a good impression on the job, she wore her black wool suit, white blouse, and heels. She clutched her small, black-leather purse on her lap.

Eyeing the people around her, Dani felt like a penguin who had wandered into the Amazon rain forest. Most of the other passengers wore jeans and sandals or sneakers, and that was not too different from the college crowd she had been hanging out with just a few weeks ago. Some of the men and even a few women wore army fatigue jackets in olive drab, but instead of military insignia they were decorated with embroidered peace symbols, marijuana leaves, and tiny rainbows. A greater percentage of the people on the bus, however, wore tie-died everything—tee shirts, scarves, sleeveless jackets, bandanas, and even formerly white cotton pants—in blended colors, heavy on the red-orange and green-blue parts of the spectrum. They flocked around her, talked over her head, even sang to each other—one man had brought a guitar and was strumming it dreamily—at seven-thirty in the morning! And they never made eye contact with Dani. It was like these birds of paradise hesitated to notice the penguin in their midst.

And then gradually, as the bus approached Market Street and the Civic Center, the people wearing the bright plumage got off and a new crowd—older, quieter, more sedate, and dressed in sober blues and grays—started to get on. By the time the bus arrived at Centennial Plaza, the end of the line, it was full of business people, some of them probably her new co-workers.

Dani had been told to check in at the security desk, where the guard would be holding a temporary badge in her name—temporary until the Personnel office could take her picture and issue a proper, laminated identification badge. Then she was to report to the same brusque young man, Michael Manuglian, she had met during the interview.

———

Manuglian looked up to see the tall young woman from—when was it, a week ago already?—standing over his desk. Yes, the woman from Personnel, Cynthia Hammond, had said she would be coming in today.

"You're Denise Wheeler," he said.

"Um, ah, no. Danielle Wheelock?"

"Oh, yeah? Well ... close enough."

The girl stood there looking flustered.

"Okay," he said. "Do I have to *ask* you to sit down? If you're here, take a chair."

Wheelock sat down, put her purse on the floor, and folded her hands in her lap.

"All right," he said. "Welcome aboard and all that. Now what am I going to do with you?"

"You said you had an engineering job ..."

"I know *that*. It's *all* engineering." He squinted at her. "Question is, what part needs to be done first? I guess the Farragut Steel Report. It's important work but not too hard, something even a—" He paused. Hammond had already warned him about his language, implying there could be legal consequences. "—even a beginner, such as yourself, can handle."

"Okay," she said. "And who is Farragut?"

"Not a who. A what. That's the David G. Farragut Nuclear Power Plant, out in Tennessee. Our contract there is for construction management, which means we oversee all the subcontractors on the site and handle all the inspections and testing in the client's name. And the Steel Report—well, Farragut's a nuke, right? Which means the Atomic Energy Commission is very particular about how it gets built. Every valve and dial, every toilet seat and doorknob, it's all mission critical. So you can't just go down to the hardware store and buy the parts, can you?"

"I—I guess not," she said uncertainly.

"That last was rhetorical, by the way."

"Yes, sir."

"Right now," he continued, "we're in month twenty-three of the on-site work, which means the seismic surveys are done, the foundations are all laid out and excavated down to bedrock, and we're now into the rebar work and initial pours for the footings under the reactor vessels, containment building, and turbine pedestal. You with me so far?"

Wheelock nodded. "Should I be taking notes?"

"Only if you think you're likely to forget."

"Month twenty-three, rebar ... vessels."

"Reactor vessels, containment, and turbine pedestal. All important to the nuclear side, especially those first two. Now, normally, rebar is rebar. They taught you about that in school, right?"

She paused. "Oh, that wasn't rhetorical? Well, I know rebar is the steel bars used for reinforcing concrete. It's usually either carbon-steel or low-alloy. You can identify it by these funny little surface ridges that anchor it in the mix and give it frictional adhesion."

So maybe, Manuglian decided, this girl wasn't stupid after all. "Ri-ight," was all he said, dragging it out.

"Anyway," he went on, "for a job like this in any other industry, even any other steam power plant, we would buy the rebar by the trainload, test one batch in five just so we don't have our heads up our asses, then stick it in the ground, cover it with concrete, and not give a damn. But Farragut is a nuke, right? So we have to be precise. The AEC inspectors will want all the paperwork in their safety review under USC—that's United States Code—Title Forty-Two, Section Twenty-Eleven. Which means they want to know the origin, tracking, and final disposition of every piece of steel, including the rebar. Producing mill, bar size, and steel type from the bar mark. But more than that, when the batch was shipped, with bills of lading along the way, when it got logged into inventory, when checked out of inventory, when tested and where and with what result, when and where it was placed on the site, and finally, when each piece of bar got covered in the concrete pour. And if they wanted to know the mother's maiden name of the guy in the hole who tied it off, then we'd give them that, too. You still with me?"

"Yes, sir. Mother's maiden name."

"Slow down, gal. We're not there yet."

"Yes, sir. Scratch that about the mother."

"And you don't always have to call me 'sir.' "

"No, sir. I mean …"

"Mike or Mister Manuglian."

"Okay. I'm Dani—in case you forgot."

"Wise ass … Now, where was I? Yeah, the guys at the site take in all this information, but they're not really clerks. And they've got a thousand other pieces of paper to deal with. So they send it all here to San Francisco for the Steel Report. Which is now your job."

Manuglian stood up and led her back to a desk in the corner of the big room.

"This is now your workspace. You share a phone with the next guy over—he's Kellerman by the way."

Kellerman looked up with the handset to his ear. "I'm Paul," he said, covering the mouthpiece, but he didn't offer to shake hands. Then he went back to listening at the earpiece and writing something.

"This is your in-basket," Manuglian said, pointing to the tray on her desk. "Every day the mail clerk will bring you notes from the field." He lifted a stack of yellow carbon copies—about three weeks' worth of reports, he guessed—from the basket and placed them in the center of the desk. "Over here—" He turned to a bookcase filled with bound journals. "—are your logs. You sort the field reports and copy the information in the appropriate logbook. 'Reactor Foundation.' " He read off the names from the spines. " 'Containment Annulus.' 'Nuclear Steam Supply.' And so on and so forth. And finally, over here—" He turned to the other wall, lined with flat files. "—are your very own set of as-builts."

" 'As-whats'? Sir?"

"Drawings from the final detailed design. The construction shack has their own set, where they mark up any alterations to the design as necessitated either by the client's change orders, the subcontractors' actual execution of the work, or the AEC's inspection results. Damn few of those, we hope. But your set is for tracking the steel. In addition to keeping the logbooks, you note the batch number on the drawing at the location referenced by the site manager.

"When you're done," he concluded, "we should be able to look at your drawings for any part of the plant and say exactly what steel's been buried where under which pour of the concrete. And from your logbooks, we'll know its complete history."

"And when will I be … done—Mike?" She fingered the stack of yellow copies.

"The last engineer held this job for six months before getting bumped upstairs. You might be here a while longer."

———

After Mike Manuglian went back to his half-cubicle, Dani sat down at the desk and picked up the first of the field reports. The paper was something she'd only read about: a thin sheet of yellow tissue impregnated with microscopic ink capsules. It took any mark and repeated it, like carbon paper but without the middle layer. The stuff had been invented by the National Cash Register Company and was informally called "NCR paper"—although they liked to say it really meant "no carbon required."

NCR … USC … AEC … She was going to be awash in acronyms on this job.

The piece of paper was actually a preprinted form, with check boxes and dotted lines for the clerk in the field to enter the data she needed to record: the manufacturer's code, batch number, issue date, waybill numbers, inspection dates and results, all the inventory data, and the drawing number for final laydown. So Dani's job, really, was to copy information from one piece of paper into a book and onto a drawing sheet, then repeat the process for the next piece of paper, and the next, "and so on and so forth," as Manuglian liked to say.

How hard could that be? She was beginning to think her engineering degree would be wasted here.

But after two hours she had cleared exactly one field report. The trouble was interpreting the plant documents. She had over sixty logbooks on those shelves, and they broke down the foundation work—where all that rebar steel was being sorted and placed—into about a dozen different types of building, stages of construction, system designation, and level of associated risk of radiation contamination. The flat files behind her contained more than a thousand drawings, again catalogued by building type, plant system, discipline designator—structural, mechanical, electrical, process piping, and so on—along with sheet type and sequence number. Copying the information took about five minutes. Figuring out where to put it—and doing it right, so that anyone else could find it again—was what took all the time.

Well, it would all make sense eventually. With enough practice, she would be able to find her way around the guts of the David G. Farragut Nuclear Power Plant as if she had actually walked across the site—if she didn't go nuts from boredom first.

And then there was the nature of the carbonless paper itself. It not only took the marks that the construction clerk made on the top sheet—which he was sending God knew where, not to her—but it also recorded every scuff, fold, and bump the document encountered in traveling from the site to her desk. Sometimes, the useful information was concealed in a blush of bruised microcapsules or a scrawl from someone writing on the outer envelope. So Dani sometimes had to study the information itself to make sense of it and not just copy down whatever she thought she saw in error. The AEC would probably take a dim view of that.

Dani sighed, picked up the next flimsy yellow sheet, and started the hunt all over again. Only a hundred and twenty of the wretched things left to process—from this day's batch.

## 2. The Grievance Committee

CASSIE PETRICK WAITED until one minute after six to begin knocking on the bathroom door. Then she waited another thirty seconds to begin pounding.

"Come on, in there. Open up."

The door opened a crack, and one pale green eye, overlaid with a skein of damp hair, peered out at her. Steam billowed out of the crack into the cold air in the hallway.

"Yes?" said the new girl. "Do you want to use the bathroom?"

"Yeah," Petrick said. "It's my turn, dummy. Six to six-twenty. Your time was up two minutes ago."

"Oh, all right. Let me just finish—"

"Uh-uh, baby cheeks. You, out. Now!"

With that, Petrick pushed open the door.

The girl inside was naked, not even a towel.

"But you can see my hair is still all wet!"

"So dry it in your room. Time's *up!*"

Petrick pulled her out into the hallway. In doing so, she was conscious of bedroom doors opening up and down the hall and more eyes peering out. Oh, well. It was still the new girl's fault.

The young woman scurried down the hallway, back to her room, trying to cover her breasts and her pubes with one hand held high and the other low while clutching her toothbrush, toothpaste, hairbrush, and other toiletries. Petrick heard muffled laughter coming from those other bedrooms.

When she went into the bathroom, she found it a perfect mess. Puddles on the floor, drips on the mirror, wet bath towel on the rack, toilet still to be flushed, and toothpaste smeared in the sink. The girl had done nothing to clean up after herself.

Well, this certainly called for a dose of House action.

———

When Dani Wheelock got back from work that evening, she found an envelope with her name on it pushed under her bedroom door. Inside was a piece of paper headed "Charge Sheet." It listed specifications including violations of the Bathroom Scheduling Protocol, of the Good Housekeeping Protocol, of Disturbing Neighbors, and of Indecent Exposure. She was invited to a hearing before the Grievance Committee at seven o'clock on the following Thursday to answer these charges and receive the appropriate Fines and Punishments.

That next Thursday, Dani approached the common room on the first floor front at the appointed time. A folding screen decorated with a Japanese print had been positioned across the archway. Tacked to the screen was a notice: "Closed for Official House Business."

Not knowing if that was indeed her business, Dani knocked quietly on the woodwork framing the arch.

"Come in," said a man's voice from beyond the screen.

Inside the room, Dani found three people seated on the beanbags along the far wall: the man she had first met, Adrian Ingalls, and two others whom she knew only from seeing their faces in the house's common areas. To the right was the woman who had rousted her from the bathroom two days earlier, Cassie Petrick.

"Take a seat," Ingalls said, gesturing to a kitchen chair that had been brought in and placed at the center of the room, facing them.

Dani sat down and folded her hands in her lap. She still wore the skirt of her business suit, so she pressed her knees together.

"One of your housemates makes serious charges against you," Ingalls began, and the two men on either side of him nodded. "So how do you plead?"

"I wasn't late in the bathroom," Dani said quietly. "By my watch, it was still five-fifty-eight. So I had two more minutes."

"Not by the clock in the kitchen," Petrick said. "And I checked it."

"This is true," Ingalls said. "In any dispute, the House clock rules."

"How was I supposed to see it?" Dani said. "From the bathroom?"

"You should set your watch by the House clock," Ingalls replied.

"All right," Dani said. "Next time. But as to the other charges, she—" Here she pointed at Petrick. "—she pulled me out of the bathroom. I had no chance to clean up, gather my towel, and cover myself."

"Not true!" Petrick said. "I just told you to come out. Then you fled."

A few steps were missing from that chronology of events, Dani noted, but she kept her mouth shut. This was going to be a case of her word against Petrick's, and the other woman was an established member of the household, while Dani was the newcomer.

"It would seem to me," Ingalls said, "that two minutes, even by your watch, would not be enough time to mop the floor, clean the sink, and leave the bathroom ready for the next person. And you shouldn't be walking around in just a towel. You should have brought a dressing gown or a bathrobe."

One of the other men, a young blond giant whose general bulk made Ingalls seem like a stick figure, leaned close to him and whispered something.

"Yes, I know," Ingalls said aloud. "She's new here and she doesn't know all the rules. But still, this should be a learning experience. The fine is twenty dollars, paid into the House Fund."

Dani sat up straighter. Twenty dollars was a week's walking-around and lunch money for her. The fine would hurt. But already the other two men were nodding in agreement. Petrick looked like she wanted more blood, but finally she nodded, too.

"That's it then," Ingalls said. "And I hope we can all try to get along better."

With that, Ingalls and the third man rose and left the room together, taking the Japanese screen and the kitchen chair with them, waiting only for Dani to vacate it. Petrick stood glaring at her for a moment, then shook her head and departed as well.

"You've made a bad enemy there," said the blond man. He finally got his feet under his center of balance and levered himself out of the beanbag. He was as tall as he looked sitting down, taller than Dani when he was standing. He moved powerfully but carefully, as if he was used to knocking over furniture. He was different from every other male resident in having a short haircut—almost a crew cut—no facial hair, and no trace of tie-dye or peace symbols. "I'm Norman, by the way," he said, putting out a hand.

"Dani," she replied, shaking it.

"Yeah, I know. The accused."

She grimaced. "Yes. I'd better keep out of Cassie's way for a few days."

"That would be the smart thing. It's what the rest of us do."

"Are all the punishments here that expensive?"

"No, it seems you're a special case."

"How so?" she asked.

"You've got a job downtown. You can afford the twenty bucks. Most of them can't. And that's how utopia works. Everyone pays the same room rent, so it's all equal. But some are privileged to pay more for their transgressions than others, so justice is done in the end. It makes everyone feel better."

"Then I'll try to have fewer transgressions, in the future."

"May not help. Obviously, Cassie was gunning for you."

"What does the 'House Fund' cover?" Dani wondered.

"Oh, repairs. Maintenance. Capital investment. Paint."

"When was the last time anyone painted this place?"

"Long before I got here." He grinned. "Grunge is the natural state of Nirvana."

"You believe this is heaven?" she asked, alarmed that anyone could think so.

"No. 'Nirvana House.' At least, that's what the first set of residents called it."

# 3. Typing Lesson

HALFWAY INTO HER second week on the job, Mike Manuglian remembered that he had a new engineer in hand and walked back to her desk to find out how she was doing on the Farragut Steel Report. When he got there, however, the desk was empty and the in-basket was full of flimsy yellow forms. So where was the girl at nine-thirty in the morning?

He lifted his head and looked around the large open-office space. Maybe she had gone to the ladies' room, but otherwise a woman that tall should be visible from anywhere. He couldn't see her at first, but he did hear an unfamiliar sound. Someone was using the office typewriter—but doing it badly.

Normally, the clacking of the IBM Selectric at the department secretary's desk was gunfire rapid—more like a machine gun, when Annie Pipps was using it. But this was the slow and distinct dot-pause-dot of a hunt-and-peck typist. Manuglian went over to Annie's desk to see what was going on.

And there he found his newest engineer, her head bent over a lined pad filled with angular, architect-style handwriting, then swiveling to the keyboard where she searched for the next letter—and twitched when the machine's type ball jerked, spun around, and struck the platen with a resounding *clack!*

"What the hell are you doing?" Manuglian demanded.

Wheelock jumped again. "Nothing, Mike. That is, I'm typing up a report."

"You don't have to issue a report on the Farragut project. Or not yet anyway. And when you do, you give your notes to Annie and she makes the fair copy. That's a more efficient division of labor." Lots more efficient, in his view, given the speed at which Wheelock was operating the typewriter.

"No, sir," she replied. "This isn't about Farragut. Paul just asked me to type up some notes for him."

"*Paul* asked you? Kellerman?"

"Um, yeah, the guy at the next desk."

"And why the hell would you agree to do that?"

"But ... didn't you tell me to do whatever I was told?"

"When the hell did I say this?" Manuglian demanded.

"When I interviewed for the job. You said that was engineering work."

"Well, yes, but you do what *I* tell you to do. Not some other engineer."

Wheelock wilted now: shoulders slumped, head down, no eye contact.

He decided to make this a life lesson. "Look, there's a hierarchy around here—and reputations to maintain. Typists do the typing. That's their job, and there's a pay grade for it. Engineers don't type, they do head work, numbers work ... solutions work. When they need those solutions written up, they go to someone like Annie to do it."

"I see," she said.

"You touch a typewriter again, and people around here will get confused. They'll think you're the new Annie—or her assistant. Then they won't respect you as an engineer. And then we all lose respect. Me most of all, because I hired you. *Capisce?*"

"Yes, sir. It won't happen again."

"Everyone gets one mistake."

## 4. Karate Lessons

FOR TWO WEEKS Dani had been scanning classified ads in the *San Francisco Chronicle,* looking for someone giving karate lessons, before she found a listing. A place on Polk Street seemed promising: the Shorinryu Academy, with classes on Mondays and Thursdays at seven-thirty in the evening. Dani figured she could get there after work. The instructor was listed as William "Big Bill" Berggren, fourth *dan.* The fee was twenty dollars a month.

She knew from her karate classes back at the university that Shorinryu was one of the three disciplines that Master Shimabuku had adapted to create the Isshinryu style. On Okinawa, before the Second World War, he had studied Shuri-te for its *kumite* or sparring techniques, Shorinryu for its *kata* or fighting forms, and Gojuryu for its hard-soft motion and muscle-tightening technique. She figured that, with its similar forms—which she had taken so long to learn and practice to near-perfection—Shorinryu would be the ideal teaching to follow if she could not find an Isshinryu *dojo* in San Francisco. And both styles extended their hand-and-foot techniques with weapons training in staff and short swords.

Dani went to the Polk Street address early on a Thursday evening, hoping to meet with the *sensei* before class started. The street number was a side door to a commercial block and had four names above the bell, none of them for any Shorinryu Academy. She was about to ring one of them, hoping at least to get information about the school, when she saw that the door was wedged open. She entered and climbed a long flight of dark stairs to the second floor. The third door down in the interior hallway had "LaSalle School of Ballet" painted on its frosted-glass window. It was the only one with light behind it. So Dani knocked.

After a few minutes and a second knock, the door opened. A small man in a white *gi* uniform stood there. The embroidered patch on the left breast showed a three-bladed, spinning scythe worked in golden thread on a dark-blue background. He had the black belt of an advanced student. He also wore a drooping, Fu Manchu–style moustache and plaited his long, dark hair in a thin braid, like an old-style Chinese queue—although he was obviously Caucasian.

"Mr. Berggren?" she asked.

"No. *Sensei* Berggren only comes up from Los Angeles for the Monday class."

"But this is the Shorinryu Academy, isn't it?" She pointed at the ballet sign.

"Oh, yeah. We rent floor space from the ballet school in the evenings."

"Are you a student here?" she asked, measuring him with her eyes.

"Assistant instructor," he said. "Are you looking for someone?"

"I've come about taking lessons. My name's Dani Wheelock."

"Call me 'Squid.' A lowly first-degree black belt," he said.

" 'Squid'? Is that what they call the students in this style?"

"Naw, just me. See, I'm a former Navy Seal. And Big Bill, he's former Green Beret." The man shrugged. "So everyone calls us the Squid and the Grunt."

"That doesn't sound very respectful," she observed.

"Respect? Then call me Mister Fiorelli, if you like."

Squid took her through the school's waiting area, with a counter and display case of ballet clothes for sale: dusty toe shoes, tutus, and leotards—all size small, as if for children. From there, they passed through an archway into the main *dojo* space. It was a large room with a parquet floor in alternating blocks of light and dark wood, heavily lacquered. Along one end was a floor-to-ceiling, wall-to-wall mirror. Along the perpendicular wall were three windows, with sheer curtains, that looked down on Polk Street. A ballet barre ran the length of the room, bolted to brackets between the windows. In the far corner was an upright piano with a round swivel stool. Old-style, white-glass globes in the high ceiling cast a smooth, almost shadowless light.

"You'll have to take off your shoes," he said, pointing at her high heels, before he let her onto the floor. "I just finished sweeping." He was already barefoot, like all proper karate students.

Dani slipped off her pumps, held them by the heels in one hand, and stepped onto the polished surface in her stocking feet.

"Changing rooms are through there," he said, pointing to a doorway on the inside wall. "You can't wear those street clothes in class."

"Oh, I didn't bring a *gi*."

"Okay, your first time?"

"Well, no. I studied two years with an Isshinryu *sensei*, John Schumacher, back at the University of Lake Ontario."

"Yeah … we don't teach Isshinryu."

"Oh, I know. I can't find a *dojo* anywhere."

"So. Do you want to switch over to Shorinryu?"

"I have a brown belt and know the first eight *kata*s."

"But Shorinryu forms and techniques are totally different."

"I understand. Still, Isshinryu is based *partly* on Shorinryu *kata*s."

"Even so. Your body, somatic memory, will probably fight you on that."

"I understand, but I still want to continue training," she said. "It's *important*."

"Okay, then, you can observe tonight," Fiorelli said. "I guess you can't sit on the floor, in that narrow skirt. So you can sit on the piano stool. We aren't using it. If you come back Monday, bring a *gi* and, yeah, buy yourself a white belt. We'll start you on the basic stances, Shorinryu style."

# 5. Rabbit Burgers

AFTER WORKING LATE at Mannheim to finish the day's load of rebar, then catching the last bus home, Dani stopped at the Arby's on Divisadero Street to buy a roast beef sandwich, fries, and small Coke. She was sitting at the kitchen table in Nirvana House, squeezing the little packet of horseradish sauce over pale, pink meat when Cassie Petrick found her.

"And what the hell are you doing?" the woman asked.

"Eating my dinner," Dani said. "What's it look like?"

"House dinner was at seven o'clock. You *know* that."

"Yes, and I had to work late. So I missed it. Big deal."

"You should have called and asked us to hold some for you."

"Rabbit burgers." Dani sighed. "Don't you get tired of them?"

"We grow them ourselves. They're sustainable. Not like that!"

*That* was Dani's sandwich, dripping with sauce. It was House dogma that beef, wherever it was grown—and those pink slices of rare roast beef probably ate their grass in Argentina or Australia—destroyed the environment. Dani could also guess that the potatoes came from either Idaho or Oregon, while the oil that cooked them was from rapeseed or cottonseed grown in either Mississippi or China. And who knew if horseradish was even a plant anymore—or just mixed up in a vat from raw chemicals? To the other members of Nirvana House, it was all processed garbage. And never ask them about the ingredients in Coca-Cola. They might start talking about rusted chrome bumpers.

"Since I'm paying for the meals here," Dani said. "I get to eat what I want."

"How can we be responsible people if you keep bringing in junk food?"

"This is my body. My choice. I can put into it whatever tastes good."

"You may think that. But this is our planet, and you're killing it."

In reply, Dani picked up the sandwich and took a big bite.

"And another thing," Petrick went on. "You never take care of the rabbits or weed the garden. Paying is one thing, but you have to participate, too. The rest of us aren't going to wait on you."

"I feed them."

"Occasionally."

"Okay!" Dani said. "So I don't take part in the slaughtering, skinning, boning, and chopping. That's just gross. And besides, after you feed them for a month and get to know them, it's hard to wring their necks and render them. It's like eating the family poodle."

"Everyone should know where their food comes from."

"Yes," she said, "but I don't have to know its name."

"You're shirking your duties under House Rules."

"Look, do we have to go through the farce of another trial before the Grievance Committee?" Dani asked. "Or should I just pay the twenty bucks right now?"

"Pay the twenty, if it will keep you from buying burgers and bringing them into our kitchen. We're trying to run a self-sustaining planet here."

## 6. Like a Palindrome

IN HER FOURTH week on the job, Dani Wheelock noted the first anomaly. It was in a group of field reports mailed from the Farragut site a week earlier. One of the batch numbers on a load of steel rebar seemed familiar.

Dani dealt with big numbers all day long, not to manipulate them with arithmetic functions or derive them from a formula, but just to read and record them accurately in her logbooks and on her set of drawings. The field location numbers were complex and broken into small chunks with hyphens and periods, relating to building codes and coordinates. But the steel batch numbers themselves were generally straight figures, and the numbers were huge, strings seven, eight, or nine digits long, most of them.

Normally, she would have no reason—and no convenient way—to remember any of these numbers. Her job was to read them, write them down, and move on. But being mathematically inclined, she tended to see patterns in any big number. Repeating groups like "123123123" would occasionally catch her eye. And, of course, straight repetitions like "8888888" would have her staring at the yellow form for whole seconds at a time. Harder to see but more satisfying, in a way, were the symmetrical inversions, which read like numerical palindromes. Such as the one she was holding now.

The batch number on a load of steel that had just been placed in the Unit 1 Reactor Containment was "9876789." She wouldn't have noticed it, except for those sevens bracketing the six, then those parallel eights, and the beginning and ending nines. As individual digits, they described a smooth downward and upward curve, like a catenary.

And then Dani realized she had seen this pattern before. No, not just the pattern itself, not just the curve, but those same bracketing sevens. She had seen them in the last week, too. The same number—she was almost sure of it. But where?

Still holding her yellow copy of the field report, she turned to the shelf of journals at her elbow. The books were arranged by the plant building and, within it, the location of the concrete pour that immediately followed the steel's placement and tie-off. The entries were meant to record what steel with what testing and provenance had been placed in which part of the site. But the query only went one way: if you knew the location, you could find the steel batch number and related details. It didn't work in reverse: if you wanted to know where any particular batch of steel had ended up—or to find a curious number some days or weeks after it had been recorded— you would have to comb through the entire set of books. They weren't cross-indexed.

"That's bad design," she said to herself. "Suppose we got a notice that something was wrong with a particular batch? Say, the manufacturer didn't put in the right alloys or something? We would have no way to trace it to placement in the site and replace it."

Well, yes, there was a way. Someone with a job description even lower than Dani's would be sent to the books and told to read through them, line by line, until she found the number under investigation. Even if it took weeks, that was better than leaving a critical plant function held together with a bad bunch of steel.

If she wanted to find that number ghosting in her head— the one she thought she had seen only a week ago—then she would have to begin such a sweeping search herself. So, for now, it was just a curiosity, and she was content to leave it at that.

But she thought she ought to mention the vulnerability of their recording system to her supervisor.

———

Mike Manuglian was just finishing up a phone call when the new girl, Dani Wheelock, approached his desk holding one of her yellow field forms. He waved for her to sit down, and she waited patiently while he completed the call.

Hanging up the receiver, he asked, "What can I do for you?"

"I think I found a problem in the way we're doing the steel records."

"You *think?*" He smiled. "You've been here how long? Less than a month? And already you're questioning the way we run the shop?"

"Isn't it an engineer's job to question things?"

"Don't be smart, missy. What's the problem?"

She started to explain how the books only went in one direction, from batch to placement, and could only be read backwards, from placement to batch. But there was no easy way to find out where a particular batch of rebar had gone in the first place.

"So?" he said. "This is the system we've got. It tells us what steel exists inside the concrete under the plant—without having to crack it open, then cut and sample the bars. That's all it's supposed to do."

"But what if we got a bad batch of rebar?"

"Bad *how?* We test it all six ways from Sunday." He paused. "Has someone sent through a report about a bad batch?" That thought troubled him.

"No, sir. I was just wondering."

"Then why bring it up now?"

"Well, I saw this particular number—" She showed him the form in her hand, pointing to the handwritten entry for the steel batch. "—and it caught my eye. You see, it's like a palindrome, but with numbers."

"So? How is that important?"

"I see these things, number groupings, patterns like that. And then I remembered that I'd seen and remarked on this particular number before. I was going to check it—but there's no way to do that, not with the system the way it's set up."

"You saw this exact number?"

"Yes, I think it was the same."

"But you're not sure. And you can't find it now."

"Well, no … not positive. But I'm *pretty* sure."

"Then it doesn't exist until you can prove it."

She sat there with lips compressed in a line.

"Look," he said. "The field team and the construction supervisor on Farragut are all experienced men. They're careful and they check their work. One man doesn't just write those numbers down and walk off. One man reads the tag and enters the number on your form there. Then a second man standing right beside him reads the form and compares it with the number on the tag. The system is foolproof."

"But it's *not!* Because unless they remember every number they've—"

"It's the way we do things. Now, why don't you go do *your* part of the job?"

He saw that the young woman was still unhappy about this. But weren't they all unhappy, at some time or another? A young man her age would have seen the logic in what he was saying and just shut up.

As soon as she walked away from his desk, Manuglian forgot the whole conversation.

# 7. Engineer in Training

AT MIKE MANUGLIAN'S suggestion, made formally as her supervisor, Dani Wheelock prepared her application, submitted the fifty-dollar fee, and arranged to take the examination that would begin her on the course of professional registration with the State of California.

"Everyone does it," he said. "And you'll need it to get ahead here."

The process was governed by the state's Department of Consumer Affairs—which made sense when you thought about what a company or a client was buying when they hired an engineer who claimed professional status. The first step was to take the eight-hour written examination called "Fundamentals of Engineering," or FE. Everyone at the company assured her that she should be able to pass it with just the knowledge she had acquired from the coursework for her bachelor of science degree—no need to study up or take practice exams. Once she passed that test, she could then apply for registration as an "Engineer in Training," or EIT.

The qualifications for that classification were three years of education with an engineering program that was approved by the Accreditation Board of Engineering and Technology, or three years of work with a consulting engineering firm or construction contractor, or some combination of education and work experience. So Dani—who had already checked that the University of Lake Ontario's mechanical engineering program was accredited—knew she qualified immediately, provided she could pass the FE exam.

Once she was an EIT, she had to work at least six years in a qualifying position before she could apply to become a "Professional Engineer," or PE, which was the basic registration. Luckily, all four of her years of education counted toward that time, so she could hope to acquire the necessary registration in as little as two more years. Taking a postgraduate degree in some field of engineering while she worked at Mannheim would help her cut into that required work experience but, either way, it looked like she would have to wait the two years.

"Qualifying experience" meant she had to be making responsible decisions—not just taking direction—on projects that the review board would consider "major" or "unique." Luckily, that meant *technical* responsibility but not ultimate *financial* responsibility, which was a whole 'nother kettle of fish. Working as a drafter, estimator, or some other "subprofessional" didn't cut it; she would have to be making *engineering* decisions. And that meant the time she put in recording batch numbers for the Farragut Steel Report, which even Manuglian acknowledged was more clerical than professional work wasn't advancing Dani toward her career goals.

When the time came to apply for professional registration, she would have to submit her university transcript, a number of work-related references, and a detailed list of the projects she had served on with a description of her own duties. The professional registration came in a variety of engineering flavors: mechanical, civil, structural, geotechnical, and so on. Since she might gain qualifying experience in any of these fields while working at Mannheim, she had options as to where her career would lead.

One other thing. Both the EIT and the PE registrations required her to affirm that she had committed no crimes—that is, either felonies or misdemeanors—related to her engineering work; had not violated any provision of the Professional Engineers Act—with which she guessed she had better become familiar; and had not faced disciplinary action demonstrating her unfitness to perform the functions of a professional engineer "in a manner consistent with the public health, safety, or welfare."

Dani looked into her conscience and tried to decide if she had any felonies or misdemeanors in her past. She didn't think so ... but then, she was still young and inexperienced. She had all of her mistakes ahead of her.

## 8. The Resident Narc

NORMAN WALL WAS more than a little interested in the new woman at Nirvana House. It wasn't just that she was pretty, although she certainly was, or smart, although that was obvious, too. She was full of energy and what he termed a "bright spirit." Norman himself was more quiet and occasionally caustic. So the vibrations of her psychic aura—to borrow the inexact phraseology of the burned-out hippies who dominated life in the residence—was greatly attractive.

And then, like him, she wasn't a believer in fantasies. Dani Wheelock was a real person, rock-solid, her own self. She was obviously raised in an old established family from the East Coast and had never seriously rebelled against them—just as Norman still respected the views espoused by his late father and never seriously defied his authority. Also, Dani had trained as an engineer, a person accustomed to finding out the facts and facing up to reality, even if it was occasionally unpleasant—just as Norman, who had taken a degree in business at the University of Pennsylvania and was currently working in the Accounting Department of Levi Strauss & Company, which made the blue jeans these hippies prized so highly, had been taught to look at the numbers and find the story they were actually telling, instead of hoping for the best or fearing the worst.

But all that bright energy and serious purpose made Dani a hard person to approach. She often worked late hours at her engineering job, and then for two nights during the week she disappeared off to some appointment or meeting that she never discussed. And on weekends she either went out to walk in nearby Golden Gate Park or stayed locked in her room, reading a book.

Norman didn't think she was seeing anyone. Rather, he got the impression that she was all alone, like him, being new in town, and that if she had left a boyfriend back in Upstate New

York, they were no longer in touch. That much was all he had been able to establish by indirect and discreet questioning of the other house members.

It was no surprise, then, to find her alone in the common room on a Friday evening. She was sitting cross-legged in one of those absurd beanbags, with her head bent over a book that was spread open across her ankles.

"I'm not disturbing you, am I?" he asked, moving to perch on the bag opposite her.

She lifted her head and smiled briefly. "Not at all. It's Norman, right?"

"Yes, Norman. The last name's Wall, by the way."

She nodded. "And mine is Wheelock."

"Yes, I know. … 'The accused.' "

"You do keep bringing that up."

"I'm sorry. Bad memory?"

"It's not a problem."

And with that, she went back to reading her book. But he got a sense, from the way her head moved more slowly, and the fact that she didn't seem to be turning any pages, not for whole minutes at a time, that she was no longer actually reading it. He noticed, too, that one finger kept moving up and tucking an invisible strand behind her ear, even though her hair was bound in a braid and no wisps were visible anywhere.

Norman wished now that he had practiced something beforehand, some line of conversation or banter to engage her. But all he could think of was to ask what she was reading.

She lifted the thick volume and showed him. The book was bound in black cloth, without a dust jacket, and across the spine he saw "Fundamentals of Structural Analysis" in white letters, with the rest in type too small to read.

"So, is it any good?" he asked lamely.

"It's for my work," she replied.

All he could say was, "Oh."

She already had the book back on her crossed ankles, and this time she turned a page.

Norman looked around desperately. And then, as if on cue, the house pest, Cassie Petrick, walked into the room.

"Well, well," Petrick said with a hard smile. "Isn't this cozy?"

Dani looked up at her and closed the book with a *thump!*

"Don't worry," Norman said. "I was just leaving."

"No, I should go," Dani said. "Getting late."

Norman levered himself out of the chair, awkward as ever. He ducked his head as he passed Petrick and hurried out of the room.

The chance encounter with Dani that evening was their second point of personal contact. It almost felt, for him, like a first date, although nothing had specifically been asked or answered. He desperately wanted to think he had made an impression on Dani, but he feared it was a bad one.

———

Cassie Petrick thought it was time to give the new girl a word of advice. It wasn't because she liked Wheelock or thought they ever might become friends, but Cassie had the reputation of the House to uphold.

"You want to stay away from him," she said quietly—in case Wall had stayed in the hallway, eavesdropping on what she might say about him.

Wheelock paused on her way out of the room. "And why is that?"

"Because he's a cop or something. He keeps a German shepherd dog."

"Having a police dog makes him a cop? Gee, isn't that … simplistic?"

"He really doesn't fit in here, and yet he chooses to stay." Cassie shrugged.

"I'm not sure I understand. Don't you all get to vote on who's a member?"

"Yeah. Most of us decided it was better to deal with the devil we know."

"Devil?" Wheelock repeated. "I still don't know what you're saying."

"We think he's a *narc*—narcotics agent. That he's looking for drugs."

"Oh. Well, plenty of drugs around here—or so I've heard. Why isn't he arresting people right and left?"

"They don't always," Cassie said. "Not at first. They play a long game, these cops. Cat and mouse. Taking their time."

"Gathering evidence?" Wheelock offered. "Building a case?"

"Yeah, something like that."

"And you really feel safer this way?"

"Well ... we get to keep an eye on him—on them."

Wheelock laughed at her. "You really are an insane bitch, aren't you?"

Then she walked out, leaving Cassie alone in the middle of the room.

# 9. Lunch with the Sisterhood

DANI WAS SURPRISED when Cynthia Hammond from Personnel called and invited her to lunch at the Tadich Grill on lower California Street. "We want to officially welcome you to the company," Hammond said—without saying who "we" might be. Dani was instructed to meet up in the lobby of Centennial Plaza at eleven forty-five, so they could walk over to the restaurant.

In the lobby she recognized Hammond right away. Standing next to her was a tall, elegantly dressed woman whom Dani judged to be in her early forties, the time when a woman's beauty either solidifies or fades—and this woman was definitely not fading. With them was a short, plump woman with her eyebrows heavily penciled and her mangled hair cut in a severe wedge at the back. She was more plainly dressed— dressed down, even. Hammond introduced the elegant woman as Missy Pearsall, from Public Relations, and the short one as Sylvia Coombs, from Technical Reports.

Pearsall offered the back of her hand, palm down, so that Dani could only grasp her drooping fingertips and give them a squeeze, like milking a cow. Dani also discovered that Pearsall was wafting an eye-watering amount of perfume. Coombs held out her hand man-style and pumped Dani's up and down. "Nice to meet you," she said. Coombs, on the other hand, smelled of roll-on deodorant.

The restaurant—an antique establishment, with a marble-and-tile front and mahogany wainscoting inside—was crowded. In fact, people were waiting outside the door.

"How do we get in?" Dani wondered aloud.

"Oh, we have a reservation," Pearsall said.

"That was kind of short notice, wasn't it?"

"My department always has a standing reservation."

"No one else was using it today," Hammond put in.

The four of them were shown to a table at the front. The three other women ordered a bottle of dry white wine to share, but Dani—not being used to drinking during the day—asked for sparkling water.

"We're celebrating Danielle's sixth week on the job," Hammond said, raising her glass.

"Hear, hear," Pearsall said and sipped.

"To sisterhood," Coombs murmured.

" 'Sisterhood?' " Dani asked quietly.

"You're only the third woman engineer the company has hired," Hammond explained. "We need more women in the technical positions if we're going to make an impact."

"*I'm* in a technical position," Coombs objected.

"Doesn't count, dear. You're an English major."

"But Technical Reports isn't exactly the ghetto."

" 'Ghetto?' " Dani repeated, feeling stupid.

"The Velvet Ghetto," Pearsall supplied.

"Departments with an over-representation of women," Hammond explained. "That's where the company wants to keep us. We have a different system of pay grades and promotion tracks than the engineering and operations groups. We look good on their hiring statistics, which is necessary for getting federal contracts these days, but it keeps us out of positions of responsibility."

"But ..." Dani shook her head. "You're in Personnel. Surely, you could get all that changed."

"Head of the department's still a man. And he reports to the Executive Committee."

"And I have to write press releases with a tag touting our diversity," Pearsall put in.

"I see," Dani said. "I guess you want me to do something about it."

"Hurry up and get promoted, so you can hire more women."

"Speak out for women in engineering and the sciences."

"Make your presence and your feminism known."

"You make it sound," Dani said, "like a crusade."

"Exactly!" Pearsall said. "Women stick together."

"Solidarity," Coombs said, taking more wine.

"Shatter the glass ceiling," Hammond said.

The other three raised their glasses, and after a beat Dani joined them with her bubbly water. She wasn't sure she wanted to join a cabal inside the company. She wasn't aware of these other two "women engineers" in the company—probably because they worked in different departments or perhaps even out in the field. Dani thought that the three women here expected her to make some sort of contact with them, form a club, hold meetings, and present a unified front. It all seemed terribly vague and … unproductive.

Except, they had invited her to lunch at this expensive place—which the menu proclaimed as the oldest seafood restaurant in town, going back to the Gold Rush—so the best thing Dani could do was keep her doubts to herself.

But when the bill came, Hammond asked for it to be divided four ways. Dani ended up paying twelve dollars for her bowl of *cioppino* and the part-bottle of wine she didn't drink. But it was all in the name of "solidarity."

———

Mike Manuglian noticed when Dani Wheelock returned from lunch half an hour late. And she had left fifteen minutes early, to boot. Not that he was keeping tabs or anything …

"Lunch hour is noon to one," he said as she breezed past his desk.

"I know," Wheelock said. "I'm sorry. I got invited by some women from the other departments."

"Oh?" Manuglian didn't know any women in the company. "What departments?"

"Personnel." She counted on her fingers. "Public Relations. Technical Reports."

"Ah … *them*," he said. "You don't want to be seen fraternizing with that group."

"They just want to empower women in the company. Isn't that a good thing?"

"But you don't want to be treated as a *woman* here. You're an *engineer*."

# 10. More Random Numbers

A COUPLE OF weeks after she spotted the first palindrome in the Farragut rebar batch numbers, Dani detected another. This one was 1234321. Again it was an inside-out number, but instead of making a graceful catenary, in her mind it described a stepped pyramid shape, or the hump of a squared-off bell curve. And she was sure she had seen it before.

Or almost sure. After her rebuff by Mike Manuglian, the last time she brought the coincidence to his attention, Dani had begun to doubt herself. Could it be that these numbers only seemed familiar because they happened to fit a pattern? Back when she had first spotted 9876789, she could recall having remarked on that pattern, down to the paired sevens and eights, somewhere before and likely in the Farragut project—although she couldn't then find the match. But this time, with the 1234321 pattern, she could not say for certain where or when or even if she had seen it. It just seemed familiar.

Although she was trained as an engineer to observe facts, search out proven principles, and draw conclusions from hard data, Dani still respected human intuition. She knew that the brain contained more information than was apparent to the surface mind. That mind governed awareness of the here and now, and directed its own draws upon active memory, searching out and recalling facts, images, and details through conscious effort. But she also believed in the role of the subconscious in daily life, as it randomly tossed up hunches, impressions, and coincidences, shading sensory perceptions with auras of meaning and imports of either protection or disaster. So she tended to credit her gut reactions and first impressions.

And her gut reaction told her that, no, this wasn't just curiosity about a pattern. She *had* seen this number before, somewhere. The new palindrome, 1234321, was a bump in the system. It was not something she should ignore. But what was she to do next?

With a sigh, her own engineer's brain told her. If she had un-limited access to the accounting on the David G. Farragut Nu-clear Power Plant Project, instead of just permission to charge her working hours to the project's billing code, she would in-stitute a full search. And that would be expensive. It would probably mean requisitioning time on the big mainframe com-puter down in the basement, the System/360 that Mannheim leased monthly from the International Business Machines Cor-poration, and for which IBM supplied and Mannheim paid a core team of experts in coding and software languages like Fortran and APL. The company jealously guarded access to that machine, because every second of its processing time was counted in tens if not hundreds of dollars and required hands-on participation from that expert team.

The only way to make use of the computer in her records search would be to feed in all the entries in all the logbooks on the shelves beside her desk—a monumental task in itself, com-prised of typing thousands of line entries onto Hollerith punch cards—and then writing a program to seek out the target num-bers, 9876789 and 1234321, and record any matches. Or rather, a more thorough approach would be to write a program that attempted to hold all the batch numbers recorded to date on the rebar job inside some vast memory reservoir—like her own subconscious hindbrain—and then scan for their duplicates by recursively sorting every number against every other number, passing any hits to a separate memory bin, and structuring a report to show the site locations of all the matches. Not being a computer programmer herself, because Dani had taken just one preliminary computer science course at the university, she could imagine how the sorting process might work, but she would need expert help to formulate it into a Fortran or APL program.

Besides, no one was going to authorize that kind of effort and computer time on what her supervisor had already dis-missed as a figment of her imagination.

That meant Dani would have to approach the problem in the old-fashioned, brute-force, labor-intensive way: read and scan the logbooks herself, noting on a separate pad the random patterns that seemed to be familiar along with their locations, and then writing it all up in a report. She would have to do it in her spare minutes, apart from her main job of receiving those yellow forms and logging them. And finally, she would probably have to do all this extra work without padding her billing on the Farragut account number and raising a red flag with the project's management.

Dani sighed once again. Well, at least she didn't have any lunch plans.

Over the next three weeks, she pursued her private project. She found that her eye and her head for numbers were still clear. She also discovered a winning strategy for herself.

Instead of trying to remember all of the batch numbers—which was obviously impossible—she noted on her lined tablet any recognizable patterns, like palindromes, straight single-digit repeats, and short, tandem, repeated sequences that were likely to catch her eye and imagination. And she wrote down not just the batch numbers themselves but also the building locations from the logbook, so that she could find any repeated number again. Then she went through her books as if she was on an Easter egg hunt, looking for colorful patterns—at least in terms of digits—keeping herself sensitive to any she might later recognize and remember. And when her memory failed, she still had her notes.

At the end of the fourth week, she had a story to tell.

———

Mike Manuglian happened to be looking in the wrong direction when Dani Wheelock dropped a load of books on his desk. When he turned, he saw the logbooks from the rebar records for the Farragut nuclear project. Without being asked, Wheelock took one of the chairs in his cubicle and plopped a blue-lined yellow tablet on the front edge of his desk. The individual sheets were thickly inscribed with handwritten numbers.

"You've got to see this, Mike," she said breathlessly.

"You know, it helps if you make an appointment."

"I didn't have the time. And this is too important."

"All right. Just this once," he said. "So show me."

"You remember when I said I'd seen a number once before in the batch records, and you said it didn't mean anything unless I could find it again?"

"Yes, vaguely. You called it a drone-something."

"A palindrome. A funny pattern. Well, I went looking for it—for any numbers, actually, that might jump out at me. And I found them, half a dozen anyway." She flipped through her pad and showed him entries that she had underlined as being duplicated in the records.

"And what does this prove?" he asked. At the same time he wondered if this might all just be a stunt to get herself promoted.

"That we're getting duplicate batch numbers from the field," she said.

"Or you're not paying attention and writing down the numbers wrong."

"No, sir. Not at all." Wheelock was flatly contradicting him. "You can see here—you can check it in the books, too—three of these entries were made before I even started working here."

"All right, so the last person who held that job got the numbers wrong."

She paused at that. It probably never occurred to her that other people had come before her. Or that they could have made the same mistakes she was making.

"I don't think so," she said finally. "I'll bet that if we ran these books through a computer, we'd find a lot more matches. Not just the funny repeats."

"And again, what would that prove?" Manuglian asked.

"That we've got the same batch of steel going into two locations at once. But then, some of these entries are weeks apart and in different buildings. How likely is it that the construction crew would use part of a batch in one place, stop, and then use the rest for something somewhere else?"

Manuglian thought about that. It might be steel that was left over when a section of the foundation was tied off and ready to pour. But the standard practice was to hold the remainder there and use it on the next section or level, the next part of the pour. If the crews were carting half-used batches of steel around the site and using them indiscriminately someplace else, that would be a bad thing in itself. But worse would be if someone was futzing around with the record slips. Much worse. It might call the whole project into question—at least as far as the Atomic Energy Commission's inspectors were concerned.

"All right," he said slowly. "Leave me your notes. And take those books back to your desk."

"You'll follow up with Harbaugh?" she asked. Peter Harbaugh was the Farragut project manager, and several grade levels above either of them.

"Yes." He paused. "And ... Dani?"

"Are you going to thank me?" she asked.

"No, I'm telling you to keep your mouth shut."

# 11. A Walk in the Park

DANI WAS ABOUT to step out for a walk on a bright Saturday morning. The day was sunny, breezy, and missing the ever-present summertime "marine layer" that people back East would have called "low clouds" or "fog." While she had her hand on the front-door knob, she heard a clatter on the stairs behind her.

"Hey, wait up!" Norman Wall called. "We were just going out ourselves."

At his heels was the strangest dog Dani had ever seen. It had the shape and size of a German shepherd, including the erect and pointed ears. But instead of the usual brown-and-tan coat with black markings, this dog was pure black all over. It looked menacing, like some kind of devil-dog, and it fixed Dani with a direct stare.

"Is that dog safe?" she asked, drawing back.

"What? Bear?" Wall said. "He's a pussycat."

Hardly, she thought. It looked like an attack dog.

Just as she was deciding this, Bear grinned at her. The dog lifted its upper lip—not to show its sharp canine teeth in a warning, but to expose the row of pearly little incisors between them. And there was no accompanying growl. The dog wagged its tail, although tentatively.

"Good boy!" Wall said. "Shake hands!"

The dog lifted its right front leg, pushed the paw forward with the toes stretched out, and dabbed at the air. Dani could do nothing except squat down, take the offered foot in her hand, and give it a shake.

"He likes you," Wall said. The dog looked up at him with obvious adoration.

"Yeah," she said. "Except, isn't 'Bear' kind of intimidating—as a name?"

"At first I called him 'Woolly Bear,' when he was a puppy, just a ball of black fluff. The name stuck."

"Well," she began. "I was going for a walk in the park."

"May we come, too?" Wall asked. Bear wagged his tail.

"Gee." She hesitated, thinking *not*. Then she shrugged. "If you want …"

Wall leashed Bear with a contraption that was like a fishing reel, a spring-loaded coil that would release a sturdy red cord attached to a flat leader. They went down the house's front steps, crossed over into the Panhandle, and walked west into Golden Gate Park past McLaren Lodge. This had been the home of the park's first superintendent and was now its headquarters. The lodge was a fortress-like, two-story building with thick walls made from blocks of blue basalt, porch and lintels of beige sandstone, and a roof of red tiles. Along the way, Bear pulled at the leash, extending its reach out to twenty or thirty feet.

When they arrived at one of the many enclosed meadows, Norman Wall reeled in his dog and unhooked him. Bear leapt into the air and dashed off.

"This really isn't an off-leash area," Wall said. "But this is the only exercise Bear gets anymore. And he generally minds his business."

"What does he do all day while you're … out working?"

"He sleeps in my room. He kind of shuts down till I get home. I've asked some of the other residents—those who don't have day jobs—to look in on him, maybe walk him. But so far, no takers."

"You know why that is, don't you?"

"What? They think he's dangerous?"

"No, because they think you're a *narc*."

"Really?" Wall laughed at that. "I'm an accountant at Levi Strauss. But I want to get into banking and finance someday. That's where the real money is."

"And I work as an engineer at Mannheim."

"Yeah …" He hesitated. "I knew that already."

"Have you been keeping tabs on me, sir?" she asked.

"Not like that. But people in the house, they talk."

"Oh, Jesus!" she said. "Don't they ever!"

———

Figuring that, thanks to Bear, he had made good contact with Dani Wheelock, Norman Wall took every opportunity to get close to her. He knew her schedule and managed to be in the kitchen five minutes before she came down in the morning for her cup of coffee and bowl of Grape-Nuts. In the evening, regardless of when the Nirvana House crew sat down for dinner together, he tried to be at the table when she rolled in—usually around seven-thirty. Then he would sit and eat his cold rabbit stew, heavy on the carrots and onions, while she ate a fast-food hamburger or chicken sandwich.

On Saturdays, he tried to recreate their walk in the park. Or if she was headed downtown to do some shopping, Norman would excuse himself, put Bear back in his bedroom, and return to join her. The first time this happened, she actually waited for him at the front door and they went downtown together. But after that, she just walked out as soon as he turned back upstairs with his dog. So it was clear she liked Bear better than him.

In the evenings, if Dani was in the common room, Norman would sit beside her and read the newspaper or a book. It helped if Bear was sitting on the floor, pressed against Wall's knee—and once against Dani's, at the edge of her beanbag. Since Dani liked the dog, Norman was willing to share the animal's affections with her.

All of this—the chance meetings, the quiet presence, the silent wooing—worked for a couple of weeks. But eventually she became wary. And then he made the mistake of being outside the bathroom door on the second floor—because his bedroom was on the third—when she suddenly came out.

"Are you *stalking* me, sir?" she asked.

"No, oh … I just happened to be here."

"Funny how our paths always cross."

And the next time he was at breakfast, waiting for her, she became more direct.

"You've got to respect boundaries, Norman."

"I'm sorry. I didn't mean to offend you."

"It's just—I need my privacy. Okay?"

Norman nodded humbly. He was terribly embarrassed to be caught out like that. At least no one else was in the kitchen. That would have made things even worse.

# 12. The Screw-Up

THE WEEKLY PROGRESS meeting of the Farragut Nuclear Power Plant Project took up all the space in the largest meeting room—other than the auditorium—in Centennial Plaza. Every chair along the two wings of the center table, even those awkward ones fitted in between the wings, and every chair along the side walls and across the back, all of them were filled. More than thirty engineers, plus engineering assistants, support personnel, and the various heads of supporting departments were present to hear the steady drumbeat of good news. Or rather, Peter Harbaugh, the Project Manager, reminded himself, the *mostly* good news.

He even had his own boss, Saul Bruno, Vice President of the Power Division, in attendance. So Harbaugh had to watch his words carefully. So far, he had made it through all but the last item on the agenda with everyone was still smiling, including Bruno.

"And finally," Harbaugh said, glancing down at his notes, "we come to a small matter regarding documentation. We don't know what the impact is yet—or even that there *is* an issue—but it's worth noting at this time."

Harbaugh took a breath and looked around the room. In the sea of faces—exclusively male, mostly satisfied faces—he noticed an anomaly. Sitting at the back was a woman, sharply dressed in a tight black skirt that showed the tops of her knees, with a short matching jacket, like the imitation of a man's business suit. She was pretty enough, too, with her auburn hair gathered in a long braid. But her face was not smiling and not satisfied. It was pale and expectant. He wondered who she was, because he didn't have any women on his team. Probably she was one of the project secretaries, sitting in and taking notes for her boss, who was either sick, out of town, or otherwise engaged.

"It seems," Harbaugh continued to the room at large, "that the reports from the rebar team are not being properly documented. There's an indication—at this time no more than a suggestion—that some of the batches have been misplaced in the reporting process. The whole thing is probably just someone seeing ghosts or engaging in fantasies. However, I assure you we will discover exactly what has happened, and we have every expectation of correcting the situation."

He looked around the room again. Most of the faces were still smiling. At his elbow, Bruno seemed almost asleep. But the woman at the back looked stricken. Her eyes were staring at him like two holes burned into a white pine board.

"For most of the departments represented here, I have nothing but the highest praise," he went on. "You are all doing an excellent job. But I cannot stress enough the importance of complete and accurate documentation on this project. It might just seem like fiddling paperwork, but the Atomic Energy Commission takes it very seriously. Nuclear power is among Mannheim's most heavily regulated and closely watched project classes—and for good reason. Each one of us must give his best in working on this plant. There can be no slacking-off, no slip-ups, no untrapped errors. Any lapse can only have the most severe and irreparable consequences."

And with that—ending on a warning note by way of a pep talk—Harbaugh brought the meeting to a close.

As people were filing out of the room, he took aside his project deputy, Jim Farley. "Who was the woman at the back?"

"Woman?" Farley said. "I didn't notice."

"Well. No matter. Probably a secretary."

———

Dani had attended the Farragut progress meeting uninvited and unannounced. It was the first regular meeting after she had reported the findings from her records search to Mike Manuglian, and she wanted to see what the reaction would be. It disturbed her that the project team and Peter Harbaugh himself were dismissing her discoveries as "ghosts" and "fantasies."

If nothing came of her work, then how was she to proceed? Just keep logging the batch numbers as they came in but not look at them too closely? Or initiate a new search on her own, gathering more evidence? That would be necessary for her own peace of mind, even if the project management was not seriously concerned.

Dani got a hint of the company's reaction three days later when she was walking back to her desk from the coffee station. Two people at adjoining desks had their heads together in whispered conversation, and the one word she overheard was "fired."

She turned to look at them, and their two heads snapped apart as if pushed by springs. The men did not look at her then but immediately busied themselves with the papers on their separate desks.

For the rest of the day, Dani found herself coming upon tight huddles in the hallway that broke up as soon as she approached. People were stepping out of her way as if she carried the plague. And she noticed an alarming absence of the nods and smiles she usually got from people on the floor. So someone was going to be fired, and no one was telling her, not even in a whisper.

Well … she could sit there and stew, or she could find out what is going on. The next morning, she approached Manuglian as soon as he came into the office.

"People are avoiding me, Mike," she said. "Has something happened around here?"

"Gee, uh … Dani. I don't know of anything." But he wouldn't meet her eyes.

"You sent my report on the duplicated batches upstairs, didn't you?"

"Yes, of course. Just as I said I would." Still no eye contact.

"You know I'm not responsible for the errors, right?"

"Um, that's for senior management to decide."

"But you *will* back me up, won't you?"

"Yes. Sure. I mean … if I can."

Joseph Fiorelli noticed that the new student, Miss Wheelock, was agitated and distracted during the Thursday-night class. She was half a beat off when he led the group through their basic exercises, and twice she started doing the wrong set of kicks. Finally, he turned the class over to a senior belt and approached her in line, casually ducking the pantomime blows of the other students as they punched and kicked the air.

"Are you okay?"

"Sure. Yeah. I'm fine."

"No, I don't think you're okay."

Fiorelli took her out of line and led her to the back of the class. He opened the door to the storage room and dragged out the sparring dummy and a stepladder. The dummy was a semi-articulated sack of olive-drab canvas, reinforced with leather straps and patches, filled with sand and kapok. The thing weighed about sixty pounds. It had just enough of a bifurcation between its legs to take a groin shot, just enough spread in its arms to let students work on strikes to shoulders, armpits, and ribs, and just enough of a face to make head and neck shots work.

He shoved the dummy into her arms. "Hold that."

Fiorelli took the ladder over to the two-by-four crossbeam that Berggren had installed in one corner of the dance studio. Wheelock followed him, half-hugging, half-dragging the dummy. He mounted the ladder, steadied himself on the beam, and reached down.

"Give me the chain."

Still clutching the dummy, she gathered the loop of stainless steel chain attached to the leather strap that was stitched around the thing's head with extensions down to its shoulders. She passed the end up to him. Fiorelli put the third link over the galvanized hook in the crossbeam while she boosted the dead weight off the ground. Then he motioned for Wheelock to let the dummy swing free. He climbed down and folded the ladder out of the way against the wall.

"You spend the rest of class putting that thing out of its misery. Use every kick, every punch you know, working both sides, high and low." He looked directly into her face. "Hit it hard. Make it suffer. You understand?"

"Yes, sir." Her jaw was set, her eyes half-closed.

"Then get busy. Knock yourself out."

By the time class was over, the Wheelock woman was exhausted and sweating. Her hair braid was coming undone, and loose strands stuck to her neck and the sides of her face. Her knuckles and even her toes were bleeding from abrading contacts with the dummy's rough canvas, and Fiorelli knew one of his jobs before he went home tonight would be swabbing off the thing's torso and spritzing it with disinfectant.

But Dani Wheelock looked a little more relaxed.

She even managed to smile at him.

––––––––

Peter Harbaugh had received, through his secretary Barbara, two requests for an appointment from some woman named Wheelock.

"Who is she?" he asked.

"Someone in Manuglian's group."

"Is she related to that screw-up with the rebar?"

"I don't know. But Manuglian's people were handling that."

"Then find out. In the meantime, I don't want to talk to anyone directly."

But before Barbara could learn anything, he was cornered in the elevator bay on the thirty-eighth floor, up in "Executive Country," by that same young woman from the meeting earlier in the week.

"Mister Harbaugh!" She was standing practically on his toes.

"Yes, miss?" He retreated until his back touched the wall.

"I'm Dani Wheelock. I work for Mike Manuglian."

"You were at the progress meeting, weren't you?"

"You know I was. You were looking right at me."

"So? What can I do for you, Miss Wheelock?"

"These are my notes about the Farragut rebar."

She held up a set of pages written in a spiky hand. These were pale photocopies made on slick Xerox paper, of course. Manuglian had given him the originals, written on lined yellow tablet paper. The implication had been that Harbaugh could use them or make them disappear as he saw fit. That the perpetrator—this young woman, evidently—had kept copies added a whole new dimension to the problem.

"I see," he said. "And why do you bring them to me?"

"From what you said at the meeting, I think you got the wrong impression. These batch numbers are not 'ghosts' or 'fantasies.' I made a careful review of the project documents— the best I could do without requisitioning computer time for a thorough search. Some of these duplicates come from before my time on the project. So I'm not the one who made these errors."

"I never said you were," he said. "I don't even know you."

"But there's talk on the floor of someone being fired."

"And you think it might be you? Because of this?"

"Well …" She calmed down. "Two plus two."

"You think we shoot the messenger here?"

"I was hoping that wasn't your way."

"Miss Wheelock …" He paused to compose himself. He put his hands on her shoulders and gently pushed her back. "When we find that there's a problem, the first thing we do is make sure it *is* a problem and we're not just chasing our tails. That's where we are right now. The team will take this up with Mike Manuglian and talk to you—formally, respectfully, and carefully. We may even do that computer search you've suggested. And then we'll act. We don't sweep issues like this under the rug. That's death on a big project—or a project of any scale. In this business, what you don't know, or won't recognize, or can't accept, usually comes back to bite you on the ass. Do you follow me, Miss Wheelock?"

"I think so, sir."

"If you've done your work diligently and carefully, you have nothing to fear. If you've made mistakes, then it would be best for you to fess up and help us correct them. Don't you agree?"

"Yes, sir." She held out the photocopies again. "Do you want these, sir?"

"You keep them. I have the originals, don't I?"

"I would hope so, sir."

"All right. So … you wait until we call you in to study this." Harbaugh let his face harden. "Otherwise, stay out of my sight. And if you ever go over Mike Manuglian's head—or any supervisor's head—again, you really will be fired. Now, *git!*"

"Yes, sir." Wheelock nodded and backed away. She looked around and found herself trapped in the elevator bay with him. She dodged into the next elevator car that opened its door, wherever it was going.

Harbaugh chuckled to himself, then sobered. If this thing sorted out the wrong way, there was going to be hell to pay.

# 13. Crisis Mode

TWO DAYS AFTER confronting the Project Manager in Centennial Plaza, Dani Wheelock received a surprise visit at her desk from the Farragut Senior Project Engineer, James Farley. Without asking permission, he pulled over the guest chair from a nearby desk and sat down in the space next to her.

"You know who I am," he said by way of introduction.

"Yes, of course," she said. "Number two on the nuclear project."

"I'm here at the express request of Peter Harbaugh—and you clearly know who he is." Farley pulled her yellow tablet sheets out of his inside jacket pocket. "And you recognize these—although Harbaugh tells me you made copies without telling anyone."

"Yes, I did," she replied. "Was that a breach of security?"

"Some scribbled numbers, unsigned, with no attribution and no conclusions?" He shrugged. "Hardly. But it does show a lack of ... faith? Trust? Belief that we would follow up?"

"I had to get someone's attention."

"You've certainly got that now—"

"And to show this isn't my fault."

"That was not our first reaction."

"I'm going to choose to believe you," Dani replied. The first rule when riding a tiger: hang on tight to its ears.

"I hope you realize, Miss Wheelock, what a pile of manure you've landed us in," Farley went on. "There are some on the team, it's true, who thought the easy way out would be to blame you for the errors. But instead, we want to find out how deep they go. I've looked at your notes up, down, and sideways, and I still can't figure them out. So show me." He handed her the papers.

Dani spread them on her desk in order, then took the first of the logbooks referenced and opened it to the right place.

She took the second book, opened it, and showed Farley the duplicate numbers.

"Two batches of rebar, see?" she said. "Same numbers, going into different buildings, three weeks apart."

He studied the numbers. She watched his lips move as he repeated the digits to himself. He nodded in agreement. For the next ten minutes, they went through the eight examples on her list, book by book, verifying each instance.

"How did you spot these?" Farley asked finally. "Manuglian said something about funny number shapes."

"Palindromes and repeated digits," she said, pointing out the patterns. "They stick in my head. Once I found one, I searched the books looking for others."

"And this is what you found just by visual inspection alone?"

"Yes, but not in one go. These took me weeks of searching."

Farley sat for a moment, lips pressed together. "You charged all this search time to the project?"

"Some. But I did most of it on my lunch hour and after work."

"That was either extremely honest of you—or very stupid," he said.

"Would you have believed me if I brought just the first match I noticed?"

He grinned. "Probably not."

"So what happens now?"

"I've already contacted the construction manager at the site," Farley said. "He's not aware of any discrepancies."

"Oh ..."

"But then, why would he be? It's not like they had anything to hide. This isn't a case of fraud. If what we're seeing here is real—and people are always going to be asking *that*—it will be more a matter of carelessness. Damnable negligence, but not intentional."

"I once thought of doing a computer search."

"That was going to be my next step," he said.

"Do you want me to code in these logbooks?"

"What? You?" He laughed. "Your time is much too valuable. Anyway, we have a team of keypunch operators in the basement. They're Filipino ladies who don't speak English, or even Spanish. Tagalog, maybe, or some Indian dialect. They are creepy-fast at data entry and totally accurate, because what they type doesn't mean a thing to them. So no word associations, no distracting ideas, no logical conclusions—and no 'palindromes.' Just in the eyes and out the fingers. You couldn't ask for a better operator."

"And once you have the logbooks reduced to punch cards?"

"We'll do a nested query to find duplicates among the batch numbers. That's the brute-force approach. Or we can do a simple bubble-sort of the numbers to put them in ascending order—or descending order—whichever would put the duplicates side by side. Then we write a structured query report to identify the duplicates and note their laydown dates and locations."

"Do you have programmers to do that?"

"Better qualified than either you or me."

———

Norman Wall noticed that Dani had been keeping odd hours. She was looking pale and nervous, not her normal self. He knew that she wanted him to keep his distance and give her space, but he was also concerned. So one day he stopped her in the front hall.

"Are you feeling all right, Dani? You look … thinner."

"I'm just working out more. Trying to keep in shape."

He held his lower lip in his teeth. "You don't look it."

"I'm fine, Norman. You don't have to worry about me."

"Sorry, but I do worry. Are there problems at your work?"

"No. No, I don't think so …" But now she looked scared.

"It's just a job, you know. You can always get another."

"Not when you've …" She shut her mouth. "Yeah, sure."

———

A week after her personal meeting with Jim Farley, Mike Ma-nuglian called Dani over to his desk. On it was a thick stack of double-wide, eleven-by-seventeen, green-bar computer paper which, when he picked it up, accordioned out at the sides and corners. It was all one continuous sheet, fanfolded and stacked as it came from the impact printer down in the basement. Across the first page, written in two-inch-high characters composed of triple repeats of each letter in the words, was the title: "Farragut Nuclear Rebar Sort 001-A1."

"Is that my survey?" Dani asked eagerly.

" 'Your survey.' " He grinned. "I like that."

"Or rather, the one Jim Farley wanted, based on my findings."

"You don't want to get too possessive about this cluster-fuck, Dani."

"Oh, sure, right. But what did they discover? It took them long enough."

"Everything with the Computer Department has a sched-ule and a turnaround time. This wasn't the only job they had to handle. Plus, those logbooks of yours took a damn lot of entry time. Consider doing it all in one week a rush job for them."

"And the findings?" she prompted.

"Worse than everybody thought."

He flipped open the stack, pointed out the parameters of the search coded in Fortran, explained how the computer printed three pages for each iteration of the search, and noted the incidence of batch number matches reported at the bottom of each third page.

"Two here," he said, pawing through the stack. "None there. Four here."

Dani nodded as he went along. Finally even she got bored. "What's the bottom line?"

Manuglian turned to the last page with its summary report. "Eighty-seven incidents of number matches that are not asso-ciated with consecutive pours."

"That's bad, isn't it?"

"Yeah. You just can't account for it—can't even imagine it—as crews holding onto random pieces from the end of one tie-off, cataloguing them in a shed somewhere, and then using them someplace else and scrupulously noting the old batch in the new location. It's just not the sensible way to proceed."

"And they never throw away part of a batch?"

"Not if they can help it. Steel costs money."

Dani thought about the issue, based on her weeks of work with the logbooks and as-built drawings. "What does all this mean?" she asked finally.

"Unless somebody can come up with a logical explanation, it means we don't know what rebar was used where in the foundations for the two reactor vessels and their containment structures."

"Can they dig up the concrete and check markings on the rebar?"

"Tear apart half the site?" Manuglian looked horrified at the thought. "Anyway, the markings stamped onto the steel itself are generic, just its size and composition. The mill name and batch number are written on tags attached to the strapping. Cut the strapping, lose the tag. Without the paperwork you've been processing, there's no provenance for the batch."

"The Atomic Energy Commission isn't going to like that."

He grunted. "This could kill the project. It's a disaster."

"Is it too late to convert it to a coal-fired steam plant?"

"What? Oh!" He seemed dazed by the question, then became thoughtful. "No, the turbine specs are all wrong. A coal-fired boiler produces steam at different pressure and temperature than the heat exchanger in a nuclear reactor. We would have to scrub the entire plant design."

"Well, it was just a thought," she said.

"But you're thinking like an engineer."

---

Jim Farley sat at the six-person conference table in his boss's office, facing Peter Harbaugh across the printout from his computer run on the Farragut rebar situation. The fanfold pages lay flopped open to the last one, with its awful conclusions.

"This is just a mess, isn't it?" Harbaugh said. He was famous in the company for his gentlemanly demeanor and decorous manner of speech, where most other project managers would have laced that observation five or six deep with theological or scatological swear words.

"Worst screw-up I've ever been involved with," Farley replied.

"You weren't here when they finished the detailed design on a hydroelectric project after relying on a third-party geological report—which nobody bothered to check and confirm. The dam had to be re-sited two miles upriver. It was a total loss on the engineering work invested to that point."

"Rio Salado. I heard about that. A bad day for everyone's career."

"We are—" Harbaugh touched the printout. "—inside the ballpark."

They sat a moment in silence together before Harbaugh spoke again.

"The best solution is that the Wheelock girl compromised her records."

Farley shook his head. "Half the duplicates come from before her time."

"Pity. Second best would be the logbooks at headquarters are compromised."

"And that they still have good records at the site?" Farley completed the thought. "Then we could just copy the site data and use it to rebuild the logs and as-builts here. All we'd lose is a couple of thousand man-hours of clerical time on the project to date."

"Who do you want to send to Shelbyville?" Harbaugh asked quietly.

"I should go myself, of course. Nate Packer already has his back up."

"Then I should go. It's my job to talk him down—and impose order."

"Actually," Farley replied, "I would like to save you for later, as our big gun. Keep things low key for now. We're still just investigating, just asking friendly questions."

"Agreed," Harbaugh said. "But you'll need more hands, especially if you have to do a snipe hunt through their office files. That could tie you up for weeks."

"I'd like to bring along the Wheelock girl," Farley said.

"Why her, in particular? Isn't she ... bad luck on this?"

Farley shrugged. "She already knows the material. She's been through the logbooks once already. And she seems to have a quick eye."

"All right—but keep her away from Packer. He'll eat her for breakfast."

# 14. Trip to Tennessee

ALTHOUGH SHE WAS supposed to fly out that morning, Dani had to make a quick detour into Centennial Plaza to pick up her plane tickets and gather her notes on the rebar situation, along with the fanfold printout from the computer run. Because the decision to include her had only been made late yesterday, the Senior Project Engineer had called her last night at home, after she already left the office, and so she was unprepared for the trip to Tennessee.

"Oh, and we'll be driving directly to the site from the airport, so wear appropriate clothing," Farley said.

"Um, okay," she replied. "Since this is my first construction site, what do you call 'appropriate'?"

The man actually sighed. "No high heels. No skirts. Wear jeans, a jacket, and boots you don't mind getting muddy."

"Gotcha. Um, how long are we gone for?"

"Overnight at least. A couple of days, maybe, depending on what we find. But pack light, because we won't be waiting around for checked baggage."

Dani also reasoned that she would need some way to carry the project paperwork, which was too bulky to fit into her largest handbag. So she spent the rest of the evening—and close to a hundred dollars—in a luggage store downtown, buying a black-leather attaché case that looked official and, in other circumstances, wouldn't clash with her purse and good shoes.

On the following morning she went into the office looking like a lumberjack weighed down with her handbag, carryon suitcase, and the attaché. And she was not just going into the converted factory building where her desk in the Power Division was located, but to the twenty-eighth floor of Centennial Plaza's main high-rise, which housed the company's Travel Office.

In the elevator going up, Dani noticed a strange phenomenon. No one would meet her eye. No one appeared to notice her. Not even people she knew and had worked with, including the department secretary, Annie. They all pretended Dani was simply not there. It was the way they would treat a bicycle messenger or a United Parcel Service deliveryman, people who should be using the freight elevator instead.

For the first dozen floors, Dani wondered about this invisible treatment. Then she realized she wasn't wearing her dark business suit, her heels, and her white blouse with the floppy bow. She didn't *look* like a professional. And these people took in a gestalt of a person's clothing before they bothered to recognize the face. Or perhaps they were just embarrassed for her, as if she had somehow forgotten to dress to code that morning.

At San Francisco International Airport, she finally met up with James Farley in the boarding area for their flight. He had also dressed rough, like her, and was carrying an overnight bag for himself. She suddenly felt better—or at least less conspicuous.

They landed at Nashville International at three in the afternoon, with the time change, and immediately went to the rental car counter where Mannheim Construction had a standing order and a fleet car reserved for engineers visiting from headquarters. The drive south through Murfreesboro to Shelbyville, where the plant was situated on the Duck River, took just over an hour. So they arrived late in the workday. That in itself put everyone on edge.

Farley showed the guard at the gate their laminated Mannheim identity cards—his own and hers together. The guard then issued them two white metal hardhats blazoned with the Mannheim logo, which showed a stylized, hexagonal-shaped world caught in the jaws of a huge wrench. The hats were one-size-fits-all, with tab-adjustable plastic bands inside. Farley put his on while still inside the car, and Dani followed his example, after fiddling with the strap three times to get it over her braided hair.

They drove along a track through muddy fields where the grass had long been beaten down and was just sprouting new shoots around the edges of things. The area was crowded with lumber stacked up in raw boards, orderly rows of pallets holding various pieces of machinery under canvas tarps, stacks of steel drums, parked construction equipment including canary-yellow Caterpillar bulldozers, graders, and front-end loaders, a blue tanker trailer for water and a green one for diesel fuel, and half a dozen various semi-trailer trucks unloading more drums and pallets of equipment and supplies from all across the country. Obvious to Dani's eye, also, was a waiting line of pink and yellow cement trucks, their barrels slowly rotating, which constituted the coming night shift's portion of the project's ongoing concrete pour.

Once they had cleared this field, which Farley called the "laydown area," they came upon the construction site itself. At first glance, it looked like a war zone with massive bomb damage. On the edge of the lot where they parked was a deep hole—three holes, actually, one for each of the two reactor containments and another for the turbine building—that extended over a dozen acres. The site stretched as far as she could see, down to the river, where foundations for the cooling-tower intakes were being laid.

When Dani looked into the first of the nearby holes, she traced out the substructure of Unit One containment in various stages of construction. First were the patches of smooth concrete, representing the already poured subfloors and the beginnings of the foundation walls. At the edges of this finished work came areas that were merely sketched in lattices of raw steel rods tied together with twisted wires, representing those parts of the slab, walls, and load-bearing pillars that were still waiting to be poured. And finally, beyond the latticework, were acres of bedrock and mud not yet prepared with the raw steel.

She was looking at the tons of steel rebar which, up to now, she had only seen referenced on her yellow carbon copies and annotated in her logbooks. It was all laid out in the intricate configurations that she had previously known only as plots in her file of as-built drawings.

"This way, Dani," Farley said behind her.

She looked around and saw him heading for a string of trailers further along the rim of the pit. They weren't any of those aerodynamic, steel-clad models that holiday campers pulled behind their station wagons. Instead, these trailers were long, narrow houselike structures with black-painted siding and tar-and-gravel shingles on the roof, all mounted on wheels and leveled with jack stands.

They climbed the steps—actually two wooden crates pushed together—to the door of the first trailer and Farley let her inside. The interior was a bare-bones space with a plywood floor, two steel desks with three telephones, a drafting board mounted on wooden sawhorses, and a wall full of steel filing cabinets. It smelled of damp wood, mildewed clothing, and stale cigar smoke.

"Dani Wheelock," Farley said as an introduction, "this is Nate Packer, Mannheim's construction manager on this job."

She focused on the older man standing back by the second desk. He had a weathered face but a pair of sharp blue eyes. His long white hair was crimped in a circle by the headband of the hardhat he was holding in his gnarled hands. Underneath his long white moustache, his lips were pressed together in barely controlled fury.

Dani smiled and stepped forward with her hand out. "I'm pleased to meet you."

He ignored her and said to Farley, "Why did you have to bring *the girl?*"

———

Nate Packer knew his business. After thirty years on big-ticket construction jobs, starting with dry docks for the West Coast shipbuilding boom during the last world war, he knew how to manage on-site activities at high-value projects like the Farragut nuke plant. And Mannheim had always respected that expertise and repaid it by leaving him, for the most part, alone.

The engineering team back at headquarters in San Francisco had designed the plant, issued the drawings, written the contracts, vetted and approved the subcontractors. And now they were keeping the government bureaucracy and its inspectors happy and at bay with progress reports and site visits. Most important, they held the client's hand—in this case, the Middle Valley Electric Cooperative—and issued their change orders, along with revised drawings and contract details, but otherwise kept the client out of his hair. So Packer could accept that San Francisco might feel they had a hand in building the plant, all right.

But when it came to how the site was run, Farragut was *his* baby. Packer and his team kept to the schedule and ran the subcontractors. His team coordinated all site logistics according to the project's Gantt chart, managed operations inside the warehouse, and tracked the project's inventory, incoming and outgoing. They kept the cat skinners moving dirt, the roughnecks tying rebar, and the cement haulers feeding the pour. And, in all things of this nature, Packer and his team took no shit from the gang in San Francisco, with their fancy suitcoats, power ties, and shiny shoes.

And now everyone on the project, from Harbaugh on down, had their panties in a twist because some junior engineer—hell, not even an engineer yet, but some college graduate new hire, and *a girl* to boot—thought she saw some numbers that looked like some other numbers. Packer didn't so much mind their asking him questions, politely, over the phone, and listening to his answers. But then they decided his answers weren't good enough and sent James Farley, Harbaugh's number-two boy and career assassin, out to snoop around. And he'd brought the *fool girl* with him.

It was damned insulting.

"Yeah, I thought you'd like that," Farley said with a grin. Insufferable bastard. "Thing is, Dani's kept the logbooks for two months now. She knows the rebar situation backwards and for—"

"From a desk in San Francisco?" Packer said. "I doubt that. Has she even *seen* a piece of number-eighteen rebar?" He picked up a one-foot length of the steel that would knit together the domes of the two reactor containment buildings.

Packer kept this sample—the largest steel made for any job—in the trailer just to impress visitors. When the time came to enclose the reactors, the Farragut team would tie this steel into a crisscross basket weave that you couldn't poke a finger through, then shoot it full of gunite. This foot-long piece was a tad more than two and a quarter inches in diameter, weighed about thirteen pounds, and made an excellent bludgeon. He tossed it to the Wheelock girl.

She tried to catch it, but for that she had to use two hands. And first she had to put down the briefcase she was carrying, and then the strap of her handbag slipped off her shoulder, tugging down on her arm. So the bar segment hit the front of her maroon nylon jacket, tearing the fabric with its rough-cut end, and fell to the floor with a solid *thump!*

"I thought so," Packer said in disgust and turned away.

"Are you done throwing your dick around?" the woman said.

He turned back in shocked surprise. If his daughter ever talked like that …

"Because there's nothing wrong with your rebar," Wheelock went on, "except we don't know where you put it. Mister Farley here and Mister Harbaugh back in the office want to figure out if *you* happen to know. Because, if you don't, then all that work out there—" She pointed to the construction site outside the window. "—is just a bunch of messed up holes in the ground."

Packer set his jaw. "You've got a mouth on you, young lady."

She nodded at that. "Have we got your attention now? Okay, show us where you keep your batch records, so I can get to work." She picked up her briefcase again. She didn't seem to know that her jacket was ripped and leaking out tiny bits of lint or feathers.

"You starting now?" he said. "It's four-thirty. We close the office at five."

"You run the site twenty-four hours for the pour, don't you?" Farley said.

"Yeah, but … she can't stay here alone. It's not safe. Not for any woman."

"All right," Farley said. "We'll be back to start first thing in the morning."

## 15. The Two-Bucket Conundrum

DANI AND FARLEY spent the night in separate cabins at a motor lodge called "Shay-Dee Acres," which was tucked into the woods outside Shelbyville. Having nothing better to do with her evening, Dani took out her emergency sewing kit and mended the tear in her favorite down jacket, which had cost her thirty dollars at L.L. Bean. She didn't mind the damage so much, because Packer's little act of aggression had shown how scared he was. His job was on the line, and now she knew that he knew it.

She and Farley took both their dinner and breakfast the following morning at a roadside diner called "Mom's Fine Eats," which had the shape of a railroad Pullman car. The breakfast specialty was biscuits and gravy, which Dani ordered, expecting to get a nice brown gravy, like her father used to make with roast beef, poured over flaky buttermilk biscuits. Instead, she got a pasty gruel made with flour and bacon fat, and she ended up nibbling around the edges of a dry, baking-powder hockey puck.

Then they drove back to the site, showed their badges, and parked next to the construction office's trailer. Nate Packer was there, sitting and drinking coffee with a young man just a year or two older than Dani. This young man wore his blonde hair cropped close to the skull, and he still suffered from acne, which seemed to make him shy. Packer introduced the boy as Jacob Aldis, the site's construction clerk.

Again, Dani offered to shake hands, and Jacob ignored her.

"Where are your logbooks on the rebar batches?" she asked.

"Those files." Packer pointed toward the row of cabinets along the wall.

Jacob unlocked the leftmost one with a key from the bunch on his belt.

"I still don't know what you're trying to prove," Packer said. "Jacob here records each tag as it comes off the bundle of rebar. He writes the batch number on his pad along with the location. He puts the white copy in his notebook here, and sends the yellow copy to San Francisco. It's all real-time and chronological. Even a monkey could do it, and there's no way he could screw it up. If we've got duplicate batch numbers, they're coming from the mill itself."

Jacob nodded at this, ignoring the comment about the monkey.

"I'm here to make sure the system works that way," Dani said.

"Why don't we go outside?" Farley said to Packer. "Let these two young people get started. You can show me the progress on last night's pour."

After the senior men left, Jacob went back to his desk and pursued whatever clerkly duties he had that morning. Clearly, Dani was on her own with the batch records.

She set her attaché case on the drafting table, took out her Xeroxed notes and the fanfold printout, and pulled a stool from between the paired sawhorses. It was a good thing that her notes and the printout included not just batch numbers but also showed their locations from her logbooks. But she still had a problem. The site notebooks were recorded chronologically, as Packer had said, not by location. So she had no easy way to correlate her records with the site's.

Her life would have been made a whole lot easier, she decided, if the Filipino ladies back in San Francisco had key-punched the dates on each form in her logbooks along with the batch numbers and locations, but Farley or one of his engineers had omitted that instruction, probably for reasons of cost and time.

Dani went to the file cabinet and pulled out the first notebook. She discovered it didn't use three split rings with a snap mechanism, like the binders she was used to, but instead had three screw-and-post fittings that bound the front and back covers together and compressed the loose pages between them. She opened the book and, yes, there were the familiar

NCR-paper forms but white, as Packer had said, while hers in San Francisco were yellow. She leafed through the first dozen or so, and confirmed that they were indeed in order by date, just as Packer had also said. The book in front of her recorded the first steel tied into the start of the foundation on Unit One, beginning at the northwest corner of the excavation.

"Do you unscrew these posts every time?" she asked Jacob.

"What?" he asked from his desk, not bothering to look around.

"These notebooks, with the screws. Do you have to take them apart every time you file a form?"

"Naw, that would be stupid. I collect the forms here at my desk, then file them when I have a bunch—and when I have the time."

"Oh." She wondered if he ever misplaced any of the records. But all she said was, "Good plan."

Dani consulted her computer printout and found that the first of the supposedly duplicated batch numbers was located somewhere toward the *northeast* corner of Unit One. So Dani had to mentally reconstruct progress on the site from the parts of the project she had observed firsthand from her tracking over the last two months, along with the parts she had skimmed in her original search for numerical palindromes. From this, she had developed a feel for the pattern the contractors had used in tying off the rebar ahead of the pour, and a sense of how fast the pour had proceeded during these months. So she made a guess, selected the notebook that covered the dates in her head, and began flipping through its pages for the batch number in question.

When she found it, she made a note on a new yellow tablet she had brought in her attaché case, tore off a strip of paper, and stuck it into the trailer's notebook to mark the page. Then she searched for the number's paired duplicate, which the computer had noted was somewhere in the foundation of Unit Two. That put her about three months ahead in the books, but she found that number as well. Searching and recording this first set of duplicates had taken about twenty minutes. At that rate, finding and noting the remaining eighty-six duplicates would take her, oh … days of work. But now she had solid evidence that at least one of the discrepancies that the computer had discovered existed here on the site and not just in her logbooks in San Francisco.

Dani worked quietly through the morning, while Farley and Packer came and went in the trailer, Jacob left to run errands and came back, and then everyone broke for lunch. In that time, she had confirmed four more of the duplicated numbers and left little yellow tags in the notebooks. But she still didn't know how Packer's "monkey-proof" system had failed. Perhaps the steel mill actually *was* shipping duplicate batch numbers. Or maybe, somehow, for some reason, the mill was sending the site subdivided portions of a larger batch, at different times, maybe from a different warehouse.

Towards midafternoon, when Jacob Aldis was back in the trailer, Dani decided to ask him how he processed the numbers. "Do you go out to the site and collect the tags as the workers start on a new batch?"

He stared at her in astonishment. "You mean, climb down into the pit and wait around in the rain and mud for them to cut the strapping? They don't pay me to do that. The guys bring me the tags and tell me where they're working."

She nodded at this. "Do they ever bring you more than one tag at a time?"

"Hell, yes. Nobody pays them to run back and forth to the trailer. Besides, the tags come in from all over the site."

"But you process each tag as soon as it comes, don't you?"

"You think that's all I've got to do? I'm really busy here."

"So … what do you do with the tags when you're busy?"

"Put them in the bucket."

"What bucket is that?"

"Under your table."

She looked under the drawing board and saw *two* buckets. She pulled them out into the open. Both were filled with metal tags stamped with coded numbers, including what she recognized as the rebar batch number.

"You put the tags in the bucket?" Dani asked. "Which one?"

"The bucket on the left, of course. The *incoming* bucket."

"How do you remember where the tag came from—what part of the foundation?"

"I remember." He nodded as if to emphasize this. "The tie-off doesn't move *that* fast around here."

Dani looked at the bucket he meant: six tags were visible on just the top layer, with more underneath. That was a lot of rebar locations locked up in Jacob's shaved head.

"What do you do with the tag once you've recorded it?" she asked.

"Put it in the bucket on the right, of course. The *discard* bucket."

"You don't throw them away?" But that shouldn't surprise her.

He shook his head. "Mister Packer said that would be illegal."

"So tell me ..." She paused, because she knew how damning and offensive her question was going to sound. "Do you ever, sometimes, maybe, reach into the *wrong* bucket, under the table, when you're sorting and recording the tags? Or maybe throw the discards into the wrong bucket, in the dark there, under the table, maybe?"

She saw Jacob's eyes go wide. "No, never! Not even once!"

———

James Farley sat at the back of the trailer, practically in the shadows, as Dani Wheelock explained her findings to Nate Packer. The construction clerk, Jacob Aldis, who had been there this morning, was nowhere in sight. Working through the day, she had confirmed seven of the duplicates shown on the computer run Farley had ordered back in San Francisco. The presumption was that more time and effort would confirm all of them. And who knew what a proper audit would show?

As to how the site's foolproof system had failed, Dani pulled out the two buckets full of steel tags and explained how Aldis had collected them from the rebar workers, relied on his own memory when filling out the forms, and had no good explanation of how he kept the two buckets separate, one with the unrecorded tags, the other with the recorded and discarded tags. As proof of her thesis, Dani displayed a metal tag that she had found by sifting through the incoming bucket and showed where it had already been entered in the most recent notebook—which would make a total of *eighty-eight* duplicates, if that particular batch form had ever reached San Francisco.

What the site had been running wasn't a proper documentation system at all, but just a hasty collection-and-disposition process relying on human memory and subject to human error. Farley wondered how many other routine processes on the Farragut site, from tracking the Gantt chart to dispensing the warehouse inventory, from billing Mannheim's subcontractors to reporting on the work's progress, were carried on with the same slipshod attention to detail.

As Dani revealed her findings, Packer at first claimed that she didn't understand what she was seeing, then that she was maligning his construction clerk and by implication his whole crew, and finally that the recording process was too complex for her to follow. So, in the end, a task that "a monkey could do" was too complicated for a college-trained engineer to understand.

Farley doubted that Packer would ever admit to the scale of the disaster he had let this pimply-faced boy create for them. The only sure thing was that documentation of the rebar steel under the site was thoroughly compromised. The next step would be decided at levels far above Farley's own pay grade.

# 16. Promoted Sideways

FOR THREE DAYS after Dani returned from Tennessee, a great silence seemed to have settled over the Power Division—at least in that part of it she inhabited inside the converted factory building. Mike Manuglian didn't speak to her, not even to ask how her trip had gone. Other people on the floor seemed to be avoiding her as well. She had not seen James Farley since they parted ways at the airport in San Francisco, and he had hardly spoken to her on the flight back. She received no communications from Peter Harbaugh or anyone else connected with the Farragut project.

On the first day, she went to her desk and continued processing the yellow copies of batch records still in her in-basket, although she sensed the job was probably pointless now. By the second day the basket was empty, and no more copies had come in from the field. But no one told her to stop work or to do something else, so she sat at her desk and tried to look busy.

All the time, she was thinking … hard. There had to be some way to correct the logbooks of those eighty-seven—or now eighty-eight—duplications and proceed with good information about the rebar placements. One thing she thought of immediately was to accept the first chronological recording of any batch number as likely to be the accurate placement. That would mean the second record, representing a tag that had been wrongly discarded into the incoming bucket in the office trailer, was the one in doubt. This approach would halve the number of doubtful placements and reduce the scope of the needed corrections.

But then, she reasoned, what batch number should have been attributed to that second placement? The one that came before it, chronologically? Or after it? And then the construction clerk, Aldis, had been collecting the tags in batches and relying on his own memory—and that of the rebar worker who ran the tags up to the trailer—as to where the teams had been working ahead of the pour when the metal tags were pulled. So how accurate were *any* of the attributions they made for the batches covering *any* number of days worked?

Dani recalled the view she had beheld from the edge of the pit, with concrete filling large areas of the foundation structure and the rest sketched out in wire frames composed of tied rebar or pits of bedrock and mud. From her plotting of the older batch numbers on her as-built drawings, she knew that each batch of steel covered an area approximately twenty by twenty feet on the ground. In her mind, those recorded duplicates attributable to Jacob Aldis's tag-pulling errors had at first shown up as red squares scattered across the surfaces of the foundation. But now, with the probability that he and the runner might have misremembered the exact locations of whole groups of batches, those single squares blossomed into splotchy rosettes of doubt.

Trying to correct the batch numbers, which she had been meticulously recording in her logbooks and on her as-builts—work in which Dani Wheelock had started to take some pride—would now require as much guesswork as deduction. Try as she might, she could see no way to fix this mess. And if Manuglian was correct in his assessment before she had even left for Tennessee, then her time on the project—and even her job with Mannheim itself—were likely finished.

———

Mike Manuglian got the word from Peter Harbaugh four days after Dani Wheelock came back from the jobsite. She should stop working on the Farragut Steel Report because the documentation was hopelessly compromised. The project would no longer accept her billing any hours to the Farragut account, which meant that her time of sitting and doing nothing, or typing up reports for the other engineers, or making them coffee, or performing whatever other tasks Manuglian might have for her, would be billed to his own overhead budget. And that wasn't going to happen for more than a day or two, even at Dani's reduced pay grade.

Still, under his brusque manner, Mike Manuglian had a heart—or so he liked to let people believe. It was a shame, really, that the young woman should be punished for doing her job, taking it seriously, and reporting upstairs when she discovered something that did not seem right. If she had kept her mouth shut, the David G. Farragut Nuclear Power Plant Project might have rolled to completion and no one would have been the wiser.

Well, no. Not likely. The inspectors from the Atomic Energy Commission were pretty sharp. They would probably have discovered the duplicate batch records themselves, ordered a thorough audit of construction practices and documentation on the site, and closed the plant down at the licensing stage. And that would have been worse, with far more money by then having been poured into the project and locked into purchased and installed reactor vessels, turbines and generators, massive amounts of pipework, complex control systems, and other major capital equipment that would just have to be junked. At least, this way, Mannheim and the client were only out of pocket on the detailed design effort and about two years of site and foundation work. That was bad enough. But scrapping a fully functional power plant would be a financial disaster that might bring down the company.

So, because he had a heart, Manuglian sent out feelers to people he knew throughout the company. Without referencing the Farragut project itself, or Wheelock's part in it, he asked if anyone had a position for a bright young Engineer in Training who wasn't afraid to speak her mind.

Then he mentally gave the old boy network two days to remove his problem before he had to solve it himself in the only other way possible.

———

Dani Wheelock was becoming thoroughly bored. Apprehension at the long silence had turned to terror for herself and others, then finally to mind-numbing resignation. She didn't care if she lost her job, she just wanted to end this long, gray week of knowing nothing and fearing the worst.

On a Thursday afternoon, Mike Manuglian came to her desk, motioned for Paul Kellerman at the next desk to remove himself, and appropriated the man's chair.

"I'm not supposed to say anything officially," he began, "but your name is now dirt in the Power Division."

"I'm … not surprised," she said. "I guessed that when you told me to stop billing my hours to them."

"It's not just the Farragut people who want you off their books. You've managed, singlehandedly, to bring down a nuclear plant with an estimated cost of more than two billion dollars. Some people in the company want to see you fired—if not prosecuted for malfeasance."

"Jesus!" she whispered. "Is that what this business has become?"

He frowned deeply. "In my opinion, you did what you had to—what any good engineer would do. But my opinion doesn't count."

"So I'm out of a job. Do I need a lawyer?"

"Not yet. There's one place for people like you in a place like this. And the Quality Assurance Department actually asked for you."

"What do they do?" she asked. "Not that it matters," she added quickly.

"They need you to write a company manual about trenching practices."

"So is this a bone you're tossing me, Mike? Not that I'm ungrateful."

"No, really, it's important. You'd be surprised how many people get killed because they jump down into a trench—even just a couple of feet deep—and the sides collapse because of improper shoring and bracing. You would be saving lives."

"Rather than building plants that matter," she said wistfully.

"Look, it's a start. And it's a bump in your pay grade."

"That makes it better. Almost. Still, QA's the leper colony, isn't it?"

"Quality Assurance is an important part of our business. So give it a few months. Let this Farragut thing die down. Do a good job. And who knows where you'll be in a couple of years?"

———

As Dani Wheelock described the outcome of her trip and its aftermath during one of their Saturday morning dog walks, Norman Wall tried to cheer her up.

"It sounds like important work," he said.

"That's what my old boss tried to tell me."

"In my line, accounting isn't just keeping track of numbers. At the highest level it's, well, troubleshooting. Like forensics. Seeing what happened in the business and determining what caused it. That's what you did with those notebooks and the buckets full of tags. You solved a problem. Isn't that what engineers are supposed to do?"

"Well, we're really more about creating and building things. Like making and selling those blue jeans that end up as numbers on your ledgers."

"But weren't you just recording batch numbers before …?"

"Yeah, but it was in support of building something bigger."

"And now you're—what? Helping people dig better trenches. That's creative."

"For as long as this manual project lasts, yeah. But after that, I'm just reviewing plans and inspecting jobsites. Checking everyone else's work, but doing no useful, creative work of my own."

"Still, everything turned out all right—after your trip to Tennessee."

"Except for the Farragut project getting shut down and hundreds of people losing their jobs?" She nodded glumly. "Yeah."

"I meant your career. At least you landed on your feet."

"In the leper colony. But I guess that's where I belong."

# 17. The Last Straw

ON AN EVENING in late September, Dani Wheelock went into her bedroom at Nirvana House and immediately sensed that something was wrong. Not knowing exactly what, she looked around.

For one thing, her bed had been remade since that morning. She always pulled the sheets, blanket, and coverlet straight, but did them one at a time, so that the top layer was perfectly smooth. Now it showed a wrinkle underneath—as if someone had pulled the bed apart and tugged everything back into place at once.

She looked in the closet and tried to remember whether the business suits and skirts hanging there had been bunched together on the rack that way when she left in the morning. Normally, Dani spaced things out as much as possible, so that clothes she planned to wear the next day would air properly.

She opened the top drawer of her dresser and found that the stack of her panties, which she always folded across the middle and aligned at the waistbands, was now catty-corner in the drawer and the bands were slightly askew. Her pile of folded bras had a strap dangling loose rather than tucked inside the cups. In the second drawer, her collection of folded tops was rumpled as if they had been shoved one way and another.

Dani still held her bunch of keys in her hand, and she went back to check the lock on her door. Nothing seemed amiss, no sign of forced entry. Yes, she knew she had locked it that morning, because she had to use the key to get in this evening. And she distinctly remembered hearing the rattle the lock always made before the tumblers clicked.

So someone with access to the house master key—or with the skill to pick a lock—had gone into her room unannounced.

Dani knelt and checked the dresser's bottom drawer, where she kept her lockbox. Its keyhole showed no telltale scratches or signs of prying. She opened it with her own key and inventoried the contents: her spare cash and emergency credit card, her most valuable pieces of jewelry including the Rolex from her father, her birth certificate, personal correspondence she wanted to keep, and other private documents. Everything was there.

So maybe the thief had failed to find the box. Or the searcher had found it but opened it with a purpose other than theft.

Either way, Dani felt violated. She no longer felt safe in the house. Even if her mother had recommended the residence, the place was no longer the friendly community of like-minded hippies it might have been when Jane lived there. The "Summer of Love" was really over.

Dani knew then that she would have to leave and strike out on her own.

————

When Norman Wall and Bear next took Dani Wheelock for a walk in Golden Gate Park, he sensed a fuming anger in the young woman. Even Bear seemed to know it and kept pushing his nose into her cupped hand.

"Something's wrong," Norman said. "Is it your job?"

"Not that. The job's good. Or as good as it can be."

"Then ...?" He waited patiently for her to speak.

"Someone broke into my room at the house."

"Oh, God!" he said. "What did they take?"

"Nothing, from what I can tell. Someone just snooping around."

"But how do you know? I mean, if nothing has gone missing?"

"Let's just say my socks weren't folded the way I left them."

"Did you lock your door? Scratch that! Of course you did!"

"Do you know if anyone has a master key? Adrian, maybe?"

"I suppose there must be one," Norman said, "like for emergencies. Say, someone locks themself in their room and ... dies ... or something. But no one ever mentioned such a key." He thought for a minute. "And Adrian would probably want a resolution of the Housing Committee before using it."

"Still, I have to leave. I'm just … creeped out."

Norman was alarmed. "Where would you go?"

"I don't know yet," she said. "I want my own apartment. With my own bathroom. More privacy anyway. And some-place closer to downtown."

"Closer in will be more expensive, you know."

"Yeah, I could find a roommate. *One*, rather than the dozen I have now."

"I've been thinking of leaving the house, too," he said—and waited.

"But I thought you were happy here?"

"Not really. I don't fit in with them."

"Yeah," she said. "The resident narc."

He laughed at that—and still waited.

"Since we're both going to be looking for an apartment—" she started.

"Yes?" He held his breath.

"We could get a bigger place if we pooled rent money," she finished.

"You mean, move in together?" His heart started to beat faster now.

"Well, yes. But on a strictly platonic basis. And separate bedrooms."

"Of course. Separate bathrooms, too. To give us both some privacy."

"We're just friends, Norman."

"Of course. That's all we are."

———

Report from Officer Cassandra Petrick, San Francisco Police Department, Badge Number 72875: "Date: September 19, 1970. Re: Danielle A. Wheelock, Final Report.

"The subject under surveillance, per the Bureau's request, appears to be unconnected with any narcotics activities at the residence identified as 'Nirvana House.' The younger Whee-lock is gainfully employed as a junior engineer at Mannheim Construction in the city (see Form W-2 and copies of pay records, attached). A search of her room revealed no recent correspondence with her mother, Jane D. Wheelock, on any topic of interest. Therefore, the imputed link to the mother's Southeast Asian drug sources should be considered unproven at this time.

"As Danielle A. Wheelock has since departed from the house and left no forwarding address, further surveillance—at least from this venue—has been terminated."

# Fall 1972

# 1. The Beast

THE CAR WAS really too big for the garage at 60 Jack London Alley, just off South Park on the sunny side of Rincon Hill. Being a coupé—if the stark, futuristic body stylings of a chrome-yellow Corvette Stingray could carry such a quaint and charming designation—the car that Dani Wheelock affectionately called "the Beast" had extra-wide doors. She could only open the one on the driver's side about halfway, and that was only when the opposite fenders were practically grazing the garage's scuffed plaster walls. Every time she brought the car home, she had to feather the clutch as the massive eight-cylinder engine pushed the low-slung chassis through the dip of the too-short driveway, over the hump of the threshold, and past the garage's wooden doorframe, which bore its share of scrapes and gouges from generations of past residents trying to park.

The alternative was worse, of course. Putting the Beast on the street—or rather, competing with other residents and restaurant patrons for the limited spaces on the oval track around this two-block-long public park hidden away in the industrial South of Market district—was simply unthinkable. Dani loved the car too much to abandon it to the elements and the careless parking habits of her neighbors. Being a totally frivolous vehicle, with not even a pretense at bumpers in front or rear, and being made of, essentially, plastic instead of metal, the Corvette for all its wide stance, internal power, and brawny demeanor was a wimp when it came to dents and dings.

And then, to obtain her privileged access to the one-car garage in the house that she and Norman Wall shared with another couple, Dani had to pay fifteen-percent extra on her share of the rent. In addition, she'd had to wait a year for the previous tenants upstairs to move out and take their beaten-up Volkswagen Bug with them. And finally, she had to convince Norman that he wouldn't have any trouble parking his ruggedly sensible and slightly rusty Ford Bronco on the street because "that car was just made for the outdoors."

Norman was such a dear that he let her have the garage all to herself. In fact, he was a dear about everything. Even though she knew he was a little bit in love with her, he always kept his hands to himself and never pressured her by word or deed. And he only pouted a little bit when she had indulged in brief affairs—two at the most, with maybe a handful of flirtations in between—and brought strange men home to the apartment. She knew it disturbed him but, damn it, a girl had her needs, just like a man. And it wasn't as if Norman hadn't occasionally seen other women—although discreetly, without rubbing her face in it—during their two years of living together.

On this hot, still morning in mid-September, Dani pushed back the folding garage doors, opened the Beast's driver-side door as far as it would go without touching the wall, slid her long legs under the steering wheel, and wedged her hips into the racing seat. When she started up the 454-cubic-inch engine, the rumble of the exhaust was deafening in the enclosed space. She shifted the transmission into reverse and backed slowly out and then halfway across the alley, listening hard for any scraping noises. Leaving the engine running, Dani got out and closed the garage doors. Then she drove the mile and a quarter downhill toward the Embarcadero and Centennial Plaza, being careful to go slowly over bumps, around potholes, and across the trolley-car tracks.

At the Plaza, her salary grade entitled her to park only down in the third subbasement, for which she paid fifteen dollars a month in fees. Sometimes reality caught up with Dani and allowed her to realize how ludicrous it was to keep such a car for her daily commute and pay that much extra to park it at both ends. She could easily have taken the bus and saved money and hassle all around. But she loved the Beast. She loved its sleekness, its sense of power, and the feeling it gave her of being able to head out at a moment's notice for distant adventures at high speeds.

And that was worth the price, even when she was just sitting still in city traffic.

## 2. Another Anomaly

"Now, what's this?" the young woman in Estimating and Scheduling asked John MacMahon, who was Senior Project Engineer of the P.T. Puncakapi Steel Project.

Mannheim Construction, Inc., had recently been awarded the reissued contract for master planning and logistical supervision of what the Indonesians proudly expected to be Southeast Asia's premier industrial facility. MacMahon was now sitting in Danielle Wheelock's office, going through a folder full of schedule fragments, contract notes, and pre-bid documents, which were all that was left from the contract's previous holder. P.T. Puncakapi Steel had originally awarded the development of their new combined smelter and rolling mill, planned for a virgin site in the jungles of South Sulawesi, to the Soviet Ministry of Iron and Steel Industry. The rumor at the time Puncakapi reopened bidding was that the Russians had completely bungled their end of the project's planning. And now that Mannheim had won the contract, everyone was finding out just how bad the bungle actually was.

"What's what?" he asked, being distracted with a different piece of paper.

Wheelock had been assigned as his liaison person in Estimating and Scheduling. The story inside the company was that she had been transferred to the department about a year ago just to keep her out of trouble. Before that, she had done time in the purgatory of Quality Assurance after bringing down a nuclear power contract worth billions—and that was as a new-hire just out of college and not even registered as an engineer yet. That story didn't inspire a lot of confidence. To boot, Danielle Wheelock was a woman. When informed of this meeting, MacMahon had hoped her assignment to his project was a mistake. And then he met her and discovered just how young she was. So he wasn't prepared to give her questions a lot of weight.

"This bill of sale," she replied, waving the photocopy at him.

MacMahon took the paper she was holding and glanced at it.

"Oh," he said dismissively. "That's just the turbine for the power plant. There's no heavy-duty grid anywhere near the site, so the Puncakapi people decided to generate their own electricity using oil or natural-gas condensates from the near-by Sulawesi field."

"Hmm!" the Wheelock woman replied. "So, they don't know what, exactly, they want to burn—and yet they've already spec'd the power plant?"

"No, they haven't. We're still hoping to get the contract for detailed design on the entire site."

"Except for the power plant turbine."

"No, that's still open, too," he said.

"Look at the paper in your hand."

MacMahon looked more closely.

"That's not pre-bid," she went on. "That's a bill of sale from Hitachi Power Systems for a four-hundred-megawatt turbine-generator set. That looks pretty detailed to me."

"What?" he exclaimed. Now he really studied the document. "This must be a mistake. How did this get in there?"

"You mean it's *not* for your project? It was sold to P.T. Puncakapi Steel."

"But dated a year ago. Maybe it's for another steel mill someplace else."

"Do the Puncakapi people even *have* another plant they're building?"

"Not ... that I'm aware of," MacMahon said. "But then where ...?"

"Well, it seems they paid thirty-two *billion* rupiahs for the thing. That's, let's see ..." Wheelock apparently knew the exchange rate for the Indonesian rupiah as of last month off the top of her head. MacMahon himself only knew it was some-where in the fractions of a cent to the dollar. "That means your client," she continued, "has already expended some three-point-two million in project dollars on a turbine-generator they acquired last year."

MacMahon had his pencil out now and was still working the numbers. "That looks about right," he said lamely.

"So," the woman concluded, "before we put the power plant on the Gantt chart, I suggest you contact our agents in Indonesia and find out where that turbine-generator is sitting as of this moment."

"Uh, yes. That would be the next logical step."

"Maybe it will even fit into the plant design."

"Jesus," he said. "What are the odds of that?"

"Thousand to one," she said. "If we're lucky."

# 3. Fukyugata One

AFTER TWO YEARS of hard training, breaking her back and her work schedule to attend classes Monday and Thursday nights, week in and week out—and with a leg up from her brown belt in Isshinryu—Dani Wheelock had earned her black belt in Shorinryu. This gave her the right to lead classes, relieving Squid of the job four times a month, which meant she was opening the *dojo* at six o'clock on those evenings and usually staying until after ten to lock up. It also meant sweeping the floor, putting away the equipment, and collecting school fees, as well as offering individual instruction to any and all students.

She got paid for none of this, although Bill Berggren did give her a discount on her own fees and spent extra training time with her, when he was in town.

This evening, after leading a class of twenty students through the basic exercises, Dani took one of the new white belts, Jimmy Tarr, aside when they broke up for the period of individual practice and sparring. It was time for him to start learning the first of the style's unarmed *kata*s, called Fukyugata One.

She led Jimmy to a free space on the floor, and the other belts quietly moved out of their way because of her rank. She turned him toward the mirror on the far wall and showed him how to stand with his heels together, head up, shoulders back, and hands relaxed at his thighs.

"That direction," she said, "the way you're facing now, is 'south.' "

"Does it matter which way I'm really facing?" Jimmy asked.

"Nope. You always start a *kata* facing nominal south. However, it's a good idea to practice with the same orientation in your workout space every time. This keeps you from getting confused."

"Got it."

"The first *kata* begins with the bow, or *rei*, and the formal attention stance," Dani continued, demonstrating. "Then you turn ninety degrees to the left, or facing east, and drop into the long stance with the left foot forward. Perform a lower leg block with your left hand fisted, simultaneously snapping your right hand back into the ready position at chest level." She performed the move. "Then step forward with your right foot in a walking stance, punch at mid-level with the right hand, and simultaneously bring the left fist up to chamber at chest level." Both sleeves of her *gi* snapped with the combined movement. "And finally step back through with your right leg, pivoting on the ball of your left foot. You are now facing to the right, or west, in the long stance with your right foot forward. And repeat the sequence of block and punch." Dani made the parry and riposte in a single blurring motion, her uniform whipping like flags in the wind.

She continued through the kata, repeating the same basic phrase with variations, facing in different directions. Jimmy followed her, not always with the same precision, his uniform folds not snapping even once the way hers did.

The whole *kata*, when performed from beginning to end, normally took about forty-five seconds. With the breaks and pauses for explanation of each move, it took about ten minutes for her to teach and for Jimmy to learn to the point at which he could practice on his own.

"I should write this all down," he said.

"Don't. It's better to commit the moves to your somatic memory—storing them in your nerves and muscles—than to verbal memory, where it won't do you any good."

"Yeah … I'm not going to *talk* my way out of a fight, right?" he said. "But will blocking and punching the air like this make me a better fighter?"

"Well … fighting is not the entire purpose of karate."

"Yes, but … we get to fight *sometime*, don't we?"

"You've already been introduced to sparring."

"Yeah, sure. Pulled punches and light taps."

"It's not like we ever go full-focus here."

"Then it's all a gyp, isn't it?" he said.

"Only if you want to kill people."

# 4. The Time Value of Money

"FINALLY," ED COOPER said, turning over a page of his notes, "what about the Poon-Cappy Steel project?" As Manager of the Estimating and Scheduling Department, Cooper had brought his youngest engineer, Danielle Wheelock, into his office for their weekly project review.

In reply, she gave a bitter laugh. "You don't want to know."

"Try me. Did they ever find that lost turbine-generator?"

"Yeah," she said. "It was right where it was supposed to be, where Hitachi delivered it for the Sulawesi site a year ago."

"But the steel mill is a greenfield project. Had the Soviets done any preparation there at all?"

"Nope. It's still just a patch of jungle. So the generator went to the next best place, the docks at Makassar, where it was pushed to one side and left."

"So, it's still salvageable—if the project can use it?"

"Hardly." Another bitter laugh. "It seems a four-hundred-megawatt turbine-generator has less value than the packing crate it comes in—at least in the local housing market, where good lumber already sawn into boards demands a premium. The townspeople took everything but the wooden braces holding up the ends of the turbine shaft. And our agent on site says they made a good job of shaving pieces off there, too. Salt air did the rest. The unit is a total write-off. So, even if we could have used it, it's gone."

"It was a stupid decision to buy it in the first place," Cooper said.

"Well, yes," she agreed. "In hindsight."

"No, even with foresight. What were the Soviets thinking, acquiring a capital item two years before it was needed?"

"According to my sources on the project," Wheelock explained, "the Soviets negotiated a forty-percent discount on the price, because the unit was returned to Hitachi from another contract, which had fallen through. The Soviets thought the cost differential was too good to pass up."

"That's their damn 'labor theory of value,' " Cooper said. "They think the only thing that makes an item valuable is the human labor that went into making it. As if a man polishing a turd for an hour would give it the same value as the diamond that a skilled artisan had been cutting and polishing for the same hour."

"And yet," Wheelock protested, "they were actually trying to undercut that human value invested in the turbine by acquiring it cheap, just because Hitachi happened to have it on hand and didn't know what else to do with it. Sheesh!"

"Sheesh, indeed. The Communists have no concept of banking and other intangibles—at least as far as they're concerned—like the 'time value of money.' They think of money as a kind of solid object, like gold coins or bars, something to be spent now or spent later and that otherwise just sits in a vault gathering dust. They can't think dynamically about interest rates, alternative investments, and the lost opportunity costs of tying up—what? Three million dollars?—in a major project asset before its time. They don't think about the lost use of that money, which they would eventually have to pay for in some way, when they've sunk it into a fancy piece of steel that, for two years and more, isn't going to generate a kilowatt or earn a nickel—ruble, whatever—in return."

"Not to mention," Wheelock said, "the costs of storing it somewhere—and guarding it against vandals—for the two years before it's needed at the site. That alone should have factored into their thinking—the labor of the guards, if not the value of the land the thing would sit on."

"Right," Cooper replied. "Count up all those costs and values, and sixty cents on the dollar is hardly a bargain. In fact, the deal would probably have gone south even if Hitachi had just *given* them the turbine."

"So that's what we're doing here?" she said. "Making people figure out the intangibles in order to save their money?"

"Yep, that's estimating and scheduling. I'm glad you're finally catching on."

# 5. The Iceman

HUGO WICHARD CHECKED his watch while he waited for his meeting with an executive in Mannheim Construction's Business Development Department. According to the wafer-thin "Pathek" Philippe on his wrist—the misspelling on the face of the dial was too small for anyone to read without a jeweler's loupe—Wichard was still five minutes early. Then he slid his French cuff forward to cover the forgery. The cuff itself was elegantly linked with an antique Greek Obol of Charon, inscribed with an image that was either a horsefly or a wasp, which the dealer in Thessaloniki swore was genuine third-century B.C., although how the man had managed to snag a pair of them, and at that price, was a genuine mystery.

Next, Wichard touched the briefcase beside his chair, to make sure it was still there. Inside, he had the details—or at least the concept, worked out with some professionally rendered architect's sketches—for a project based on an idea that was plausible if not, technically, at this point in time, according to some experts, achievable. He also had a letter of support signed by a prince from a cadet branch of the House of Saud. The emir's commitment to the project was sincere and effusive if not, technically, at this point in time, according to some experts, binding on the kingdom.

For the purposes of the upcoming interview, however, these project documents were the hook, and the prince's letter was the bait.

———

Dennis Denbridge took his position as Special Assistant to the Vice President of Business Development seriously. And the position, as he saw it, was to clear his boss's desk of meaningless paperwork and his calendar of unprofitable meetings. That included the man Denbridge was about to meet at ten o'clock this morning. In preparation, he reviewed the letter sent to his boss's attention a week ago.

It was signed by one Hugo Wichard, an expatriate French-man whose résumé, attached to the letter, included advanced degrees in hydraulic engineering from the École Polytechnique in Paris and in electrical engineering from the Karlsruhe Institute of Technology in Germany. His work experience included artfully vague participation in a string of development projects in sub-Saharan Africa: a water distribution system in Léopoldville, Democratic Republic of the Congo; a generating station in Accra, Ghana; and agricultural studies in Kenya and Tanzania. The project on offer today was similarly vague but promised to be of "immense scientific and technical interest, as well as the solution to a pressing worldwide problem."

It was exactly the sort of flyblown rubbish that Denbridge was tasked with keeping from ever reaching Avery Winston's desk.

He checked his watch. Well, time to begin this sideshow—and end it quickly.

The man whom Winston's secretary Martha showed into the office had to be in his mid-forties, according to his résu-mé. And yet Wichard's was a preternaturally young face, with smooth, perfectly tanned skin that stretched tight across his high, narrow forehead and over his cheekbones, accenting the man's wide, staring, ice-blue eyes. His nose was aristocratically long and thin, and his jaw was long with a pointed chin—almost like a rat's quivering snout. His dark hair, showing decorative streaks of gray at the temples, was brushed back from his hairline in a generous sweep, around ears that lay flat against his skull, and down to his collar in the back, where it was cut off in a straight line. Wichard was not a big man, either in height or girth, but the way he walked into the room, with his torso and arms in constant motion—including a turn and a dismissive wave to Martha—seemed to fill the space with his presence.

When he reached the desk, Wichard leaned over it and ex-tended his hand.

"Very pleased to make your acquaintance, *M'sieur* Denbri'e."

Denbridge only had time to half-rise from his chair, trapping his knees beneath the desk's central drawer, and take the extended hand from his half-crouch. And that hand was long and thin, with hard bones and knobby knuckles—just like a rat's grasping paw.

"Likewise, I'm sure," Denbridge murmured, then cleared his throat. "I understand you have brought us a project for evaluation …?"

"Oh, but this is more than a project!" the other man enthused. "This is the salvation of the world. I bring you nothing less than a way to satisfy the thirst of arid nations and to make their deserts bloom."

"That's a pretty strong claim. What do you have to prove all this?"

"Ah, this is conceptual design only. But for a man of your imagination …"

Wichard moved aside Denbridge's telephone, the picture of his wife, and the desk set that commemorated his fifteen years with the company, all to make room for Wichard's own black-leather attaché case. Its corners and edges showed the cuts and scuffs of hard usage. The man released its snaps with two sharp clicks and opened the lid. From inside, he took out a comb-bound report and a stack of engineering drawings that had been folded four ways to fit inside the case. He spread the latter on the remaining desk space, pushing aside Denbridge's papers to do so.

It turned out the drawings were not mechanical schematics at all, not plans and elevations, nor technical diagrams. What Denbridge was looking at were architect's renderings, in perspective and presumably to scale, of scenes intending to show activity on a completed set of works. In one, a crew of men in fur-lined parkas ran a drilling rig—with a derrick that had to be fifty-feet tall, according to the scale, yet was mounted on caterpillar treads—across a snow-covered plain that had been carved into curlicue drifts by sharp winds. In another rendering, a seagoing tugboat—no, more than one, with the others made tiny by distance—pulled taut cables attached to a floating mountain of ice. In the third, more tugboats pushed another ice mountain through a lock gate, which was much wider than those on the Panama Canal or any other ocean-shipping point, and into a basin the size of a large lake.

"You're ... moving icebergs," Denbridge said.

"They are from the Amery Ice Shelf—sea ice, true, but still fresh water, completely pure. All you have to do is go and cut them loose. Thousands of cubic meters—millions, actually—just there for the taking."

"And you are taking them ... where?"

"Why, due north, of course. Up the east coast of Africa, into the Red Sea, and up to the port of Jeddah in Saudi Arabia. We can place all that fresh water right on the kingdom's doorstep, ready to melt in the desert sun."

"I see ..." Denbridge considered, for a moment, what the man was offering. "This is not a particularly new idea," he said at last.

"But I have worked it out—with both technical and economic feasibility—in some detail."

Here Wichard opened the engineering report and pointed out maps he had prepared showing the permanent bases to be established on the east coast of Antarctica; the prevailing ocean currents—with a narrow northerly and easterly route traced inside the Madagascar Current and the Southwest Monsoon Drift, against the more southerly and westerly direction of the Indian Ocean Gyre; and soundings along the Red Sea coast. Wichard turned the pages and trailed his fingers down tables that showed the cost-per-meter for drilling in solid ice—which, based on Denbridge's own experience from early in his career, as a hard-rock miner, compared poorly to drilling in solid granite; the cost-per-kilometer for operating heavy-duty tugboats in subarctic conditions on an annualized basis; the seawater temperature taken at every ten degrees of latitude in the Indian Ocean; and the current costs of excavation and general construction in Saudi Arabia, according to estimates prepared by the Saudi Binladin Group.

"You've been in contact with Mohammed bin Laden?" Denbridge was surprised.

"Some of his people have consulted on the project." The man smiled modestly.

"Well then, if you have Binladin's backing, you don't need Mannheim for—"

"I have something better," Wichard said, producing a letter from his case.

The letter was on thick vellum paper, the color of old parchment, with one edge left ragged. Embossed at the top in green and gold inks was the national emblem of Saudi Arabia: two crossed swords, inverted, below a palm tree. The letter was addressed "To Whom It May Concern" and expressed both personal and financial support for the "Antarctic Hydrological Project," as presented by *Sayyid* Hugo N. Wichard, Professional Engineer. The letter was signed by His Highness Ali bin Muhammad al-Kabir al Saud, Emir of the Kingdom. Next to the signature was a stamp in green wax with silk ribbons, and the design pressed into the wax was a tangle of Arabic writing with another sword beneath it.

"You have the backing of a prince!" Denbridge said.

"Indeed."

"And his commitment is binding?"

"As that of any other prince ..."

"Oh, my!"

Mannheim Construction, Inc., had been trying to get into the expanding and highly profitable Saudi construction market for more than twenty years. Despite some early work that the company's founding partners had done for the kingdom right after the Second World War, Mannheim's presence in the Middle East had been blighted by a single project, a half-mile of breakwater in the harbor of the Israeli port of Jaffa in 1952. That contract, worth about a hundred thousand in current dollars, had made Mannheim and all of its personnel and operating branches *persona non grata* throughout the Arab world and blocked their access to billions in lucrative contracts backed by the kingdom's oil riches.

"I'll have to turn these documents over to someone in our estimating department," Denbridge temporized. "Just to go over the details and check your numbers."

"But of course."

"However, on the whole, I'm inclined to say—" Denbridge paused just short of committing himself. "—I *think* we may be able to do business."

———

Dani was at her desk when the man from the thirty-eighth floor—instantly recognizable by his sober, navy-blue suit and buzz-cut hair—knocked on the jamb of her open door and then walked right through.

"Can I help you?" she asked after he was already in her office.

"Hello! Dennis Denbridge. This is the estimating department, right?"

"Estimating and Scheduling. We do both here—they're kind of associated."

"Right, right. Well, I only need the estimating part at this point in time."

"Excuse me, but ..."

"I'm from the office of the Vice President of Business Development. We have a new project we'd like you to evaluate."

"Projects are scheduled with Mr. Cooper, our department head. He's just around—"

"I understand all that. But he's not there. This will only take a moment of your time." Before she could respond further, Denbridge stepped back out into the corridor and brought in a second man.

This other man was as different from the thirty-eighth floor as a person could be. For one thing, he wore a linen suit in a color that most men could not name, called "ecru." It reminded her of a soft chamois skin or old ivory. The fabric was more attuned to the tropics than to San Francisco, although September was one of the two notably hot and sticky months in the city, the other being May. The suit was cut with a shawl collar and patch pockets, much more casual than the men's business suits she saw everywhere at Mannheim. And yet this man had a developed sense of style, with an expensively thin gold watch and large, oval cufflinks, also made of gold.

His haircut was unlike that of anyone else at Mannheim, too. It was more like the artistic types she saw in the cafés around her South Park neighborhood: long, swept back, and dragging on the collar. Except that kind of hairstyle among the men in her life went with a four-day's growth of stubble and an air of social-democratic poverty. This man radiated something else, something foreign and sophisticated, something European and vaguely aristocratic.

His face was young and smooth, at once both grave and smiling, and totally confident. He came forward and then slipped around the corner of her desk, his eyes gazing directly into Dani's. It seemed as if he was fixing her face—no, her soul—in his photographic memory. The effect was both flattering and unnerving.

"Ah, sweet lady!" he exclaimed. He took her hand off the edge of her desk, where she was about to push her chair and herself back out of his range, and held it firmly in his warm, dry grip. He actually bowed over her hand—to the point at which she thought he was going to kiss it. "I know we will accomplish wonderful things together!"

"Sir!" was all she could think to say.

"Excuse me," Denbridge said from across the room. "To the point. This is Mr. Hugo Wichard, an engineer from … well, Saudi Arabia for now. He has brought us an interesting proposal that needs your evaluation."

"What is it?" Dani asked.

From under his arm, Denbridge took a slender report in a plastic binding and laid it on her desk. "Antarctic Hydrologic Project for the Kingdom of Saudi Arabia" she read on the bright-green cover.

"I see," she said. "Antarctic?"

"Exactly so," Wichard replied.

She flipped open the cover and examined the table of contents. The chapters—none longer than three pages and most of them a single page—covered topics like Exploration and Drilling Costs, Towing Practices, Practical Sea Routes, Marine-Based Infrastructure, and Land-Based Infrastructure. She skimmed one or two of the tables and maps—the latter crudely drawn to the scale of about two hundred miles to the inch.

It was all about things to be done and built, with no obvious economic analysis except for one table of drilling costs, an estimate of fuel consumption during towing at sea, and a breakdown of various labor categories inside the kingdom, all to be performed by "third-country nationals." There was no hint of economic alternatives like current water resources on the Arabian Peninsula and desalination strategies.

After a moment, she sensed the combined gaze of the two men—but especially Wichard's blue-white stare—on the back of her head. She closed the report.

"There's not much to go on here," she said. "It's a pretty slim definition of what seems to be a major undertaking."

"That's why we need you to flesh it out," Denbridge said.

Which was a distinct change from where he had started the conversation—with a request for Dani's "evaluation."

"I … well, yes," she said. "I suppose you can leave this with me and I will discuss it with Mr. Cooper."

"That's—" Denbridge began, then sighed. "Very well."

"I am sure," Wichard said, "you will give it your complete attention."

Dani found herself smiling at him. And Wichard's gaze lingered on her face as Denbridge turned the man around and practically marched him out of the room.

After a moment, the Mannheim executive reappeared alone in her doorway.

"Miss Wheelock?" he said. "Make this work. It's important."
And then he was well and truly gone.

———

According to the rules established between Norman Wall and
his roommate Dani, the first person to get home from work in
the evening was supposed to start dinner. Norman usually extended "work" to include taking Bear for a walk around South
Park's circle of grass and trees. But after he had brought the
dog back with still no sign of Dani, he put a pot of salted water
on to heat, dumped two jars of A.G. Ferrari's Bolognese meat
sauce into a pan to simmer on a back burner, and opened a
package of dry spaghetti, ready to put it into freshly boiling
water whenever she did return.

At seven-thirty he finally heard the rumble of her car's engine in the alleyway and the creak of the garage doors under
the house. Norman turned up the heat under the water and
opened a bottle of Chianti to let it breathe. Dani came into the
kitchen two minutes later.

"Smells good," she said. "Is it spaghetti again?"

"If you want something different, then get home early."

"Spaghetti is fine. And I had to pick up the Beast at the
shop."

"What was it this time?" he asked. He had never trusted
that Corvette.

"Just an oil change," she said. "And brake pads. They wear
on these hills."

"All that took you two hours?" he asked. "Not that I'm
checking up on you."

"Had to stay on a bit after work. I got tossed a new project
today."

"Something that needs so much attention on the first day?"

"Something from the thirty-eighth floor. Really big."

Norman smiled. "Congratulations, I guess."

"Well … don't congratulate me yet."

"Why not? Is there trouble?"

"Because the thing they want to build is looney-tunes. Hauling icebergs up from Antarctica to Saudi Arabia. Supposed to be a new source of fresh water."

"Aren't icebergs made of salt water?"

"No, freezing drives out the crystals."

"Oh, then the science is valid, right?"

"Yah!" she said, disgusted. "Except the iceberg melts on its way north. If it could be allowed to sit in a puddle of cool water just as it came out of the glacier, insulating the berg from the surrounding tropical water, then it might last. But these icebergs are in constant motion, as they're being towed. The cooler water gets left behind and all that nice, warm seawater continually bathes the ice, causing it to melt quicker. Plus, there's an amount of energy produced by the towing motion that I haven't yet figured out."

"Oh. So … not feasible?"

"Even if the berg could be brought back whole, the person or people who thought this one up never considered the *nature* of an iceberg."

"And what nature is that?"

"It's seven-eighths under water. For everything you can see above the surface, it goes down seven times deeper. If you want to bring a big iceberg into Jeddah, you're going to have to dig a basin a thousand feet deep, to and below bedrock, and that's *after* you gouge a channel just as deep into the seabed leading up to the port. And *then* you have to build a lock gate a thousand feet tall so you can isolate the berg, drain the remaining seawater that came in with it, and begin collecting fresh water as it melts."

"It sounds like an engineering challenge," he said.

"It's an engineering *nightmare*," she replied.

"And they want you to make it all better?"

"They're expecting the impossible."

"It's a sign they trust you, isn't it?"

"They don't know me, not really."

"But if you could make it work—solve the engineering problems—then wouldn't this be your ticket out of purgatory in Estimating and Scheduling? Wouldn't they have to make you part of the team that will actually build this thing? Isn't that what you've wanted all along?"

"But this project is just not possible," she insisted.

"So?" he said. "Make it something that *is* possible."

# 6. Redefining Feasibility

DANI WHEELOCK SAT at her desk surrounded by volumes borrowed from Mannheim's third-floor Engineering Library. Some were flipped open to the pages of interest, weighted down with the edges of other volumes, and marked with slips of paper underlining key passages and the relevant lines in tables of data. Some had pens from her desk arranged strategically pointing to facts she wanted to use. On the yellow tablet in a cleared space in front of her, she was writing—trying to write, trying just to formulate—a set of equations.

She was attempting to figure out how fast an iceberg would melt if she towed it the 7,698 miles from, roughly, the South Pole to the Port of Jeddah at 21° 35´ North by 39° 10´ East. That distance, she noted, would put the point of the berg's arrival on the *other* side of the equator and almost up to the Tropic of Cancer at 23.26° North.

To know how long an iceberg would last under normal drift conditions, she had found some references to bergs that had calved from the various Greenland glaciers and drifted with the currents into the North Atlantic—most notably the one that RMS *Titanic* had struck. Given the average size of these bergs and the surrounding water temperature, such a mass of ice might endure for two or three years. The text also noted that icebergs which calved from Antarctic glaciers were larger and tended to live perhaps several years longer—although none survived for very long in the warmer waters north of forty degrees of southern latitude, which put them well away from most shipping lanes except those that ventured around Cape Horn.

So, theoretically, a large enough iceberg, moving fast enough, might survive in the warmer waters, even crossing the equator, and arrive in Saudi Arabia with some of its ice—perhaps even most of its ice—intact. But how fast could a team of oceangoing tugs tow a massive berg? Dani had a reference showing the mechanics and economics of ocean towing, and it suggested five or six knots, or nautical miles per hour, as a reasonable speed. The travel distance in nautical miles, which she knew were a bit longer than standard miles, was 6,689 miles. So, at a steady five knots, the trip would take 1,337 hours, or about fifty-five days, or just short of two months. Of course, that was absent any contrary forces like winds and currents. Still, it was not an insurmountable travel time.

But then, she had yet to take into account the energy of towing, or inducing all that mass to move forward, and figure out the heat generated by the friction of moving it through the water. Given that each iceberg would have a unique underwater shape, generating pockets of drag, eddies of turbulence, and other almost incalculable factors, she needed a shortcut to estimating the deterioration involved.

Well, the power of the tugboat engines, measured by the fuel they used in towing the iceberg—because the fuel to move the tugs themselves would be negligible in comparison— would be a good stand-in for the heat of friction. She found tables of engine power and fuel consumption in her reference book that showed a large tugboat towing a barge at five knots was operating at sixty percent power—which made sense, as no one wanted to run a large engine at maximum power for days on end. At that rate, an oceangoing tug burned 141 gallons of diesel fuel per hour.

The energy density of a gallon of marine diesel fuel averaged 36.7 kilowatt-hours, or 132 megajoules. A joule was a tiny amount of energy, about a quarter of a standard calorie. But a hundred and thirty million of them was a lot of energy to pack into a single gallon of fuel. Burning those 141 gallons of diesel for an hour yielded almost nineteen billion joules, or just short of five billion calories. Multiply that by, say, three large tugs pulling a single berg, and you had fifteen billion calories per hour. Multiply that by thirteen hundred hours of travel time, and you had two times ten to the eleventh power calories. That plus the warmer water around the equator would be enough to melt any iceberg.

Or would it?

What Dani had to do now was write a program in Fortran that translated ice volume into exposed underwater surface area. She would then account for the rate of melting at the interface between the frozen surface of the berg and the surrounding water, throw in a factor that accounted for residual cooling from the still-frozen interior of the berg, and remove the cooling effects of the meltwater lingering at the interface, because the ice mountain would be continually moving north into new and warmer water. She could then adjust that function for the range of different water temperatures at different latitudes, supplied by the tables in Hugo Wichard's original report, and calibrate it for a range of anticipated towing speeds. And finally, she could throw in a heating variable from those two-to-the-eleventh-power calories—based on the standard definition of a calorie, as the amount of energy required to raise a gram of water one degree Celsius—that would be generated by a minimum of three tugboats, factoring up or down for their optimum speed, and adjust that calculation up or down depending on the size of the anticipated berg to be moved and the number of tugs required to tow it.

When she had all of these different variables properly stated, she could program a series of test cases, from the smallest possible berg that could make the trip and still have a usable frozen core, to the largest possible berg that a team of wranglers could separate from the Amery Ice Shelf and attempt to move without burning out the engines of the tugboats.

Then she would turn the program over to the coding team in the basement, for them to punch it into Hollerith cards and feed it into the System/360. And when the machine had spat out its report on green-lined, fanfold pages, she would have an answer in the form of an engineering sweet spot between an iceberg too small to survive and one too massive to move.

Or that was the theory.

————

After nearly three weeks of waiting, Dennis Denbridge called down to the woman in Estimating and Scheduling to whom he had entrusted Mannheim's analysis of the Saudi Iceberg Project. Or that was the way Denbridge thought of it in his own mind, as something already in the corporate backlog, with its own account number and billing cycle.

"You'd better come down and see this," was all the Wheelock woman would say.

When he arrived in her office, he found the young woman sitting behind three stacked piles of green-bar computer paper.

"What do you have for me?" he asked.

"I've run the numbers three separate ways," she said. "I've eaten up a lot of computer time on your overhead account—"

"*Your* overhead. I never authorized a computer study."

"—well, the *company's* overhead. And I still can't make it work."

"What part doesn't compute?"

"I still can't get an iceberg from the waters off Antarctica to a port north of the equator."

"I should think that's the easy part, and *Monsieur* Wichard has already worked it out. The iceberg is floating freely, so you just tow it with tugboats."

"Yes, of course," she replied. "But as the iceberg gets into warmer waters, it melts. Or the little ones do anyway. I've run different scenarios with different-size bergs. The ones you can manage and can tow fast—say, taking two or three months on the trip—are gone before you cross the equator. The big ones that might survive such a trip are just too big to move. And if you can get them moving, then they're too big to control. Where the currents are right, the winds are wrong, and *vice versa,* you end up in a tangle. So the trip takes you a year, and even the biggest icebergs melt when they stay that long in tropical seas."

"I don't believe it," Denbridge said. "Wichard brought us an *engineering* report."

"No, sir. He brought you a bunch of engineering suggestions along with some pretty sketches. There's nothing in there—" She pointed to the document bound in bright-green covers, the colors of Saudi Arabia, that lay to one side on her desk. "—that constitutes a real technical or economic analysis."

"There's got to be some way to do it." He felt the project was slipping away.

"There is no sweet spot between an iceberg's size and its maneuverability."

"So? Think creatively," Denbridge said. "The ultimate goal here is to harvest the meltwater. After all, we're selling the Saudis water for the desert, not the ice itself for their scotch. Maybe you can cover the berg with a plastic bag or something. Let it melt under wraps while you tow it north."

"But ..." Wheelock's eyes went wide, and he was pleased to have found a way to shock this smug young woman. "But the major part of an iceberg, seven-eighths, is *under* water. These things go down hundreds—sometimes thousands—of feet. We have no way to get a bag under and around it, let alone seal the bag tight enough to keep the fresh water in and the seawater out. Not under the stress of towing."

"I can see you've already considered other options. That's good. Now find one that *will* work, because Mannheim really wants this project. So think outside the box."

He watched her stiffen, then relax and sigh. That, too, was pleasant to see.

"Finding the solution may require more computer time," she said slowly.

"I'll talk with your boss about charges. You just get this thing done."

———

Dani Wheelock wrestled for a day with Denbridge's suggestion about wrapping an iceberg in plastic. She got books about materials science out of the library and studied up on various plastics and other flexible, bag-making fabrics.

The main trouble was not, as she had thought at first, getting the mouth of the bag down to five hundred or a thousand feet deep, so as to catch and cover the berg's jagged bottom, and then sealing off the opening to make it watertight. Yes, those were all problems. But commercial fisheries managed nets that were nearly as big. Hell, they could drag the ocean floor with them to scoop up bottom fish or clams or whatever. So the mechanics of bag handling were probably workable.

Another issue, which Dani had been putting aside for later and which wrapping the iceberg in a bag would only partially address—involved the dynamics of hauling a massive berg in the first place. If you simply anchored cables to the surface ice, the parts you could easily reach above water, or threw a cable around it at the waterline, you weren't pulling at the center of mass. Surface cabling might work for moving the ice mountain very slowly, with just a suggestion of force, but any stronger effort would end up being divided between forward motion and tipping motion. In the worst case, you would invite the iceberg to roll over on itself. That would foul your lines disastrously and perhaps drag one or more of your tugboats under. For a stable tow, you had to dive deep and place your pitons and cables near the center of mass. But aside from hiring a team of deep-sea divers or a manned submersible, she didn't have a solution for that problem yet.

Perhaps she wouldn't have to, if she could work out a way to bag the iceberg as a whole, but there the real issue was the strength of materials. Trying to create a watertight barrier meant that the tugboats could no longer anchor pitons directly in the ice or throw an exposed cable around the backside of the mountain. Pitons would pierce the bag material, and cables would quickly abrade, wear holes, and create tears in it. So all the strain of towing would have to be borne by the bag itself. The team would have to sew patches with loops onto the bag's surface—and that was only after cutting loose, surveying, and modeling a specific piece of ice. Those draw points and the surrounding fabric would each have to take their share of the strain, based on however many tugboats might be involved.

And then the ice mountain would still have spikes and sharp points that could pierce and cut the fabric. And those rough spots would surely change shape—sometimes becoming sharper—as the berg melted inside the bag. The whole iceberg would change shape, too, meaning that the draw points might have to be shifted during the trip to distribute the strain more evenly. And then, when the berg was gone, melted away, and the tugs were simply towing a bag full of fresh water—which was less dense than the surrounding salt water—the bag would adopt a new configuration, tending to flatten out in a pancake shape that would again foul the hauling lines. The tug crews would be grappling with a bag that was constantly changing its configuration, and that would slow down the trip and complicate operations.

Dani tried to find a material that was tough enough to stand up to all that pulling, stretching, and tearing. She could figure the strains in pounds per square inch by calculating the mass of a large iceberg and the energies—which she had already worked out—for towing it. Nothing made of plastic film would last even a day or two. Some woven fabric might have more tensile strength, but then she was up against the strength of the individual yarns that were used in weaving it. Even heavy cotton canvas with a rubberized coating would eventually fail. Only rubberized canvas over a net of steel cables would do the trick, but that would add to the towing weight and be hell to manage in terms of flexibility. The only material that would seem to work was Kevlar® aramid fiber. And that was going to be one expensive bag!

But then she remembered the last thing Denbridge had said: that old chestnut about "thinking outside the box." But what if, instead of a bag, they designed a box, a barge, a rigid structure with easily defined towing points? Such a structure could also be designed with a more hydrodynamic shape than a jagged old iceberg, too.

The project could make its icebergs any shape they wanted. After all, Wichard's sketches showed teams cutting a chunk out of the floating ice shelf, rather than waiting for an irregular berg to calve off and drift away. So why not cut a square berg, the way quarrymen took out a block of granite?

They could design a barge with underwater doors at one end. Then just slide the ice block inside, close the doors, and pump out the seawater that came in along with it. Tow the barge north to Saudi Arabia as if they were hauling a load of coal or oil. And if they made the proper size adjustments between the cargo's frozen and liquid states—so that the expanding meltwater didn't put undue pressure on the barge cavity and the doors—they wouldn't have to worry about the barge leaking or approaching its point of negative buoyancy and sinking.

Dani wasn't thinking *outside* the box—she was thinking *inside* it.

And barging blocks of ice solved another problem, too. Building an iceberg-sized holding tank at or near the port of Jeddah, including a sea lane to approach it with a berg extending for a couple of hundred or a thousand feet under the water's surface, and then sealing the basin with massive lock gates extending deep enough to accommodate the floating mass—that had always been a colossal stumbling block. Aside from the engineering difficulties, the capital investment of building such a huge piece of infrastructure before the project produced its first gallon of fresh water—that had continually brought the economics of the plan into question.

But ice barges, with icebergs that were cut to fit them, could be built anywhere, towed anywhere, and unloaded anywhere. Even more important than the logistics, they made the entire project *scalable*. One massive basin could take and melt only one iceberg at a time. But a string of barges could provide more water over any period of time just by building and floating more of them. On top of that, the technology of building barges with watertight doors and pumps was already available in the shipbuilding industry. And the operations involved with towing them had been part of the human experience for a hundred years or more, since the dawn of steam power.

Dani had just redefined both the technical and economic feasibility of the entire project.

# 7. Yes … and No

DENNIS DENBRIDGE LISTENED to the Wheelock woman describe a whole new plan for bringing ice—or rather, barges full of freshly melted water—to Saudi Arabia. He didn't know whether he liked the idea or not, because the days when he had to study engineering problems and come up with a solution were many years in his past. Denbridge had spent the last decade or more sitting at a desk, talking with prospective clients, and then turning their problems—or in this case their proposals—over to worker bees like Danielle Wheelock. But he did know that this was a complete redefinition of the project, one not covered by Hugo Wichard's green book.

"I think I told you," he said at last, "to make this project work. Not to go totally blue sky and think up a new one."

"But …" There was that wide-eyed look again. "There's no way to get a naked iceberg across the equator and into a warm-water northern port without it melting down to nothing. And there's no way to bag an iceberg—at least not economically—so as to capture all the water as it melts *en route*. Maybe someone else can do it, but I've run the numbers and they don't lie."

"No, you've just run the *negative* numbers, where the iceberg just disappears. But what about the costs of your new project—for building all these 'ice barges' and then towing them across the ocean?"

"It will certainly cost less," she replied, "than digging a hole a thousand feet deep in the coastline of Saudi Arabia."

"So you claim. But where are your numbers? If I'm going to take this idea to the Executive Committee, I need a report like the one Wichard provided, with cost estimates, schedules, and a rate of return. Come on, you're supposed to be the estimator and scheduler. This is your *job*."

"But … I can't keep fudging this thing on Ed Cooper's overhead budget. You're talking about a conceptual engineering study." Wheelock blew out her cheeks and lips—which was hardly an attractive facial expression on a woman. "Business Development's got to help me out here."

"That's … not … " Denbridge began slowly, hesitant about committing himself.

"Then the answer from the Estimating and Scheduling Department—and Cooper will back me up on this—is that your iceberg project is neither technically nor economically feasible." She smiled. "And no skin off my nose."

"I'll … have to see what I can do."

"Everyone will be much obliged."

———

Hugo Wichard admitted to himself some qualms when Dennis Denbridge invited him back to Mannheim Construction, Inc., for a second interview. It was more than a month since their first meeting, when the Business Development assistant had immediately passed his iceberg project off to some low-level flunky—and a woman—to evaluate. In the meantime he had returned to France. First, because he could not afford to remain in a San Francisco hotel room to await an answer, even on a project that was worth, potentially, millions of dollars. Second, because he had other irons in the fire, and he could tend to them better from his third-floor walkup in the *banlieue* of Corbeil-Essonnes than from some third-rate and still expensive suburban motel in California.

When the call finally came from Denbridge, Wichard tried to divine the construction company's intentions from the tone of the man's voice. But this was harder with Americans, who were always so positive and upbeat in their most casual conversations. Still, Wichard heard hesitations and reservations in Denbridge's call. That was a bad sign. For five long seconds, Wichard had considered turning down—politely, with many heaving sighs—the invitation to return, based solely on the cost of international round-trip airfare, even in tourist class, although he would never have mentioned that as his reason. But at the last second, he thought of some other business he might conduct on the West Coast, and so Wichard unclenched, relaxed, and agreed to a date.

Now he sat in the office of the Wheelock woman with a sheaf of photocopied pages on his lap. The estimator sat across from him, holding the originals in front of her. And Denbridge sat beside him in the room's other guest chair with more paper, which he didn't even pretend to read.

At first, Wichard had felt insulted as this woman—this girl, in fact, and just how many years away from her école technique?—explained why his iceberg project was infeasible from both a technical and an economic viewpoint. He felt the frown forming on his face, but he kept his head down, studying the pages in his lap, and controlled his temper.

It was good that he did so, because in the next sentence, not a minute later, she was explaining another way, a better way, to work the problem. It was not *his* way, of course, but the fact that Denbridge had called him back, as if they expected to need his approval of their new plan, with its slabs of ship-sized ice cut from the glacier and floated aboard covered barges for the long haul across the ocean. The Mannheim people—or this woman herself, it would appear—had taken his idea and made it smaller, more compact, less grandiose, less imaginative, but also more practical, and still potentially profitable. What she was proposing was a shipping operation rather than a salvage at sea. But why would the company take his idea, shred it, and then offer it back to him—rather than kicking Hugo Neville Wichard, unknown foreigner and failed hydrologist, to the curb and running with it themselves?

Ah! The letter in his briefcase. His access to the House of Saud. They still needed that. And so …

He followed along with her pages of cost estimates, timetables, the metrics of towing capacities, and the descriptions of potential barge construction sites and pump-out stations. He still had to keep his head down, so that neither Wheelock nor Denbridge might see his growing smile and the gleam in his eye, of *le chat qui a mangé le pigeon*. But when the woman finally did finish and then waited, expecting a response from him, Wichard lifted his head and gave her his patented, client-pleasing smile.

"But this is simply brilliant!" he exclaimed. "You have found the nut, the kernel, the *essence* of the proposition and refined it into facts and figures."

He watched as she lowered her sheaf of papers and smiled back.

"This is a proposal of which I am *positif*—I am certain—the Saudi Supreme Economic Council can approve. I will take it to them at the first opportunity—"

"Um, before that," Denbridge said, and then paused to clear his throat. "For this to become a project with Mannheim's backing, I will have to obtain approval from our Executive Committee."

"Oh, yes. I see." Wichard swallowed. "Of course. And how long do you think that will take?" Or rather, how long would he have to sit in an expensive San Francisco hotel room, to keep up appearances? Or fly back to Paris and sit in his rat-trap of an apartment in the suburbs, waiting for another answer?

"Oh, not long," Denbridge said. "The committee meets monthly, and the next meeting is the Tuesday after this coming Monday. I can still get this proposal on the agenda, as the Vice President of Business Development practically runs that meeting, and I manage his schedule."

"I understand," Wichard said. "I suppose we can wait until then."

In the meantime, he would console himself with the vision of millions of Saudi petrodollars effortlessly converted into French or Swiss francs by the melting of icebergs.

———

A week after her second meeting with the French engineer Hugo Wichard, Dani Wheelock was summoned to Dennis Denbridge's office on the thirty-eighth floor. Since the iceberg—now ice *barge*—project was the only thing she had going at the moment with the people in Business Development, she knew this meeting would be about the verdict from the Executive Committee, which had met the day before.

The offices up here were a lot nicer than hers: thick, gray broadloom carpeting instead of vinyl laminate, walls paneled in mahogany or rosewood veneer instead of painted steel partitions keyed into tracks in the concrete floor, furniture made of genuine hardwoods instead of Steelcase and Formica. These nice surroundings came with taking on more professional responsibility, demonstrating proven performance in solving problems, and making the big things happen. Dani was eager to begin tackling that kind of challenge—in fact, thought she was doing just that with the Saudi project—so she could rise above her current station on the lower floors and work in this kind of rarified environment.

Wichard was already sitting in Denbridge's guest chair, and as she entered he rose immediately, took her hand, and performed his little bow over it. Denbridge himself stood up a fraction of a second later—and it was obvious from his face that he was puzzled by the reflex—but he did not come around from behind his desk to greet her.

As she seated herself and the two men settled into their chairs, Denbridge began talking. "I am very much afraid that I must be the bearer of bad news."

Dani drew her head back: this was not the result she was expecting.

Wichard, she noticed, had fixed Denbridge in a kind of death glare.

"No," the Business Development man went on, "the Executive Committee heard your proposal—or *Monsieur* Wichard's proposal, as modified by Miss Wheelock. They considered and discussed it at length, and in the end they decided that the project was not something Mannheim wants to pursue."

"Is there some question we might be able to answer?" Wichard asked quietly.

"No, they are quite clear on the concept. Have no fear on that account."

"What were their specific objections?" Dani asked next. "If any."

"Basically, that it's just not our kind of project. The consensus was that the plan is essentially a shipbuilding and ocean transport operation. And when my boss, Avery Winston, pointed out that Mannheim has a lot of experience constructing dry docks, slipways, and ocean terminals, the response—put rather brusquely, I thought—was that these are not the same things as running a barge service."

"Mannheim could contract to build those parts of the project's infrastructure," Dani suggested.

"It would not be enough," Denbridge replied. "And those elements might not be built inside Saudi Arabia proper. No, the committee has taken a set against the idea. One member even noted that, with this proposed solution, it would be easier and more logical to take a tanker ship into the mouth of, say, the Nile, pump it full of river water, and run it back through the Suez Canal and into Jeddah. Of course, then you'd have to deal with the burden of silt, industrial sludge, and *E. coli* colony-forming units—the hazards of drinking from any of the world's major rivers. But cleaning up those contaminants would still be cheaper than setting up a base camp at the South Pole."

Dani sighed. "I guess that's it then."

"Yes, exactly so," Denbridge said.

But Wichard still had said nothing.

———

As he walked out of the twelve-foot-tall, brass-bound, darkened glass doors of the Centennial Plaza lobby and into the late-morning sunshine of downtown San Francisco, Hugo Wichard's mind was still churning. But he was finally getting his emotions under control.

In his briefcase, he carried his original engineering report in its bright-green cover and the folded drawings of the icebergs being cut and moving in stately procession across the ocean. For these original project documents he had paid a junior architect in Kinshasa thirty thousand Congolese zaires, or about thirty French francs. Denbridge had been good enough to return them—not that they were worth anything now. What Wichard did *not* have was a single piece of paper describing or costing out the new barge concept as developed by the Wheelock woman, because that remained a Mannheim work product, and Denbridge had collected all those materials.

But Wichard still held the letter of introduction from Ali bin Muhammad al-Kabir, and that had been the heart of his proposal all along.

He had hoped to eventually connect Mannheim Construction, Inc., with one of the more centrally placed royal princes, one who could actually speak for and sign contracts on behalf of the Saudi government. Once this bond was established and the two parties were negotiating together, Wichard expected to be paid a finder's fee from one or the other, and perhaps from both. At that point, he could step back and let the project find its own course, for good or ill.

But now that was not going to happen.

It looked like he was left holding worthless paper on a defunct project. He could not take the iceberg scheme across the street to the next largest engineering and construction company, because he knew from experience that these big firms kept no secrets from each other. In fact, at the senior level, they gossiped among themselves like *des nounous*—a group of baby nannies pushing their strollers through the *Bois de Boulogne*.

*Alors ... bien.* There was always more than one way to remove *la peau du chat* or, in this case, *les plumes du pigeon*.

# 8. And Yes

IT WAS TWO weeks after Mannheim's Executive Committee had turned thumbs down on the Saudi deal. Dani was in the middle of a new assignment, corralling the cost elements and developing the work breakdown structure on port improvements for containerized shipping in Chile. She had almost forgotten the extracurricular effort she had put into the aborted iceberg project, although she had not completely overcome the sting of its rejection. And then she received a phone call on her outside line.

"It is I, Hugo Wichard," said the same grave but somehow lilting voice. "We need to talk, you and I."

"I'm sorry, Mister Wichard, but I don't know what else there is to discuss. The decision of the committee is final in these things."

"This is not about your committee. Not about Mannheim Construction at all. Can you meet me at the Grill of Tadich in, say, half an hour? I am at a table in the back."

"I don't know if that's appropriate."

"It's not appropriate. It's *important*."

Dani decided she could take time off from the container port to be polite to the man. Anyway, it was almost lunchtime, and Ed Cooper wouldn't mind her slipping out a bit early.

She found Wichard, true to his word, holding a table in the shadows at the back of the dining room, where his lightweight suit—a pale blue this time—stood out against the dark wainscoting. As before, he leapt to his feet and bowed over her extended hand, as if she were visiting royalty. When they had seated themselves, he folded his hands on the table's edge, as if to help compose his thoughts.

"First," he began, "I was very disappointed that Mannheim will not join us in this venture. I can sense that you, too, share in that disappointment."

"Yes, I'm sorry things turned out this way."

"Of course, but the situation still exists. The Saudi people still need fresh water if they are to reach their full potential. And with your ingenious improvements to the methods of iceberg wrangling—'wrangling' is the right word, yes? like a cowboy?—as described in the original project, providing that water is now even more possible."

"But Mannheim won't back it," she said.

"No ... and yet their participation is hardly necessary, is it? Not since you have removed most of the major deepwater infrastructure requirements of the project. As your committee people have said, this is now an exercise in shipbuilding and ocean transport. With your concept, and with your expertise in cost estimating and scheduling, not to mention the research you have already done, the project can now proceed."

"I don't understand how. Have the Saudis agreed to put up the money?"

"Not yet, and I will be working on that, when I have a more developed picture of the plans to present. In the meantime, I can approach the Organisation of Islamic Cooperation, which has an interest in developing the region, or the U.S. Agency for International Development. They will be eager to find and showcase infrastructure projects that improve living conditions."

"What about our committee's alternative suggestion?" Dani was still stung by the memory of it. "About running a tanker ship up the Nile for fresh water?"

"Ah!" Wichard smiled, then frowned deeply. "You Americans do not understand the national perspective on this. You would be asking the Arabs to drink the effluvium—that is the word? sewer discharge?—of Egypt. It is not a thing that is possible. The Saudis would rather go to the ends of the earth, or in this case the South Pole, for their water."

"I can see you understand the cultural issues," she said.

"Oh, I have worked all over Africa and the Middle East."

"And you already have contacts in Arabia?" she asked.

"A prince of the House of Saud has endorsed this work."

"But there is still one problem—a major one, I'm afraid. You see, I don't own the conceptual design for barging the ice. It doesn't really belong to me."

"It was your idea."

"Yes, but I developed it on Mannheim's time, while on their payroll, using their budget and their computer resources. So the concept and all that goes with it is their work product."

"I'm not sure I understand," he said, again frowning. "Using barges instead of hauling raw icebergs is just an idea, is it not? A notion. You and your legal people have not taken out a patent on it, have you? Have they?"

"No, an idea like that is not patentable. I don't think it would even qualify as a new application of existing technology."

"Then where is the harm? Besides, they have already rejected the proposal. They cannot now sit like the dog in the manger and forbid others to follow it."

"It's a matter of principle," Dani said. "If you were to go ahead with the ice barges on your own—especially as a project being showcased by the Organisation of Islamic Cooperation—then Mannheim would recognize their past involvement. They would charge you with stealing their—my—work, my time and effort. And, if I gave you the calculations and supporting documents, they would dismiss me out of hand."

"I understand. But this is not insurmountable. When the time comes, and with the backing of the Saudi royal family and the international bankers, we will pay Mannheim for their services. Call it a quitclaim. Call it a conceptual design fee. Everyone will be satisfied."

"Then I'm not sure why you need me," she said.

"Because I cannot do this thing without you. You not only have the background, the numbers in your head, but you had the—do I say?—the genius to see the original project's flaws in the first place and then to fix them."

Dani felt a glow at that. No one—certainly no one at Mannheim Construction, Inc.—had ever called her a genius. And besides, the whole reason she had worked so hard on the ice-barge concept, aside from Dennis Denbridge's urging and insistence, was that she sensed something big in it, something worthwhile. This project in Saudi Arabia was the proverbial ground floor, the unexplored territory, a new world of engineering expertise. And she could be central to it, if she could earn the confidence and gratitude of senior-level executives like Denbridge and, through him, Avery Winston. And after them, of a man with international development and banking connections like Hugo Wichard. This project could be the elevator that took her out of the engineering services basement, up from a support function like Estimating and Scheduling, to a full-blown project management position. With this under her belt, she could be somebody in the profession. And if the company would accept a quitclaim on the ice-barge idea, then everything was all right, both legally and morally.

"Are you offering me a job?" she asked for the record.

"We will make a good team," he said with a smile.

————

Norman Wall saw that Dani was upset—or scared, or nervous, or excited, or *something*. Although she had said she was starving when she came home from work early and made them a big dinner of load-your-own tacos and a three-bean salad, she then picked at her plate and had taken no more than a bite of her first taco. And all the while she talked—not fast, not anxious, but in a low, reasonable tone, as if she was trying to convince herself.

"… I mean, it's not like I'm not *happy* at the company. It's a good place to work, although they're kind of hard on women, and it's one of the biggest construction outfits in the business, with a worldwide reputation, which means that even working as part of a small contract, for them, is the equivalent of taking on the largest and best jobs at any other firm."

"You've always said you liked Mannheim," he put in.

"Yes, I *like* it there. But progress is slow, you know? And slower for a woman. It will take me years to get up the ladder. And I kind of hurt myself with that nuclear project. I mean,

*Jesus!* My first job out of school and I bring down a multi-billion-dollar power plant. And then, working in Estimating and Scheduling has been interesting. And I've learned a lot there. But it's not like a real engineering job. Not like I'm actually *building* anything."

"And this job offer from what's-his-name, Richard?"

"Wi-*shard*. It's French. And his first name is Hugo."

"Do you think this iceberg thing will really take off?"

"I can *make* it happen," Dani said. "It's not a new technology, after all. There's nothing we have to invent or prove. We just build the barges, hire the tugboats, and go cut blocks of ice out of a glacier. By the time they get to Saudi, we're just pumping clean, fresh water into the city pipeline system."

"So why is this exciting?" Norman asked.

"Because it's never been done before. It will get write-ups in *Engineering News-Record, Construction Today, International Builder*—you name it. And I'll be central to all those stories. Not just because I thought of the idea—that's the easy part. But because I made it happen."

"With the help of this Wichard fellow. And, presumably, a lot of people at the South Pole cutting the ice and driving the tugboats. ... I notice you haven't said much about this Wichard, either way."

"Oh … he's nice. Kind of old-fashioned, with I guess you would say 'Old World' manners. For instance, every time he sees me, he takes my hand and—" Here Dani leapt up from the table, came around, grabbed Norman's own hand, and bowed over it. Then she planted the faintest of kisses on the back of his knuckles. "—or at least I *think* he's going to kiss my hand every time. But he never actually does."

"What is he like? As a person?"

"Very sincere. Sure of himself."

"And?" He pressed, with a grin.

"Fortyish. Tanned. Graying hair."

"Handsome?" Norman dared to ask.

"In a sleek, sophisticated, European way."

"And you're in love with him. Just a little bit?"

"Oh, no! Or, well, every girl finds such men attractive."

"What is he like as an engineer? That should be the question."

"I ... don't know. His résumé is impressive. But, well, *thin*. He's been involved in a lot of projects, mostly in Africa, but he never says what, exactly, he did on them. I think it's mostly consulting. But that doesn't really matter. What's important is that he has the connections with bankers and money people, and within the House of Saud. And he understands the culture—which is something that has kept Mannheim out of the running for decades. He has the inside scoop. So I can do the engineering work for both of us."

"And, like every girl, you find him attractive." Norman knew he was pushing a boundary here. But what the hell. "If not the man himself, personally, then what he can do for you, for your career. So you *are* falling in love, just a bit."

"*Really*, Norman. I've given up on the idea of love."

————

Dani lay awake in her bed at three in the morning and stared into the darkness above her head. That hour of the night, she knew, was when the doubts came. It was a time that the mind—when it wasn't dreaming of terrors and confusions and strange regrets, when it was still wakeful—confronted the harshest of realities. If she went through with this, if she left the company to join Wichard in this iceberg venture, what was going to happen?

Her first thought was that she might have to go to Saudi Arabia right away. Would she have to *live* there? And for how long? Everyone said the country was like a prison for women. She knew engineers who had come into Mannheim from other companies that had projects in the kingdom. They lived inside walled compounds, kept separate from Saudi society. It was like living in a distant suburb of a city you could never actually visit. They said their wives—if they relocated with their husbands and tried to make a home there—found it tolerable enough, if a bit boring. And they put their children in boarding schools, usually in Europe, most of them in Switzerland.

But Dani wouldn't be a dependent wife. She would be a single woman, an executive, someone who would have to go out into that foreign society, work alongside Arab men, and tell them what to do. The expatriates from other companies also said that Saudi citizens seldom took actual working jobs inside the kingdom. And then they only wanted high-level positions as sinecures and secondary sources of income, apart from their oil wealth. All the Saudi executives wanted to do was play at being businessmen and chase the company secretaries. Unless they could drive D9 Caterpillar tractors—that was supposed to be honorable work, like riding a camel or something. But most of the real labor in the kingdom, even at middle levels of management, was performed by "third country nationals," usually from Asia, most of them from Korea.

However, as a key executive in the iceberg venture, Dani would have to deal with those high-level Saudi princes and sheikhs. And she would get no respect from them. If they decided to pay attention to the business and challenge her on technical or financial issues, who would stand up for her, without the support of a big company like Mannheim behind her? How, for example, would she have gone into that confrontation at the Tennessee nuclear plant if it had been just her, without James Farley and Peter Harbaugh backing up her findings?

And then there were the personal questions. What would happen to her life in San Francisco? If she went away for the months—no, years—it would take to make the iceberg project work, how could she keep their lovely little house in South Park? Could she still afford to pay her share of the rent and not live there, just to have the place to come back to in a couple of years? Would Norman stay there alone after she left? Or would he bring in someone new to live with him and take over her role in a relationship that was more than a friendship, for they were actually living together, but was not really love?

And what would happen to the Beast? Could she pay to keep her Corvette in storage somewhere? Would it survive being parked in a garage for years at a time? For all its raw power, the 454 engine was a demanding piece of machinery. Could it stand not being in even semi-constant use? Or would it deteriorate over time? And what about the tires, the leather interior, and the other non-metal parts? Would the fiberglass body weaken or get brittle with age?

And what about her karate training? Now that she was a black belt in Shorinryu, she could take her skills to a *dojo* anywhere. But did Saudi Arabia even have *dojo*s? And would they accept women? And if she didn't go to the *dojo* and work out at least once a week, would her skills deteriorate the way her car might?

But these personal questions were ones she had always faced as an engineer in a company doing civil contracting around the world. She could not be a key player in a big project from behind a desk in San Francisco. Or not until she became a senior project manager like Harbaugh. Real, working engineers did their jobs in the field. And with a company like Mannheim, that field might be on any continent, usually in undeveloped places not that different from Saudi Arabia. Even in Antarctica. So leaving San Francisco had always been a possibility, if she was ever offered the chance to build something big and important—the kind of work she had always said she craved.

But to leave Mannheim now, to go with a man like Wichard, in an unknown venture, to a place she had never been, without the backing of a large and stable organization, without the support of knowledgeable professionals in service organizations like estimating and scheduling, computing and drafting, import and export, financial and legal—that was daunting.

But with the chance of doing something big and important came the risk of doing it badly and falling on her face. Risk and reward were the *yin* and *yang* of a professional life.

And then ... Who was to say that the stark thoughts, the terrors, and the doubts a person experienced in the dark at three o'clock in the morning were any more real than the determinations and resolutions she made in the cold light of day?

With that thought, she rolled over and composed herself for sleep.

———

Ed Cooper sat in his office going over the monthly computer printout of billable hours charged by members of his department to various Mannheim project accounts. He was just shaking his head over the number of overhead hours—to his own account and to Avery Winston's—spent on that absurd iceberg scheme, when the reason for those hours knocked once on his door frame, walked in, and seated herself in front of his desk.

"Hello, Dani. I was just thinking about you."

"There's something I need to discuss ... I need to tell you, Mister Cooper."

"All right, but you used to call me 'Ed,' once upon a time. What's up?"

"I think I have to leave the company," she said slowly, as if only just then making up her mind.

"What for? If you're worried about that business with Denbridge and all these overhead charges—"

"Huh? What about them? They were approved, weren't they?"

"Yes, by Winston's people, and only after the fact," Cooper said, sorry he'd brought up the matter. "But you're not here about that, are you?"

"Well ... not directly. I have been offered a position in a new venture to make the iceberg project a reality."

"Really? And by whom?"

"By Mister Wichard."

"That Frenchman!"

"He's done a lot of work in the Middle East and Africa. He understands hydrological work. And he has contacts in the Saudi royal house and with the Islamic bankers."

"And he has your idea for putting the ice in barges, doesn't he?"

"Well, yes. By taking the ice up north in ready-made tanks, we overcome a lot of technical and economic difficulties."

"And that *ipso facto* makes the project economically feasible?"

"Yes, the numbers are very favorable."

"Compared to what?"

"Well, compared to wrangling the free-floating icebergs and hauling them seven thousand miles through tropical waters."

"But not compared to other alternatives," he said.

"If you mean taking Nile water into Saudi, the Saudis wouldn't stand for it. Not as a matter of national feeling."

"What about desalination?" Cooper suggested. "All you need for that is a plant, which you can build, and seawater, which you can pump. Oh, and an abundant source of energy, of which the Saudis have oodles in the form of their oil and its byproducts. Did you think about that?"

"Well, we can take a look at it. But the icebergs—"

"I know, Dani." He sighed. "They're the horse you can ride, aren't they? They're the one good idea you bring to the party."

"When you put it that way—"

"Our business, the engineering business, is to look at all options and pick the one that works best. That means least cost, greatest return, lowest risks, ease of constructability, fewest moving parts—you know the drill by now."

"But ... don't you *see?*" The girl's face was twisted with something like grief. "This is my chance."

"Chance at what, for heaven's sake? Some kind of brass ring? A shortcut to—?"

"To get out from under," she said, and now she sounded truly desperate.

"What exactly are you 'under' here? Are you in some kind of trouble? Do you have debts? Because if you—?"

"From under the shadow of Farragut. You know I've had the word 'Fuckup' tattooed on my forehead ever since then.

It's why I was assigned to Estimating and Scheduling in the first place. To keep me out of trouble."

"That's not true," Cooper said. "You've done valuable work here. And your discovery of the faulty foundation steel was a plus for the company, in the long run. People of importance recognize that."

"Then why won't they assign me to projects that are worthwhile? Where we're building something? I've applied and applied, and each time I get shot down."

"Your time will come, Dani."

"I think it's come now, sir."

"I can't stop you, can I?"

"Please don't try, Ed."

———

The woman who processed Dani's paperwork and conducted her exit interview was named Kathy Jenner. It said so on the plaque in front of her desk, although she never really introduced herself. She was young, too, like Dani, somewhere in her mid-twenties. When she smiled—which she did a lot—her cheeks showed dimples.

"Your final paycheck," Jenner was saying, "will be cut on the fifteenth and mailed to your home address." She held out another form. "And we need your signature here to authorize taking your accrued pension benefit as a lump-sum amount. This is common for employees with less than ten years of service. That's the point at which vesting kicks in."

Dani took the form and signed it. "Does anyone stay here that long?" she asked.

"Oh, quite a few, actually. Although mostly in the support functions."

"Like, in Estimating and Scheduling?" Dani suggested.

"Usually, the non-engineers," Jenner replied.

"And what do the engineers do?"

"After a certain point, they move around a lot. They're working within their specialty, right? So they go where the jobs are. If you're a transportation engineer, and Mannheim doesn't have a highway or rail transit project opening up, you'll likely go to some other outfit—one of our competitors—who just got a big contract and needs the talent."

"And the company is okay with this? Do people ever come back?"

"Oh, all the time! Especially if they are good at what they do."

"The company doesn't think people who leave are traitors?"

"If we did, then we could never staff up for the big jobs."

"That's good to know ... if I ever had to come back."

"You know," Jenner said, "I envy people like you."

"How so? I mean, I'm leaving under a cloud."

"No, you're heading out on your own. Or that's the story I hear. Taking off for adventure in the real world. Starting your own company. Working directly with foreign clients and investors. Doing something no one's ever done before. I would try it myself, but with a degree in anthropology—alongside four thousand other anthro majors with undergraduate degrees—and only a handful of digs being funded in any given year—well, that's why I'm here in Personnel. The pay is steady."

"Speaking of pay," Dani said, to change the subject, "how much is that pension?"

Jenner looked through her papers. "Six thousand, two hundred, fifteen dollars, and thirty-eight cents."

"That's hardly enough to live on, is it?"

"Depends on how long you plan to live."

## 9. Making It Real

HUGO WICHARD HAD arranged for the meeting to take place in Café de la Presse on Grant Avenue, because the lawyer he had hired to prepare and file the necessary documents, Augustus Slezak, had said he liked French food, and the restaurant was an easy walk from his office on Bush Street. The two men arrived at the scheduled time of twelve noon, and Danielle Wheelock came in ten minutes later.

"Sorry," she said. "I had trouble finding a place to park."

"You keep a car in the city?" Wichard asked, surprised.

"I'd never try to do that," Slezak offered over his menu.

"Yes, I know," Wichard replied. "Anyway, *Mad'moiselle* Danielle Wheelock, this is *M'sieur* Slezak, our lawyer. Gus, this is our new partner."

The lawyer nodded his head but did not offer to rise.

"We are here today," Wichard continued, "to formalize the relationship of our new venture. Now, I have proposed 'Saudi Ice Partners' as the business name."

"Wouldn't do that," Slezak said from behind the menu. "Is the *Steak Frites* good here?"

Wichard shook his head. "Yes, it's very good. But why not the name?"

Slezak lowered the menu. "It's just not a good idea to use 'partner' in the title. And identifying anything as 'Saudi,' first, it limits your scope; second, it will offend the royal house; and third, it makes you a target for some groups. Keep it general. Keep it vague."

"How about 'Antarctic Ice Ventures'?" Wheelock said. "Or does that limit us, too?"

Wichard shrugged and turned to Slezak.

"Fine by me," the lawyer said.

"Now, as to the membership and shares," Wichard went on. "I propose we divide the ownership and profits in the venture according to the level of responsibility. I will take fifty-five percent, as the managing partner and originator of the concept. Miss Wheelock will take twenty-five percent as our chief engineer and project technical lead. His Highness Ali bin Muhammad al-Kabir will take twenty-five percent as the source of our startup capital. And *M'sieur* Slezak will take five percent as general counsel."

"That's more than one hundred percent!" Wheelock objected.

"Don't make me part of this!" Slezak said at the same instant.

"More than a hundred?" Wichard blinked. "Ah, I see the error."

"You'll pay me a fee," the lawyer continued, "and I stay out of it."

"All right!" Wichard put up a hand. "How about fifty-five to me, twenty-five to Danielle, and twenty to Prince Ali? Does *that* make the numbers square?"

"Okay by me," Wheelock said quietly, "if it works for the prince."

"I'm sure he will agree," Wichard replied. "He is most generous."

"Will I get to meet this prince who's now my partner?" she asked.

"Yes, but not right away. Prince Ali never travels out of the kingdom."

"And," she went on, "as for being partners, how does that actually work? I mean, we are bound to have liability issues—industrial accidents, storms at sea, missed deliveries. How do we account for those?"

"You each take responsibility proportionally," Slezak said.

"You mean," she replied, "I could get personally sued by a welder who burns his hand in a shipyard somewhere in Egypt or Pakistan?"

Slezak pursed his lips, as if considering representing the welder.

"It will never come to that," Wichard said quickly. "We will work through subcontractors, like all the big outfits. They will do the hiring and assume the risks to their personnel."

"Still," Wheelock insisted, "for other things, like lost cargo and late deliveries, shouldn't we form a corporation to absorb those risks?"

Wichard looked at Slezak, who shrugged.

"Either way," the lawyer said.

"In theory, we could form a corporation," Wichard temporized. "Of course, that is a lot of extra expense for filings, taxes, and such." He glanced at Slezak again, whose eyes had acquired a stony glaze. "Large corporations, like your Mannheim Construction, might be able to afford these things. But I am not sure the prince, with his position in the royal family, would be able to support incorporation outside the laws of the kingdom. And you yourself, *mad'moiselle,* in order to buy shares in this hypothetical corporation, would be required to put up substantial amounts of your own money—instead of creating the work product as your share."

He saw the woman was not happy with this. She sat with a frown on her face. And finally she said, "Well, who takes the responsibility then?"

"Prince Ali," Wichard offered. "He is making the major investment. And his participation guarantees our project in the eyes of the Saudi government, which is to say the royal family."

Wichard saw her glance at the lawyer. Again Slezak shrugged.

"That will have to be good enough," she said. "I guess."

———

The office was one large room, entered through a vestibule not much bigger than a broom closet. This entry space would serve as a reception area only if the receptionist sat behind a folding tray table instead of a real desk. The hallway outside was right at the top of the stairs up from a side door on Filbert Street. The office was one floor up, above a Chicago-style pizza restaurant, and even at eleven o'clock in the morning Dani smelled the odors of garlic and tomato sauce wafting through the floorboards.

On the plus side, the place had two windows that looked out on the street, which the offices further back in the building did not offer. It was in a building supposedly designed by Bernard Maybeck, although what she would be renting was a barren room, square and unadorned in the modernist Bauhaus style, with varnished woodwork, hardwood floors, windows that raised manually on sash weights, and no air conditioning. But the office did have phone service—or at least one outside line that could be reconnected once she got a phone.

The real-estate saleswoman, whose name was Mandy, had explained all these features. She ended with, "This space is a steal at the price."

"And what is that?" Dani asked, wondering how much the landlord would ask for ten by fifteen feet with entrance through a closet.

"Seven twenty-five a month, with first and last, and a security deposit."

So a room in a once-prestigious building cost more than her house rent.

"I'll have to think about it."

"It's going to be snapped up."

"Yes, but I need to think first."

Hugo Wichard had insisted that Antarctic Ice Ventures set up its local offices quickly: one in San Francisco to handle engineering and design, one in Jeddah to obtain permits and develop shipbuilding and pumping sites. He had tasked Dani with the former while he and Prince Ali arranged the latter.

"How will I pay for this?" she had asked him.

"You have resources, yes?" Wichard said. "You can put up the ready money until we get a letter of credit from the Organisation of Islamic Cooperation."

"I have *some* resources," she had replied. "Not a lot."

"It will all be worked out in a month or two."

And so Dani had gone hunting for office space in San Francisco's North Beach, which was supposed to be less expensive than downtown and still trendy enough as an address to impress bankers, project backers, and subcontractors.

That seven hundred and twenty-five a month—plus last month and security deposit—would just be the start, of course. Then she had to reconnect the phone, have the partnership's name painted on the door, get stationery printed up, and apply for a business license, which she would do herself rather than pay Gus Slezak a fee for the job. After that, she had to buy—or probably rent—office furniture, a typewriter, drafting tables and tools, and some desk lamps, because the room had switches but no installed ceiling lighting, and she couldn't work by the sunlight coming in from the east-facing windows.

All of that was going to make a big dent in her Mannheim pension payout. But, hopefully, it would not be for long. No longer than three months, at the rate her money was going out.

And there was so much to do. Wichard wanted her to begin designing the semi-submersible barges that would take aboard the icebergs and pump out the excess seawater. At this point, she was not just producing the basic idea—which was still all in her head, because she had not been allowed to take any documents out of her old office at Mannheim—but Wichard now wanted developed capacities, measurements, and detailed designs that he could take to the Islamic bankers and then to the shipyards to begin cutting and welding steel plates. On top of that, he wanted her to develop the specifications for ocean towing, which depended on the size and displacement of the barges. And then would come the designs for docking and receiving facilities in Jeddah, and a strategy for either cutting slabs from the Amery Ice Shelf or capturing and carving up newly floating bergs. Out of that strategy would come a plan for an Antarctic base camp with a list of its necessary equipment and supplies. But the barge design came first and defined all that.

Dani was not only working out of her head, but she didn't have access to support groups like drafting, estimating, and computer services to do the donkey work. She was looking at a bunch of late nights stretching into the distant future. So she decided to make those desk lamps a priority. After that, she could begin thinking about hiring a receptionist and maybe a draftsman to begin making the technical drawings. By then, maybe the money would have come in to pay their salaries. And hers, of course. In the meantime ...

"Okay, I'll take it," she told the real-estate woman.

———

"I don't know if I should even be talking to you," Paul Kellerman said, as Danielle Wheelock seated herself in the straight-backed chair beside his desk. He wasn't even sure if it was okay for him to approve her signing in at the guard station downstairs, not after the stories he had heard. What if anyone checked the logbook and found his name there?

"That's all right," she said. "We hardly talked two years ago, when I was sitting right next to you."

"I think we talked ... back then."

"That was supposed to be a joke."

"So ... what do you want, Dani?"

"How's your career going?" she asked brightly. "Here at Mannheim?"

That was the question, wasn't it? Kellerman knew he once had a promising start, back in the Power Division. But then the woman sitting right here had singlehandedly shut down the Farragut nuclear plant and kicked everything sideways. In the resulting reorganization, Kellerman had been traded to Urban Planning, which wasn't really his specialty, and where they really didn't have a slot for him. He had spent the last eighteen months running the numbers on power distribution systems and locating substations for hypothetical cities in Malaysia, instead of building thermal power plants in Nebraska.

"I'm doing all right," he said.

"In other words, not so great."

"Just what are you doing here?"

"I'm offering you a way out."

"That iceberg thing? Really?"

"We need engineers, people who can plan and execute," she said. "From what I could see, while I was pawing through those rebar reports, you were pretty good at scoping out large projects. And you had a fair hand at the drafting table, when you couldn't wait around for Engineering Services to finish up a design."

"And, with you, I would be scoping and designing … what?"

"Barges. Semi-submersible containers. And places to dock them."

"How is a barge like a power plant? Or an electric distribution system?"

"I don't know." She frowned. "They both move stuff around?"

"Please! That was a rhetorical question."

"I'll tell you how they're different. One is something common, that you can find in every state, and connecting every town. While the other is something that doesn't exist yet, that will provide a service nobody's offered before, and will end up in the record books."

"Huh!" That jibed with the rumors then. Dani Wheelock had gone off to hunt the great white whale, the engineering project that had never been attempted before.

"How much are you paying?" he asked.

"Well, I don't know that I can match—"

"I make thirty-six thousand a year here."

He saw her doing sums in her head. The answer didn't look good.

"Not that much, not to begin with, but when the project comes in—"

"You mean, after the barges are all scoped and the dock is designed."

"There'll be follow-on work for a good engineer. This will be *big*, Paul."

"And in the meantime, it pays peanuts and we buy our own health care."

"With great reward comes risk," she said.

"I'll think about it," he said, making his decision.

"Just don't think too long," she warned.

"How about I call you?"

———

Dani Wheelock sat at one of the long tables in the Reading Room of the San Francisco Public Library. She was surrounded by bookshelves that reached above her head, under a coffered ceiling with stone beams that had been cut in a vine-like pattern—or so it appeared from where she sat—and with pendulum lamps that hung too high to help anyone with their reading. Most of the light in the room that morning came from a series of arched windows along one wall, throwing a pale, fog-diffused brightness against the mural on the opposite wall, which depicted some kind of religious ceremony.

It would have been so much easier if she still had the resources of Mannheim's Engineering Library, but that perk came with the status of an employee rather than an entrepreneur. She sighed and returned to the stack of books in front of her.

Before she could run after icebergs, she first had to work out the principles of constructing barges. And that meant involving herself with questions of capacity and buoyancy, the gauges of various grades of sheet steel, the methods of construction and internal bracing, the mechanics of hull shape and fluid dynamics, and a thousand other details. And all this was before she got into designing watertight doors and pumps fast enough to remove excess water before the barge capsized and sank.

So she had checked out at the desk Attwood's *Theoretical Naval Architecture*, from 1922; MacBride's *A Handbook of Practical Shipbuilding: With a Glossary of Terms*, from 1921; and Durand's

*The Resistance and Propulsion of Ships,* from 1909. All this was to ground herself in the basics. When she understood everything she didn't know now, then she would get on to more modern texts, hopefully with current pictures, that could guide her in designing her capture vehicles.

And then Dani also had to design a port for offloading the fresh-water cargo. She discovered from a set of maps, based on a British survey done in 1923, and references in the memoirs of more recent travelers including Idries Shah's *Caravan of Dreams,* published half a dozen years ago, that Jeddah was an antique port, more decorative than functional. It might have been suitable for Arab dhows and coastal shipping in the nineteenth century, but the harbor was blocked by reefs that kept out larger, oceangoing vessels. She found articles in the Middle Eastern news journals about plans in the kingdom to develop a major port at Jeddah, but no ground had yet been broken.

So before Dani could think about docks and holding tanks, she had to study up on cutting a ship channel through the reefs and building a harbor. She located a slender volume from Texas A&M University titled *Port and Harbor Development System,* from three years earlier, that dealt mostly with projects in Houston and Galveston—but it was a start. She also had the more recent *Port Planning Design and Construction,* from last year, by the American Association of Port Authorities. If all else failed, she could locate the association, call up some of its members, and pick their brains.

Dani had expected that Hugo Wichard would provide most of the knowhow for the project, having lived and worked in the Middle East. But her senior partner had disappeared almost as soon as the ink was dry on their partnership contract. He sent her encouraging telegrams, through the lawyer's office, about his progress in lining up funds through Prince Ali's contacts with the Organisation of Islamic Cooperation. The subtext of these messages was that she should hurry up with a more formal description of the project and its costs, as the negotiations were reaching a critical stage as to technical and economic feasibility.

She had already regurgitated as much as she could remember from the proposal she had put together while at Mannheim. She had rounded off the numbers to the closest million when more exact figures escaped her memory. And her design for the "semi-submersible barges" was still based more on imaginative fantasy than established shipbuilding theory. But at least Wichard had something on paper as a talking point.

It would have been better if Hugo Wichard, whom she once had thought of as an older head and a steadier hand in the business, were able to guide all this work and make sure it would come out all right. But Dani saw now that he was more of a salesman and promoter than a thinker and doer. She was not even sure he was as good an engineer as she was—and that was with just two years of quality assurance and estimating experience, and a freshly minted professional registration, under her belt.

Well, no help for that now. She was in the soup, and the only thing she could do was swim. She opened Edward Attwood's book on naval architecture and started reading.

---

"But you're *not* a bad engineer," Norman Wall told Dani over their bowls of cioppino, which he had bought as takeout from the seafood bistro across the park. It was one of her favorites, and he got it as a treat—along with their special chocolate decadence for dessert—because he knew she was feeling stressed at work. But now she just stared into her bowl, frowning, without touching her spoon.

"I know," she said after a moment. "But I just can't seem to …"

"I don't know anyone else who can pick up a new technical specialty, like shipbuilding, and create an award-winning design the first time. And you're trying to do two specialties—that and harbor building—both at once. I don't know anyone who would even try."

"Then perhaps I shouldn't have."

"That's your frustration talking."

"And what chance do I have now?" she said. "I made this choice. Jumped in with both feet, without thinking. Imagining I could design a submerged barge."

"You came up with the idea," he pointed out.

"Yeah, just as an idea. A fantasy concept. But when I try to put it on paper, the thing looks like a Lego block. I have no idea how to balance it. How to keep it from capsizing."

"Maybe … you could hire a marine engineer?"

"I've tried. The engineers I can afford are right out of school with no experience, and at this point they know less about barges than I do. The ones with experience specialize as consultants and will charge an arm and a leg."

"Then apply to your partner Wichard for the money. That's his end, isn't it?"

"I don't know. He'll think I'm not doing my job. That I'm not up to the challenge."

"Well, you can have your pride, or you can fix the problem. I don't think there's a third alternative."

She shrugged, took a spoonful of soup with a shelled prawn, tasted it.

"It's good cioppino," she said, trying to smile. "Cold by now, though."

———

"Oh, I think you are doing *marvelously*," said the crackling voice—but still with that European lilt—from the other end of Dani's long-distance call to Riyadh.

"I don't know," she said. "I still haven't got a complete design—"

"Prince Ali loves what you've produced," Wichard said. "In fact, he and I made a presentation last week at the Ministry of Environment, Water, and Agriculture. Of course, it doesn't hurt that Ali's uncle runs the place."

Dani tried to think what they could have shown to a full-blown government ministry. All she had given Wichard so far was her notes from memory of the proposal she had worked up while employed by Mannheim, and that was intended for their own business development planning. She could not believe that any rational government agency would be impressed by her rough sketches and round numbers. It was all pie in the—

"The minister approved an initial payment of ten million to the partnership's account in Zurich," Wichard had been saying while she daydreamed about her inadequacies.

"Excuse me?" She faltered. "Ten million? Is that in dollars?" As opposed, she imagined, to some fractional amount in Saudi riyals.

"Yes, in dollars. What else?"

"And which bank is this?"

"It is the Habib Bank."

"I've never heard of it."

"They are Karachi based. Very big. Multinational."

"That's good to know," she said. "Look ... I have some payments coming due. There's rent on our office space in San Francisco, plus utilities. And I need to hire some outside expertise for the detail design." She paused. "Marine architects ... to certify the barge design. And some port and terminal experts ... just to verify what we need to do at Jeddah."

The other end of the line went deathly quiet.

"Hello?" she said. "Are you still there?"

"Oh, yes," Wichard replied. "I am here."

"So ... do you think you could get me some money?"

"Ah ... that would be difficult. Not for a while yet."

"But you said there's ten million in the Swiss bank."

"Yes, but stateside transfers are hard to arrange. They take a long time, and there are tax implications to consider. In addition, the foreign exchange rates are unfavorable at this time."

"The exchange rate from dollars to dollars?" she said.

"The Swiss treat dollars at a disadvantage right now."

"All right. But these are necessary expenses. I have to—"

"Danielle! We must all live off our humps from time to time. This is the nature of venture capitalism. I had thought you understood this."

"Yes, of course," she said. "But that with money in—"

"I need you to cope for now. That is the word? *Cope?*"

"Yes, that's the word." She set her teeth, trying to decide what to say next. She really needed a cash infusion.

"So, we cope with what we have," Wichard said, then paused. "*Alors* ... I will get you something, a transfer to your bank—but you must proceed with the work, yes?"

"Right. Of course," Dani said with relief. "The work goes forward. No question."

# 10. Progress Payments

JOHN MARTIN LIKED having offices on Pier 9 at the Embarcadero. His windows overlooked the docks for the San Francisco Bar Pilots association and had a longer view of the ship traffic going south, under the western span of the Bay Bridge, to the Port of Oakland. As a marine architect, he valued all that maritime ambience, because it kept his customers relaxed and confident.

But maybe not this customer. The young woman seated before him was tall with a long, reddish-brown braid, almost the color of Rust-Oleum primer paint. She seemed confident enough, except for a slight trembling in her hands and a warble in her voice. She was scared and uncertain, he saw that, and no amount of harbor vista was going to calm her. As she described the project before her, the one she wanted him to take on, he knew she had a reason to be afraid.

"You want a barge with doors that open up the whole back end—or front end, whichever works better—to take on an iceberg," he summed up. "Do you know how far down underwater those things go?"

"Of course I know," she said. "I've run the numbers. But we're going to be shaping these icebergs into slabs, wide and long but not too deep. I calculate the average draft of our floating ice to be not more than twelve meters, thirty-odd feet."

"All right, but still a big barge. To move the kind of tonnage to make your deal profitable, you're looking at a barge the size of a small oil tanker."

"Yes ..." she said, although clearly she hadn't thought of that. "Yes, that would be about right."

"You'll need four or five ocean tugs to haul a vessel that size at nominal speed, with one or two in reserve in case you run into foul weather or adverse currents."

"Yes, I would imagine so."

"So, you have your barge in place, you've shaped your iceberg which is the size of a city block, and you want to open these doors and slide the berg inside, right?"

"That is the plan," she said. "Actually, it's floating, not sliding."

"And all the while your barge is sinking, because you've let in all that seawater."

"Well, no. It will have positive buoyancy with the tanks I've sketched." She flipped through the binder she had laid on Martin's desk and unfolded a technical drawing.

"Those round things on the bottom?" He pointed. "Like knobs on a Lego block?"

"Yes, they're tanks. Pump them full of water for ballast when the barge is empty. Pump out water and let in air for buoyancy when the doors open."

"And you placed them on the bottom because …?"

"To optimize the lifting force, or so I figured," she said.

"Why not make the thing double-walled, like a floating drydock?"

"You could do that, too," she acknowledged.

"Save you a ton of grief if you ever run your barge aground. So, you essentially want to build a drydock for an iceberg, a special kind of iceberg. Why not just haul the thing directly?"

"I've already run the numbers. The berg melts before you can get it to port."

"I see," Martin said. Then he thought of another objection. "What are you hauling when you're deadheading back to Antarctica?"

"Excuse me? Deadheading?"

"Returning empty."

"Nothing, I guess."

"So you're running in ballast. Your iceberg hold is empty, because you don't want to be hauling the weight of all that seawater for no profit. Just a big empty shell. Do you know what the water pressure is at a depth of thirty meters—which, as you know, is actually closer to forty feet?"

"I could do the math."

"Don't bother. It's two hundred and twenty kilopascals, or thirty-two pounds per square inch. Something more than two atmospheres. You're going to need a pressure seal on those end doors. And bracing equivalent to anyplace else on the hull."

"That's—" He watched as her mind worked in response. "—why I need your help."

"And who's paying for all this? It concerns me, because I have bills to pay myself."

"We already have an initial installment from the Saudi government for the project."

"The Saudis are backing you? That's good. But, boy, they must be pretty thirsty."

———

William Mason looked across his desk at the tall young woman, not much older than his daughter, who had brought him the fantastic plan for taking icebergs—or what was going to end up as tankers full of fresh water—into the Port of Jeddah on the Red Sea coast. Or rather, into the sleepy little town with a bad harbor that was something out of the Sinbad stories in the *Arabian Nights*.

"But the infrastructure over there is nonexistent," he told her.

"That's why I need help from an expert on harbor design."

"Yes, so why don't you offload in one of the oil ports?"

"Because … they are already in use for shipping oil?"

"Yes, but you can probably find a wharf somewhere in there," he said. "Two wharves, actually. Because you'll need one for offloading product and one held in reserve, in case a loaded barge comes in before the one that's unloading is empty.

"But with this scheme—" Mason pointed to the binder she had brought him. "You not only have to build a long tanker wharf, millions of gallons in storage tanks, and sizable pumping facilities—you also have to dredge the entire harbor and excavate a ship channel through the outer reefs. That must, oh, triple your front-end costs, if not more."

"But Jeddah is closest to the population centers of Mecca and Medina," she replied. "They need water for all those pilgrims on the *hajj*. The oil ports are mostly to the east, in the Persian Gulf."

"And the Saudis don't mind paying to get what they want, hey?" he observed.

"We already have an installment on the project, if that's what you're asking."

"If you have their backing, then my firm is happy to do business with you."

———

After three weeks of waiting and essentially twiddling her engineering thumbs at her barren office in North Beach—aside from answering a few follow-up questions from her consultants—Dani Wheelock received the first results of their labors.

From the office of John Martin Marine Architect, she got a package of drawings and specifications for an improved barge design, complete with pressure doors rated at three atmospheres for a margin of safety. The vessels themselves were big, but not bigger than the profile dimensions—especially the depth of draft—she had given to Mason & Mason Marine Solutions as working parameters for a shipping channel and wharf structure. And that firm had supplied a preliminary, map-based survey of the Jeddah harbor and a tentative location for the offloading terminal.

Dani spent a week going over the two sets of specifications, comparing details and checking computations as a form of quality control. She knew that their designs had vastly improved on her early sketches, but they were still incomplete and needed further work.

For example, John Martin's design for the barges indicated a grade of sheet steel for the hull plates, but the material specs and detailed designs for internal bracing and external reinforcement points were still lacking, as were all the mechanical details of systems like ballast pumping and door activation.

And William Mason's proposed pathway through the reefs would require an on-site, underwater survey to verify its accuracy. His location for the terminal would require a land survey, soils and bedrock analysis, examination of existing property deeds—if they had such things in Saudi Arabia—or review of local rules about eminent domain, and a hundred other details. And he had yet to produce a workable design for the terminal itself.

But the documents in hand were good enough to show progress to the Saudi Ministry of Environment, Water, and Agriculture and to the Organisation of Islamic Cooperation. With that in mind, Dani made full-sized, E-scale copies of the drawings and a booklet of the specification pages for filing in North Beach and sent the originals off to Hugo Wichard at his current mailing address in Riyadh.

Along with their technical packages, both Martin and Mason had included invoices for the work performed to date. When Dani opened them, her jaw dropped. The marine architect was charging a cool fifty thousand dollars for the revised barge design, while Mason & Mason wanted sixty thousand for work that Dani herself could have done with the 1923 British survey maps. But that was the price of an expert opinion.

"And we're good for it," she said aloud, thinking of the Antarctic Ice Ventures partnership's money in the Habib Bank. "Or we soon will be," she added, thinking of Wichard's promise to transfer the funds.

———

Norman Wall had watched his roommate mope about the house and fret for two weeks before he spoke up one morning at breakfast. "Something's clearly wrong," he said.

"I'm sorry," Dani said. "I don't mean to be a downer."

"You used to be so optimistic about this venture."

"Well … the truth is, I'm running out of cash."

"Can I help? You know I'd do anything."

"You don't have this kind of money."

"How much are we talking about?"

"Nobody has this kind of money. More than a hundred thousand dollars."

"But I thought your partner said he had a payment of ten million."

"He does, but it's all tied up at the bank in Switzerland."

"Can't he send you some of it?"

"He says he's made a transfer."

"When was this?" Norman asked.

"Weeks ago. But Wichard says the process takes a long time."

"My firm transfers a lot of foreign money. It takes a couple of days."

"Well, he says these things are just different with the Swiss."

"Do you have a passport, Dani?"

"No. I mean, Mannheim never assigned me overseas. And I don't travel much."

"Then I suggest you apply for one right away, and expedite the processing."

"Why?" she asked.

"Because you're going to Saudi Arabia or Switzerland in the very near future."

———

After three tries at calling the contact number in Riyadh, Dani at last got Wichard on the phone.

"Ah, it is so good to finally hear your voice," he said. "We have *such* good news!"

"That's wonderful, Hugo. But look, it seems we are running out of money, and the bills are piling up for the work I've already contracted."

"And such marvelous work it is, too! The Organisation of Islamic Cooperation has made a progress payment of one hundred millions—also in dollars—based on the drawings you sent. I have arranged with a Dutch shipyard to begin fabricating the first of your barges. And next week we break ground in Jeddah for the terminal complex."

"But no, wait! Those were just preliminary designs," she explained. "I only sent them for approval. You can't start building anything yet!"

"Why not? We are simply taking the first steps, baby steps really. Ordering the steel and pacing off the wharfage. But we need the details to come pretty quickly, yes? So that the real work can go ahead."

"And that's the problem, the marine architect and the port designer have both sent invoices that need to be paid before they will finalize their designs."

"So? Go ahead and pay them."

"But I haven't got the money."

"I sent you a transfer weeks ago."

"It never came in. And I've been waiting."

"Have you? Perhaps, then, I transferred it to the wrong bank. Your account is with the Bank of America, yes?"

"No, no!" she said, "Bank of the *West*."

"Ah, well, that was an easy mistake to make."

"But I sent you the routing and account numbers."

"Did you really? I don't remember. This thing is easily fixed."

"I'll be sure to call Bank of America," Dani said. "And find that money."

There was a sudden emptiness on the line. "Do so," he replied at last. "But get your contractors back on track, because we need to file for another progress payment, and we need to do it soon."

And with that, Wichard hung up on her.

# 11. The Thing Unravels

DANI WHEELOCK KNEW the contents of the Antarctic Ice Ventures partnership account at Bank of the West down to the penny because, so far, she had made all the deposits and withdrawals herself. But still, the next day after calling Riyadh, because of the time difference, she drove down to the branch on Mission Street and had one of the tellers confirm the balance, which was still just four hundred sixty-two dollars and twenty-two cents.

On the possibility that Hugo Wichard had made an honest mistake and sent the money to the wrong bank, she drove the six blocks west to California Street and up Nob Hill to the Bank of America World Headquarters at No. 555. She entered the building's underground parking and paid six dollars to park her Corvette for two hours. Inside the bank, she had to wait in line, and when she got to the teller's window—the nameplate on her jacket said "Maisie"—Dani wasn't sure how to begin.

"May I help you?" the woman said, smiling.

"I need to ask about a possible money transfer."

"All right then. And what is the account number?"

"That's just it, because I don't have an account here."

"I see. You want to set up an account and make a transfer?"

"No," Dani said. "Some money has been transferred here in error."

"I don't believe that's possible." Maisie's smile was starting to slip.

"Well, could you check? It will be a large amount, over a hundred thousand dollars, sent from the Habib Bank in Zurich, sometime in the last two or three weeks."

"And you sent the money here?"

"My partner did. Or says he did."

"This was without an account number?"

"Well, to the *wrong* account number. We're at another bank entirely."

"That's ... not the way it works," Maisie said. "An amount of that size—any amount, really—has to be deposited into an existing account. Especially a transfer from overseas."

"Maybe it went into a Bank of America account with the same number?" Dani said. She took the partnership's checkbook out of her purse and showed the woman a blank deposit slip. "Could you see if this bank has a similar account?"

"But then the routing would be different. This is for a different bank. We can't just receive foreign money into general deposit and hold it until somebody calls for it."

"So," Dani said, "you don't have any money sent from Habib Bank."

"Not in the way you describe. It's just not possible."

Dani was starting to feel discouraged. She decided to walk—because she still had time on her parking pass at the bank garage—two blocks back and a block east on Bush Street to the office of the lawyer, Augustus Slezak. She had not been there since signing the partnership documents because, so far, everything had been proceeding smoothly and there was no need to involve him.

The one-man office was two flights up in a building without an elevator. Dani remembered the way, because once again she was navigating the steep slope of Nob Hill and then climbing stairs, which both times left her breathless. But when she arrived at Slezak's door, the interior beyond the frosted glass was dark. She tried the knob, but it was locked. She raised her hand to knock.

"Don't bother," said a voice behind her.

Dani turned to find an older man in gray coveralls. "Who are you?"

"Building superintendent. Don't bother knocking, because that office is empty. If you're here about renting it, you need to make an appointment with the realtor."

"Where is Gus Slezak?"

"Gone two weeks ago."

"But his name is still on the glass."

The man shrugged. "I'll scrape it off when I've got something else to put up."

"So did Mister Slezak leave a forwarding address?"

"Not that I know. Locked up one night and just walked away. Rent was two months in arrears by then, so we took the furniture—such as it was—in partial payment."

"What about his files?" she asked. "My firm had papers with him."

"Everything gone. Just empty drawers. Like he'd never been there."

Dani thought hard. "You must have a regular stream of people asking about him."

"Nope." The superintendent poked his cheek with his tongue. "You're the first."

———

"I think you've been taken," Norman Wall said bluntly, after Dani described her parallel discoveries at the bank and the lawyer's office.

"You mean, some kind of fraud," she replied. From the way she pulled her eyebrows down and drew her mouth in, Norman knew she strongly resisted the idea.

"Is there even money in that Swiss bank?"

"Wichard said he had a progress payment—"

"Yes, based on work you did. But is that *true?*"

"I have to believe …" Dani's two fists clenched.

"Look," he said. "You can try calling him again."

"There's no answer at his phone. It rings and rings."

"Then how about your other partner, this Prince Ali?"

"I don't have a number for him. And I never met him."

"But he signed your partnership agreement, didn't he?"

"I don't know. Wichard took it to Saudi for him to sign."

"And the lawyer disappeared. That looks like fraud to me."

"But if there was no prince, and no Saudi money, then what was the point?" she asked. "What would Wichard get out of it?"

"Other than some pretty good designs for an iceberg scheme that he can now peddle somewhere else? He's got your work product and doesn't have to pay for it."

"But he *was* in Riyadh. The operator connected me. That part is genuine. He was there in the Saudi capital."

"So? Did you apply for that passport yet?" Norman asked.

"Yes, I have one now," she replied "Why do you ask?"

"Because you have to see this thing face to face."

# 12. Coming Face to Face

DANI WHEELOCK WAS not sure how to go about a face-to-face meeting with the people funding the iceberg venture in Saudi Arabia. She wasn't sure she could get a visa to enter the country. And with no answer to her calls at Wichard's private number, she did not even know where to begin.

So she called the Saudi consulate in San Francisco, and the young woman there—Dani was surprised to have a woman answer the phone—heard her out and suggested she contact the Ministry of Environment, Water, and Agriculture directly. "After all, they are your client," the woman said. "Why not let them arrange these things?" She gave Dani the ministry's outside line in Riyadh.

Dani called the ministry that same day, introduced herself to the young man at the other end of the line as "the Antarctic Ice Ventures' local U.S. partner," and explained that she would like to "come and confer on progress." She expected him to object, because they already had Hugo Wichard in Riyadh to handle all their business. But instead the young man asked politely if he might put her on hold. After three minutes—which was almost immediately, in bureaucratic time—he returned to greet her warmly and tell her that the ministry would arrange a visa for her. It would be available at the consulate the next day.

Using her own money, what was left of it, for plane fare and hotel bills, she arranged with a travel agent to fly Pan Am on the overnight polar route to Cairo and transfer there to Saudi Arabian Airlines. Because she had read up on the country and its customs in preparing for the project, Dani knew to dress conservatively: flat shoes, long skirts that almost touched the floor, long sleeves, high collars, and a head scarf. She knew not to wear too much makeup, but then she normally wore hardly any makeup at all.

On the second leg of her flight, the Saudi airline announced, first in Arabic and then in English, that they would be landing at the Riyadh Air Base of the Royal Saudi Air Force. Dani thought this might be because of a security problem, but the steward assured her that all air traffic for the capital went through the base.

Outside the terminal, a man in a blue business suit and a checkered *keffiyeh* headdress was standing beside a black Mercedes and holding a sign that read "Whee Luck."

"That's me," she muttered. She approached him with her suitcase. "*Salaam Alaikum,*" she said, trying out her first words in Arabic.

"And peace be unto you," the man said and took her bag. "The Ministry sent this car for you, Miss Wheelock. I hope you have a pleasant ride."

Riyadh was a city of white masonry, with low buildings of three to five stories each, situated on a flat and dusty plain. Most of the buildings boasted some small architectural styling—a lattice-screened balcony or an entrance flanked by plaster columns—but all of them had flat-roofs and a frayed look. The Ministry of Environment, Water, and Agriculture, when the car arrived there, was different only for being larger, six stories, and having a portico and carriageway with a turnaround in front.

The driver delivered Dani to a male secretary waiting outside. This young man, who also wore a *keffiyeh* with *agal* ropes, greeted her courteously by name, led her inside to a second-floor conference room, and asked her "please to wait."

In a few minutes, the secretary came back with two gentlemen, one older and one younger. He introduced the elder as Emir Abdullah bin Yousef al-Kabir and the other as Emir Ali bin Muhammad al-Kabir—presumably the same "Prince Ali" who was her business partner. They wore identical suits of dark-gray silk but without the headcloths and ropes—perhaps they dispensed with such things indoors—and both had neat, black Vandyke beards. She thought of the older one as "the

Emir" and the younger as "the Prince," although she knew by then that the two words meant essentially the same thing in Arabic, and that all members of the royal family were styled as princes.

"We are so pleased to meet you at last," the Emir said.

"A person of such imaginative genius," the Prince said.

"And a woman!" exclaimed the Emir, nodding.

"And so young!" exclaimed the Prince, smiling.

"And I, too, am pleased to finally visit your country," Dani replied. "I wanted to see the land that our project will help to bloom with water from the South Pole."

"Bloom," the Emir replied, with a tight grin.

"Indeed," his nephew rejoined, still smiling.

"So, how do you think it's going?" Dani asked.

"Ah …" from the Emir.

"Well …" from the Prince.

"We understand that *you* asked for this meeting," the Emir said.

"Yes," Dani replied. "When I last heard from Hugo Wichard—"

"Your partner," the Prince put in, clarifying her relationship.

"And yours," she replied. "Or so I was led to believe."

At this the Prince hesitated, then nodded gravely.

"Hugo had said you were already starting the site work in Jeddah," she continued, "and I wanted to go there and inspect it. Also, he said you had arranged with a shipyard in Holland to begin fabricating the semi-submersible barges."

"*Sayyid* Wichard has been very busy," the Emir said vaguely.

"All to your design," the Prince said, as if confirming that.

"Well, yes. And I wanted to know—" Dani was about to explain that the drawings and specifications she had sent over were only preliminary work, just about one step beyond conceptual designs. But something in the manner of these two princes, some suggestion of emotional distance or abstraction, made her pause. Perhaps it was just a cultural thing, a polite aversion to getting down to business too quickly. But her gut instinct was to leave her qualms about the state of the drawings for later, after she had inspected what the site teams were actually working on. She also sensed that this was not the time to bring up the matter of the money she needed to issue the detailed design.

"I wanted to see your progress," she finished lamely.

"We, too, would like to see that progress," the Prince said.

"The thing is," she continued, "I haven't yet received from Hugo the name and address of the shipyard. Or, for that matter, the exact location of our office in Jeddah, nor the land picked out for the terminal site. I have tried to call Hugo—*Sayyid* Wichard—but he has not been answering his phone. Not here in Riyadh. Not anywhere."

"We have tried to contact him ourselves," the Emir said, almost sadly.

"He told us he had to leave the country," the Prince explained. "But he did not leave us a means of further contact."

"I see." Dani suddenly thought this absence might mean some trouble had befallen her partner. She hoped that was not the case, but she also sensed it would be bad form to voice her fears to these two men.

"Well, I'm here now," she said, trying to sound confident and in charge. "If you have those addresses, I'd like to go out there and see how far the work has gone."

"Of course," said the Emir. "Our files should have that information.

"We will help in any way we can," the Prince assured her.

"As a matter of hospitality," the Emir finished.

———

Mustafa Tawfiq was sitting in the office of his family business, the Jeddah Land and Property Development Company, when a European woman came in from the street. She was dressed appropriately, with head scarf, sleeves, and skirt covering every inch of skin except for her face and hands. In addition, she wore dark sunglasses that completely covered her eye sockets from brows to cheekbones. And this, too, was appropriate to the time of year and of day. It made her virtually anonymous, as was also appropriate for a young woman.

"May I help you?" Tawfiq asked politely, first in English, although he was prepared to transfer the conversation to French, German, or another of his languages if he had guessed wrongly.

"Yes … maybe," she said, taking off the glasses. She had dazzling green eyes, which were most disturbing in that pale face. "They gave me this address in Riyadh, but I don't think it is right."

"Who gave you, please?"

"The Minister for the Environment, Water, and Agriculture—or his nephew did—and he said it was the local office of Antarctic Ice Ventures. But clearly—"

"Ah!" Tawfiq said.

One month ago, a Frenchman had come into this office, asking about property along the shoreline outside of town. He wanted to put in a bid on a parcel with access to the harbor. Tawfiq had explained that prices were very dear at the moment, because the royal family was rumored to have plans for building a deepwater port on the Red Sea, and Jeddah was the prime candidate. This news did not discourage the Frenchman at all. He merely sought a small parcel, he said. A foothold on the shoreline, he called it. Large enough to post a sign, with the exact specifications and requirements to come later. And it did not have to be a completely competitive bid, he said, simply enough to show interest.

The Frenchman had scribbled the text of the sign while sitting at Tawfiq's desk: "Future Site of Antarctic Ice Ventures" was to be the boldest line, in both English and Arabic, with below that in smaller lettering the words "Fresh Water Discharge Terminal and Pumping Plant." The sign was to give Jeddah Land and Property Development as the contact point for further information. The Frenchman had paid him with a fistful of riyals to have the sign made and posted. He also produced a letter of intent above his own signature, Hugo N. Wichard, to purchase a minimum of two hundred acres whose only requirement was access to the current shoreline within a maximum distance of two hundred meters.

"This is the place for such inquiries," Tawfiq now told the young woman.

"Well, good," she said. "I am one of the partners in Antarctic Ice Ventures."

"Ah, then you must know Mr. Hugo Wichard."

"Yes. You have had dealings with him?"

"He is working through Jeddah Land."

"Well, that's a start," she said.

The woman opened a large purse that was slung over her shoulder and pulled out a sheaf of folded technical drawings. "I wanted to inspect the work on the property to date," she said. "To make sure it conforms to our specifications."

"Excuse me, please?" Tawfiq was confused.

"You *are* managing the site work?"

"We have posted the sign he requested."

"The sign? But what about the groundbreaking?"

"No ground has been broken. No ground has been purchased."

He saw her jaw and lips moving. If Tawfiq had possessed better skills with the English language, he might have said she was silently mouthing his last statement: "*No ... ground ...*"

Finally, she said aloud, "Do you have a car?"

"Of course, I have an off-road vehicle."

"Then we better go see this sign."

Tawfiq left his nephew in charge of the office while he took the American woman—whose name he learned was Danielle Wheelock, a very Arabic-sounding name—behind the building to where he parked his 1963 Willys CJ-5. The desert sun, salt air, and sandblast winds had turned its original ruby-red paintwork into a compound of burnt orange and rust. But mechanically, the machine was in perfect condition, and the tires were new.

They drove south out of town along the edge of the harbor, to the tiny parcel that had been leased to put up *Monsieur* Wichard's sign. And true to Tawfiq's pledge, the billboard stood there in glaring white and already-peeling black paint. It was two meters tall, three and a half meters wide, and included—out of Tawfiq's imagination and at his own expense—an outline of the continent of Antarctica, for authenticity.

The Wheelock woman studied the sign for a full minute, although it did not have much writing, and half of that was in Arabic script. Then she turned and looked around, first at the distant shoreline, then at the inland horizon. "There's marsh between this spot and the open water," she said.

"Yes," Tawfiq agreed. "*Monsieur* Wichard's letter of intent specified only a maximum distance from the harbor, not the type of ground."

" 'Letter of intent,' " she repeated. "What does that entail?"

"A willingness to buy, if this land or a suitable site should become available."

"So, as you said, Hugo Wichard has not actually purchased any of this land."

"Not even a hard-money option. As a contract, his letter is worth nothing."

She pulled at the drawings in her purse, then shoved them back. "And how much land was mentioned in this letter?"

"Two hundred acres, of no particular length or depth."

She shut her eyes. "Did he pay you anything?" she asked.

"For the sign. I had to lease the patch of ground it stands on."

"And do you know where *Monsieur* Wichard is at the moment?"

"I have only seen or heard from him the once. That was a month ago."

She sighed. "I'm beginning to understand. Will you drive me back now?"

———

The glass-walled executive offices of Nederland Scheepstechniek BV looked out across acres of cranes, slipways, and
scaffolding, with the squared-off launching basin and the river—one hesitated to call it a harbor—beyond that. The view
reminded Dani of pictures she had seen of the Richmond shipyards in California during World War II, except that everything
here was larger and, if anything, busier.

Johannes Pieterzoon, who was in charge of Nederland
Scheepstechniek's sales and marketing, held her business card
by the edges, between the tips of thumb and forefinger, as if he
was afraid of smudging the white pasteboard. Or perhaps he
thought the card might contaminate him.

"Yes, I remember *Meneer* Wichard," Pieterzoon said.
"Vividly."

"He does tend to make an impression," Dani agreed. "But
can you tell me what terms you and he arrived at, about building our semi-submersible barges?"

"Terms?" the man asked. "You're his partner. Don't you
know?"

"Mister Wichard handled the European end of our business. He is required to travel widely. Unfortunately, he has
been out of touch." *In more ways than one,* she thought.

"I see." Pieterzoon shook his head. "It is hardly accurate
to call our discussion 'terms.' He described a project he had
in hand for fabricating two of these ice-hauling barges. He
showed me some sketches." The man shrugged.

Dani touched her purse, on the floor beside her chair, almost by reflex. She stopped the impulse to bring out the improved design concepts from John Martin. They did not seem
relevant now.

"Did you enter into any kind of a contract?" she asked.

"Not at all. We talked scheduling, and I told him I had one
launch ramp available in the next sixty days. We discussed a
price to reserve it for his project, pending receipt of the final
plans."

"What was the price?"

"Fifty thousand guilders."

"And what is that in—?"

"Just short of twenty thousand of your dollars."

"And did he pay it?" she asked. She *had* to ask.

Pieterzoon gave out a knowing chuckle. "Of course not. He hemmed. He hawed—I think I am using the correct English terms? He said he would have to consult his partners about making such a commitment."

"Do you think he went anywhere else to get the barges built?"

"Rotterdam is a big place. The most active shipbuilding port in Europe," he said proudly, then shrugged again. "But I ask you, how did you know to come to Nederland Scheepstechniek in the first place?"

"Because Wichard gave our other partner your firm's name. He said it was the place where our barges were actually being built."

"Then I think that answers your question."

"More than one," she said with a sigh.

# 13. The Trail Ends

AT THE DIRECTION of the Ministry of Environment, Water, and Agriculture, Ahmed al-Hashim and his team from *Al Mukhabarat Al A'amah,* or the Saudi General Intelligence Presidency, had been following the American woman for three days now.

At first, they had remained invisible, moving two steps behind her, when she went to the port of Jeddah on the Red Sea. This was possible because the ministry had already given them the address Danielle Wheelock was likely to visit. She spent the morning at the office of a local land developer and then accompanied him to an empty stretch of sand at the southern end of the harbor.

From there, she had traveled back to Riyadh, spent the night in a hotel that catered to Europeans and was also thoroughly invested with the General Intelligence Presidency. The next morning she went out to Riyadh Air Base and arranged for passage on KLM Royal Dutch Airlines—where the GIP had an arrangement with the ticketing agents—for the next connecting flight to the Netherlands. Al-Hashim and his subordinate agents, Orimer and Radwan, flew on that same flight but stayed well in the back of the plane, out of her line of sight.

In the Netherlands, they took turns tailing the woman to the next address, a shipyard in Rotterdam, where she stayed for less than an hour. When she emerged from that office, Wheelock took the train back to Amsterdam Zuid, with the three Saudi agents trailing at intervals of twenty meters. She boarded the *Zuidtak,* or "south branch" train, and they could all relax and take the next car back, because Al-Hashim guessed she was now headed for the airport. The only question was, where would she fly to next?

He had one more address on his list, the Zurich branch of the Habib Bank. It was a gamble—less than fifty percent, in his estimation—that she would go there. After all, the account of the Antarctic Ice Ventures partnership had been cleaned out six days before, all one hundred and ten million dollars of the ministry's advance money. If the Wheelock woman knew this, then she was guilty, and would have no reason to fly to Zurich. If she did not know of the withdrawal, then she might be innocent, and would possibly go to check on the money. At this point, al-Hashim had no opinion in the matter. He merely watched her.

The third possibility was that she would fly back to Riyadh and report to the ministry about what she had found in Jeddah and Rotterdam, as she had promised to do. That was the option al-Hashim was hoping for, because it would make his task easier. The fourth possibility, that she would flee to America and go into hiding, was the one to be dreaded. His instructions from the GIP were to prevent that if possible, because the Kingdom of Saudi Arabia had no extradition treaty with the United States.

But, in any event, he and his team were to follow her for as long as possible, hoping that she might make contact with Hugo N. Wichard—about whom al-Hashim had full particulars, including photographs, physical description, French passport number, and partial fingerprints. If they encountered the man, they were to take him, regardless of the legal situation.

Schiphol Airport was therefore the crux of their operation. Al-Hashim had instructed his agents to stay close to the woman as she emerged from the train station and entered the main concourse. Where she was planning to go next would be indicated by her choice of airline ticketing window. But they were now in Europe's third busiest airport, traveling at midday, and the crowds were dense. He knew he could follow the woman easily, but Orimer and Radwan were less sure of their tracking skills, and so they tried to stay close to her.

That turned out to be a mistake.

———

Dani Wheelock picked up on the three men as she passed through the Amsterdam Zuid station. In a crowd of mostly blond, mostly pale European faces, three dark-skinned men with long hair, Vandyke beards, and the same dark business suits and white, collarless shirts buttoned to the throat were hard to miss. They looked like Arabs, but not the kind who dressed in full desert robes and rode in limousines.

In fact, she thought she might have seen one of them—but which one?—outside the shipyard gate in Rotterdam. So ... perhaps seeing that man and two more at the exact same time as she was transiting through Amsterdam was not a coincidence.

With her awareness heightened, Dani got off the train at the Schiphol Airport station. Out of the corner of her eye, she saw the same three men—or their identical cousins—move up the platform behind her and follow her at a distance of ten or fifteen feet. As she entered the concourse, she casually turned her head—once to read a sign, a second time to check her hair in the reflection from a window. With these sideways glances, she saw that they were keeping her in a triangular formation: two flankers, one follower. To her woman-trained senses, any man or group of men taking covert notice of her in a crowd spelled danger. To her karate-trained reflexes, a formation moving on a parallel and possibly converging course spelled enemy action.

When she was in the middle of the airport's vast, open concourse where the crowd was thickest, one of the flankers started moving in on her.

Dani had to think fast. Luckily, she was in Europe and not in the Middle East. Instead of the full-length dress, she was wearing a miniskirt that came up six inches above her knees. The garment was tight across her hips and ass, but the fabric was stretchy enough that she could get her legs into action. The problem was her shoes. The outfit had called for good shoes, and she had chosen a pair with at least three-inch heels. She could walk in them easily enough, but she wasn't sure about performing a side snap kick. She thought of taking off her shoes and getting back to basics in bare feet, but that would mean stopping, reaching down, and holding the heel of the shoe to lever it away from her arched foot, and doing that not once but twice, each time balancing on the opposite foot. There was no simple method for relaxing her feet and just slipping out of her shoes—otherwise she would be falling out of them half the time. So now she had to learn the essence of street fighting *versus* training practice: performing under less than favorable circumstances.

While she was weighing her options, Bogie Number One came alongside and actually reached out for her right arm.

Without breaking stride, Dani dropped her suitcase, let the purse slip off her left shoulder, brought her left hand across and down with force to block the grab, and spun on the ball of her leading foot, which she timed to be her right when she burst into action. She felt the leather tip of that shoe's high heel scrape as she turned on the ball of her foot. The heel snagged on the edge of a floor tile, broke off entirely, and collapsed sideways beneath her foot. No matter! She completed the move by planting the top of her left knee, smoothly, with focus, in the attacker's midsection. She missed his groin by a good three inches of elevation—because her ranging was off by the height of the shoes she was wearing—but the unexpected impact doubled the man over anyway. She reached forward, took hold of his shoulders to steady both his forward motion and her turning motion, then pushed off hard, so that he fell sideways between two people passing in the opposite direction.

Dani tried to resume her walk then, as if nothing had happened. But she was working with a broken shoe, which made her gait uneven. She limped forward two steps, swiveling her head to see where Bogies Two and Three were now.

As her head was in mid-turn, something struck her in the back of the neck.

She tried to react, but her feet were no longer underneath her.

Dani was falling toward the hard ceramic tiles.

She knew that was going to hurt.

She didn't feel a thing.

———

Ahmed al-Hashim watched in dismay as Radwan tried to touch the Wheelock woman. It was too soon to make their presence known. She had not visited the bank. She had not come into contact with her co-conspirator. And the General Intelligence Presidency had no authority to arrest or even to apprehend and detain her in Europe.

His dismay turned to horror as, from a distance of three meters, he saw Wheelock turn and attack his agent. She moved so fast that al-Hashim did not quite see what she did, but Radwan was suddenly falling away and the woman was making her escape. No one at the ministry had told him that she had the fighting skills needed to elude capture. Clearly, she was more dangerous than his superiors knew.

From his pocket, he took an object that would be hard to explain under normal circumstances. It was a dart, used by veterinarians to tranquilize large animals, anything from a horse to an elephant. For safety in carrying, al-Hashim had covered its needle tip with a rubber cap. Because it would never be loaded and shot from an air gun, he had stripped off the feathered plume designed to stabilize the dart in flight. What he had then—for use only in emergencies—was a portable hypodermic loaded with twenty cc's of a cocktail that included pentobarbital to induce coma and an acetylcholine suppressor to block neuromuscular activity. The dart was designed to put the animal both *down* and *out* within a matter of seconds.

Al-Hashim judged that this was such an emergency.

He flipped the rubber button off the needle with his thumb, reversed his grip on the barrel, and rushed forward through the crowd. He struck the Wheelock woman with a downward stroke from behind. He was aiming for her neck, as close to the spine as possible without actually impacting on her vertebrae and possibly breaking the needle, or penetrating her spinal cord and doing permanent damage. He felt the compressed air in the dart pulse once and knew the cocktail had been injected successfully.

As she collapsed forward, he motioned Orimer forward. Together they lowered the woman to the ground, as if she had fainted.

Al-Hashim looked around, to see if anyone in authority had noticed the incident. He saw only stolid Dutch faces, moving purposefully in all directions, going about their business, and incurious as to the story of a woman fallen between two men.

Radwan came over, still holding his stomach.

"Find a porter and get a wheelchair," al-Hashim told him.

He turned to Orimer. "Take her to a lounge area. Say to anyone she is sick."

"What are you going to do?" Radwan asked. "We cannot fly with her now."

"Call for backup," al-Hashim said.

He went to a pay phone, dialed an international number, identified himself, and explained the situation. His contacts in the network that the GIP had spread throughout Europe then called in a favor from the transportation manager of the Saudi Binladin Group. Within ten minutes, one of the construction company's private jets was rerouted on its flight to London and requested an unscheduled landing at Schiphol.

Al-Hashim, his agents, and his comatose prisoner met the plane at the private gate for general aviation. Because they were leaving the country, they could avoid the usual inspections for customs and documentation. He knew that when they arrived in Riyadh—which was the plane's new destination, according to a change in flight plan—there would be no difficulty about visas and passports.

What happened after that was out of his hands.

# 14. In Detention

DANI WOKE UP on a hard bench in a white-tiled cell. She had a splitting headache and, taking stock of herself, she discovered bruising on her forearms, a stiff shoulder, and tenderness on her face that she supposed would show as another bruise if she had a mirror with which to see it. All of these injuries were from a fight she could not remember. The left knee of her pantyhose had a bad snag, and the heel of her right shoe was broken off. But she did remember how those damages had occurred.

She wondered where she was. The cell was empty, except for a white-painted bucket with a sheet-metal lid in the corner. She supposed it was for her bodily functions, although she didn't want to investigate it yet. Light came from a fluorescent tube inside a metal cage in the ceiling. A horizontal window high up in the wall behind the bench had no bars, but it was too narrow to pass a human skull anyway. She stepped up onto the bench to look out, only to discover it was nighttime and all she could see was a blank wall ten or fifteen feet away that might have been made of concrete or stucco. The cell had a door without a handle and a peephole covered from the outside. And that was it—except for a grated drain in the tile floor that seemed ominous to her.

Dani wanted to know the time, but her watch—the Rolex Orchid her father had given her—was gone, either stolen or lost in the fight that had caused all the bruising. She thought about yelling for a guard or warden or someone, but she suspected the cell's walls and door were soundproofed. After all, the window had been double-paned. She decided to save her strength.

After what must have been hours, she heard a click from the other side of the door—so it wasn't all that soundproof—and then a public address system in the hallway started up with a weird wailing that, after the first three notes, she recognized from her cultural studies for the iceberg project as the *adhan,* or the Islamic call to prayer. Since it had been full dark before, she assumed this was the *salat al-fajr,* for prayers just before sunrise. She also knew that, if they were piping the voice of the *muezzin* into the prison, she was being held somewhere in the Middle East. Probably back in Saudi Arabia.

After more hours of complete boredom, she heard the *muezzin*'s call again and knew the time must have been just after noon. The view from her window remained the same, except for hard sunlight slanting onto the concrete. In all this time, she had received no water to drink and no likelihood of food or human contact anytime soon. Dani resigned herself to playing some sort of mind-body game with her captors. She went to relieve herself in the bucket again, knowing she was probably courting dehydration. She wondered if they were going to make her drink her own filth.

After another hour or so, she heard the first sound—other than those she had made herself and that weird, echoing call to prayer—when a scraping noise came from the door. She looked up quickly and saw that the cover on the spy hole had moved aside. She jumped to the door but could not see anyone or anything beyond that circle of darkness.

In a moment, however, the lock clicked and the door swung outward. She stepped back, knowing it would be foolish to rush whoever was outside and try to escape.

A dark-haired man with a beard—possibly one of the three she had first seen at the train station—came into the cell. He was wearing khakis that might have been military fatigues. The uniform, if it was one, had no insignia.

"I know you," Dani said. "You were at the airport with the others."

"I am Colonel Ahmed al-Hashim," he said. His English was perfect, without an accent, but the inflection was still foreign, maybe British. "Of the General Intelligence Presidency."

"That's … that's the Saudi government, isn't it?"

"Yes," he said and paused, waiting for her to speak.

"But I'm *working* for the Saudis!" Dani exclaimed.

"Are you, indeed? That is not what we understand."

"Then what *do* you 'understand'? Why am I being held here?"

He looked at her expectantly, as if she might supply the answer herself.

After a minute of this standoff, he shrugged. "You are not dressed appropriately," he said, pointing to her miniskirt and her sleeveless blouse with its low-cut neckline. Her matching jacket lay on the bench, where she had been using it as a pillow.

The colonel walked out into the corridor. Clearly, someone else was waiting out there, because he came back in a few seconds holding a shapeless mass of black cloth and a pair of flat canvas shoes, also black. "You will wear the *abaya* instead of your lewd and ridiculous European clothing."

Dani took the garments but she was not satisfied. "Where is my purse? And my suitcase?"

The man simply turned away and walked out. The cell door started to close.

"And where the hell is my father's watch?" she yelled.

But her captor was already gone.

---

James Roberts was second attaché at the U.S. embassy in Riyadh. Two days ago he had received a note from the switchboard about a call on the embassy's public line. It was from a young man, surname Wall, first name Norman, in San Francisco, asking about his girlfriend traveling alone in Saudi Arabia, and could the embassy look into the matter? Roberts had put the note aside at the time, although it wasn't for lack of interest.

The State Department was still dealing with the aftereffects of the Six Day War from 1967 and the humiliating loss of territory the participating Arab nations and their backers in the Saudi kingdom had suffered. The United States had been caught on the wrong side of that conflict—morally right, but politically and economically disastrous—and Ambassador

Nicholas Thacher was still working to mend fences in the region, particularly with regard to oil supplies and commitments. At least, the local situation had since gone from playing catchup to working cleanup. And so, in the middle of all this, the situation of a young American woman lost in the desert had to go on the second burner, if not the third.

Anyway, young western women simply did not vacation in the kingdom. And even if they traveled there for cultural, educational, or business purposes, they were always part of an organized group, moved around together *en masse,* and were quartered separately, with chaperones. There was just no way an American woman could have encountered any kind of real trouble during her visit.

And even if she did, with the current political situation, she was too small potatoes to represent any kind of bargaining chip or political leverage. Unless, of course, someone on the outside managed to turn her into a media celebrity and a bleeding-heart cause in the court of public opinion. That was unlikely, however. Or less than likely. But even then, it would be a disaster—*another* disaster—if her case took a turn in that direction.

And so, finally, in the spirit of performing his due diligence, Roberts checked the embassy's records and learned that one Danielle Wheelock—for that was the name the caller supplied—had indeed applied for a visa with the Saudi consulate in San Francisco. Her request had been approved under the auspices of the Ministry of Environment, Water, and Agriculture. And she had traveled alone on a flight departing from San Francisco to Cairo. That was a week and a half ago.

Roberts contacted the ministry in question and was referred to the *Mabahith,* the General Investigation Directorate. This was the police arm—some would say "secret police"—of the Presidency of State Security. Before inquiring further, Roberts considered whether he should stop and turn the matter over to the American Central Intelligence Agency, on the off-chance the Wheelock woman was one of theirs. But doing so would open up a layer of complication and confusion that was probably not in the State Department's best interest.

Sometimes, he decided, it paid to be naïve and unassuming—so long as one proceeded slowly. James Roberts called the *Mabahith* on their public line and made his inquiries—just following up on a call, closing the loop as it were, and not a matter of any *political* concern.

The next day he traveled to al-Ha'ir Prison, twenty-five miles south of the capital.

———

Dani had been held *incommunicado* for four days. She never saw the colonel from the airport again. Neither was she approached by anyone in a position of authority. And so she never heard the charges against her, nor did she have the opportunity to demand a lawyer and receive her one phone call, as was the right of every accused person. The only human beings she saw were uniformed young men who brought her food and took away her waste bucket each day, and they either could not or would not respond to her in English.

By the fourth day, Dani had begun to entertain the dark fantasy of a white woman disappearing forever into a Middle Eastern prison and not being discovered for years or even decades, not until she was old and gray and half-blind, humming the call to prayer to herself five times a day as her only way of keeping time. ... But then the door of her cell opened without the preceding scrape of the spyhole's cover.

Two of the men in uniform were standing outside, which was a departure from routine, because usually it was only one man. Instead of entering the cell to attend her needs, they beckoned for her to come forth. Their faces were not exactly smiling, but they lacked their habitual frowns. In fact, they seemed uncertain.

Dani slid her feet down off the bench and into the ratty canvas shoes. She gathered the black cotton robe around her hips and stood up. But she hesitated to go with them.

"*Min fadlak* ..." the nearer guard said, which she understood to mean "please."

She relented and walked out into the corridor for the first time. Unlike the cells, the walls here were stucco or rough cement, although the floor was still tiled. The same strip lighting in wire cages lined the ceiling. After several turns, which led into a more genteel part of the prison—indicated by wooden wainscoting and painted plaster on the walls—they took her to a room with a glass door and a mirror along one wall that she supposed was two-way glass. One of the guards pointed to a metal chair on the far side of a shiny metal table in the center of the room. He made a squatting motion, suggesting she should sit.

Dani complied with as much dignity as she could muster. Then they closed the door, and she waited.

After ten minutes, the door opened again and another guard ushered in a young man with sandy hair and a clean, beardless face. He was wearing a dark business suit and carrying a briefcase. He sat down opposite Dani, on the door-side of the table.

"You are Danielle Wheelock?" he asked in what she now thought of—since her time in the Middle East and Europe—as an American accent.

"Yes, I'm Dani Wheelock. Can you tell me what I'm doing here?"

"First, I'm James Roberts. I've come from the American embassy, back in Riyadh."

"So then, am I still in Saudi Arabia?" she asked.

"Yes, in a prison just outside of the capital. You don't know why you're here?"

"No one will tell me anything. I'm an engineer, working for the Saudi government. I was in the Netherlands checking on a project that we have when three men attacked me. One of them is here—was here—in the prison. He said he's a colonel with the intelligence services."

"First, have they harmed you? Beaten you or ... or ..."

"I haven't been raped. Just drugged and kidnapped."

At this point, she expected Roberts to open his briefcase and take out papers: a charge sheet, some diplomatic forms, anything official. Instead, he folded his hands on the table.

"The ministry you've been working for—the ministry in charge of water and the environment—claims that you stole from them," he said. "One hundred and ten million dollars, which was put into your charge in a bank in Switzerland."

"That was a progress payment," she explained. "It was made in two parts, ten million about a month and a half ago, to get us started with the design work. And then the hundred million in the last two weeks, to begin construction. But ..."

Dani was suddenly struck by the implications of what she was saying. No major project moved so fast from design to construction. And from what she had recently learned in Jeddah and Rotterdam, no work on the project was actually proceeding, or even contracted for—nothing, in fact, except the work she had been doing on her end in San Francisco. She didn't even know for sure that there *was* any money in that Swiss bank, other than what Hugo Wichard had told her.

"So you took out progress payments," Roberts summed up. "On what? A project to transport ice from Antarctica?"

"I never took any money. I never *saw* any money."

"Well, the ministry checked, and that account is empty."

"But the minister's own nephew was a partner in our project."

"Yes? So? That is often the way things work here in the kingdom."

"So my partner must have taken the money." It was the only explanation.

"You and the nephew were partners? That makes it your word against his."

"No, we also had a *third* partner, Hugo Wichard. He brokered the deal."

"Is this man Wichard an American?"

"No. French, I think. Or naturalized."

"Let me understand. Two outsiders—an American and a European—get together with a Saudi prince to build—what? Ships, is it? And a port facility? You take out a progress payment that suddenly disappears. And now the Saudi government is detaining you." The embassy man sighed. "How much progress have you actually made?"

Dani bit her lower lip. "None. Or that is, I have design firms in San Francisco working on the ice barges and the harbor and terminal designs. We already owe them more than a hundred thousand for their work to date. It was about getting payment for these consultants that I came to Saudi."

"You haven't taken any of the money?"

"No, I haven't. Right now, I'm out of pocket, too."

"So your partner, this Wichard, he must have done a lot of work on the project."

"That's what I was traveling in Europe to find out. It turns out, he had made some inquiries, both here in the kingdom and in Rotterdam, but there was no real investment. He has nothing under contract."

"Tell me truthfully," Roberts said quietly, "because I can't do anything for you otherwise. Is this whole iceberg thing a scam?"

Dani glanced at the mirror. She had no way of knowing who might be watching and listening on the other side.

"It might seem like that, I guess," she admitted. "But not by me. I thought we were going to bring in millions of gallons of clean, fresh water. We were going to make the desert bloom."

"But you can see how this looks, can't you? Two westerners take a Saudi ministry and a naïve young princeling for a hundred million dollars that suddenly disappears."

"It wasn't … I need a lawyer, don't I?"

"Do you happen to know one?" he asked.

"Can't the embassy help me out? I'm an American citizen. I have a passport—had one, in my purse, before I was attacked in Rotterdam."

"We know that you're a citizen. But the thing is, the United States has no extradition treaty with the Saudis. You are here on their sufferance. Even if your iceberg scheme had broken laws in the States, there's nothing we can do for you, officially."

"Then I'm cooked, aren't I?" Dani saw again that vision of a wraithlike old woman, mumbling Arabic prayers.

"We will keep track of your case," Roberts offered.

"Can you call my family? At least let them know where I am?"

"We knew about you only because a man in San Francisco said you were missing."

"Norman," she said. "That would be Norman Wall. He worries about me. Tell him I'm … well, not all right, but alive."

"I'll do that. We can also advise him about what he and your lawyer can do, working through the Saudi judicial system."

"And what *can* they do?"

"Not much, I'm afraid."

## 15. The Helping Hand

WHEN NORMAN WALL hung up the phone after talking with the man from the State Department, he sat for ten minutes and thought.

Dani's situation was pretty bad … very bad.

And he wasn't sure what he could do about it.

Norman had known all along—well, perhaps not from the beginning, but soon after it started—that the iceberg venture was some kind of confidence scheme. For one thing, it had always sounded too good to be true, that an oil sheikdom in the Middle East, let alone the Kingdom of Saudi Arabia, would pay a junior engineer big bucks and make her a strategic partner in a major project, creating a set of new and untested technologies, eventually employing hundreds of people, who would travel thousands of miles and establish a permanent base in far-off Antarctica … just to get a few million gallons of fresh water—which they could have from any nearby river using proper purification methods, or from the ocean itself with current desalination technology. But Dani had been hungry for the work. She was desperate for the fame—no, for the chance to do something big and important. And she had believed the promises of this Frenchman, Hugo Wi-*shard*.

Dani Wheelock thought she could do anything.

That was one of the things he loved about her.

And now the whole project had turned out, for real, to be a huge scam. Apparently, the Frenchman had left Dani holding the bag. And now she was in a Saudi prison without a hope of rescue, because the Islamic justice system didn't recognize American legal standards, and this country had no extradition treaty with which to bring Dani back and try her in a fair court. So the State Department was only going to wait and monitor the situation. No sympathy there. Norman himself could hire a lawyer, either here in the U.S. or someone in Saudi Arabia. But without the support of his own government, Norman wasn't sure what good that would do.

The Saudis would end up cutting off her hands—or her head.

And everyone involved was supposed to stand by and watch.

Norman didn't know much about Dani's family. He knew she had a mother back East, in the college town where she grew up. Jane was the mother's name. Dani was in irregular contact with the woman, calling her only two or three times a year. Something was wrong there, because Norman used to call his own mother once or twice a month, at least before his father died and she had remarried disastrously. Dani actually spoke more about her father, recalling things he would say and lessons she learned from him. But Dani had called the man only four or five times and received only two letters in all the years Norman had known her. Something was wrong there, too.

Although it was a violation of her private space, Norman knew Dani kept her personal phone book in the drawer of her nightstand. He would never go into that drawer, or look through the book, unless it was an emergency. But this situation seemed to be the definition of emergency. Not that he thought there was anything her family could do for Dani, either. But, estranged or not, they should know their daughter was in danger.

That evening, he opened the book and called the home number listed for Jane Wheelock. The phone at the other end rang and rang. Norman looked at his watch. Eight o'clock in San Francisco would be eleven in Upstate New York. Late enough for everyone to be at home. Not so late that they would be in bed and dead to the world.

He checked the book again and saw an alternate number for something called the "Third Base." It was either a baseball reference or some kind of sexual code. He called that number.

The line was picked up on the second ring, and he heard background noises: voices talking over one another, recorded music in the distance, the clink of glassware up close. And then a female voice cut across it all.

"Third Base! Don't ask! He's not here. Wouldn't tell you if he was. Now, what can I do for you?" The voice delivering this obviously practiced spiel was bright, hard, and businesslike.

"Um, can I speak to Jane Wheelock, please?"

"You're talking to her," the woman replied.

"Hi! Well, my name is, uh, Norman Wall. And I'm calling from San Francisco about your daughter, Danielle?"

"Are you her boyfriend?"

"Well, that's not exactly—"

"Shoot! ... So what's this about?"

"I'm afraid your daughter's in trouble."

"Now, *that's* a surprise. What has she done?"

Norman began telling the tale from the beginning, about Dani's promising career with Mannheim Construction but her frustration with the way she had gotten sidetracked into a support function. He told Jane about the arrival of the man Wichard and his fantastic iceberg scheme. Norman described what he knew of the partnership deal and details about the shady lawyer and the Saudi prince. He recalled how Dani had done everything on her end, but the project had started to come unraveled all at once. He told about her traveling to Saudi Arabia, trying to assess and fix the situation, but that she disappeared soon afterward. Norman finished with what he had learned from the State Department.

All through this recitation, Jane Wheelock listened quietly. Although she was clearly standing in the middle of a busy work environment, she didn't try to hurry him along or insist he come to the point. She kept up her end only by murmuring "Uh-huh" when he finished a long sentence. Or she asked "And then what?" when he paused to gather his thoughts.

Once, she turned away—Norman heard the rattle of her earring against the telephone handset and a rustle as her fingers tried to cover the mouthpiece—and shouted, "Take care of table twelve, will you?"

Another time, she cut across him to say, "No, you make that one with Chivas."

But otherwise, Norman seemed to have the woman's undivided attention. The funny thing was, she never asked for clarification on any point, either. She didn't seem to care for his explanations or want him to make excuses for her daughter.

When he had come to the end of his story, when he had nothing more to say, there was a long pause on the line. The background noises seemed to go dim, too. Finally, Jane said, "Okay, I'll see what I can do."

"I'm not sure what anyone *can* do," he said. "Internationally speaking."

"I'm pretty resourceful," Jane replied. "Let me make a few calls."

With that, she hung up. No thank-you, no goodbye, nothing.

———

Three days after Dani's meeting with James Roberts from the embassy—days in which nothing happened except the arrival of food, removal of the honey bucket, and the call to prayer five times a day—the guards again took her out of the cell, through the prison's corridors, and into the room with the steel table and the two-way mirror.

This time the room was already occupied. It was an Asian man, thin and unsmiling, with long, slicked-back hair. He wore gold-rimmed eyeglasses and a black business suit. As she entered, he rose from his chair and gave her a stiff, formal bow, like a *karateka* at the start of a match.

Dani pulled herself straighter, brought her heels together, and returned the bow.

"My name is Phan Van Khiem," the man said in unaccented English. He extended his right hand—but not far enough for her to reach it across the table. The gesture was merely a Western courtesy. "You may call me Mister Khiem."

"Danielle Wheelock," she said, nodding. When the guards had withdrawn, she asked cautiously, "Are you … from the embassy?"

"No, and not from any particular country."

"A lawyer, then?" He looked like a lawyer.

"I have practiced law," he said, "but not today."

"All right." She sighed. "Why are you here?"

"I have come to bring you this." He pushed a brown envelope over the metal surface, to her side of the table. "And this." From the floor next to his chair, he lifted a linen sack, like a laundry bag, and set it on the table. "It contains your personal effects. Clothes and things. They did not have your suitcase. Nor your handbag."

Dani opened the envelope and found her passport, an airline ticket to London on British Airways, one hundred American dollars in crisp twenties, and a piece of thin, wood-pulp paper, of the kind she used to have for doing her math homework. The paper was full of printed Arabic with two stamps in purple ink. One of them she recognized as the crossed swords and palm tree of the Saudi national emblem.

"What is this?" she asked, pointing to the math paper.

"That is an official release from the government. You are free to go."

"I'm free. ... Just like that?"

"Yes, like that."

She pulled over the bag and sorted through it. Someone had simply dumped the contents of her suitcase and purse. After a minute she was certain it did not contain the most important item.

"I don't see my watch in there."

"This was all they gave me."

Dani imagined some security officer's wife wearing her Rolex Orchid with the decorative seashells. "I want that watch back. It was my father's gift. Someone took it off my wrist after they drugged me."

"The return is not possible. Only what you have here."

She had to make a hard decision then. She could fight for the watch, which was probably untraceable by now. Or she could take what she had and run. But still ...

"I don't understand," Dani said. "The government charged me with fraud and embezzlement. They claim I stole millions of dollars. Why are they releasing me now?"

"The reasons are not your concern," he said stiffly.

"But will I be arrested again? Say, by the Swiss?"

"All charges against you have been dropped."

"I still would like to know why," Dani said.

He sighed. "It is a matter of cartel business."

"The Saudi oil cartel?"

"No, one I represent."

She shook her head.

Mr. Khiem sighed again. "Your mother has asked me to explain to the royal family that you are too young, naïve, and stupid—her choice of words, not mine—to steal any hundreds of millions dollars. That you are no more guilty than the young Prince Ali, who also signed onto your partnership. And then we, the people I represent, asked which the Saudi royal family wanted more, you in their prison as a hostage and a hood ornament—her phrase, whatever it means—or continued access to their supply of recreational pharmaceuticals. Our trade with the kingdom is chiefly heroin, although certain members of the royal family now have a growing taste for Colombian cocaine, which is also under our control. The answer was easy for them."

"I can't believe my mother has that kind of power," Dani said. "I thought she was out of the drug smuggling business."

"Oh, she still had one favor left to call in. We owed her a debt for arranging the elimination of a colleague, the uncouth and violent Mister Bell—whom I believe you met under unfortunate circumstances. The man had gone rogue and needed to be dealt with. Your mother provided both the pretext and the solution. For that, we are grateful."

"I'm ... grateful, too," Dani replied quietly.

Mr. Khiem held up a finger before his face.

"But this is a matter of discretion, yes?"

"Oh, I'm as discreet as the grave."

"I see that you *do* understand."

# 16. Back Home

NORMAN WALL MET Dani's plane from London when she arrived at San Francisco International Airport. She came through the swinging doors on the public side of customs inspection looking no more rumpled and discouraged than any of the other passengers from the twelve-hour flight. Tall as Norman was, it took Dani a moment to spot him among the crowd of people waiting outside to greet their friends and family. But then her face brightened, her shoulders lifted, she dropped her brown duffel bag—not the expensive leather suitcase she had left with—and ran to meet him.

It was a postcard moment, except that Dani did not offer up her mouth to be kissed. Instead, she hugged him around the middle and buried her face in his jacket lapels.

"I'm so glad to be back home," she murmured.

"And I'm really glad to have you," he replied. "Did they treat you very badly?"

"No, not really. I mean, they didn't beat me or anything. After they roughed me up and tranquilized me in Amsterdam, the Saudi secret police were actually pretty tame. Just a lot of solitary confinement and no chance to take a bath."

"Now that you mention it ..." He held her at arm's length. Her loosely braided hair and wrinkled clothing were somewhat pungent. Norman worked hard not to make a face.

Dani made it for him. "I tried to wash up in the lavatory at Heathrow's International Transit Lounge. But there wasn't any dry cleaning, and this outfit's three days beyond wearing." She was dressed in her dark-blue wool suit with the miniskirt, short jacket, and a white silk blouse. But her pantyhose were ripped, and her shoes were fraying, black canvas slippers. Norman wondered if the shoes were something complimentary from the plane. "Right now," she went on, "I'd kill for the tub at home, about fifteen gallons of really hot water, and my bath salts."

"All that can be arranged," he said. "Plus dinner."

Dani picked up her bag. "But my bath first, please."

"Whatever you want. You're home and free now."

As they went to the car—his beat-up Bronco, not her shiny yellow Corvette—she said in a low voice, almost as if he wasn't supposed to hear, "You called my mother, didn't you?"

In the same low tone, he answered, "It was the only thing I could think to do."

"Well … it was the right thing. This time. But please don't make a habit of it."

———

Dani Wheelock walked out of the United States Courthouse at 450 Golden Gate Avenue, which housed the federal Bankruptcy Court for the Northern District of California. The morning fog had finally burned off. The sun was bright in the sky. It was springtime—although with Bay Area weather you could hardly tell one season from the next. Except for winter. At least it wasn't raining.

She had just received judgment on her filing under Chapter 11. Since she still hadn't found a job and had no regular source of income, she did not qualify for the more lenient terms of Chapter 13. Not that it would make a whole lot of difference.

The three months of past-due rent on the North Beach office of Antarctic Ice Ventures, before the landlord finally evicted her, was the least of her indebtedness. She still owed more than a hundred thousand dollars in invoices to John Martin Marine Architect and to Mason & Mason Marine Solutions for their work on the project. The court would not expunge these claims or limit her liability as member of a partnership whose other partners were beyond reach. But the two firms—out of the goodness of their hearts, she supposed—had agreed to waive their usual guarantees, inspections, and other service add-ons. That brought the amount she owed down to seventy-five thousand dollars.

It was still too much for her. Not even if she had an income to attach or could work out a payment plan. Her only real property was the Beast, and after selling it to pay off the financing, she could probably realize only about five or six thousand. The rest of her debt would just sit there, not going away, like a millstone around her neck—and a disclosable obligation on any employment application—until the creditors themselves went away or hell froze over, whichever came first.

But at least she wasn't in jail. She didn't owe the Saudis their hundred million dollars. And nobody was going to cut off her hands.

A month ago Dani had received a letter from the California Board for Professional Engineers, Land Surveyors, and Geologists in Sacramento. Because of her involvement in what had become a notable international scandal—even without official prosecution—her professional registration was being suspended for two years, pending a clean work record. That meant she could not earn her living as an engineer. So it was back to schlepping drinks. Probably.

Norman had been there when she opened the letter. Predictably, he had immediately become all gallant. "Don't worry," he said. "I'll take care of you."

"I can't let you do that. It wouldn't be right."

"I don't think you have a choice at this point."

But she wondered if what he said was really true.

Wasn't life always about—and nothing but—choices?

# Winter 1974

# 1. Petals on a Wet, Black Bough

THE BART TRAIN from Richmond, which would be heading south to her stop in Oakland and then on to its posted destination in Fremont, was late this morning. Of course, Dani Wheelock knew, the system's trains couldn't ever be *late*, because they all ran on a frequency or headway—usually twenty minutes between trains, whether during commute hours or at other times of the day—rather than on a schedule. But this morning the last train had already come through twenty-five minutes ago, according to comments passing up and down the Berkeley Station platform, although the public-address system had as yet made no formal announcement.

People who pretended to know said the problem was the heavy overnight rain. When the tracks got wet, they said, it interfered with the train sensing system, which was based either on impedance or conduction—there was disagreement on this point—between the track rails and the car wheels, rather than on some kind of electromechanical switching system. Dani didn't know or care, except that the train was late, which meant she would get to her job at Rayburn International after the official workday start at eight-fifteen.

Then Bob Tanner, Manager of the Technical Reports Department, would just happen to position himself alongside his secretary Cathy's desk, pretending to discuss a memo or something meaningful with her, but actually keeping his eye on the double doors that led into the department. He did this every morning to take note of late arrivals. Supposedly, there was no penalty for starting late, as the department's technical writers—all of whom held salaried and supposedly "management level" positions—had the option of making up fifteen-minute increments on their billable hours by skipping lunch or working past five o'clock without registering for supplemental overtime. But everyone knew Tanner kept a secret log of who was punctual and who was not, and he would use it against people at review time.

Working as a technical writer was the best Dani could find after the fiasco with the Saudi iceberg project. The trouble was that the collapse of her engineering career had come right ahead of a major worldwide recession, brought on by the OPEC oil price squeeze, rising inflation, and stagnation in the U.S. economy. Every day she had to remind herself that she was lucky to be working at all, when so many others had lost their jobs—and not because they had been duped by a slick-talking Frenchman working a con game on Saudi princes.

Actually, her job wasn't even as glamorous as any kind of writing. She was more of a technical editor, correcting the spelling, punctuation, and grammatical glitches of Rayburn's real, working engineers as they wrote up sections of a new engineering report or marketing proposal. And pushing a red pencil to polish their prose was actually the least part of her job.

The technical editors were charged with ramrodding those reports and proposals through the Rayburn International document production system: ordering graphics such as a proposal's organization charts and schedules from the graphic arts group; getting engineering drawings printed at reduced size; sending the various report sections to typing, proofreading, and printing; seeing that everything got bound into book form; and arranging for shipping the finished documents by express mail or courier to the client, all under an ironclad deadline. Since the report process was the tail end of an engineering effort that might have gone on for months and sometimes years, everything coming into the Technical Reports Department was a last-minute rush. So Dani's job was more like that of an air traffic controller: keeping a dozen pieces and parts of the document in the air and moving forward, trying to bring them all together at one time, and getting them out the door by a promised delivery date.

This morning she was scheduled to oversee binding the proposal on a Libyan aluminum smelter project: two volumes, fourteen sections, twenty-three personnel résumés, and forty pages of qualifying project descriptions. Ninety percent of these pages were already printed and stacked on her desk, with the last couple due back this morning from the printshop. Now she had to get them all into the bindery, arrange them in the collating racks, double-check the order of the pages, and team up the clerks who would gather by hand, punch, and comb-bind the finished books. That part of her job was like an old western cattle drover's: keeping those documents rolling, rolling, rolling along.

Now she looked at her watch, a well-worn Timex on a leather strap. At least the BART system managers hadn't given up yet, shut the trains down, and suggested over the loud-speakers that everyone on the platform—who had already fed their tickets through the gate machines and started pay-ing their fares—"find alternate means of transportation." Then Dani really would be late, by an hour or more. And that would be actionable because, if she missed her place in the bindery this morning, the Libyan proposal would miss its arranged pickup with the courier service. Such a thing had never hap-pened in the history of the Technical Reports Department. The consequences of that failure—missing the proposal deadline in Tripoli, after which the Libyan Investment Authority could no longer open bids on a project worth more than a billion U.S. dollars—were simply unthinkable.

The rain from the night before had continued heavily into the morning, so everyone on the platform was wet, glum, and anxious—with Dani more anxious than most. Everyone was fumbling with a furled and dripping umbrella, because even though the station was underground and protected, peo-ple had to walk to BART in the first place or take a bus that stopped a block away from the main entrance to discharge its passengers. There was just no way to stay dry.

When the Fremont-bound train finally came into the station—seven cars instead of the usual ten—Dani saw through the steamed-up windows that every seat was already taken. Passengers were standing in the aisles, clinging to the little handhold attached to the seatbacks, because the sleek, new cars had nothing like a subway strap. Well, waiting for the next train was not an option.

As she pushed through the crowd to secure a place for herself inside the doors, Dani rubbed against the damp lapels and dripping sleeves of dark raincoats. She passed unseeing gazes from the pale, unhappy faces of other riders. A phrase floated up in her mind: "petals on a wet, black bough."

Dani knew it was from somewhere, something she had heard or read before. It took her a moment to define the phrase as having to do with the Paris Metro. It was a line from what had been billed as the shortest poem in literature, back in her required English course in freshman year. She always knew that stuff would come back to haunt her. But the title and the author escaped her completely.

Never mind. At least she was now moving forward, by jerks and starts, in a crowded subway train on its way to an office tower in Oakland and her appointment with the bindery.

## 2. The Best Man for the Job

HADLEY AMES, VICE President for Minerals Development at Rayburn International, was just getting on the executive elevator in the second subbasement garage when someone from fifteen feet away called out, "Hold the door!" Ames immediately pressed the door-closing button, but not in time. He turned to see Leslie Trimble approaching the still-open elevator car.

Trimble was a principal engineer in Ames's division with expertise in mining and a specialty in ferrous ores. He had recently been assigned as project manager to the new study of the Gâra Djebilet deposit in western Algeria, and from the way Trimble was acting, he thought the project was going to be the salvation of the division. Perhaps so, but only if, first, the study proved the deposit was economically feasible; second, the American-based client was happy with the results, was agreeable to their presumptive Algerian partners, and was impressed by Rayburn's work on the study; and finally, third, the client decided to go ahead with mine development and actually picked Rayburn to dig the hole and build the infrastructure. That was a lot of ifs.

"Good morning, Les," Ames said as the other boarded the car.

"You're just the person I wanted to see," Trimble said.

"Can it wait 'til I've had my first cup of coffee?"

"This won't take but a minute of your time."

"All right, say you've got two minutes."

"You know this Gâra Djebilet is going to be a massive study," Trimble began.

"So I've heard. That's why we put a man of your experience on the job." Ames saw the other stand a little taller at that, but the compliment did not deflect him.

"All of the components—mine facilities, ore processing, slurry pipeline, pelletizing, shipping port—each one is equivalent to an engineering report in its own right. This project is going to require someone really talented in Bob Tanner's group to pull it off."

"I'm sure his people are up to the task."

"Well, it's good that you think so. I'm not completely sure. Most of them are former English majors. They ask a lot of stupid questions and still get things wrong. And the client, Mesabi Iron and Steel, aren't going to brook a lot of mistakes on this one."

"I'm aware of the client's needs, Les."

"So I was hoping you would intervene with Tanner and get him to assign his best person. Someone who knows what questions to ask and, otherwise, when to keep his mouth shut."

"You know Tanner assigns his editors as they become available."

"Yes, of course, but I thought a suggestion from you …"

"I'll consider what might be done," Ames replied.

The elevator stopped at the sixth floor. Trimble's time was up.

"Thank you very much, sir."

"Goodbye now."

After he'd had his coffee, cleared his phone messages, and found five free minutes in his schedule, Ames decided it wouldn't hurt to put in a call to Tanner in Technical Reports.

"What can I do for you, Mister Ames?" the other man said politely.

"You know my division is working on a new project, Gâra Djebilet."

"Yes, I read about it in the company newsletter. Congratulations, sir."

"Then you know this one is going to be a massive effort. The engineering report will run to ten or twelve volumes. And the final report will be in both English and French, to satisfy our client's Algerian partners."

"I didn't know about the French."

"Well, yes. That's not the worst of it. The client, Mesabi, is an old, established mining company out of Duluth. This is their first overseas venture, and their first time working with a foreign partner. So you could say the Mesabi people are a bit on edge, nervous about the outcome. They want everything to go right—as do we."

"Of course, sir."

"It's going to require a special member of your technical editing team. Not just one of your English majors, who will get all balled up in dangling participles and such."

"No, sir. None of that."

"We need someone with a cool head, who understands the engineering business, and won't make foolish suggestions."

"I may have just the person," Tanner said. "Just come off the Libyan aluminum smelter proposal and ready to take on a major new assignment. And Dani Wheelock is a mechanical engineer by training, so she won't get in your people's hair."

"*She?* You have a woman engineer down there?"

"But she's good, though. An experienced hand."

"All right then, if she's the best man for the job."

"Or woman."

"Yes, that."

# 3. The Tinkertoy Approach

ONCE THE LIBYAN proposal had been delivered to the hands of the courier service, Dani Wheelock was called into the office of Stephen Calder, who supervised the team of editors in Technical Reports.

"Everything go all right on the smelter proposal?" he asked.

"Yes, sir. Finished books went out on time. No glitches."

"Good. We were counting on you." He paused. "Now there's another thing."

"Some problem?" Dani asked.

"No, more of an opportunity."

"I'm glad to hear that." Maybe, for once, she would get the chance to make a contribution as an engineer instead of a glorified traffic cop. "What's the project?"

"Minerals Development has asked for you—you particularly—on a new engineering study, an iron mine in Algeria."

"Gâra Djebilet," she said, and her heart beat a little faster.

"That's the one. You're meeting with the project manager at two this afternoon."

"Gosh. I should have my hair done." Dani touched her ever-present braid.

Calder squinted. "Is that a joke?"

"Yes, sir."

At two o'clock, she went up two flights to the three-thousand square feet of office space that had been opened on the sixth floor for the Algerian Iron Ore Project. That was what the gold-lettered decal on the double doors said, probably because no one in Building Services could be trusted to spell "Gâra Djebilet."

Inside, Dani found teams of engineers setting up drafting tables, arranging desks, and unpacking boxes of books. She stopped the first person she came to. "I'm looking for Les Trimble?"

The man nodded. "He's not here."

"Well, I have an appointment."

"Then see Mike Chambers."

The engineer pointed to an enclosed cubicle set in the middle of a string against the inner wall. It was not the biggest one and not in the corner with its own window. The sign next to the door, written in felt-tip on the back of a manila file folder, read "Assistant Project Engineer." Dani knocked on the doorframe. "Mister Chambers?"

Inside, an older man with graying hair and a round, pale face marked with reddish blotches looked up. "That's me." Dani judged him to be late fifties, maybe even early sixties. She wondered what it was like to be that far along in your engineering career, almost at the end, and not yet having reached even full project manager, let alone any kind of executive level. The thought crossed her mind that maybe the blotches were from heavy drinking.

Chambers put aside the document he was holding. "What can I do for you?"

"I was supposed to meet with Les Trimble this afternoon?"

"And who are you?" He blinked as if he might not believe whatever she told him.

"I'm Dani Wheelock. From Tech Reports. I'm going to be putting together your engineering study document."

Chambers cleared his throat. "Funny, I guess. We all thought 'Danny' would be a man."

"Surprise, surprise," she said evenly. "Where is Mister Trimble?"

"He's back in Minnesota, meeting with the client. I don't suppose you'll see much of him, because this client requires a lot of facetime. But don't worry. Your group will do most of its work through me. I'm kind of the project secretary for this job." Chambers indicated a guest chair for her to sit down, then noticed it was stacked with bound reports. He jumped up, scooped up the reports, looked around, and finally dropped them on the floor behind his desk. "We're still getting organized," he said.

"I can see that. So, what can you tell me about Gâra Djebilet?"

Chambers blew out his lips. "Well, to start with, it's a rich deposit. Three lenses of ore with assays averaging about fifty-four percent iron content. The estimate is one-point-seven billion metric tons of recoverable material. That's a great mine in anyone's book."

"Then I guess our study is going to be an easy one."

"Well, there are some drawbacks—maybe 'contingencies' is the better word. For one thing, the deposit is far off in the desert, in Tindouf Province, at the extreme western edge of Algeria, just south of the Atlas Mountains. The region shares borders with Morocco, Western Sahara, and Mauretania."

"So logistics is going to be a problem?" she asked.

"Logistics is going to be an interesting challenge."

He picked up the document he had originally been holding, which turned out to be Rayburn International's original bid on the study. He opened it to a map page and unfolded that to a full eleven by seventeen inches across his desk.

"From the mine's location, eighty miles southeast of Tindouf, the shortest route to a seaport for shipping out the ore is probably two hundred miles northwest, to Agadir in Morocco, on the Atlantic Ocean. Some low mountains, a river to cross, but otherwise easy traveling. However, the client, Mesabi Iron and Steel, is partnering with the Algerians, through their *Société National de Recherches et d'Exploitation Minière*. They have no interest in building a processing plant, stockpile, and shipping port in Morocco. They want the ore to go out through Oran in Algeria, on the Mediterranean."

Dani studied the map. "That's nine hundred miles across the desert."

"So you've noticed," Chambers said, smiling grimly.

"Is it profitable to truck the ore that far?"

"They're not going to truck anything. You see, Algeria is energy rich. They can sell their oil readily, but their natural gas resources are harder to export. The gas has to be collected, liquefied, shipped out in special vessels, and then received and regasified at special plants. So the Algerians end up with more of the stuff than they know what to do with. Someone in the *Société National* came up with this scheme."

Dani focused on a set of parallel lines running across the desert. "Those look like pipelines. Are you supplying water to the population in Tindouf?"

"They are indeed pipelines. And no, not much for the town. The plan is to use excess natural gas to run a reverse-osmosis desalination facility at Oran. This will make clean water from the salt water of the Mediterranean. The project will then pipe that water down to Gâra Djebilet, where we will use it to slurry the ground-up ore and pipeline it back to Oran. We'll be using more of their gas in pumping stations to move both water and slurry. At Oran the project will dewater the ore and pelletize it for shipping. Then the water itself—wastewater in any other project—will finally be purified for agriculture or domestic use. It's a win in every way. Algeria uses excess gas to get fresh water for drinking and iron ore to sell on the international market."

Dani whistled. "Who thought up this tinkertoy? Rube Goldberg?"

"Some bright boy in Algiers who's no doubt read Jules Verne. But you don't want to be too critical, Dani. Everyone here is very gung-ho about the prospects."

"But … can the price of iron ore, even at fifty-four percent metal content, support all this infrastructure?"

"That's what we're here to find out," Chambers said.

"So how do I fit into all this?"

"We'll have different teams out there—" He waved a hand beyond his own office. "—working on different parts of the project. It's all conceptual design and preliminary cost, mind you. We have teams for the mine planning, ore processing, the two pipelines—there and back—with pumping plants, de-salination, dewatering, pelletizing, stockpiling, and shipping. Those separate facilities, plus ancillaries and the economic analysis, will come out in a dozen volumes of the report. The project will also generate about four hundred engineering drawings. These all have to come together at once, and the deadline is just ten weeks away."

Dani whistled again, this time on a dying note.

Chambers nodded. "The client wants both an intermediate draft, which they will review and approve, and then a final report, which will go to their Algerian partner."

"All right," she agreed. "That's a challenge."

"In French," Chambers said.

"Excuse me?"

"The final report is to be delivered in two sets of volumes, one in English, the other in French."

"That's … going to be … I mean, do your engineers even *speak* French?"

"I had a year of conversational French in high school," he said deadpan. "You'll have to find an expert translation service once the initial draft has been approved. Maybe even before then. The good news is that we only have to produce one set of drawings, because they'll all have callouts in both languages."

"So who is doing the translation on the drawings?"

"We're giving our draftsmen French dictionaries."

"That might even work. … But you know, of course, that otherwise this whole thing is impossible. Not just the documentation, but the project plan itself, from every angle."

"I'll thank you to keep that opinion to yourself," he said.

"Yes, sir. Right, sir." Dani grinned. "Three bags full, sir."

# 4. Home Late, Again

"PHONE FOR YOU, Dawson," the shop manager called out. "It's the wife."

"She's not my wife," Dawson Powers muttered. But he put down the Del Orto 38-millimeter carburetor he had just taken off a new Ducati 900SS that had somehow gotten clogged up—maybe some packing grease left over from assembly—and needed a thorough cleaning. He ambled over to the service desk and took the handset. "Yeah?"

"Hey, honey," said a too-familiar voice. "It's me."

"I know, Dani. I'm sort of busy. What you want?"

"Just to say I'm three days into that big assignment, and there's already a pile of work on my desk. So I'll be home late, again. Can you take care of yourself? Get yourself dinner?"

"Sure, I'll rustle something up. You okay with all this?"

"I don't know what else there is to do but be okay."

"Right. I'll see you later. Don't strain yourself."

"I'll try not to." Then she hung up her end.

So … that left him alone, in the city, on a Thursday night, with nothing to do, but also with no obligations—at least not until, maybe, ten o'clock tonight. Well, there was no sense in fighting traffic back across the Bay Bridge just to sit in an empty apartment and see what Dani had put away in the freezer.

There was a bar downtown, Los Lobos, which everyone said was crawling with fresh meat, secretaries down from the office towers in the Financial District. They were bound to be lookers, because that's what the corporate types paid for. And, from Powers's experience, they all liked a man with a little grease on his knuckles. Somebody real. Somebody … authentic.

Oh, yeah. He could take care of himself. And so what? If Dani could hang out for the evening, then so could he.

---

Dani finally got out of the office at nine forty-five, which was plenty of time to catch the BART train back to Berkeley, because the service didn't end until midnight. But she would have trouble finding a bus to take her the last mile or so to her apartment in the hills north of campus. Well, it wouldn't be the first time she had to walk.

The center of downtown Oakland was deserted at night after about nine o'clock. No street life. No restaurants closing out their last seating. Not even much vehicle traffic, except for the distant wail of sirens, either from police or ambulance, and in any case trouble.

Dani had to go three blocks over and two blocks down to get to the 12th Street Station, and she walked them quickly, with her purse held close against her side. She was still dressed for the office, which meant an A-line midi skirt, hose, and shoes with medium heels—not a good outfit for running and dodging.

She didn't see anyone on the streets, or going down the escalator, or even on the upper concourse where she added money to her BART ticket and then fed it into the gate machine. But at the head of the stairs leading down to the Richmond-bound platform she saw a man leaning against the wall of glazed red brick that enclosed the stairwell. He was dressed shabbily in loose, paint-spattered trousers and an army fatigue jacket. He might have been homeless and just keeping himself warm in the gush of heated air that moved with the trains through the subway tunnels. But the funny thing was, the man didn't look at her. She was the only other person in sight, and a not-unattractive young woman, yet he paid her not even a glance. That, in her experience, was a warning sign. But still, she had to pass right by him if she was to get to the platform.

Because of her work schedule, it had been some months since Dani had been able to get to the *dojo* in San Francisco. She did manage to run through the basic exercises and the Shorin-ryu *kata*s whenever she could find free time and floor space. So she was not personally afraid. She just did not want a personal confrontation after spending a long day at her desk.

Dani ducked her head—bad form, because it signaled submissiveness—and moved around the man to the head of the stairway. She even muttered, "Excuse me"—which he might interpret as an acknowledgement, even a kind of greeting.

He still hadn't seemed to notice her, but as she moved her foot out into the open air over that first step, she felt his hand clamp on her upper arm, right where she was holding her purse. The grip was strong, too—not a vagrant's tentative touch but a fighter's first move.

The purse, she reminded herself, was not a priority. Everything there could be replaced. Her objective was the defense of her person.

That forward foot, which was poised above a drop of perhaps ten feet on hard concrete steps, was her point of vulnerability. It had the potential to throw her off balance. So, to change the direction of her momentum, she pulled her foot back fast, as if recovering from a forward kick, and placed it solidly back on the concourse level. She used her recovered momentum to pivot back and around, using the man's grip as her axis point. That movement, carrying her whole weight, bent his fingers back away from the thumb. His hand opened rather than let her break the small bones of his wrist.

Like a dancer with a reluctant partner, Dani spun completely around the man and brought her hands up to brace herself against the brick parapet on his other side. Her attacker had also turned with her, to preserve his hand and arm, and his back was now against the low wall.

With her forward leg now planted, she let her opposite leg swing with the momentum, passing around and behind her, tapped the toe of her shoe on the wall beyond her, then brought that leg forward again and up, directing her knee into his exposed groin. As the man started to double over, she hit him again with a double-pump of the same leg, this time striking him in the face, and that snapped him back erect. With her free hand, and using not much effort at all, she pushed him backward over the wall and down onto the stairs, where he took that eight-foot drop with two awkward bounces.

Dani walked around the end of the wall and moved carefully down the stairs to see how badly she might have hurt him. The body was lying face down and not moving—always a bad sign. The man did not appear to be breathing. She crouched above him and extended a hand to touch his neck and check for a pulse.

From the folds of the jacket, his own hand shot out and clawed at her wrist.

Dani broke the attempted hold immediately and backed up a step.

A train horn sounded below, along with the squeal of steel wheels on steel rails. If she delayed further with subduing this mugger, she was going to miss her ride home.

She grabbed the stair's handrail, vaulted over the man's still-prostrate form with her skirts flying, and continued down the steps, taking them two at a time. She arrived on the platform just as her Richmond train was slowing to a stop. When the doors opened, she boarded and took the first available seat. She was still breathing fast from the encounter and then her rush down the stairs. She was fighting for internal stability.

"I've got to stop beating up guys in train stations," she said under her breath.

As she grew calmer she wondered if, without the man's receiving immediate medical attention, she had just performed an act of willful murder, or at least manslaughter. And then, if the homeless man was still alive and not all that hurt, would he want to press charges against her for aggravated assault? She wondered if the BART station had any kind of surveillance cameras, and if any of them were in a position to have captured the fight, and finally whether the police could identify her from the blurred images—mostly the back of her head, with her braid flying around her face—that the cameras were likely to show.

Somehow, she didn't think so.

———

Dawson Powers eased his Moto Guzzi Daytona 1000 into the space he had set aside for it, just behind the dumpster in the garage of their apartment building on Euclid Avenue. The fit was tight, because he had to maneuver between parked cars and a concrete wall, and he was careful of the bike's bright-red fiberglass bodywork. But even three-quarters drunk, Powers could still paddle the low-slung chassis around—although his foot slipped briefly on the closest turn and a patch of grease, almost dumping the thing. And then he had to try three times with the heel of his left boot to get the kickstand down. Still, no scrapes or scratches—no harm, no foul.

He made his way up to their second-floor apartment, one bedroom with a galley kitchen and a breakfast nook, but the living-room balcony had a view between two eucalyptus trees that showed a slice of the North Bay and Angel Island. At least Dani liked it. Powers himself couldn't care less about views.

The lights were on when he opened the front door, which meant she had gotten home before him. Uh-oh.

He found her sitting on the couch with a couple of paper towels spread across her lap. She was daubing liquid polish on the toe of one of her shoes.

"Little late for that, isn't it?" he said.

She held up the shoe. Even from this distance, he saw parallel tears that showed up gray in the black leather. In his professional opinion, as a mechanic who dealt with torn motorcycle seats and riding leathers all the time, no amount of polish was going to fix those scratches.

"I scuffed it," she said. "These were new, too. Dammit."

"How?" he asked, hanging on the door for support.

"Oh, I got mugged in the BART station tonight."

"Your shoe got scuffed kicking someone?"

"No, I bumped it against a brick wall."

"But you always could take care of yourself."

Dani squinted at him. "Thank you for your concern."

Powers ambled across the room and sat down on—or rather fell into—one of the chairs at the dinette table. He rocked for a moment until the room stopped spinning.

"Did you ride your bike back across the Bay Bridge in that condition?" She shook her head. "Of course you did."

"You know … I can take care of myself, too." He held out his hand to prove his steadiness.

"Did you get anything to eat?" she asked.

"Sure, some … shrimp things."

"Appetizers? Like at a bar?"

"Yeah …" And he belched.

"Downtown? Which one?"

"You don't want to know."

"No … I probably don't."

# 5. Easy Money

ALISTAIR MEACHIN AND Rocky Chvotkin sat in one of the two conference rooms on the sixth floor of the Rayburn International building that had been assigned to the Algerian Iron Ore Project. They had their reference books and maps spread across the big table.

Technically, they were squatting in what was supposed to be a meeting space open to all of the teams on the project. Technically, they were supposed to do this kind of work at their desks out on the project floor. But because someone had put Meachin's desk in one corner of the large room and Chvotkin's in the other, they had to come to this common area to get any work done together. Or that was their story. Otherwise, they would only budge if Les Trimble or Mike Chambers called a project-wide meeting and reserved the room for it. They simply chased out any lesser groups that wanted to use the space.

"So what am I missing?" Meachin asked his partner.

"Not much," Chvotkin said. "It's Algeria. It's *dirt*."

"Well, isn't some of it the Sahara? That'll be *sand*."

"Sure, hinterland. Between the mine and the coast."

"Except for that coastal mountain range, Mahgreb."

"That's just alluvial debris. With occasional ridges."

Meachin lifted his left eyebrow. "Hell of a place to build a pipeline."

Chvotkin hunched his shoulders. "Yes—but is that really our problem?"

"What do you mean?"

"Look at our charter."

"Roads and grades."

"Within the plant."

"Ah!" Meachin said.

"Finished roads, within functioning areas of the plant," Chvotkin elaborated. "Our job is to say how people will move around the working areas of the mine and inside the processing plants at both ends of the pipeline. Ours is not to say how they get to these sites. Or what kind of temporary access roads the construction team will need across nine hundred miles of desert and mountain range in order to build the fucking pipeline."

"Well, when you put it like that …"

"It's an iron mine in a third-world country. The staff will drive around in Jeeps, or some European equivalent. The ore will go from the pit to processing in two-hundred-ton mine haulers that would chew up any paved surface. All the roads will be at grade. We're not going to be building any bridges, because there aren't any rivers. And all the roads inside the plant boundaries will be scraped and rammed earth because— well, what else is there to work with? It's not like we're build-ing a superhighway."

"I suppose we ought say what kind of dirt it is," Meachin said.

"Laterite, with high concentrations of iron and aluminum."

"You're just quoting from the original survey, aren't you?"

"Do you mean we should go to Tindouf to confirm with samples?" Chvotkin asked.

"Not even as far as Algiers. But I could happily study soils from as close as Paris."

Chvotkin put his feet up on the table. "This will be the easi-est job we've ever had."

Meachin gazed at the ceiling, then suddenly sat up straight. "Just don't tell anyone."

———

The first of the actual drafts from the Gâra Djebilet project— a set of sixteen typewritten pages for the third chapter in the projected Ancillary Facilities volume titled "Roads and Grades"—was delivered to Dani Wheelock's office by the most mismatched pair of civil engineers she had ever met.

Alistair Meachin was tall and willowy, with elegant, sil-very gray hair. He wore a three-piece suit in fine gray wool with tiny white pinstripes. He actually had a gold watch chain threaded through the third buttonhole of his waistcoat. Presumably a pocket watch and either a heavy Masonic medallion or a Phi Beta Kappa key anchored the chain's ends in the two vest pockets.

His partner, Rocky Chvotkin—although Meachin introduced him as "Rockwell"—was short and wiry, with bristling dark hair that was only gray at the temples. He wore khaki chinos, a sports jacket in a rough tweed, and ankle boots. While Meachin's tie reeked of some regimental or school significance, Chvotkin's was too wide and decorated with tropical fish.

"Here is our work product," Meachin said, handing over the pages with a little bow.

Dani took the set and riffled through it. The subsections were labeled with headings such as "Mine Proper," "Ore Processing Plant," "Water Receipt and Slurry Processing Plant," and on through each element of the project. The odd thing was, for a section on roads and grades, there were no drawings—or even references to drawings—showing where the roads would actually go or how each plant site would be leveled and graded.

"Oh, those things will be shown on each of the main facility drawings," Meachin said when she inquired about this.

"So your input here is mostly technical?"

"Yes, technical description, based on a soils review."

"Do you expect much change at the review stage?" she asked.

"I don't know how anyone could object to our work." Meachin sounded defensive.

"Agh, she thinks the Mesabi people are going to stiff us," his partner suggested.

"I assure you," Meachin said to Dani, "this is all solid analysis."

"I'm sure it is," she said with a smile. "I only ask because, maybe, we can get this section, at least, off to typing and then to the translator and save some time."

"There should be no problem," Meachin said.

His partner nodded vigorously.

That afternoon, with her first real project document in hand, Dani sat down with the pages and her red pencil to edit them for the production typists. She read through the first section on the mine, which told how all the roads would be "at grade"— which her technical dictionary translated as "ground level"— and the underlying soil was "hard-packed laterite." The text described preparing the roads by, first, clearing the ground of loose rocks and overburden, leveling the surface with a road scraper, saturating the remaining soil with a binding agent such as pozzolana or commercial portland cement, and then compacting it with a road roller. Even to her untrained eye, it all made obvious sense. And she supposed that the mine drawings, when they came, would show the various routes into and out of the developing pit. She made a few punctuation corrections with her pencil and moved ahead.

However, when she turned to the next section—dealing with the plant for receiving, grinding, and screening the ore before it was to be slurried for the pipeline—she found the exact same wording, point for point and line for line. She flipped to the next section and the one after that, and each set of paragraphs was the same as the first.

Dani had learned as a technical editor that one of the keys to her job was clarity. The other was brevity. It would offend anyone to have to read through page after page of the same stuff. She got to work with her red pencil, putting like things together, removing redundancies, and noting exceptions. When she was done, Meachin and Chvotkin's sixteen pages of rolling thunder on the subject of "Roads and Grades" had melted away.

What she had left, and what she would submit for typing, was just two paragraphs. One described the soil at all the plant sites—which she listed in bullet point order—as hard-packed laterite. Since laterite was just another word for "dirt," she considered substituting that for the more technical term, but she decided to give the engineers their little bit of grandeur. The other paragraph described all roads at the above-listed sites as being prepared at grade through the processes of clearing, scraping, binding, and compaction.

It was going to make for a short chapter. But those two paragraphs would be clearer to the technical and financial teams who would ultimately read the engineering report. They could then focus on the real issues in making their decisions about the project's feasibility.

With a light heart and a clear conscience, Dani turned the text section in for typing.

———

Mike Chambers had in his office two of the angriest project engineers he had ever seen. Well, Rocky Chvotkin always seemed a bit angry, but now he was waving a single piece of paper around as if he was swatting flies. Alistair Meachin was tight-lipped and shaking, and his furrowed brow reminded Chambers of a disappointed Roman emperor. The source of their anger was the paper in Chvotkin's hand, which was a copy of their report section, returned from Technical Reports for approval—which they were definitely not going to give.

"Let me call the editor and find out what happened," he told the two men, pointing them toward his office's guest chairs.

"Technical Reports, Wheelock speaking," the young woman's voice came over the line.

"Dani? This is Mike Chambers. I'm calling about the section you just returned, on Roads and Grades."

"Oh? Yes?" She sounded utterly bland.

"My engineers and I want to know what the hell happened. They say they turned over sixteen pages to you for editing."

"They did."

"And ...?"

"It was the same sixteen pages, over and over," she said. "I just boiled it down to something intelligible."

Chambers took the handset away from his ear and covered the mouthpiece with his hand. "She says it was full of redundancies," he told the two engineers. "Did you, by any chance, try to pad your work?"

"Of course not!" Chvotkin exclaimed. "There was no issue of 'padding' there."

"We merely described the roads and soil conditions at each plant," Meachin said.

Chambers had been warned about these two, of course, even before the project got under way. He personally couldn't see soils and road conditions as taking up more than a fraction of one engineer's time—and probably from one of the mining engineers or geologists who were assigned to design the pit. But Meachin and Chvotkin were a well-known pair within the company. They always worked as a team, and they got themselves assigned to every major project. That alone told Chambers the two of them must have had something on somebody upstairs.

He put the phone back to his ear. "Dani? I think you should put through the original section as submitted."

"But that's not good editorial practice," she said stiffly.

"As may be," he replied. "But it's not your call to make."

"All right. But I tell you the client won't like the result."

"And that will be my problem to deal with, not yours."

## 6. Not Home At All, Again


NORMAN WALL WOKE up to his alarm clock at five-thirty in the morning in an empty bed. Worse than empty, he sensed that Molly's side hadn't even been slept in, because the bedspread and blanket were still flat and the pillows undented.

Sometimes his wife worked late at her artist's studio, which was in a warehouse off East 12th Street in Oakland, in a questionable part of town. Sometimes, too, she camped out on a daybed there, rather than risk driving at night through bad neighborhoods to reach their stucco-walled and red-tile-roofed home in Piedmont. Obviously, last night was one of those times.

Norman untangled himself from the sheet and blanket, leveraged himself off the mattress, and stood upright. It was still dark outside, but that was to be expected. He rose early every morning, because between then and seven-thirty he had to shave, shower, dress, eat something, and get down the hill to the MacArthur BART Station for his commute into the city. He still worked at Levi Strauss, of course, still in accounting, and not yet a manager. That was because Norman knew he was a boring person who lived an unexciting life.

He didn't have to walk his dog Bear in the morning anymore. Molly had objected to the animal two weeks after they were married. She had not been raised with pets and discovered she was allergic to them. So Norman had to find a home for Bear with some people living up in Grass Valley. At least Bear was happy, out in the country.

"Guess that's why I married an artist," he said aloud.

Molly Hungerford—she had kept her surname for professional reasons—was a sculptor who worked in hot metal. Her chosen profession was welding, casting, shaping, and polishing everything from stainless steel to high-carbon steel to copper and bronze. "All the metals from antiquity to the present," she liked to say. It was hot, dirty, exhausting work. It was also

249

a labor of love that generally required a second pair of hands, and they generally belonged to her assistant David—Norman never exactly knew his last name—a muscular young man who labored alongside her. And some nights he slept in the studio, too.

Of course, Norman had already put two and two together. People who worked closely, shared an artistic vision, and sweated through the heat of the day sometimes had ... unchaste relationships. But that was the artist in Molly, too. The free spirit.

Still, she always came home to him, eventually. At least, she had for the eighteen months since they were married. Molly was petite, gray-eyed, and honey-haired, with a compact body that had developed some serious muscle from all her pounding on hot metal, pulling around heavy equipment, and hauling on chain hoists to move her artworks. And she always *said* that she loved Norman. But Molly was an artist, and her affections and concerns were changeable from day to day.

But one thing Norman could count on was the steadying influence of money. He had a good job that paid well. Molly had an artistic passion that required regular infusions of sheet steel, ingots of iron, silicon bronze, and copper alloy, tanks of acetylene gas, a natural gas hookup for her forge and annealing furnace, packets of steel wool and Brillo pads, and buckets of polishing compound, not to mention the rent and electric bill for her studio. So long as he could keep her supplied with these necessities—at least until the commissions started coming in, if ever—Norman knew he had a wife who would always return.

And that had to be good enough for him.

————

On a Saturday morning, while Dawson Powers was out racing his big red motorcycle up and down the twisting mountain roads of Napa and Sonoma counties, Dani Wheelock went to visit her old friend and sometime housemate, Norman Wall. When he had called her late in the week, he sounded distressed. Well, not weepy or whiny, because that was never Norman's reaction when he was in serious trouble. But she heard a tightness in his voice, the sign of tension or confusion being repressed, and that had alarmed her.

Over coffee—Peet's Major Dickason blend, from a drip pot—in the brightly tiled kitchen of Norman's Italianate house on tree-shaded Greenbank Avenue, the story came out. She learned how Molly, of whom she at first approved as a good fit for her friend, had turned out to be a tramp—Dani's summation, not Norman's words—and a manipulator. How the woman spent more time in her studio down in Oakland than in her lovely home with her husband. And how that studio came with its own live-in stud, with whom Molly appeared to be in a *delicto* that was pretty obviously, if not provably, *flagrante*.

"It's not my place to say anything, Norman," Dani murmured, although she had a lot to say about all this.

However, as to the charge of manipulation … Dani remembered a time, right after she had returned from her Arabian adventure, dead broke and owing money, when she had let Norman carry her share of the rent and groceries—and a good deal more—because she sensed, deep down, that he loved her and would let her live in their house for free. When he found Molly and became infatuated, Dani had gradually been eased out of the picture. And, truth to tell, that was like having a weight lifted from her conscience.

"Please," he said. "I'd really like your interpretation."

"Uh-huh! Well, how are things between you two, otherwise?"

"Pretty good. When she's here. Molly is awfully busy with her art."

"And is that going anywhere? Does she have any shows or maybe sales?"

"Not yet," he said. "But she is very close. The Alameda County Art Commission invited her to interview for a possible placement at a park in Pleasanton."

"That's something. Pleasanton's south of here, isn't it?"

"It's over the hills, in the Livermore Valley."

"Still, it sounds important," she said.

"I'd hate to cut her off just as her career was starting out."

"Has it come to that? I mean, are you really thinking divorce?"

"Yes. No. I don't know. I don't know how to handle any of this."

"Talk with her? Be honest with her? Ask the same from her?"

"That sounds so easy in theory. But, you know …"

"Yeah. Any advice I give will sound too easy."

"But thank you for coming and listening."

"Least I can do. You've always been there for me."

He gave her a tight smile. Nothing had changed.

# 7. Economy of Scale

PHILIP KOZICKI WAS the owner and day-shift manager at Sparkle, Inc., a five-press job printer in Emeryville, just north of Oakland. He had a standing contract with Rayburn International, the big engineering and construction firm downtown, to handle work that was too complex for their own reproduction services, including report covers on special stock or with special finishes and photo-reduction of their out-sized engineering drawings. Usually, the editors from the Technical Reports Department just gave him a phone call and messengered over whatever copy they had that needed printing. But on this Monday morning, one of them actually came to visit his shop.

"Hi! I'm Danielle Wheelock, from Rayburn?" She was a tall young woman with a long, auburn braid. Not bad looking, either, except for that curious dent in her left cheekbone.

"Okay," he said. "What can I do for you?"

"I have a big job that's coming your way."

"Of course you do." Kozicki grinned at her.

"No, this one is *really* big. And serious. And we're on a tight deadline."

"All right. We can handle it, sure. What are you planning?" He noted that her hands were empty. Maybe she had left a carton of stuff out in the parking lot.

"Nothing just yet. Maybe nothing till the end of this week. But I wanted to come here, see your plant, and sort of make eye contact."

"You know we've done work for you before, Miss Wheelock. Drawings for the Libyan smelter. Wasn't that job ... satisfactory?"

"Oh, everything was fine. But that was small potatoes compared to this." She nervously pulled the braid over her shoulder and stroked the loose tassel of hair at its end with her fingertips. "I'm working on an engineering report for an iron mine in Algeria. It's a big project, a dozen volumes, and we'll print most of the pages in-house, as usual. What we'll need from you is sets of covers, front and back, on heavy board, maybe cloth laminate, with post-and-screw binding."

"Do you have the text for them yet?"

"Not yet. Not for a couple of weeks."

"All right. Let me know when you have the dimensions, and I can send out to have the boards made. Then we'll silk-screen them with George Litho in the city."

"And we will have drawings, ANSI E-size, thirty-four by forty-four, to be reduced to eleven by seventeen and gatefolded."

"I can do those here. How many drawings."

"The count right now is four hundred. Maybe more."

Kozicki whistled. "I may have to put on a third shift for that."

"And we'll be printing everything in two waves—a draft for the client's internal review, and then a final set to present to the client's Algerian partner."

"How many copies in each?"

"Twenty-five for the draft, one hundred in final."

"Huh! I'll run off twenty-five just doing make-ready on the press."

"Look, these aren't my specs. I'm just telling you what the client wants."

Kozicki thought for a moment. "How much change do you expect between draft and final printing?"

The woman tucked her lower lip behind her front teeth. "Not much … probably."

"Well, if that's the case, I think I can save you some time and money. We'll print a hundred and twenty-five for the draft version. It's practically the same cost. So we do the job once, and you hold the extras after you send out the review copies. Any drawings the client doesn't change, you just bind into the final report."

"That sounds like a plan," she said. "And if they do change something?"

"Then you reprint—but you came in here planning to do that anyway."

"I think I can make that work. So do we have an understanding?"

Kozicki nodded. "When will you have the drawings ready?"

"I'll send them just as the project people release them."

"Okay ... not all at once—not if you can help it."

"That may not be my call."

"And when is this all due?"

"Draft report goes out in six weeks."

"Then I *will* have to put on that third shift. You'll pay for it."

"I don't think anyone on this project is worried about costs right now."

Kozicki bared his teeth in a grin. "You really don't want to be telling me that."

# 8. Still Dead Broke

DANI SAT AT the dinette table, going over her monthly accounts. Even with a steady job, which paid well for a technical writer, she was having a hard time meeting her commitments. This month, she was going to have to choose between rent and groceries.

It wasn't that she was a spendthrift. Dani was always careful about her money. There just wasn't enough of it to go around.

The biggest chunk, of course, was the debt she owed to the two marine consultants over the iceberg project. She was still paying that off gradually. Right after she walked out of bankruptcy court, Dani had taken out the largest personal loan she could get. That had begun the payoff process. And she put more of the debt on her credit cards, and now they were maxed out. She was still out of pocket to John Martin's and William Mason's firms—small businesses, and she hated the thought of stiffing them for the money—to the tune of fifty thousand dollars. She had made a promise to herself to pay them at least five hundred each on the first of every month, and that was breaking her. But they were obviously encouraged by this and didn't press her for faster payback. In fact, they sent her Christmas cards every year, and she took that as a sign of their good will.

Dani wished she could get paid for all the overtime she was putting in at Rayburn International. On the Algerian project alone, she was already racking up about fifteen extra hours a week, and that was going to skyrocket as the draft-review deadline drew near. But the company had her signed on as a "salaried, exempt employee." Like the professional engineers on the staff, she was supposed to do the job, whatever it took, and not expect to be paid for it—although the company did track her hours and billed them to the project, which meant they were ultimately billed to the client.

Because Technical Reports was tail-end charlie on every project, and the technical editors moved from one crash-rush deadline to the next, accumulating a lot of overtime hours, Bob Tanner, head of her department, had worked out a process with the company's senior management. On projects that demanded large amounts of overtime—calculated at more than twenty hours in any one week—his editors were allowed to take compensatory time off at the rate of one for two. That meant for every extra hour she worked, Dani would get thirty minutes of paid time off. The engineers in the company complained about this, of course, but it was Tanner's way of keeping his people sane and holding down department turnover. At the rate the Algerian project was going, Dani figured she would get a week or two of vacation time on the clock after the final report went out.

But really, she would rather have the money.

Dani had considered going to her mother for a loan, but Jane never had much money herself, which was why she worked full time at that bar. And, after the chits Jane had to call in to get her daughter out of Saudi Arabia, Dani was afraid that approaching her mother for such a big chunk of money would have … consequences. The cartel that had negotiated her release was probably itching to get their hands on a young person with serious business connections. Even though Dani sat in an Oakland office all day, she presumably knew people who were out in the field working on construction projects across the country and in foreign places like Libya and Algeria. With enough incentive—or coercion—she might be forced to arrange for muling or distributing drugs or laundering the cartel's money.

No, better let that dog sleep until it woke up and bit her.

Still, Dani was on a glide path to a financial crash. Unless she could work up the nerve to rob a bank, she was going to have to decide whether to pay her share of the rent or the grocery bill this month.

———

Dawson Powers was sitting on the couch, across the room from the dining alcove where Dani was bent over her checkbook and credit-card statements. She had been at it for an hour when she finally lifted her head and looked at him with a frown.

"I'm afraid I'm going to have to go light on the rent this month," she said.

Powers felt his face scrunching up. "What? You mean, *again?*"

"It's just … I'm in a bit of a squeeze, you know?"

"No, I *don't* know." He and Dani had never seriously talked about money. When they first moved in together, she had never bothered to tell him about this huge debt she was carrying. And yet there she was, doing scut work as a technical editor— a kind of glorified clerk—instead of practicing the professional career and making the big bucks that were guaranteed by her college degree. None of this made sense to Powell.

"You know I can't carry this place on what I make as a mechanic," he said.

"I'm not asking you to. Just spot me a few hundred this month."

"And last month. And next month. Is that it?"

"Well, you do what you have to."

What Dawson Powers had to do was issue a bit of physical correction. He had already advanced halfway across the room as the argument progressed. Now he took two more steps, drew back his right hand, and slapped Dani across the cheek.

That was when he discovered another lie in their relationship. She didn't even move to stop him. Some big, badass karate black belt she was. Just another girl …

———

Dani saw the blow coming, of course. Even though she was sitting down, with the corner of the table intersecting the space between them—effectively pinning her in the chair—she could have blocked it. But she also knew Dawson was going to give her an open-hand slap, not a serious attack. And he wasn't all that strong anyway.

When it landed—well clear of her eye, which was the important thing—the slap stung her skin. But she had suffered worse in sparring matches, especially when she stepped *in*, toward an oncoming strike rather than *out*, and took a shot to the face. Still, that slap was going to leave a red mark. It would probably require some makeup in the morning.

Dani kept her eyes on him the whole time, and when she failed to react to the blow, she saw him smile. That was a bad sign.

He drew back his left hand this time, to slap her again.

She waited until he had committed himself. Then she almost casually brought up her right hand in a head block that put the back of her clenched fist and stiffened wrist in jarring contact with the more delicate bone, the ulna, in his forearm. She knew at once that she had hurt him. If she had moved any faster, she might have broken his arm. And all this was from a sitting position.

Dawson backed off, holding his arm with his free hand.

"What the hell did you want to do that for?" he yelled.

"You get one free shot. Don't ever try to hit me again."

Dani knew she was in a bad personal situation. And she liked Dawson a whole lot less at this point. But she still needed him to pay the rent. And that just sucked.

## 9. *Toutes les langues françaises sont les mêmes*

JEAN-PIERRE DUVAL SAT in his one-room office on the third-floor of a walkup building on Grant Street, two doors south of Bush, in San Francisco. With the name "European Language Institute" blazoned on the frosted glass of the hallway door, it sounded a lot more sophisticated and established—more "institutional"—than his business actually was. In reality, Duval was a "one-man band," to use the American expression, backed up by a floating stable of foreign language majors and graduate students drawn from San Francisco State, Cal Berkeley, Stanford, and the points in between where he left his flyers.

For this reason, he was hesitant about the meeting he had arranged with the young woman, Danielle Wheelock, from the engineering company in Oakland. He sensed she had a job in hand that was larger than he could really commit to—suggested by the fact that she wanted to meet and interview him in person, rather than just send over her document for translation. But Duval's cash flow was down to the last thousand or so of those fat American dollars in his bank account. He needed the work.

At the knock on his office door, he got up from his uncluttered desk and opened it. A tall young woman in a dripping raincoat was standing in the hallway. She had dazzling green eyes and auburn hair pulled back in a bun or braid—he couldn't see which, because she was wearing a rain hood, but he would have guessed a braid.

"Won't you come in?" Duval said. "Let me take your coat."

When she slipped out of it, he saw she was wearing a dark-wool business suit with sensible, straight lines, like a knockoff from Chanel. Under the open jacket, she wore a puffy white blouse in some shiny, satiny material, tied at the neck with a large, flowing bow. Her clothing said big business and, perhaps, some kind of executive. She was carrying a slim attaché case in black leather.

He stood there holding her dripping coat until he realized the office had no coatrack and nowhere for him to put the garment. As a substitute, Duval opened the top drawer of the farthest filing cabinet and draped the coat across its front panel.

He indicated the only other chair, and when she was seated, he took his place at the desk. "I understand from your call that you are from Rayburn International, in Oakland, and you have a project for me—for the Institute."

"Yes." She put the case on her lap, unsnapped the latches, and took out a one-page document.

Duval breathed a little easier. One page he could translate himself, probably in less than an hour. But when he took the sheet, he saw it was not a flyer or announcement but a paragraph of description with a list of what had to be chapter headings. "What is this?" he asked with an uncertain smile.

"This is the outline of an engineering report and economic analysis on the Gâra Djebilet iron-ore deposit in Algeria. My firm is preparing the report, and the client wants it both in English and French, to accommodate their Algerian partner. We are preparing the initial draft for review—about seventy percent has already been submitted by our engineers—so I thought it would be good to get started on the translation."

Duval nodded as if he understood, but inside he was panicking. "And ... how big are each of these chapters?"

"Oh, not chapters! Those are the volumes."

"I ... see. And how many pages in all?"

"About five hundred. Single spaced."

He made a rapid calculation. Maybe if he called in his every contact, anyone who had majored—perhaps even minored—in French, he could just about cover it.

"How did you come to choose ELI?" he asked. "We haven't worked together before."

"Frankly, I picked you out of the Yellow Pages. This is our first dual-language job."

"And does your firm, by chance, have any French-speaking engineers on staff?"

"No, but you don't have to worry about translating the engineering drawings. They're already being prepared in English and French."

"How did you accomplish this?"

"Gave the draftsmen French dictionaries."

"Oh …" Duval's heart sank. "That could work."

He saw her looking around at the office. He was painfully conscious that the one room had no connecting doors, indicating no busy back office full of chatter in French, German, Spanish … all people hard at work on other projects—which he didn't have at the moment.

"This is just our business office," he explained.

"I can understand that," she replied.

"I draw on teams of translators all over the Bay Area. All over California."

"Oh, that's good. Because we don't have a lot of time on this project."

"And how much time is that?"

"We're nearly done pulling together the draft report, which the American client will then review. Once we get their approval of the English version, we have four weeks to produce the final set in both English and French."

"So … five or six weeks to translate twelve volumes?"

"Something like that. But once we get approval, it will go really fast."

"Yes, I would hope so." Maybe if he advertised for anyone who had taken French in high school …?

"But I have just one question," she went on. "Your institute is supposed to handle all European languages. Are you sure your people can do Algerian French? I ask because I know Castilian Spanish is not the same as Mexican or Argentine Spanish. Different words, different idioms …"

"Oh, no!" he said. "All French languages—" What a ridiculous notion! "—are the same. That is one of the benefits of having an *Académie française* to keep our language pure."

"Good then. That makes me more comfortable with the drawings, too."

"When will you have something for my team to translate?"

"In another week or so," she said. "Is that all right?

Duval gulped. "Of *course* it is all right."

# 10. Ee-aye, Ee-aye, Oh!


STEPHEN CALDER CAUGHT up with Dani Wheelock as she carried another carton out of her office and placed it on the growing stacks along the corridor wall. There were more of her cartons stored against the back wall of the elevator bay, too. On the end of each box she had taped a piece of typing paper with an alphanumeric code written in black marker. The one in her arms read: "04-20-P-03." It was all Greek to Calder—and he had studied Greek in college.

"Say, Dani ..."

She stopped. "Yes, sir?"

"Mr. Tanner has asked me to check with the fire marshal about this."

"The fire marshal?" she repeated. "What does he have to do with it?"

"Well, this is all paper, isn't it? And it's blocking an escape route."

She looked at the stacks against the wall. "Not exactly blocking."

"You know what I mean," he said.

"It's only for a couple of weeks."

"That may not be the issue. Can't you find someplace else to keep them?"

"You know how small my office is," she said. "Before we're done, I'm going to have four hundred of these boxes."

"How about an offsite storage facility?"

"Then I'd be going back and forth every two or three hours."

"Is Sparkle delivering finished prints that often?"

"Prints, reprints, corrections to reprints ..."

In addition to the stacks of boxes here, Calder knew that more of her drawings were ending up in the dumpster down at the loading dock. Every time the Algerian mining people made a change to one of their drawings, she had to send out for another printing. He had once suggested she wait until the project was finished before sending anything to print, and Dani had replied that then they would be pushed two weeks past their deadline. Besides, the project people knew about and were willing to pay the extra printing charges. He wondered if anyone in management had considered the security implications of sending multiple copies of drawings on an economically sensitive project like Gâra Djebilet to a landfill. Somehow, he didn't think the project team was thinking that far ahead.

"It seems to me like your project is out of control."

She shook her head. "I've got it. I'm handling it."

"I know you are. But try to keep down the amount of clutter. And please don't go stacking these things on other floors. It just looks bad."

She flipped her braid from one shoulder to the other. "Sure thing, boss."

———

Dani was at her desk, working over an engineer's description of the mill line in the ore-processing plant, when her phone rang. She knew it would be Mike Chambers, because he was now the only member of the Gâra Djebilet project who called her directly, and the mining project was the only thing on her calendar.

"So what's up, Mike?"

"How did you know—?"

"It's always you, Mike."

"Oh, yes, I guess. Well, the Mesabi people have called for another set of changes."

"Of course they have," she said. "And we're not even up to the draft report."

Chambers sighed. "Please don't get snippy with me."

"Sorry, I'm just … What do they want?"

"It's in the ore plant. They want four ball mills in the processing line, not three."

Dani looked at the piece of text in her hands. That would be changed, too. "Okay," she said and put the document aside.

"Do you want the drawing numbers?"

"I think I've got them memorized."

"The plant number is oh-three, the mill line forty, and the changes will be made to the structural, piping, and electrical drawings. The current revision on the first two should be oh-three, and on the electrical, oh-four. Got that?"

Dani made notes. "Those drawings went out to print last week, I think. So it's too late to stop Sparkle from working on them. The copies should already have come back." She checked her cheat sheet on the press runs. "Yes, they were delivered Monday."

"Well, destroy them and let the printer know we'll have new revisions Friday."

"Have them whenever! He's running three shifts on this job by now."

"Just keep your temper, Dani," Chambers warned.

"I'll try, Mike. Always try."

With that, she went out in the hallway, looking for the cartons of freshly printed and folded drawings, with enough copies for both the draft and final report, that were now just wastepaper. As she scanned the labels on the carton ends, she started humming and then sang her little song.

"Oh-three, forty, E, oh-four! Ee-aye, ee-aye, oh!"

# 11. Between Husband and Wife

NORMAN WALL THOUGHT it might bring him and his wife closer together if they invited some new people into their diminished social circle. He decided on Dani Wheelock, as a known quantity, and asked her to bring along her boyfriend. Just one couple visiting another, as soon-to-be old friends. The occasion would be the completion of Molly's first paid commission, for Alameda County at the Mission Hills Park in Pleasanton, and so he asked Molly to host them all at her studio in Oakland.

On the day of their little party, a Saturday, Molly had made an effort to clean up the studio, clear some space in the middle of the scrap metal and acetylene tanks, and put out a card table with cheese and wine along with four folding chairs. Next to it was her sculpture, a life-sized horse assembled from pieces of rusted iron that she had welded together. The bright scars from the welds made the creature look like some Frankenstein resurrection, but they also made it oddly beautiful. If Molly was making any artistic or political statement with the work, Norman couldn't see it. However, he could see that the horse was a stallion and anatomically so equipped. He wondered how that would go over in a neighborhood park with a playground and barbecue pits.

Dani and her boyfriend arrived on a bright-red motorcycle that didn't look any taller than Norman's kneecap. Dani was clinging to the driver's back and perched on what looked like the bike's rear fender. When she uncoiled herself, dropped her left leg to the ground, and swung her right leg free, Norman saw she had been sitting on a pink satin pillow that was bungee-corded to the rear cowling of the plastic bodywork. Both she and the driver were wearing blue jeans, leather jackets, gloves, and bucket-style helmets.

"Hey, there!" Dani called, flipping up her face shield. Then she started unfastening the hooks that held her pillow on the cowling.

The boyfriend quickly snapped up his own shield. "Watch it, *bit ... ba*by! Don't scratch the fiberglass."

"I'm being very careful, Dawson."

When the couple had shed their motorcycle gear, Norman and Dani exchanged introductions with Molly and the boyfriend, whose name was Dawson Powers. It seemed he was a motorcycle mechanic in the city, which explained the racing-style bike. Then they all went inside to admire the stallion.

"Wow," Dawson said. "That's sure a lot of welds."

"You're a mechanic," Molly said. "Do you also weld?"

"Naw, we replace parts instead of repair them. Is it hard?"

"Really, welding's easy, once you get the touch right. Come back here sometime and I'll teach you."

While this exchange was going on, Dani leaned over to Norman. "Is that horse as male as I think it is?"

"It's supposed to be in proportion," he replied, deadpan.

"Well, artists are supposed to use their imaginations, I guess."

After that, they sat down to taste the cheese and wine. Norman noticed that the couples seemed to have paired off again, Dawson with Molly, himself with Dani. He also noted that, despite the chill outside, Molly had chosen to wear a pair of skintight jeans and a loose, silky top that was more like underwear, a camisole. Well, it was warm enough inside the studio, because the fire was banked in the forge.

After another twenty minutes of parallel conversations with almost no crossover, Molly stood up and put out her hand to Dawson. "Come on, I have something to show you."

Dani's boyfriend stood up and followed her to a curtained alcove where, Norman knew, Molly kept the daybed and a few personal items. For the next half hour, Dani and Norman sat in embarrassed silence, listening to muffled coughs—and then a strange, rhythmic creaking—from behind the curtain.

"Does this happen often?" Dani finally asked.

"I think this is the first time she's met him."

"Yes, but I mean ... right under your nose?"

"Please, this is between husband and wife."

"Yeah. Except Dawson's not my husband."

# 12. The Go-Ahead

WHEN IT CAME time to assemble the draft report on Gâra Dje-bilet, Dani Wheelock realized what a massive project it really was. Although they were preparing only twenty-five copies instead of the full one hundred, and using printed cardboard covers instead of silk-screened cloth laminate, the bindery was jammed with her boxes of printed and folded drawings, and stacks and stacks of printed text pages.

Just to keep everything straight and make sure that chapter one from the mine report didn't get swapped with chapter one from the ore-processing report, Dani had to supervise the team of clerks—closely supervise, as in watch where every hand placed every stack of twenty-five sheets—as they put the printed copies into the collating racks. Then she instructed that they should only gather the pages for one volume at a time. Well, they had to anyway, because the bindery area had only one collating table, with room to gather about half a volume at once. But if she had more room to work, there would have been more opportunity for confusion, and more chance of an embarrassing error.

To hurry the process along, Dani herself took a collating tray—actually, the top from a box of printing paper, cut to size with two remaining perpendicular sides to hold the pages square—and helped collect the first half of the first volume. This meant she was in line behind the bindery clerks, walking down one side of the table, across the end, and back up the other side, pulling first the cover, then title page, contents page, first text page, second page, first drawing … and on and on until she came to the end of the rack. She emptied her tray at the binding station and went to collate another set. Around and around, until all twenty-five copies had been pulled.

At the binding station, other clerks aligned each stack of pages by thumping the set on the countertop, then punched the left edge of the stack with a line of closely spaced oblong holes for comb binding. And when the two halves of the volume were brought together, another clerk set them in the binding machine with a black plastic comb, stretched the comb open, and inserted its teeth through the holes. A skilled clerk could bind a volume in about twelve seconds, five volumes per minute, the whole twenty-five in about five minutes. That alone would keep them on schedule.

And then Dani realized that binding the one hundred copies in the final report would use the post-and-screw system instead. That meant feeding aluminum posts through three holes in the side of the page, holding them in place, threading on the screw cap, and tightening it with a screwdriver. But it also meant that the final copies would have to be printed on paper that was pre-drilled with those three holes, like notebook paper. And then she realized that all of her printed drawings, which had plain edges for the comb-binding method, would have to be punched with three holes—or at least any of them that survived the review and revision process. Well, she could set a clerk to doing that before the final report came into the bindery. Or she could do it herself in her copious spare time. As she walked down the line of the collating table, Dani laughed at the idea of "spare time."

"Something funny?" Mike Chambers asked. Dani didn't realize he had come into the bindery—or even knew where it was.

"Just thinking of something," she said.

"And are we going to be done on time?"

"At this rate, yes—unless you're bringing me some more changes."

"No, we're done for now. This report just about covers the ground."

———

A week and three business days after the draft report had been sent by special messenger to the Mesabi Iron & Steel headquarters in Duluth, the marked copies came back from the client. Mike Chambers stood beside Les Trimble behind a desk that had been cleared at one end of the project's open-plan work area. Seated at other desks and standing around the perimeter walls were the entire project team and the support personnel involved from other departments. Right at the front, at a desk normally belonging to a junior engineer working on the mine site, sat Hadley Ames, Vice President for Minerals Development. He was there to hear and weigh Trimble's discussion of the client's reaction to the work so far.

On the desk before Trimble and Chambers were twelve stacks of the cardboard-bound reports. Some stacks had only two or three copies, some six, and one—about the slurry pipeline—had twelve. Each copy was marked with annotations and text changes from reviewers in the Mesabi home office and from their paid consultants.

Trimble was explaining all this to his team, while Chambers stood by to handle any logistical questions. "I have talked with the Mesabi people," Trimble concluded, "and they are generally pleased with our first effort."

Chambers saw Ames nod at that.

"Of course," the project manager went on, "they have a few changes ..."

That brought a laugh from the group.

"But these are nothing we can't handle and factor into our economic analysis. The good news is, the client has no major disagreement with our overall plan and technical analysis. And for that you should all be proud."

He then stepped aside and let Chambers explain that each team should pick up the volume or volumes relating to their project area, read the various comments, come up with a consensus draft and an approach to handling any serious modifications, and turn their revisions in to Dani Wheelock—he pointed her out, standing against the wall, and she gave a little wave—as soon as might be practicable. Chambers refrained from saying "possible," because many things might be possible that were not permitted in good engineering practice.

After the teams had picked up their work, and Ames and Trimble had gone back to their offices, Wheelock came over to see him.

"Tell me, Mike," she began, "does the week that the Mesabi people took to review this draft push back the final report deadline at all?"

He mentally reviewed the contract. "That is nowhere stipulated."

"Okay, so the answer is 'no.' But do you think they are done making changes? I ask only because I've got all twelve volumes out for the French translation, and it's going to be a squeaker just with what your people have to do with these current revisions."

He grinned. "Knowing how Mesabi worked in the past, what do you think?"

"Again, the answer is 'no.' Then I can't guarantee making the deadline."

"You have to. You find a way to do it. That's your job on the line now."

He saw her frown, but wisely she didn't say anything, just walked off.

## 13. Hip Deep in the Swamp

DANI GATHERED THE first batch of the project team's revisions—a hundred and forty-two separate cases of reworked sentences or added paragraphs in three different volumes, plus two completely rewritten chapters, which she also had to re-edit. From the number of changes that appeared to correct errors of which Rayburn's project engineers hadn't seemed to be aware, Dani concluded that perhaps her company wasn't as good at evaluating an iron mine in a foreign country as they were at, say, building cement plants, hydroelectric dams, and less complicated, U.S.-based projects. Maybe the Rayburn engineers just didn't understand the work.

When Dani carried their revisions into the typing pool, the production supervisor, Joe McPhee, took her aside. "So, no let up from the client, huh?"

"These are just from the draft review."

"But after this, the changes stop, right?"

"Well … that is not my impression."

"Then let me show you something."

He walked her over to a corner of the room, where two of his best typists were sitting at wide, desk-like consoles that Dani had seen somewhere before. Then she flashed on the computer room on the second floor, where keypunch operators typed code into Hollerith cards. These were the same sort of machine—except instead of a card feed and punch mechanism, they had a spinning printwheel that impacted against a page of green-bar, fanfold paper on the roller platen, which fed from a carton at the typist's feet and dumped into a basket behind the console.

One of the women, Judy Busch, was typing on the keyboard and the printwheel was simply reproducing her keystrokes, just like a normal typewriter. The other woman, Sarah McLaughlin, was sitting with her hands in her lap, watching as her machine worked itself, spitting out lines of typewriting three times faster than any human typist.

"Um, is this some kind of teletype?" Dani ventured.

"They're linked to the IBM Three-Sixty downstairs."

"That's all very neat, but why are you showing me?"

"These desks were installed two weeks ago, while you were binding your draft report. We call it the Administrative Terminal System—ATS for short. With it, we don't have to retype every page where you make a change, or retype to the end of the chapter if you add a paragraph. The whole chapter, the whole volume, the whole *report* is stored in the mainframe's memory. To revise it, the operator just calls up the proper text file and the line number—" He pointed to a column of digits to the right of and separate from the text on Sarah's machine. "—and makes the change. Then the revision is stored inside the document and the machine can print out everything fresh. No more retyping the whole thing and having to proof everything to catch new typing errors." He put a hand on Sarah's shoulder. "Not that my people aren't the best, fastest, and most accurate typists in the world." At this, Sarah smiled up at him.

Dani was impressed. "Does it have to be on that green paper with the line numbers?"

"Oh, no. The final copy can be on a letter-sized sheet or stencil. No numbers then."

"But ..." She had to think about this. "How do you get the rest of the volume into the system? The pages where we haven't made changes would still be on stencil. And they would be in a different typeface."

"Well, yes," McPhee said. "But from what I can see, your engineers are already rewriting almost the whole report anyway. Why not capture it now and be ready for the second wave of changes?"

"That makes sense." She made a snap decision. "Do it."

"Of course," he said. "I only have these two operators trained up."

276 • Thomas T. Thomas

"A big project like this would get you budget to train more, wouldn't it?"

"There is that," McPhee agreed.

After Dani had messengered a photocopy of the same revisions to the European Language Institute, she got a call almost immediately from Jean-Pierre Duval.

"This is all becoming very confusing," he complained.

"How so?" she replied.

"I have to remember which of these sections, in which of the volumes, I sent to the different translators."

"So how many people do you have working on this job?"

"Seventeen. One is in Redding and another in Fresno. The others in between."

"That's more than one translator per volume! How do you maintain consistency?"

"Consistency?"

"Yes. It means—"

"I know the *word*," Duval said coolly. "But at this stage, you just have to hope that everything gets finished and returned to me on time, *n'est-ce pas*?"

"I see. … Well, do the best you can."

"That has been my goal, *mad'moiselle*."

This exchange gave Dani an idea, which she took back to McPhee.

"Can your typists—excuse me, ATS *operators*—work on the translation, too?"

"You mean the French version?" he said. "Oh, no! None of my people reads French, so their input speed would be very slow and their accuracy rate very, very low. Besides, the ATS is not equipped to store and reproduce the proper diacritics. We've already had to drop the circumflex in Gâra Djebilet."

"You mean, the little hat thing on the *a*?" Dani said.

"You don't want to try proofing this project in French."

———

As his girlfriend's project at work moved into its later stages, Dawson Powers found himself more and more alone.

Dani would come home late at night, catching the last train out of Oakland and exiting the Berkeley BART station just as the agents were rolling down the steel gates. Then she would gobble something from the refrigerator and climb into bed, because she would be getting up early to arrive at work on time the next morning. She promised him that things would start going better—she would have free time to do whatever he wanted—when the iron mine project was finished. But Dawson was bored and frustrated *now*.

One night, knowing that Dani wouldn't be home until after midnight, he took his motorcycle out and raced down the freeway to East Oakland, where that artist who had wanted to teach him how to weld had her studio. He killed the Moto Guzzi's engine for the last hundred feet and coasted up to the warehouse. There he backed into the curb, set the kickstand, and took off his helmet.

The building's one outside door, when he tried it, was unlocked. And that meant the woman—Molly was her name—would be inside and probably working. He pushed the door open and walked into the studio. It was dark inside, lit only by the lamp over the desk against the far wall, where she sketched out her designs, and by a red glow from the fire exit sign above his own head. That, and diffuse light came from around the edges of the paisley-printed drapery hanging in front of the alcove where she kept her bed.

Thinking he would find her sleeping—and knowing just how to wake her—Dawson made his way across the studio. But as he neared the alcove, he heard voices, hers and another, a man's. He moved closer to listen, but his boot brushed against a piece of steel scrap on the cement floor, and it made a tiny, chirping sound.

The two voices paused.

Dawson's body froze.

Time just stopped.

After a while, when no one came out to investigate, the voices resumed.

Dawson turned as quietly as he could, straining his eye-sight to spot any more obstructions, walked carefully back to the door, and out into the night. He pushed his motorcycle a hundred feet down the road so that, when he started it up, with its distinctive exhaust note, Molly the artist and her new boyfriend wouldn't know he had ever been there.

————

Mike Chambers went down to the bindery area in Tech Re-ports while the final draft of the Gâra Djebilet report was being assembled, just to see how things were going. He found Dani Wheelock once again taking a hand, even though the bindery crew had set up two tables this time and were collating two volumes at once. The people with the cut-down box tops were moving at a fast walk around the tables, pulling sheets of text and folded drawings as quickly as a card shark could deal cards.

Without getting in anyone's way, Chambers leaned in to do a spot check of the pages, just to make sure no one was mix-ing things up. Right away he saw a problem. On the table he was looking at, the team appeared to be collating the middle chapters of the volume on the pelletizing plant. But the pages didn't match. Some chapters had been typed with the famil-iar IBM Executive typewriter that Tech Reports used for all of its documents. Other chapters were reproduced in a smaller typeface, angular and without those little hooky things that usually appeared at the tops and bottoms of letters. Those strange chapters were also typed with even margins on both sides, while the older material had the ragged edge down the right side common to all typewriting. Any two chapters put together looked like a complete mismatch.

When Dani had come to the end of a round and dropped off her stack of pages with the binders, Chambers drew her aside and pointed out the problem.

"It's not a problem," she said.

"But it looks just terrible."

"That can't be helped. The chapters with major revisions were entered on our new word-processing system, which runs on the computer downstairs and uses a terminal for output. We had to do this to save time. The chapters with no changes were left in their original typewritten form. And those 'hooky things' are called 'serifs,' since you're so concerned."

"The client's not going to like this."

"Then they need to give us more time."

"Les Trimble is not going to like it, either."

"Then he has to factor in time to work on the text."

Chambers realized it was no good arguing with this young woman. And she wasn't exactly wrong. In all the planning for the project, everyone figured Tech Reports could do its job in about a week, which was their usual turnaround. But nobody took into account the scale of the project or the number of volumes.

He went over to the second table. Here, he noticed, the pages were in French. And when he looked more closely, the mismatch was even greater. He couldn't find either the familiar Executive typewriting or the new computer-printed text. Every chapter was prepared on a different machine. Sometimes separate pages within a chapter were typed differently. And each typist had followed a different style for margins, spacing, and page numbering. This was a complete disaster.

Again, he called Dani over to discuss the matter.

"Look, Mike," she said, obviously trying to control her temper. "If we had precious little time to work on the English draft, imagine what the translators went through. No one person, not even two or three, could translate twelve volumes of technical French in a couple of weeks. The European Language Institute had whole teams working on different chapters. And there was no time to have one person go through and type up a fair copy. You're just lucky we got it all done and didn't end up with a mess of 'Franglish.' "

"What's that?" he asked.

"Try reading *'deux* Chevrolet pickup trucks *seront néces-saires.'* That actually came through in one draft—but we fixed it to *camionnettes.*"

"Lordy! And you trusted our work to these guys?"

"We had to. And, as I said, we fixed it. It's all good French. It just looks a little messy."

"Nothing we can do about it now, I suppose."

"Rope 'em, roll 'em, brand 'em," Dani said.

"What's that supposed to mean?" he asked.

"It's a *joke*. Never mind. I've got to work."

As she went back to the conga line of collators, Chambers looked around. It really was too late to complain. And anyway, maybe the client wouldn't notice. The fact was, the economic analysis on Gâra Djebilet stank, and that had nothing to do with the typeface. Even in a good world market for iron ore, even with a mine producing fifty-four percent ferrous content, Gâra Djebilet couldn't support all that infrastructure. A water desalination plant, new purpose-built gas pipelines, nine hundred miles of fresh-water pipe going south, slurry lines coming back north, and pumping stations in between … the sheer scale of the project had doomed it.

In Mike Chambers's experience, when the feasibility study found that a project was simply unworkable, everybody's instinct was to bury it as soon as possible and forget about it. And then how gracefully it had been typed up didn't make any difference. None at all.

## 14. Skinned Alive

TWO WEEKS AFTER the Gâra Djebilet report had gone out, Dani was sitting in her office editing the qualifications section for a proposal on a cement plant. The promised weeks of compensatory time, granted on a one-for-two basis, covering her overtime on the iron mine study had not yet materialized. Bob Tanner had explained that the department workload just did not let up, and the company could not spare her. At the precise moment she was thinking about him, the department manager appeared in her open doorway.

"Dani?" he asked in a shaky voice. "Mister Ames would like to talk with you." Then he flattened himself against the door panel.

"Where is that Wheelock woman!" an angry voice bellowed down the hallway. "I'm going to skin her alive!"

Two seconds later, the Vice President of Minerals Development brushed past Tanner and charged into her office. "There you are!" Hadley Ames exclaimed.

Dani put down her red pencil, stood up, and straightened her skirt. Inside, she was trembling, but she knew she couldn't show it. After all, she had been attacked, drugged, and held for ransom in an Arab prison. What was this middle-aged white man going to do? *Kill* her?

"If you're going to skin me, Hadley," she said, "first you'll have to catch me."

That caught the man off guard. She saw him begin to relax. He even smiled—although it was more like a death's-head grin.

She pointed to her guest chair, a square frame of chromed steel with a thin vinyl seat cushion. "Now sit down, please, and tell me what's wrong."

"The Mesabi people say our report was an absolute disaster," he began.

"I don't see why," she replied. "We made every change they asked for."

Tanner still stood against her door. In the corner of her eye, he flinched.

"They say," Ames went on, "it was typed up on two different machines."

"That is an unfortunate artifact of the short deadline. We couldn't retype the whole thing just to make it *pretty*. A week and a half isn't nearly enough time to process a report that big. I told Mike Chambers all this."

Ames wrinkled his brow. "Who is this Chambers person?"

"The project engineer on Gâra Djebilet? He's your man."

"Oh, well, then he never told *me* anything about it."

"Too bad. Other than typefaces, what's wrong?"

"The client claims the translation was done in grade-school French," Ames said. "The Algerians were plainly insulted."

"Again, it's the timing. We used an outside contractor who had to call in a dozen different translators to complete the job. You should be thankful we had a French version at all."

Tanner drew a hissing breath. She knew she was scaring him.

"It's not your business," Ames began, "to tell me what we—"

"I read the report, you know," Dani cut across him. "I edited every word of it. And you and I both know that the real reason they're upset is in the final chapter on economic analysis. The project, as Mesabi had defined it, can't make any money. The thing was dead before we took the job. We could have had monks hand-letter the report on parchment and translate it into medieval Latin. Mesabi's people and their partners would still be unhappy with it."

"That is as may be," the older man said. "But you are responsible for presentation and reproduction. You have failed in your job. Worse, you have forced me to defend this company to a valuable client. Do you know how embarrassing that is?"

"I have a fair idea." Dani could *not* tremble now. She *had* to remain calm.

"I'll be talking with Tanner here." Hadley Ames stood up, towering over her, because she remained seated in her office chair. "We'll have to see that this department does better next time. *Hopefully,* without an incompetent technical editor like you."

The man nodded as if to make his point. He turned and stalked out.

Tanner slumped, still backed up against the door. "Dani, really ..."

She held up a hand. "What more can you add to all that, Bob?"

The "more" came through interoffice mail two days later, a yellow carbon form that was her notice of termination. Dani wasn't surprised. She had been unemployed before. She just regretted that she wasn't going to spend any of that comp time. But, on the other hand, she was going to have loads of spare time now—just not on somebody else's dime.

# 15. Things Fall Apart

AT MIDDAY ON a Thursday, Norman Wall was feeling rotten: headache, stiff joints, itchy eyes, and a tingle in his throat that might be the onset of the flu. His department manager told him to go home and get in bed. When Norman arrived at Greenbank Avenue and opened the front door, he heard water running in the shower upstairs, so he knew Molly was home. Maybe she would stay long enough to make him some honey-lemon tea with a shot of brandy and offer him a little mothering. But before he disturbed her, Norman went to the kitchen to get a glass of water for his throat.

There he found a man. From the gray in his dark hair, the man was closer to forty than thirty. He was of medium height and flabby build, with a paunch. Norman saw all this because the man was naked except for a bath towel wrapped around his hips, curving under that paunch. He was fixing himself a sandwich, as if he lived there.

"Who are you?" Norman asked.

The man turned. He didn't seem at all surprised.

"I'm with the art commission. She invited me. Who are *you?*"

"I'm the husband."

"Tough luck, guy."

And then the man smiled. It might have been a smile of embarrassment or commiseration, but in this wretched moment Norman saw it as a smile of triumph.

With his imposing height and big frame, Norman was always careful around people, trying not to scare or alarm them with a sudden, aggressive movement. But now he decided to use his physique to advantage.

Norman strode into the room, right into the art commissioner's face. He ignored that the man was holding a sandwich spreader in his right hand, as if that were any kind of weapon. Norman towered over him, and the older man cowered in return.

But that was as far as the aggression went, because Norman was not going to hit anyone, despite any amount of provocation. Then he thought of something better. In the drawer beside the man's right hip was a disposable camera that Molly had bought to take photos of her horse sculpture before it was shipped off to Pleasanton. Then she had brought it home and left it. Norman thought there might be one or two unexposed frames on the roll.

Pinning the man with his glare, he reached down, opened the drawer, and took out the camera. Then he stepped back and put the thing to his eye.

"Keep smiling like that," he said and snapped off three quick shots, with flash.

By the time the third flash faded, the art commissioner was no longer smiling.

"Now get out," Norman said.

"But what about my clothes?"

"There's a raincoat in the front hall closet. Take that. And keep the towel."

"But my car keys! And my shoes."

"Find a pay phone. Call a cab."

When the man hesitated, Norman stepped back in, as if to strike him.

The art commissioner slid sideways past him and ran out to the hall. A moment later the front door slammed. And all this time the shower upstairs continued running.

In that moment, Norman Wall made a decision that had been brewing for a long time. He went to the wall phone and called his lawyer. He was going to ask for a divorce. And with the evidence in his hand, he didn't think Molly would be able to contest it.

The shower was still running when his lawyer came on the line.

———

After Dani had gone home in the middle of the day, carrying a carton of personal effects from her office at Rayburn International, and then told Dawson she was unemployed, things had gone bad—no, gotten worse—between them. Money was still the issue, of course—her sudden lack of it, his ongoing need for it—if they were to continue living together in a nice—well, just *okay*—apartment anywhere in the Bay Area.

Dawson was drinking more in the evening. He had started adding bourbon chasers to his beer, even though they made the habit more expensive. He and Dani hadn't made love in weeks—actually, since before she lost her job, and really some months before that—and now even the occasional kisses and hugs on greeting and parting, and the friendly touches in between, were long gone. The small pleasantries that greased any relationship, the "please" and "thank you" accompanying small personal requests, the smiles of appreciation and comfort, had disappeared from the apartment on Euclid Avenue.

On a Friday night, when they used to go out for burgers and a movie, or down to Freight & Salvage for some country music, Dani was sitting at the dinette, reading a two-week-old copy of *Engineering News-Record*, trying to get a sense of where the jobs might be in this stagnating economy. Dawson was splayed out on the couch, halfway to drunk, and his resentments were bubbling up, again.

"Are you even *looking* for a job?" he demanded.

"In my line, these things take time. You know that."

"Oh, '*in my line*'—what line is that? Fucked up engineer?"

"*Mechanical* engineer. And yes, it takes résumés, interviews—"

"So? Why don't you try getting a *real* job—a *woman's* job—for once?"

"And what sort of job would that be?" she asked, controlling her temper.

"Waitress. Or secretary." He belched. "Shoe clerk. Sumpin' like that."

"Even those jobs require some level of skill. And you still have to—"

"You're not pretty enough to be a stripper. You can't even dance."

Dani suddenly had enough of this inane conversation. "Dawson. Shut up. You're *drunk*. And I will not discuss my professional career with someone who plays with motorcycles all day."

"You too ladylike to get dirt under your fingernails ...?"

"I'm not listening to any more of this. I'm going to bed."

She folded her magazine, stood up, and turned away.

"Don't you turn your back on me, you bitch!"

Dani had seriously misjudged his level of intoxication. Before she could take a second step, he had launched himself off the couch, crossed the room, and locked a hand on her arm. Her reaction was completely instinctual. She spun back, raised that arm in a sweeping block with open palm, hitting him in the bicep with the hardened edge of her hand and breaking his grip with the change in leverage. Then she countered with a straight punch just under his sternum, to the solar plexus.

Of course Dawson wasn't ready for it. He folded up and dropped to his knees, wheezing for breath. And then he vomited a pale froth of beer and the remains of his dinner onto the shag carpet. She studied him from her standing position, where she had relaxed into a loose guard stance. Dani knew that, in his impaired condition, the chances of aspirating his own vomit and drowning were pretty good. But with his diaphragm in continual spasm because of the impact to that nerve center, he wasn't going to be taking in much of anything for another minute.

"I told you never to hit me again."

In response, he flapped his arms.

She knew then that their relationship was well and truly over. It would take her ten minutes to go into the bedroom, pack a suitcase with a few clothes and some toiletries, and leave. He wouldn't be in any shape to stop her. She could fig-

ure out what to do about her other stuff later. There only remained the problem of where she would spend the night. She
could find a hotel in Berkeley or downtown in Oakland. She
probably had enough credit left on her various cards to pay for
at least a couple of nights. And after that—well, things would
just have to work themselves out.

# 16. Things Come Together

JULIANA BONNER HAD a sudden inspiration—or perhaps it was just desperation. Anyway, she made the call.

Bonner had gotten the name of Danielle Wheelock from the Mannheim Construction, Inc., Human Resources Department. The woman there said that a Danielle Wheelock was one of three female engineers the company had employed over the years. But she had left some time ago to start a private business in the city and then dropped out of sight. Maybe she had gone back to New York State, where she originally came from and might still have family. But the woman didn't think so.

Next, Bonner canvassed the engineering and construction firms around the Bay Area, asking if they had employed Wheelock anytime in the last four years. She hit pay dirt on the third call, to Rayburn International in Oakland. Yes, the man in Human Resources said, they had signed her on as a technical writer doing engineering reports, but she had left the company some weeks ago. Company policy forbade him giving out a home address. However, Rayburn's location did narrow Bonner's search.

She turned to the East Bay phone book and found a "D. Wheelock" listed at a Berkeley address on Euclid Avenue. She called that number during the day and let it ring ten times before giving up. She called later in the evening, and a man answered. When Bonner explained the reason for her call, his only response was, "Yeah, well, that bitch is long gone." And there the trail ended.

But the ugly nature of his response might have been a clue in itself. And with that slender lead, she called the Berkeley Women's Shelter on Acton Street. The receptionist there agreed to check her records, and Bonner held her breath.

"Yes, we have served a Danielle Wheelock," the woman said. "But I really can't tell you anything more."

"Can you at least get a message to her?" Bonner said. "Please, it's important."

"Well ... give me your name and number. I'll see if she wants to contact you."

"That's good enough. Say that I have a job for her."

"A job offer is always good news."

And then Bonner waited.

Two days later, when she was almost out of hope, her telephone rang.

"This is Dani Wheelock," said a woman's voice. "You called about me?"

———

The woman on the other end of the line introduced herself as Juliana Bonner, one of three partners in a new startup called "Bay Environmental Services." Then she told Dani she was a hard person to find.

"Yeah, I seem to move around a lot. But you have a job?"

"Our firm is going to be researching and writing environmental impact assessments for property developers and city planners in Northern California. A lot of these efforts will touch on unbuilt areas, mostly wetlands fringing the San Francisco Bay. According to the California Environmental Quality Act of 1970, these developments all require an assessment."

"And why do you need me? I trained in mechanical engineering."

"Yes, but you are also a woman. Our firm is women only."

Dani was impressed, but ... "Why would you do that?"

"Advantages in federal contracting, for one thing."

"Okay, but I still know nothing about the environment."

"You know how to write a report, from your experience at Rayburn," Bonner said. "And Mannheim was in the construction business, so you have familiarity with building things. You can learn the environmental angle with a few courses on biology and ecology at UC Berkeley Extension—for which we would both provide the time and pay tuition. But none of that's why we selected you. Cynthia Hammond at Mannheim said you don't back down. Not ever."

"And is stubbornness a job requirement?" Dani asked.

"Our work will be the toughest fight of your life."

"You make that sound like a challenge."

"So come interview with us."

"Where and when?"

———

Norman Wall had lost track of Dani after she was fired from her job at the engineering company. He tried calling her apartment in Berkeley, but Dawson would only say that she had gone and he didn't know where. So Norman waited and fretted, holding to the belief that she would contact him and renew their friendship when she was ready.

A couple of weeks after that, she called his home phone.

"My goodness, gal!" he said in relief. "Where've you been?"

"Oh, out and about. It's a long story."

"But you're safe now? No trouble?"

"Yeah, and I think I have a job."

"Tell me about it. Everything."

Dani explained she had interviewed with an environmental services company that was going to be employing only women—for tax and contracting purposes. They would be evaluating development projects in the Bay Area and assessing the environmental impacts. The partners expected a lot of pushback from developers and land owners, so it was going to be a tough job.

"But you're up to it," he suggested.

"Oh, yeah. I'm the original roughneck."

"So … where are you living? Not with Dawson."

"Not anymore. I'm at the Berkeley YWCA now."

"There's a guest bedroom here, you know."

"What would Molly say to that?"

"Not much. I'm divorcing her."

"Hey, hey! Isn't *that* about time!"

"I got tired of being her doormat."

"Good. And where is the girl now?"
"Staying at her studio. Making ends meet."
"About that room. You know I can pay you now."
"Are you still carrying that hellacious debt load?"
"Probably until the day I die." And she sighed.
"Then your rent's negotiable," he said.
"Fair enough. I live lightly these days."

**Spring 1976**

# 1. Meeting an Old Friend

ON AN AFTERNOON in early April, Jane Wheelock stood on the floating dock of the Lakeshore Yard with two of her senior distributors. The three of them were staring into the mist that filled the narrow inlet extending inland from Lake Ontario.

It was cold on the dock. Even though the mist might almost classify as rain, the trees around the inlet still had patches of crusty snow under them. Jane shivered inside her winter coat. She knew that in another minute the man who owned the yard, Bill Gibbs, was going to come out of his nice, warm office and ask what they were doing.

"There she is," Scott said at her right elbow. He pointed to a form that was barely visible, the suggestion of a curved white bow and long aluminum bowsprit coming out of the gray mist.

"Gotta be ours," David said on her other side. Jane had been given the New York registration of the boat as backup confirmation, but the mist was still too heavy and the license numbers on the hull's side were too far away to be sure.

And yet, who else would be coming in to this particular creek along the lake's southern shore at this particular time?

"Not a good day for boating, is it?" said a voice behind her. That would be Gibbs, arriving on the dock at just the wrong time.

Jane turned, knowing that he would probably recognize her. Well, let him. He had no proof of anything.

"We're just meeting an old friend," she told Gibbs.

"Aye-*yuh*," he said, nodding as if he believed that.

As the length of the hull became clear, Jane saw that the sails were down, flopped over, and folded on the foredeck and cabintop, rather than neatly furled along the jib stay and the boom. She also heard the quiet mutter of a small engine. All of this suggested the boat was not going to stop at the dock for long.

When the sailboat got within twenty feet of them, a man came out of the cabin, went up to the foredeck, and pulled a length of rope from under the jib. When the boat was ten feet away, he held out the rope's free end and shook it for someone to take hold. Jane nudged Scott, and he leaned out to catch it. David moved down the dock to take the line from the man who operated the tiller at the stern. Just before the hull touched the padded rubrail along the edge of the dock, the man at the stern cut the engine.

As soon as the boat was held close against the dock, a woman emerged from the cabin. She wore a heavy coat, like Jane's. She was clearly Asian, with dark eyes and black hair. Unlike most Asian women of Jane's experience, however, this one had her hair permed into ringlets instead of wearing it straight. The woman brought out two suitcases, leaned over the rail and set them on the dock. She went below, came up with two more, went back, and brought out a fifth. Significantly, the two men running the boat did not offer to help. They didn't even bother to look at her.

The suitcases were expensive models, black canvas with black leather piping. They even had personal name tags— which Jane saw at a glance were blank.

When the woman had put the last case on the dock, she disappeared into the cabin and did not return.

The man at the stern started the engine and gestured for David to give back his end of the rope. The man at the bow took the rope from Scott, then stepped off onto the dock long enough to give the hull a hard push out into the stream. As the bow cleared the dock, the man grabbed a stay and climbed back aboard.

"Isn't your friend coming ashore?" Gibbs asked.

"No," Jane said. "It's a good day for a sail, after all."

"But what about her luggage?" he asked.

"She doesn't need it just to go boating."

"Okay … so it's none of my business."

"Unless you're charging a docking fee."

"Are your guests planning on staying overnight?"
Jane just looked at the man, willing him to disappear.
"Then I guess not," Gibbs said and turned away.

# 2. Saving the Least of These

JULIANA BONNER WAS becoming concerned about her newest partner at Bay Environmental Services. Dani Wheelock was a pleasant enough person and apparently a competent engineer, but she could be a little dense sometimes, a little obvious—or oblivious. Bonner herself was none of these things, having a background in law and a specialty in courtroom tactics, which she viewed as part mathematical chess, part advanced street fighting.

But it was Wheelock's basic niceness and her engineering skills that had charmed Bonner's other partners, Melissa Wade and Catherine Perkins. They had wanted Wheelock as their fourth partner, and the position of vice president went with it. That made BES a firm with more generals than soldiers, but it was the nature of small, specialty consultancies to be top-heavy with committed players. Bonner had not been sure about Wheelock at the time, but she went along with the other two as a courtesy, in order to make the vote unanimous. She had always hoped Dani Wheelock would grow into the job. Now, she wasn't even sure of that.

"Look, Dani ..." Bonner said, bringing Wheelock's draft assessment over to the young woman's desk. "Our clients are environmentalists. They oppose ongoing work on the California Water Project and its supporters on solid environmental grounds. But since the various dam, canal, and pumping stations were all approved in legislative acts and public bond measures, we have to think outside the box. That's where the recent Endangered Species Act comes in. We want to identify species that will be harmed by draining water from Northern California and sending it south."

"I thought that's what I did," Wheelock said. "I've studied historic patterns of waterfowl migration and the annual salmon run, but nothing significant shows up with the past construction projects. The Bay Delta is mostly farmland now, on diked islands resembling the Dutch polders. Their largest populations of wild animals seem to be rats and the occasional horned lizard. And nothing the State Water Project does will change that. I'm afraid the tule elk, beaver, and other aboriginal species left the area long ago."

"You're not looking at this thing the right way," Bonner said.

"How so?" the other replied. "What am I doing wrong?"

Bonner took a breath. "It's not the impact on the ecology as a whole, or the parts of it that the public knows and cares about, that will win us—or win our clients in the Sierra Club and Friends of the Earth—an injunction against further development. The point is not that the environment as a whole is being endangered, although it is. What we need is a vulnerable species, some plant or animal that is found nowhere else that will go extinct if we keep taking water out of the ecosystem."

"You mean, like a fish?"

"That's a place to start."

"But there's plenty of fishing in the Delta. It's one of the most popular recreation areas—"

"Dani!" Bonner exploded. "Listen to yourself."

The young woman sat back in her chair.

"Stop thinking popular! Stop thinking of game fish and beavers! Start thinking of some uniquely adapted insect or frog or something that can't live anywhere else. I'd even accept a specialized rodent that burrows in the levies, so long as a lowered water level makes its life harder."

"Are we saving rats now?"

"Not the point. We're saving the environment. We're protecting the basic nature of the Delta and its waterways—such as they are, after a hundred and thirty years of human intrusion—against what taking more water out of the system will bring. Less fresh water flowing into and through the Delta allows salt water from the ocean to come further upstream. And the pollution from upstream will settle out and silt up, rather than passing out to sea. The nature of whatever animal or fish—or plant—doesn't so much matter. The law has given us a lever. It's our duty to find out where it hinges and to pull it."

"Well ..." Wheelock paused and chewed her lip, thinking. "Well, if we're talking about minute effects, small-scale damages ..."

"Think of canaries in the coal mine," Bonner suggested.

"Then coming at the problem from that end—rather than finding an obvious, publicly acknowledged effect—will require a massive population survey," Wheelock said. "We'd have to catalog every plant and fish in an area of eleven hundred square miles."

"So? The place is a California landmark. It has been thoroughly studied. You just have to go to the library, find the reports and monographs, and cross reference the species with other wetlands to find the ones that don't exist anywhere else."

"Gee," she said. "That will take ... months."

"Yes, dear. But I'm afraid that's the job."

"Then I guess I'd better get cracking.

———

After getting chewed out by her senior partner, Dani Wheelock needed to absent herself from the Bay Environmental Services office on Mission Street. She walked across Market Street to the Mechanics' Institute Library and Chess Room on Post Street. She had bought a membership there as soon as her finances stabilized after rising to her current position with the environmental group. Dani still owed a whopping debt to the two marine architects and the bank that had financed it, but she was paying that burden down steadily and felt she could afford a few of the city's luxuries, like a membership in one of its oldest establishments.

The Mechanics' Institute had a pretty good technical library, too. So Dani figured it would be a good place to start her deeper search for the obscure fauna and flora of the San Francisco Bay Delta. Because the institute was founded in 1854 as a service to young men heading off to the California gold fields, she thought its library might specialize in the inland area and its features, describing everything that a young person transplanted from the East Coast might hope to learn about this new land. At least the trip got her out of the office and from under the disapproving stare of Juliana Bonner.

She spent the afternoon reading from the Thompson & West series on Solano and San Joaquin counties, which encompassed about two-thirds of the Delta—everything but the southern fringes in Contra Costa County. She discovered that the historical series, published in the 1880s, was mostly an illustrated book of the farms and houses belonging to rich subscribers, with occasional snippets of county history added for color. But the content was interesting and gave her a sense of the place in an older time, even if it did not help her biological search at all.

At five o'clock, Dani walked to the cable car turnaround on Powell Street and took the Hyde Street line up to the house on Russian Hill where she had a small apartment. The rent on that place was another reason her debt was getting paid off steadily but not as quickly as her current salary would suggest. She unlocked the door, dropped her coat and purse on the end of the sofa, and went into the kitchen to see what she could make for her dinner.

Dani's refrigerator was depressingly neat. She had it well organized, according to her nature, with cold cuts and packaged meats in one cooler bin; bagged vegetables including carrots and green beans in the crisper; opened jars of condiments including sweet pickle relish and black olives on one shelf; milk, yogurt, butter, and cheeses on another. Everything was lined up in its place, oldest in front, newest in back, with an inch margin of space between items. Everything was tightly sealed, so that it might not spread or absorb flavors. Her refrigerator had none of the clutter that accumulated when two people shared a kitchen. It had no leftovers and no mystery packages wrapped loosely in foil. It was the refrigerator of a neat old maid.

As she considered turning a package of hamburger—well, half a package—into a poor man's chili with cans of pinto beans and tomato paste from the pantry, half an onion from the bin under the counter, and paprika from the spice rack, Dani remembered the dinners she would cook with Norman Wall at the little house they had rented in South Park. The food then wasn't much different from what she was making now—in fact, Norman had really liked her fake chili. But their dinners had the savor of being shared.

That was something she missed. Not the passion, the kisses, and the frantic couplings she had experienced with Dawson Powers—along with his snarls and bursts of temper. But the simple togetherness, the quiet companionship, she felt when she was with Norman.

He still had the house in the Oakland Hills. He had acquired another dog—a Newfoundland named "Boots" from a rescue shelter, who could follow but never replace Norman's beloved Bear. When Dani had been renting a room from him, they had taken turns walking the new dog in the morning and evening, and sometimes took him out together. Dani missed having a dog around, too.

When the saucepan of chili was almost ready, and seasoned to her taste and nobody else's, Dani thought about going whole hog, dicing up a tomato, grating some cheese, slicing lettuce from the crisper bin, and opening a package of store-bought corn tortillas to make herself a mess of tacos. But that was really more like party food, something you enjoyed dipping, spreading, folding, and trying to eat without spilling on yourself while you talked and joked with somebody else.

Instead, she carried the pan and a fork to her breakfast nook, set it on a potholder so as not to scar the tabletop, and started eating. After a moment, she got up and took a beer from the refrigerator and remembered to take down a napkin for herself.

It was just different, eating alone. Like an old maid.

# 3. Person of Interest

CASSANDRA PETRICK SAT brooding in her cubicle at 850 Bryant, the San Francisco Police Department headquarters in the Hall of Justice. Once again, she was being tasked with putting on a persona and going undercover, but that was not the problem. The issue was her being asked to return to a venue—at least metaphorically, not the place, but the target—that she had left years ago and to presume upon an acquaintance that, for tactical reasons, had never risen to the level of friendship. Quite the opposite, in fact. The situation made Petrick feel vulnerable. It offered the possibility of her exposure—but not in any productive way. In her view, there was zero possibility of an arrest, either by her own Narcotics and Vice Division or by the Federal Bureau of Investigation itself, and lots of possibility for a screwup that would flash over onto her career.

She held up and rescanned the memo that had come through that morning. It appeared that the newly established Drug Enforcement Administration, with which the FBI was pledged to cooperate, had been tracking a former South Vietnamese national, now on the run from the new Communist government, named Phan Van Khiem. "Phan" was one of the more common Vietnamese surnames, which Petrick knew because of the recent influx of immigrants into the Bay Area. And "Khiem" was a popular boy's name. But no matter, the DEA wanted their man.

They had a report, now four years old, from the State Department about a Phan Van Khiem visiting Riyadh in Saudi Arabia. A young second attaché in the U.S. embassy had noted that this Phan—*the* Phan, *a* Phan, whatever—had met with a young American woman in al-Ha'ir Prison, where she was being held by the kingdom on charges of fraud and embezzlement. Shortly after Phan's visit, and for reasons unknown to State, the woman had been released without further explanation. Her name was Danielle Wheelock.

So it took the DEA—or the agents assigned to it from various federal departments—four years to read their mail, did it? Or maybe it just took them that long to cross-reference the name of their person of interest with the name in a report that Petrick had filed for the Bureau two years earlier—at this point, six years ago—concerning negative findings about one of the residents of Nirvana House in the Haight District. But now, they wanted to know, could Detective Petrick please re-establish contact with this Wheelock woman and find out what connection she had with the Phan Van Khiem who flew to Riyadh on her behalf? And also, was it the same man?

Cassandra Petrick certainly remembered Dani Wheelock: young, pretty, privileged, impressionable, innocent ... and stupid. Petrick had hated her on sight, but still she found nothing on her. And the Division's files had shown that Dani's mother, Jane Wheelock, left the drug business some years earlier, well before the Controlled Substances Act of 1970 consolidated federal policy on narcotics, if not before the statute of limitations kicked in on any particular state or federal law regarding importation and distribution.

Petrick would stand by her judgment back then, that Dani wasn't involved in any drug conspiracy. And she wasn't likely, in the two years since then, to have become a drug kingpin in the same league as this Phan character. But a simple reply, that Petrick personally didn't believe in the connection, wasn't going to pass muster with the DEA, or with their connections inside the Bureau. When tasked, one was supposed to put on a polite smile and comply.

It wouldn't be hard to track down Danielle Wheelock. The charges against her in Saudi Arabia would be one starting point. And then again, when Wheelock had lived on Haight Street she was an educated person, an engineer just hired on with one of the world's biggest construction firms, Mannheim. That would be another starting point. And in between, Petrick knew, people like Wheelock would leave a trail of professional assignments and registrations that a monkey could follow through the public databases. It would be the work of a morning to find and contact her target.

Petrick just didn't know if there would be a payoff, other than a smidge of professional courtesy between government departments—at the risk of a really embarrassing blowback.

———

Dani studied the woman sitting on the other side of her desk, who had invited herself for a visit that morning. Cassie Petrick looked older than she had when Dani knew her at the house on Haight Street, older than the passage of just six years would suggest. She had a streak of gray in her hair that had not been there before, but it could have been covered by hair coloring then, or it might be a modish fashion statement now. The skin around her eyes and mouth betrayed tiny lines that might have been caused by too much play in the sun, or they could have been covered with makeup—persistent and careful use of moisturizers and foundation—back then.

But the most disturbing thing was how friendly the woman was being. The Cassie Petrick who had haunted Nirvana House like an avenging spirit of rules and regulations had not been at all friendly. Quite the opposite, in fact. She had persecuted Dani from day one. But now everything was sweetness and light. Huh!

"What do you hear from the old gang?" Petrick asked. "Any juicy gossip? Any love stories?"

"I don't know," Dani replied. "I was only there for a couple of months."

"You were pretty thick with that accountant fellow. Norman Wall?"

"Well, yes. Norman and I have kept in touch over the years."

"And you've been pretty busy yourself, haven't you? Wrangling icebergs for the Saudis, wasn't it? I heard a story about that not ending so well. You were in jail in Riyadh for a time, weren't you? Fraud and embezzlement—or so I heard."

"How did you hear about that?" Dani asked.

"Oh, I still have friends from the house."

"Yeah, I guess bad news travels."

"How did you ever get out?"

The woman was leaning forward now. Her mouth was shaped in a smile, which seemed to make the Saudi experience out to be some fantastic joke. But her eyes were too bright, too focused, too probing. And that put Dani on her guard.

"Well, first of all," Dani said, "it was just a mistake. I had a business partner who, it turned out, wasn't at all on the level—although I knew nothing about that at the time—and he took the money."

"Of course it wasn't your fault. But how did you get the Saudis to release you?"

*Caution,* Dani told herself. "The iceberg project and its aftermath were some sort of wrangle within the royal family. One of their business contacts ... someone in the oil business from Southeast Asia, I think ... was brought in as a kind of mediator. I guess he made the ... feuding parties ... see reason. I was let go soon afterward."

"Really?" Petrick said, apparently surprised. "Someone who buys their oil has that much sway with the royal family? I would have thought it was the other way around."

"Believe me, business is really strange over there."

"I guess so." Petrick uncrossed and recrossed her legs. "So, how's old Norman?"

"Same as ever ... really the same. He doesn't seem to change." Dani thought about telling her about Norman's unfortunate marriage to the artist Molly, but that wasn't her story to tell. Not to this woman.

"Well." Petrick sat up straighter, suggesting the visit—or maybe it was more like an interview—was now over. "It's been fun catching up. We should do this again soon."

"Sure," Dani said without enthusiasm.

After the woman had left, Dani thought for two minutes. Then she put in a call to Norman in his office at Levi Strauss.

"Hey, Dani!" he said happily. "What do you need?"

"I just had the strangest visit from you'll never guess who."

"You know I'm not good with these games. Who was it?"

"Cassie Petrick. Remember her from Nirvana House?

"Oh, that place on Haight Street, where we met?"

"The same place. And the same woman. ... Well, she asked about my time in Saudi Arabia. She seemed to know all about it, too. And I was wondering ... You didn't tell anyone from the old house about my being in jail there, did you?"

"No, why would I? I figure that's your business and nobody else's."

"Yes ... thank you. It's just strange. She seemed really interested."

"Cassie was always a snoop. You remember how she acted then."

"Right. Royal bitch, as I remember. Well, thank you anyway."

And after she hung up with Norman, Dani sat at her desk, staring into space. The whole visit, the interview, smelled wrong. It was off balance. Faux friendly. And too pointed. But toward what ...?

Then Dani remembered the rumors that had been swirling around Nirvana House that summer. People were talking about a mole, a narc, an agent from the police who was supposedly there to sniff out drug trafficking. For a time, people said it had to be Norman, because he was so square and squeaky clean. But what if the agent was someone less conspicuous—or else, so conspicuous and ridiculous that no one would think she was an undercover cop?

And now, all these years later, Cassie Petrick had come looking for Dani and the one thing she wanted to talk about was her experience in the Riyadh prison. Which had been Dani's one brush, distant and second hand, with somebody in the heroin business who was *not* her mother.

Yes, the whole thing smelled.

———

Jane Wheelock was awakened by the phone ringing at ten-thirty in the morning, after she had pulled the late shift at the

Third Base downtown. It took her three rings to rouse, two more to come fully awake, two more just to locate the phone under a pillow, and another two rings to hope that whoever was calling would finally give up. Then she picked up the receiver. "Hello—and this better be good!"

"Mother? It's me, Dani, calling from San Francisco."

"Do you know what the hell time it is?" Jane asked.

"Three hours later than here. I thought you'd be up."

"You know I work nights. ... What's so important?"

"Someone from that place you sent me to when I first came out here, Nirvana House, showed up in my office yesterday. She was making all fake nice and asking about my time in Saudi Arabia—which she had no reason to know anything about, because it happened long after I left Haight Street. She wanted to know how I got out of jail."

"What was this woman's name?" Jane asked.

"Cassandra Petrick—and she is *not* a nice person."

The name rang no bells. "What exactly did you tell her?"

"I told her about Mister Khiem."

" 'Phan,' dear. That's his family name."

"Okay, but *he* told me to call him 'Khiem.' "

"Then he was being polite—or possibly devious. Anyway, what did you tell this Petrick woman about him?"

"Nothing real. Not his actual name, and not who he really was. If she has records, she could check out my story. But I said he was someone in the oil business, a customer from South Vietnam, who helped get me released as a favor to the royal family. I kept it all vague."

"Why would she have records?" Jane asked.

"Because she knew too much. And because Khiem—Phan—told me he represented the drug cartel, the people you used to work for, and that he was paying back a favor, because you helped finger Eric Bell for them. And ... because I think Cassie Petrick is a narc."

"Why would you think that?"

"Because everyone at Nirvana House said there was a narc on the premises but nobody knew who it was. And then Petrick comes calling, and the one connection in all of this is your drug cartel. Two plus two, Mother."

"That sounds like a long and involved chain of reasoning," Jane said. "Not at all simple."

"Please tell me you're clean. Tell me I don't have to worry."

Jane pressed her lips together. She wanted to do just that. But this was her daughter.

"Okay, so what are you dealing?" Dani asked finally. "Not that it matters."

Jane gave up, but just enough. "Only some heroin, and a little cocaine, to the college crowd, in town. Not that it's any of your business."

"It is my business if the Feds are asking."

"You are assuming this woman is a Fed."

"Jesus, Mother! This isn't the Sixties anymore. The whole country's getting serious about drugs now. They've got an entire federal agency dedicated to hunting down drug dealers."

"I know that, dear. But nobody cares about a little college town out in the sticks."

"All right. I'll let it go. But I'm on somebody's radar, and it has to do with your favor paid off in Saudi Arabia. I thought you would want to know."

"I appreciate the thought, dear. Now just forget about it."

———

After her visit to Danielle Wheelock's office, Cassandra Petrick took time to consider before filing her meeting report with the Division, which would also be an answer to the Drug Enforcement Administration's request for identification of this Phan Van Khiem.

On the one hand, Dani Wheelock appeared to know nothing about any drug connection. She believed Phan—her Phan, the person she met in Riyadh—was an oil buyer from South Vietnam. In 1972, that would have made him one of the last functioning businessmen in Saigon under the corrupt regime of Nguyen Van Thieu, before America pulled out and the regime collapsed. And *that* would have made this Phan a probable agent of the U.S. government, or certainly someone operating with its knowledge and authority. The DEA or the State Department could trace that connection in a heartbeat. So it would appear that Dani Wheelock was either lying or misinformed. Or perhaps she was simply as uniformed as anyone else. Petrick would bet on the latter possibility.

On the other hand, if Phan wasn't an oil buyer, then it was possible he was the person the agents at DEA thought he was: a member of the South Vietnamese cartel, which after the fall of that country to the Communists had switched its base of operations to points further west across the Indochina Peninsula. Or perhaps they were tracking someone else entirely.

At any rate, Petrick had done her job, made the contact, and gotten her informant's story. What it might mean and where it might lead was up to the people who had made the request in the first place.

# 4. Turning in the Wind

JULIANA BONNER RECEIVED a package in the mail that included a three-page proposal to place a series of windmills in the Altamont Pass and a request for proposals issued by Alameda County to conduct an environmental and engineering study of the proposal and the wind resource of the surrounding area.

She was intrigued. It took her less than ten minutes to read over and absorb the proposal, which was prepared by a group called "Altamont Wind Ventures." Basically, they wanted to place twenty-four Darrieus-type, vertical-axis wind turbines—which in the sketches looked like a much-simplified eggbeater—at or near the summit of the pass. Each unit would have a vertical shaft of twenty meters, or about sixty-five feet, and a blade diameter at its widest point of fifteen meters, or about fifty feet. At a rated twenty-five percent efficiency, and with steady winds, each unit was capable of producing an output of nineteen kilowatts, or about fourteen thousand kilowatt-hours per month, give or take. The document claimed that one unit would be able to supply ten average homes in the area with two kilowatts of power apiece on a continuous basis.

"So long as the wind is blowing," Bonner muttered to herself.

Then she wondered where this Altamont Pass was supposed to be.

Bonner took the package of documents with her into the small room that served Bay Environmental Services as a reference library. She pulled out the world atlas and turned to the page showing California with both political boundaries, including county lines, and elevation contours, depicted as colors ranging from deep green to dark brown. She searched the East Bay within the limits of Alameda County and found the pass—part of the Diablo Range—between the towns of Livermore and Tracy. It didn't look like much compared to the mountains of the Sierra Nevada Range farther to the east.

Next, she reviewed the county's request for proposals. They wanted a complete review, not only of the project but also potential effects and the prospects for further development of wind energy in the pass. They specified a meteorological study showing daily, monthly, and yearly average wind speeds and directions. And they wanted an analysis of adverse effects under such topics as—but not limited to—bird migrations and radio and television communications.

It all looked like something Bay Environmental Services could do. And Bonner knew just the person to give it to. Dani Wheelock was not just an engineer, but she had previous experience—or so her résumé stated—with nuclear energy.

This job should be right up her ally.

————

For a couple of days after her daughter's call, Jane Wheelock chewed over its meaning. If someone from Nirvana House came asking Dani about her release from the Saudi jail, and Phan Van Khiem's name or nationality—or even a whisper of him—had come into the conversation, then Jane had no doubt that this Cassie Petrick woman was a federal agent. That was bad enough. It meant they knew the Southeast Asian cartel was involved with Dani, which meant they knew about Jane's connection with the cartel—or at least they knew some of the story.

Phan had told Dani a half-truth when he said he was repaying Jane a favor for eliminating Eric Bell. That act had simply kept Jane on the plus side of the column, but it wouldn't have bought her any favors later on. No, when she called her old bosses in the business, the price of their support had been her help in establishing them in the relatively virgin territory of Upstate New York.

And Jane had been telling a half-truth when she said she was dealing a little heroin and cocaine on campus. It had started that way, with covert sales to knowledgeable buyers out the back door of the Third Base after hours. But in the year and a half since Jane renewed her deal with the devil, the volume of her business had grown. By now, she was managing a distribution network that encompassed much more than the University of Lake Ontario and the college town of Byzantium. It stretched from Rochester to Syracuse and employed half-a-dozen mid-level distributors and hundreds of local runners and sellers.

Jane had never been busted, not even back in the days when she was riding with Eric Bell. But if the Feds had a link between her and the cartel—this Phan Van Khiem—then it was only a matter of time before they started rolling up the supply chain, either from its source in Southeast Asia or the transshipment point in Vancouver. Or they might come directly to Jane's end in Byzantium.

If she were arrested and prosecuted, Jane would probably serve the rest of her life in prison. If she testified against the cartel under a plea deal, then she would either die quickly in prison or wither away in witness protection. But if she disappeared now, silently cashed out and bought a new life with the stash she had been quietly putting aside, there was a chance to live normally. She would be looking over her shoulder wherever she went, but at least she would be gone from this mess. And then maybe, in ten or fifteen years, she could find her daughter again. She had done that before.

And after all, what was holding her in this place? Her husband, William Henry? She had come back to him when she was on the run the last time, and it had not exactly worked out. It was three years since Jane had seen him last, six months since she had any word of him at all. He was never coming back from his fling with the Welsh woman. And it was not as if Jane herself hadn't skipped out on him before. William Henry was durable and everlasting, a constant. When she needed him—if she ever needed him again—Jane knew she could find him and win him away from the witch woman, or from whatever other fantasy he was pursuing. So William Henry was not a factor in her decision.

All she had to do was gauge the wind that was coming, sense its mood and changes, and make up her mind to go.

———

Dani was reading through the proposal by Altamont Wind Ventures. She read it with interest, because wind energy was a technology that she felt sure was underutilized in the country's generating mix. She knew it was actually an old technology: Europeans had been using windmills to grind their flour and pump their water for centuries, and the Dutch had used wind power to drain tidelands that they had surrounded with dikes and reclaimed for farmland. So she was enthusiastic about the project until she came to the last page, with the names of the partners in the project.

"Damn!" she said. And again, "Damnation!"

There on the page, bold as a fart at the opera, was the name of Hugo N. Wichard. Even after four years, just seeing his name made the hairs on the back of her neck stand up.

Without pausing to think, she gathered up the document package and marched into Juliana Bonner's office. Her senior partner was on the phone when she entered, so Dani had time to stand and fume and mutter to herself. Finally, Bonner hung up and nodded for Dani to speak.

"Did you see who's behind this wind project?"

"I saw their names. But nothing in particular—"

"Hugo Wichard is on their Board of Directors."

"And this man is …? Oh, yes, now I remember."

"We cannot do this project! It has to be a scam."

"You sure it's the same person?" Bonner asked.

"Who else could it be? Anyone else with that name would be hiding his head in shame after what Wichard did with the Arabs and their icebergs. This wind project is just another way for Wichard to take his partners and investors for some ungodly amount of money. And he will use our environmental report to help him do it. He will make fools of us. It will damage our reputation in the business."

"Well, be that as it may," Bonner said, "you will notice that we aren't actually being asked to contract with Altamont Wind Ventures. The request for proposals is from Alameda County. They are looking for an evaluation of the environmental impacts, nothing more."

"Good," Dani said. "Then let's cut short the bullshit and tell them it's a scam."

"That is not our business," Bonner replied. "We evaluate the proposal itself, the wind resource in the Altamont Pass, perhaps something about the proposed technology and how efficiently it harvests that resource, and how doing so will affect the environment. We're not studying the project's economic feasibility. And we're not asked to evaluate the project team and their intentions. Come on, Dani! This is a plum. A groundbreaking project to work on. And wind energy could become a big market for our services."

"All right," Dani said, holding the document against her chest. "But I can tell you this will turn out badly. We're going to regret having our name on this."

"Just do your job, please. And try to be dispassionate about it."

---

Norman Wall was having his usual Sunday brunch with Dani, this time at the Magic Pan in the reconstructed chocolate factory at Ghirardelli Square. He was having a pair of crêpes with diced ham and the Swiss cheese with a French name, *Gruyère*. She had ordered what looked to him like blintzes, or something with sweet cheese and no meat. As usual, they would split the bill when it came.

This particular morning Dani could talk about nothing except her situation at work. It seemed that her boss—actually, "senior partner"—had taken on a project that was backed by the infamous Hugo Wichard, and the woman had assigned it to Dani without even thinking. Dani had tried to tell her what a danger the man posed, both to herself and the firm, but Juliana Bonner had been adamant.

"It's as if I had this irrational fear of the man," Dani was saying, now for the second or third time, "and she wanted me to face him and get over it."

"She doesn't understand the problem," Norman said.

"She doesn't believe how dangerous Wichard really is."

"Uh-huh," Norman said around a mouthful of food.

He really didn't want to get into this discussion.

If anybody in Dani's life understood her frustration—and the anger, despair, and alarm bells that were now going off inside her head—it was Norman. He had been the first person she called from the Saudi jail, after she figured out that the U.S. embassy wasn't going to be any help. He had met her plane when she flew back to the States in tatters. And more, he had spent those months before the downfall watching Dani put her entire career in this man Wichard's hands and then seen him toss her aside like a gum wrapper. But there was nothing Norman could do to change her situation. He could only listen, nod, and occasionally—sparingly, in this case—agree with her.

He wished there was more he could do. It was a continual heartache for Norman that he could not protect her, could not strap on shiny armor and slay her dragons, challenge Wichard to a duel or a fistfight, just make things all right.

Norman had loved this young woman from afar from the first time they met. And then—to a wonder—they had become housemates, although that was more like a brother and sister or first cousins sharing communal space and cooking chores, but sleeping in separate bedrooms and trading access to the apartment's one bathroom. Then, after she came back from her overseas adventure, they had been married to—or in her case, involved with—other people. And finally, they had briefly—only as an emergency measure—been housemates again, but living as landlord and tenant in his house, not even sharing. Now they were friends who saw each other once or twice a month.

These brunches, or the occasional dinner and a movie, were more like two acquaintances getting together for old times than actual dates. They talked and joked. They barely touched, other than the accidental brush of hands. They had never gone so far as to share a kiss, not ever. But this was the best he could do, the most she would allow. And it was killing him inside. Still, he wouldn't have given up these moments of contact for the world, even if all she wanted to talk about was the men in her life—this poisonous Frenchman, the hapless motorcycle mechanic Dawson Powers, and others of her experience—and how they had hurt her.

Norman would never hurt Dani by thought, word, or deed.

But then, he would never get the chance to prove it.

———

Hugo Wichard received the letter from Bay Environmental Services at his motel room in Hayward, California. He was staying there because the town was geographically closer to the Altamont Pass than anywhere else inside the Bay Area, without being situated a dozen kilometers out in the middle of farmland and abject wilderness.

He looked at the front of the envelope, turned it over, and looked at the back. He didn't know the company, who they represented, or what they wanted. It was addressed to him in care of Altamont Wind Ventures at the motel's address. So he figured it was not some random solicitation—"junk mail" in the American vernacular. It wasn't a law firm or a creditor, either. So he might as well open it.

Inside he found a short letter informing him that Bay Environmental Services had been sent a request for proposals from Alameda County "to investigate the wind resources of the Altamont Pass area and any environmental effects" in relation to his group's proposal for installing "turbines of the vertical-axis type known as 'Darrieus.'" Because he was one of the venture partnership's directors, BES wanted to meet with him on the twenty-fifth of the month to "discuss details of the project."

It was all well and good, until he came to the letter's signature block. There the name "Danielle Wheelock" leapt out at him. He briefly wondered if it could be the same woman—but of course it was. How many female engineers in this part of the state of California would have that same name? Then he wondered what having Dani assigned to examine the project would mean for his group's chances of getting the project approved. It certainly wouldn't help.

He noticed that her name was typed under the closing but not signed in ink. Perhaps the letter had been typed by someone else, some secretary in a large organization, after Dani had somehow been assigned to the project but before she was actively involved. But no, even American businesses did not operate in such an impersonal fashion. She had to know. It was her letter. That meant she was expecting him. And she would certainly recognize his name and remember him.

The only remaining question was, would they meet alone? Or would the police be present? And would representatives from the Saudi Arabian consulate be far behind?

———

Dani had reluctantly agreed to meet with Hugo Wichard in his role as one of the directors and lead partner in Altamont Wind Ventures. She had consented to do so, not just because, in Juliana Bonner's words, it was her job but mainly because—as Juliana later told her, and more kindly—"for the sake of your soul. This is your story, Dani. It's been eating up and destroying you. So you need to put it to rest."

On a late April day, with the rain coming down in San Francisco, Hugo Wichard entered the Bay Environmental Services offices and their receptionist Janine showed him into the conference room Dani had reserved for their meeting.

The man was wearing an old black raincoat that was dripping wet. His long hair hung in strings from the back of his head. When he removed the coat and draped it over the back of a chair, she saw he was wearing khaki chinos, a blue Oxford-cloth shirt with knitted tie, and a rumpled tweed jacket. Gone was the pale tropical suit with shawl collar. Gone, too, was the man's personal aura of suave elegance. All through this performance of tending to his raincoat, he studied the ground or the chair or the coat itself and never once looked at her. Finally, he pulled out another chair and sat down to face her.

"Hello, Danielle. I did not think you would want to meet with me."

"I didn't. I don't. But it looks like I don't have a choice in the matter."

"I know you think I am *le diable*, the devil, for what happened to you."

"That would be putting it mildly. Your confidence game ruined my career."

He nodded slowly. "But you seem to have recovered." He waved a hand to indicate the well-appointed room, the offices, and the position of authority she now occupied.

"Only after much work," Dani said. "And meanwhile, you took—what? A hundred and ten million dollars." She paused and considered his clothing again. "I thought you would have more to show for it."

Wichard's eyes were down again, focused on the table. Then he looked up at her, directly into her eyes.

"I never took that money," he said. "I never got but a fraction of it. The iceberg project was not my idea. Not originally, at least, and not completely. It was the creation of Prince Ali bin Muhammad al-Kabir, one of the men you met in Riyadh. He invented the plan in order to take the money from the royal family."

"So … it was Prince Ali who went to Switzerland and withdrew the money from the Habib Bank?"

"No, I did that—but at his direction. All I received out of the deal was a one-half-of-one-percent handling fee, just over half a million dollars. Not much, in the greater scheme of things, for fronting the project and taking the blame."

"Oh, poor you!" Dani flared. "While I had to take the blame, get hunted down by Arab assassins, and go to prison. Not to mention my assuming the debt for the work we contracted— a debt I'm still paying off." That led her to another thought.

"I don't suppose any of that half a million is left to help out there?"

Wichard gave her a weak smile. "I'm sorry. There have been ... expenses."

"Of course. There always are." Then she relaxed. "So, tell me. What kind of scam is this windmill venture? Who are you fleecing this time? And who gets the boodle?"

"The boo—?"

"The money."

"This project is actually on the level, as you Americans would say. Or, in this case, it's a mountain pass." He gave her a weak smile, which she did not return. "There are investors, of course, but they are being very sparing with their money. As you can see from the documents we sent, they are not paying for the environmental statement. The county has asked for and will pay for that. I will not be touching any of the money under that contract."

"Well, *that*'s a good thing," Dani said.

"Does this mean we can work together?"

"In a pig's eye—as we Americans say."

# 5. Various Declarations

LATE AT NIGHT, after she had finished her shift at the Third Base, Jane Wheelock finally came to a decision. She pulled back the area rug that covered a set of floorboards in the bedroom of her apartment, in the space right beside her bed, where she would normally touch the floor for the last time at night and put her feet down first thing in the morning.

Most of the planks in the bedroom floor were a standard eight feet long, but in this particular space a series of fine cuts—made at first with a wood chisel, then a hand jigsaw, sanded smooth, flushed with a matching wood filler, and finished with varnish—interrupted the pattern. The cuts created a patch of staggered boards roughly four feet by four feet. Hence the rug.

Jane now knelt beside the patch and used a steel nail file to pry at one edge. When she had that edge started, she scooted around and worked on the opposite edge. With two minutes of prying, she was able to get her fingernails into the sides of the exposed seam and lift out the patch.

There, between the joists, were stacks of bills bundled with rubber bands. They were mostly hundreds, but with occasional fifties and twenties. Jane had sorted the bills herself and taken care to keep nothing smaller than the rare twenty. The money was totally untraceable. And it had better be, because it represented her private skim from the drug business she had been running for the Southeast Asian cartel. If they even suspected she had kept back this money, she would be a dead woman.

Jane had always known this day would come. The money before her was not riches she had kept back for herself out of greed. It was not intended to buy her a better lifestyle, a nicer apartment, a new car, or release from her nights tending bar. She might have lived well on her take, but she did not want to waste it—and anyway, working at the bar was her cover. No, this stash was getaway money, life savings in every sense of that phrase.

It had been a while since Jane had bothered to count it, but the last time she opened the floor and spread out the bundles, she had a bit more than $980,000. With recent additions, it was probably north of a cool million. Now she eyeballed the stacks themselves, their number and their height against the joists. If she had to pack it all for travel, it would fill two or three attaché cases, or a medium-sized suitcase. She picked up one of the larger bundles and felt its weight. Jane was no expert, but with it packed in a suitcase, she would probably be carrying forty or fifty pounds. It would be a handful to haul around, much more than a suitcase full of clothes or even shoes. More like a case full of books.

But that was what she had before her. No way was she going to ship that block of cash through the U.S. mail or a parcel service, let alone deposit it in a bank and take a cashier's check. She wasn't ever going to let it out of her sight—especially since she didn't know where she would eventually end up.

Luckily, Jane had taken out a passport when she first started working for the cartel. They had insisted, because it enabled her to travel internationally and mule their drugs, which was her first assignment on her own and not under Eric Bell's thumb. She had kept the passport up-to-date with renewals. She also had her New York driver's license. But she didn't plan to use either one to leave the country, only to establish herself in wherever the hell she was going.

Now, she just had to figure out some destination where the United States had no extradition treaty, the Drug Enforcement Administration had no authority, and the Southeast Asian cartel had no active presence. Oh, and somewhere she could live in relative comfort for the rest of her life on a million tax-free, untraceable dollars.

———

Juliana Bonner was sitting in her office, looking out the window at the traffic snarled on Mission Street in the rain, when she heard a soft knock on the doorframe. She turned to see Dani Wheelock standing there. The young woman was frowning deeply—almost a scowl—with her shoulders slumped. Her whole demeanor reminded Bonner of a guilty child who had done something wrong, or a petulant one who was not getting her way.

"What is it, Dani?"

"I met with Hugo Wichard, as you asked."

"And how did that go?"

"Not … well. I don't feel I can work with him."

"Why not? Other than your past association, which you need to put behind you."

"I just can't," Dani said, raising her hands. "The man makes my skin crawl. I can't be in the same room with him without wanting to throw up."

"But I've explained, you would be working with the county, not the partnership."

"I know, but … just knowing that he will benefit from my analysis makes me uneasy. And there will be times when we would have to confirm their data, go over their plans, ask for specifications—and then I would be working with the man directly. I just can't be fair in all this. But I do support the idea of wind energy, and I don't want my personal bias to stand in the way."

"I see," Bonner said. "So … what do you want me to do?"

"Assign the project to someone else. Another partner."

"We're a small shop, Dani. Everyone else is busy."

"I understand that. But I just … can't do this."

"All right. I'll have to see what I can do."

———

Norman Wall had given the situation a lot of thought. Eighteen months after his marriage had officially ended, and two years since Dani broke up with her live-in boyfriend, Dawson Powers, Norman had been seeing her on and off as a friend. They talked about their work, about the advantages of living in the City versus the East Bay, about politics and the environment. Not once did Dani talk about a new boyfriend or the other men

324 • Thomas T. Thomas

in her life—which meant she was either being uncharacteristically discreet, or she was actually living alone.

The question was, did this come about by choice or lack of opportunity? And was Norman going to do anything about it?

On a Saturday evening at the end of April, he made reservations at the Ben Jonson, an English-themed pub in The Cannery, which was a remodeled factory adjacent to Fisherman's Wharf. The restaurant was famous for its Beef Wellington and for its giant martinis, served in a two-handed goblet with a stick of pickled brussels sprouts for garnish.

According to their rule, he and Dani had just one drink each before dinner. In this case, they ordered a single martini and two little red cocktail straws. The straws brought their faces close together as they sipped.

"Dani …" he began, after they had ordered—prime rib for him, catch-of-the-day for her. "We've known each other how long?"

"Since the summer I came to San Francisco. That house on Haight Street."

"And I want you to know, in all that time, I've—"

———

Dani Wheelock touched Norman's hand on the big, frosted glass. "I know," she said. "I think I know what you're going to say."

"Then let me say it, please," he replied patiently. "I love you. I've always loved you, from the first day." He paused. "My marriage to Molly was a mistake. An infatuation. Maybe a rebound. But it's always been you, in my heart, and in my thoughts."

"Norman, I …"

But what *did* she feel?

Really, down in her heart?

Norman Wall was the best, most stable, most reliable, most understanding man she had ever known, after her father. When she reached out, Norman was always there. He never criticized her, never blamed her. He always offered her sound advice and encouragement. She even loved his dogs. And Heaven knew, they had lived together on and off over the years, although never as man and wife. More like brother and sister.

Was that enough? Was that *love?*

Dani didn't know. Certainly, she had experienced her own infatuations. Dawson was the prime example of appearance and style over substance. And look how that turned out.

Maybe life with a good and kind man was what love became after the fire and the passion, the secret intensity down in the loins, had all burned out. Maybe she could love a man like Dawson but not bear to live with him. So ... maybe she could live with a man like Norman and learn to love him, passionately, down in the loins.

Dani also knew that this was her moment of decision. If she refused Norman now, she would lose him forever, perhaps even as a friend.

So ... what was she going to do?

"Does you proposal come with a ring?" she asked.

For the first time, Norman looked flustered. "I, uh, didn't think—?"

"That you were proposing something serious? Well, you are. And I am if you are."

"Then yes, let's get married, together, death do us part, the whole thing." He paused. "Uh, what size ring do you wear?"

"The ring is optional. But size six and a half, if you want to surprise me."

———

The first week in May, with the sun shining and San Francisco heading into one of its two most temperate and summerlike months—the other being September, bracketing the cold and foggy days of what everyone else called "summer"—Juliana Bonner waited in the conference room at Bay Environmental Services. She was prepared to meet with the mystery man, this Hugo Wichard, the person with whom Dani Wheelock refused to do business. Because Bonner was taking over the windmill project herself, at least until they had actually won the contract with the county and could begin the grunt work, she wanted to see what they would be up against.

Right on time, Janine showed Wichard into the room.

He was tall, with straight shoulders and a slender waist. He wore a three-piece suit of fine black wool, lightweight for the season, with tiny white pinstripes. His shirt had a French collar held with a gold bar that supported the knot of a silk tie, yellow with tiny red flowers. His shoes, or what she could see of them, were highly polished lace-ups with square toes.

More important than his dress was the man's face. Bonner detected an Old World elegance in his long hair, prominent cheekbones, thin nose, and drooping lids over eyes of a startling and piercing blue. When he looked at her, she felt he was peering into her soul.

Wichard came around the end of the table to where she was sitting, took her hand, and bowed over it. "Madame!" he exclaimed, then looked into her eyes again and smiled.

"Mister Wichard," Bonner replied, hoping she had the pronunciation right.

He retreated to his side of the conference table and seated himself. His posture was relaxed, confident, and he sat with his shoulders at a slight angle, as if the chair itself and the table were immaterial, just props to his decision to sit.

Bonner hid her face in the folder before her, which held Alameda County's request for proposals and the project definition from Altamont Wind Ventures. It was an opportunity to collect herself.

"Well," she said after a moment. "I have some questions about your proposal."

"By all means," he replied. Wichard didn't seem bothered by Dani's absence.

"First of all, you plan to site just twenty-four of these windmills. And that, by your reckoning, would supply the power needs of less than two hundred and fifty homes. Hardly a dent in even a small town like Livermore. That's not much of a resource."

"Ah, but this is just the first stage. A test, if you will. The Altamont Pass area has much more wind to harvest, but we need to prove the technology first."

"And why did you choose this Darrieus turbine design?"

Those piercing eyes opened a bit wider. The man smiled.

"Because it offers to be the most stable, with the weight of the turbine at the bottom, at ground level, and the shaft and blades supported vertically. There is some question of efficiency—" He shrugged, as if that was not important. "—because the blades are curved and change their attack angle on the prevailing winds as they turn around. But we are satisfied enough with the design to use it in our first effort. Other designs may be tested later."

"I see," Bonner said. The room was getting warm. If it weren't for the potential intrusion of traffic noise from below, she was thinking of opening a window.

In all, she spent just over an hour with Hugo Wichard. At the end of their meeting, she was satisfied with the project details. And she trusted this man completely.

# 6. And Resolutions

DANI SPENT THE next three days after Norman's proposal trying to reach her mother to tell her the good news. She called the apartment at various times during the day when she thought Jane would be home and not sleeping. Each time, the phone rang and rang, eight, ten, twelve times. With each call, she figured her mother was just busy, or out, doing errands, or whatever. After all, Jane had a life.

On the fourth day, which came after the first of the month, Dani got a recorded message about the number having been disconnected. That shocked her. So she decided to call the bar where Jane worked, the Third Base, and talk to her there.

"Hello, Third Base," answered a young male voice.

"Hi, I'm trying to reach Jane Wheelock, your lead bartender?"

"Don't know her."

"Excuse me?"

"Sorry, I'm new here. I understand there was an older woman who worked the bar. I never met her. I don't know what happened to her."

"Well," Dani tried to absorb that. "Could you have the manager or the owner give me a call? I'm in San Francisco—" She read out her home and work numbers. "—and tell him he can reverse the charges."

"Okay ... sure."

"It's important."

"I will *tell* him."

A day later she got a call at work. Janine had to yell to her through the open office door that it was from New York, and the operator said it was collect. Dani replied, yelling back, that she would cover it.

"This is Jim Barnes, owner of the Third Base. My guy said you wanted me to call?"

"Yes, about my mother, Jane Wheelock. I've been trying to reach her, and—"

"Yeah, she quit. Or I think she did. She disappeared about a week ago."

"Just like that?" Dani asked. Something in her stomach turned over.

"Exactly. Signed out of her shift one night and never returned."

"Did she give any reason why? Or did she talk to anyone?"

"Not that I know. But ... one of my guys said some federal agents were in the day before, asking about drug dealing, or maybe about a drug ring. Now, you know, I don't allow that kind of stuff in my bar."

"Was one of them a female agent named Petrick?" Dani asked.

"No, my guy said two men, FBI or DEA, one of those agencies."

"I see." Dani wanted to hang up fast. "Thank you."

"Do you know anything about this?" Barnes demanded.

"Apparently, nothing at all." Dani had her finger over the phone's plunger.

"So ... you're her daughter. Next of kin? What do you want me to do about her last paycheck? It's short, because she didn't work the entire week. Still, it's something."

"Don't you want to hold it for her?"

"Look, lady. I'm not a banker."

"All right, mail it to me." She read him the address. "And if you hear from Jane, or anything about her, *please,* give me a call."

"Yeah, okay ... if I remember. People come and go in this business, you know?"

———

Norman Wall got out of work at five o'clock and went up to Dani's apartment on Russian Hill. He was helping her pack for the move to his house on Greenbank Avenue in Oakland. He let himself in with the key she had given him, but she was already home—which he did not expect. Normally, with her workload at Bay Environmental Services, Dani often stayed late, sometimes into the evening. Now she was sitting on the couch with her face in her hands.

"You're here," he said.

"Yeah, here for good."

"What do you mean?"

"Juliana just fired me."

"What? For *cause?*"

"She said," Dani began, wiping back tears, "because I refused to work with that creep Wichard, she could 'no longer trust me' to be part of important contracts. For that, and some other differences we've had in the past, she says I am 'not sympathetic to their program,' although I never said that. I never even implied it."

"But they can't fire you," Norman objected. "You are a partner. You have equity in the firm, don't you?"

"Equity?"

"A share in the investment. You're an owner."

"They helped me pay for my partnership by putting something aside each month. Juliana offered to buy me out by canceling that debt and reimbursing the amount they've already collected."

"Doesn't she need votes from the other partners to do that?"

"She has them, apparently. So … I'm gone from there."

"I'm sorry. It looked like a fit for you."

"I'm not sorry. It's kind of a relief."

"But you've been crying," he said.

"That's from … Oh, anger, embarrassment, frustration—not from sadness."

"Are you telling me you weren't happy there?"

"I haven't been happy, really *happy,* since I was designing those ice barges."

"That didn't work out so well, did it?"

"At least I was building something. I was making something worthwhile—that I *thought* was worthwhile. I was making my mark. I was creating. I'm not an environmental advocate or a technical editor. Those are just jobs. I am an *engineer*."

"So? You're all of, what, twenty-eight now? Hardly washed up."

"But getting another engineering position with my history—"

"Oh, Dani! *Screw* history! You've got brains and talent. You've got the degree and the registrations. So find a place that's doing the things you really need to do and convince them to hire you. They won't come to you—not like Wichard or Bonner did. You have to go out and go after the thing you want."

"Well ..."

"Come on. Go take a hot shower. Put on your best dress. We'll go to dinner and start strategizing your next move."

"Well, if you really ..."

"Just go. We'll do this."

**June 1976**

# 1. Hello!

Two weeks after Dani moved into the house in Oakland, she and Norman were still living "chastely." His word. They had made their wedding plans for a small ceremony—probably in a judge's chambers—rather than a big church service with a grand reception. First, because neither of them was very religious. Second, because their families were far away and ... distant. Norman's father had died a few years ago, and his mother and new stepfather were now estranged from him.

Dani had called her own father at the resort on Lake Simcoe. After exchanging a few guarded pleasantries with the Welsh woman who owned the place, Morwenna Daffyd, she got William Henry on the line. He was greatly pleased to hear that Dani was getting married, wished her well, and promised to send a wedding present. No, he had not heard anything from Jane, who seemed to have pulled another of her disappearing acts. And yes, he would certainly get out to the West Coast, if not for the ceremony itself—because they were still finishing winter repairs to *Crwydro Gorffen,* which was Welsh for "Done Roving," as the hotel and spa was called—then for a visit later in the summer.

Their third reason for choosing a small ceremony was that the number of Dani's and Norman's close friends, even after all this time together, would be easier to seat in a neighborhood bar for a celebratory drink than fill a hotel ballroom.

But between them there still remained the issue of "compatibility." Her word. Yes, since Norman's declaration they had spent their evenings kissing and cuddling on the couch. They held hands when they went out walking or saw a movie. And his touches were always gentle and firm. But at night they parted at the bedroom door. His door. And each night she took to the double bed alone while he slept on the couch in the living room.

Dani wanted to know if those firm touches were backed up by anything stronger and more vigorous. And so she had put her foot down. She wanted a physical commitment, coupling—sex—before she made her existential vows and committed herself to him for life. She was sure of their love and affection on an intellectual and emotional level, but now she wanted proof in the flesh.

So this night was now "the night." Dani made her preparations alone in the master bathroom. She had bought a pretty camisole in red silk with satin ribbons to go along with a sheer bra and bikini panties. She had always heard that red was the color of men's desire, although Dawson never seemed to notice or express a preference.

Now she lay on her back on the bathroom rug and fitted her diaphragm and applied the spermicidal jelly. She wanted sex and commitment; the decision about children would come later.

When she was as much dressed as she was going to be, and ready, she opened the bathroom door.

Norman was lying on the bed, on top of the covers rather than under them. He was wearing a pair of green-striped flannel pajamas, the kind he always wore. She knew that because their relationship had extended to Saturday morning breakfasts together in their bathrobes. She recognized the pattern from the cuffs at his exposed shins and the collar above the robe's lapels at his throat. So he had taken no special care or extra effort there tonight.

He rose from the bed, came to her in the doorway, and took her hand. He pulled her close, right up against him, and kissed her on the lips. He led her back to the bed.

"How do you want to begin?" he asked.

"Gently but firmly," she replied.

———

When they had completed their lovemaking, Norman and Dani lay back on the pillows, with the bedclothes tangled around their waists, and their discarded nightclothes nowhere to be seen. Even though the moment was complete, he felt moved to say something.

"How was that?"

"Just wonderful!"

Norman remembered all the times that Molly had seemed satisfied with their physical relationship, and yet clearly she had felt he was an insufficient lover. So he had to ask.

"Did you—um—?"

"Come? Oh, yes!"

"Then you think we're 'compatible'?"

"Yes. But let's try it again—just to be sure."

# 2. And Goodbye

"WELL, HERE I am," Jane Wheelock said to herself as she stepped off the Greyhound bus at the station in Nogales, Arizona.

She was still carrying the red American Tourister suitcase, with the double locking latches and the key on a chain around her neck. It had been a pain to her—and a notable eccentricity to the other passengers—that she struggled up and down the bus's inside stairs and narrow aisles with the thing, paid a full-fare ticket to put it on the seat beside her rather than consign it to the cargo hold, and even carried it with her into the tiny washrooms. She had made this same effort aboard that bus and every other one she had taken in her roundabout journey across the country. But, knowing what the suitcase secretly carried, Jane would never leave it for a moment. Her other suitcase, containing her clothes, a few cosmetics, and some sentimental pictures and pieces of jewelry—that one could be checked as baggage.

Jane had come to Nogales because it was out of the way. It wasn't an important tourist crossing into Mexico. It wasn't on the smuggler routes into the United Sates, which currently went by sea into the Florida swamps—as she should know, being an expert in these things.

She carried her passport, her New York driver's license, and her Social Security card, if she should ever again need to prove her identity. But for now, she had no intention of showing these at the border and crossing legally into another country. She wanted no record of her ever having left the States.

The bus station was just off Interstate 19, a few blocks from the international border. She could walk the distance in five minutes, if she wanted to stay on the main roads.

Instead, after she had collected her other bag from the bus's hold, she took her bearings by the sun and started walking east. She used the city streets at first, although this area already felt more like suburbs, even this close to the center of town.

She passed one-story buildings dedicated to light commerce and warehousing, and then people's homes on winding streets further out. When she came to the last house, she sat down on the curb and traded her scuffed, flat-heeled pumps for a pair of hiking boots from her second suitcase.

Jane faced off into the hills and scrublands beyond the end of the road. It was a hot day in June with the sun beating down. She was weighted down with everything she owned in two heavy suitcases. But she figured she could make it, oh, five miles out into the desert, beyond the sight of any roads or buildings, before crossing the invisible line of the border, turning around and entering Nogales, Mexico, which by then would be somewhere to the west.

And after that ... she would see what came next.

# About the Author

THOMAS T. THOMAS is a writer with a career spanning forty years in book editing, technical writing, public relations, and popular fiction writing. Among his various careers, he has worked at a university press, a tradebook publisher, an engineering and construction company, a public utility, an oil refinery, a pharmaceutical company, and a supplier of biotechnology instruments and reagents. He published eight novels and collaborations in science fiction with Baen Books and is now working on more general and speculative fiction. When he's not working and writing, he may be out riding his motorcycle, practicing karate, or wargaming with friends. Catch up with him at www.thomastthomas.com. *(Photo by Robert L. Thomas)*

### Books by Thomas T. Thomas
The House at the Crossroads
ME, Too: Loose in the Network
Coming of Age, Volume 1: Eternal Life
Coming of Age, Volume 2: Endless Conflict
The Children of Possibility
The Professor's Mistress
The Judge's Daughter
Sunflowers
Trojan Horse
The Doomsday Effect (as by "Thomas Wren")
First Citizen
ME: A Novel of Self-Discovery
Crygender

**Books in Collaboration**
An Honorable Defense (with David Drake)
The Mask of Loki (with Roger Zelazny)
Flare (with Roger Zelazny)
Mars Plus (with Frederik Pohl)
Between the Sheets (with Kate Campbell)

**Excerpt from**
*The Professor's Mistress*

# 1. Putting Galatea to Bed

GEORGE AND MARIAN Kirkeby stood on the dock at the Lakeshore Yard, near Byzantium, New York, and watched their ship come in. The couple had driven up from Rochester for the annual ceremony of bedding her down for the winter while the paid crew, Captain Emmet Gallagher and First Mate-Engineer Andrej Haraszthy, brought the steam launch *Galatea* along Lake Ontario's southern shore, a trip of sixty miles from her summertime berthing in Irondequoit Bay.

"I still get a thrill seeing her from the land," George said. "We don't get this view of the grand old vessel—coming into dock like this—when we're already aboard and picking up our guests."

"Emmet's hung out all the bunting, I see," Marian remarked, pointing to the string of pennants flying on the forward stay, from the bowsprit to the top of the first mast, then all the way back to the second mast. "What do they say?"

"Spell it out, darling," he urged.

"You know I'm no good with signals."

"But you should recognize a few by now."

"Well, I see two of those blue-with-white-squares. Is that the 'blue peter'?"

"Yes, and that stands for …?"

"Peter … Papa, the letter P!"

"Speaking of blue peters, gosh, that wind is cold!"

"You came out here without your long johns, didn't you?"

"I didn't think wind off the lake in October would be so keen."

"A couple more days like this and we'll be seeing ice on the creek."

"Back to your spelling lesson."

"But *you* distracted *me!*"

"Two Ps together?"

"Well, I see just two flags before them," Marian went on. "The first one's white-and-red, so that's either Foxtrot or Hotel. And the second is white-and-blue, which I'm sure is Alfa. It can't be F-A-P-P-anything, so it must be 'happy.' "

"Very good, m'dear!"

"Now give me the rest."

"After that comes 'ending' and the numbers one-nine-five-two," he said. "Then 'golden,' 'summer,' and 'days' in 1953."

"What a lovely thought, George! Did you put him up to it?"

"I may have had a hand," he said modestly.

As *Galatea* came parallel with the dock, the first mate jumped ashore with a line while Captain Gallagher finished up his business in the wheelhouse. They each greeted the owners with a nod, then went off to confer with the yard manager, Mr. Gibbs.

As George and Marian stepped aboard, he carried the picnic basket that had been at their feet. They went down into the main cabin, where Haraszthy had already put dust covers over the furniture and cleaned out the galley. Further forward, Gallagher had blown down the boiler. Whatever else they might need to do in preparing engine and hull for winter storage could be done once the boat was drawn up on shore.

George retrieved a vacuum bottle from the basket. "May I pour you a libation, darling?"

"Of course. About time, too!"

He unscrewed the cap, which did double-duty as a plain metal cup, and filled it with a clear liquid. He offered the cup to her.

"No ice?" Marian said, taking it. "Mmm, cold!"

"Ice seemed redundant today," he replied.

"And why dilute the good stuff?"

"Sorry about the olives," he said. He tipped the container's mouth toward the light coming in the cabin windows. "They appear to be stuck at the bottom."

"I don't see why we bother with them anymore."

"It's traditional, darling," he said. "People would miss them."

"People don't miss the vermouth in your martinis—and what's your recipe now? One drop? Or is it two?"

"I tip the vermouth bottle ever so slightly toward the shaker, being careful not to spill any. Besides, you don't need any of that wormwood-flavored wine when you serve really good gin."

"Nobody's complained yet."

"Well, Gretchen Meyers ..."

"Gretchen wouldn't know a good time if it fell on her."

"She likes drinks with floating fruit and a little parasol."

"Enough said," Marian agreed.

"Excuse me, sir—ma'am?" Captain Gallagher said from the entry. "We're about to pull her over to the ramp."

"Do you want us to go ashore?" George asked.

"It might be more convenient, sir."

So the owners went back onto the dock and walked the long way around, to the other side of the yard and out onto one of the concrete piers flanking the boat ramp. By the time they arrived, the workboat had maneuvered *Galatea* over to the ramp, and Mr. Gibbs's crew had ropes on her for aligning bow and keel with the notches and supports of her cradle, which was already down in the water.

At the top of the ramp, a tractor started up and slowly backed away, pulling two lengths of iron chain out of the water. The cradle followed, and the men with ropes pulled the hull forward until it settled into the timber skeleton with a series of muffled groans. A few minutes later the long, white hull with its dark-red underbelly was out of the inlet and freely dripping water and a summer's growth of hanging weed.

"Excellent," George said, "just like delivering a baby."

"And what, pray tell, would you know about *that?*"

"Why, just the usual—I mean, hypothetical—"

"Oh, hush! Say goodbye for another year."

"Sleep well, my beautiful *Galatea*."

And he blew a kiss to the boat.

## 2. The War of the Drums

THE OUTHOUSE STENCH had struck the moment his plane from the States landed at Kimpo Airfield in Korea. It was a sense memory of place and time that William Henry Wheelock carried to his dying day. The Koreans fertilized their rice paddies with human waste, politely called "night soil," and the odor had dug itself into his brain and never let go.

Through all seasons the foul vapors slipped under the flaps of his tent at night. They fought with the taste of his eggs at breakfast and smothered his steaks for dinner. Among the troops it was said that only kimchi could stand up to the smell coming off the paddies, and kimchi was disgusting. The only time the odor seemed to diminish was now, in October, when the paddies froze with the onset of winter. The farmers still spread their steaming muck, of course, but it had a chance to freeze before making headway on the wind.

But now the smell was coming back stronger as his jeep followed the Honton River up to the southern edge of the Iron Triangle between Ch'orwon and Kumhwa. The terrain on all sides was really too hilly and arid for rice farming, but Wheelock knew well enough that night soil could fertilize any kind of field. Perhaps his nose was playing tricks, and the smell only seemed stronger. Over his months in country Wheelock had become a connoisseur of stenches, and he could now identify something more. From somewhere close at hand came the sweet miasma of bodies left too long above ground and then buried in shallow graves with too little lime. And—yes!—mingled with the smell of bodies was a lighter, more penetrating aroma that he knew well.

God, he was going to be glad to get out of this country!

"There's one, sir," said his driver Binns, who could also smell the difference. The man pointed to a dark, square-shaped mound along the side of the road.

Wheelock sighed. "Pull over, Sergeant."

Operating this close to the nearly static front lines, they went fully armed. In addition to Wheelock's Colt Model 1911 sidearm, he had laid an M1 Carbine across the jeep's back seat with the stock ready to hand. Just in front of it, with stock and barrel reversed, was the standard M1 Garand rifle issued to Binns. The driver also carried a couple of grenades clipped to his belt. Of course, none of this weaponry meant much if they came upon a probing Communist patrol. Still, as the jeep skidded to a stop on the muddy road, William Henry reached back for his carbine before getting out.

The blocky cache was covered by a tarpaulin weighted with rocks and stood much taller than a man. Wheelock could count by the semicircular bulges along its upper edge that it was nine wide by five deep. He could estimate the height of the stack as three tall, because he knew exactly what he was counting: fifty-five gallon fuel drums.

But before he became too excited by the find, Wheelock had to make sure this wasn't an unregistered storage dump of full drums. He lifted the bottom edge of the tarp. Up close and freshly released, the sweetish, knifelike smell of gasoline and the deep, bitter scent of lubricating oil again cut through the stench from the fields. He rapped on a drum in the lowest tier and got a hollow *boom* in return.

They were *empty* fifty-five gallon drums, left by someone at the roadside for the Drum Fairies to come along and collect. … That would be Wheelock and Binns.

He made a notation on his map: 135/55, with an estimate in yards to the last milepost he and Binns had passed. Now all he had to do was coordinate this sighting with the other pencil notations that stretched from here back to Inch'on. Then he could fashion a truck route that would pick up all the drums in the shortest distance with the least amount of unladen travel. In this way the effort would take the least time and consume the least fuel. It was just a matter of linear programming, really.

Wheelock had landed in country in the summer of 1951, immediately after the Allies had beaten off the last of the Communists' spring offensives around Seoul. On his collar tabs flashed the gold oak leaves of a major, which he always suspected had been a consolation prize for the unglamorous duty to which he had been assigned. Packed in his luggage were folio-sized page proofs of a book titled *Methods of Operations Research*, co-authored by one George E. Kimball and based on work the man had done for the U.S. Navy during the war. As the text had recently been declassified and was about to go on the presses at MIT, Wheelock carried a mockup of the book pages "rather than carting classified documents all over the Pacific Theater"—as the colonel in charge of Stateside petroleum operations had explained at the time.

The Quartermaster Corps must have figured that a graduate student in the classics, who could read fluently in two dead languages, would find the statistical abstractions of operations research a breeze to decipher. Wheelock tacitly agreed to treat the analysis of resource allocations as just another form of esoterica and plunged himself into the study of probability theory, strategical kinematics, operational experiments in logistics, and gunnery problems. The book was filled with diagrams and tables—some of the latter reminding Wheelock of fragments from Cretan Linear B. Well, at least it had kept his mind occupied while he waited for transportation to the Korean peninsula.

And so it turned out that William Henry Wheelock's war in Korea had been a war of the drums. A modern army marched, not on its stomach, but on wheels and tracks turned by gasoline and diesel fuel, anointed with lubricating oil. These materials were brought into Inch'on's treacherous harbor, which was plagued by thirty-foot tides, in small coastal tankers. They were offloaded at a transfer station for petroleum, oils, and lubricants—or POLs, as the armed forces knew them. Avgas went out by pipeline or rail car to the airfields. But fuel for the forward areas went by truck in fifty-five gallon drums and, less often, in five gallon jerry cans. The trouble was, maintaining the POL supply was under the joint jurisdiction of the Quartermasters Corp, the Corps of Engineers, and various units of Transportation.

Everyone wanted to see as much gasoline and diesel moved to the front as quickly as possible. Not everyone saw returning the empty drums for future refilling as a priority. The limiting factor—as Kimball's book had taught Wheelock to think—was not the supply of fuel, but the availability of empty drums to carry it. Shipping out an endless supply of new drums from the States, even for an organization as rich and wasteful as the U.S. Army, was not an option. Wheelock's assignment, before he ever set foot in Korea, was to establish a system that would get the empty drums back to the depot with the least effort and inconvenience to all concerned. The system that seemed to work best was for Major Wheelock and Sergeant Binns to drive around the forward areas—the rear of the front, as it were—locate caches of empty drums, and mark them for return.

From the back of the jeep, he took a can of white paint and a flat brush and marked a large I-in-a-circle on the front of the tarpaulin facing the road. That was the agreed-upon mark with his drivers: "I" for return to Inch'on.

"Not too many, are there?" Binns said.

"Enough," Wheelock replied.

"Fewer than before."

"What are you trying to say, Sergeant?"

The man stared off to the horizon. "Maybe we're getting ahead of the game? Fewer caches this month than last. More barrels must be finding their way back to base."

"We're still a few thousand short," Wheelock grumped. "At the very least."

"But … when we find them all, they'll let us go home, right?"

Wheelock thought about that for two seconds.

"Nope," he said. "Not a chance."